The Godmother Sanction

Patricia White

Hard Shell Word Factory

©1998 Patricia White
Trade paperback ISBN: 0-7500-0284-4
Published August 2001

Eboook ISBN: 1-58200-054-9
Published December 1998

Hard Shell Word Factory
PO Box 161
Amherst Jct. WI 54407
books@hardshell.com
http://www.hardshell.com
Cover art © 1998 Dirk A. Wolf
All electronic rights reserved.

All characters in this book have no existence outside the imagination of the author, and have no relation whatsoever to anyone bearing the same name or names. These characters are not even distantly inspired by any individual known or unknown to the author, and all incidents are pure invention.

Prologue

ONCE UPON A time, in a very different place, there was a boy. Fierce and proud, untouchable as a new-fledged eagle, only his amber eyes betraying the dark and aching sorrow of innocence lost, he stood beside the looms and embroidery frames in the candle-lit solar and waited. It wasn't a long wait.

"Marcus, I will not bless your going."

Although it added to his inner hurt, the boy didn't flinch away from the disappointment, anger, and grief that twisted together, marred the strong planes of his father's handsome face, making him seem suddenly old and oddly defenseless. Marcus lifted his head a little higher, stiffened his skinny back, and said, his voice carrying only the faintest hint of a tremor, "Father, I have to go. You must know that." He was young enough to want to plead for understanding, even though he knew it would not be forthcoming, but he didn't dare allow himself that small weakness. Even that much would prove his undoing.

Narrowing his eyes, glaring at Marcus, his father stood mute. He just tightened his fist on the hilt of his sword and shifted his stance ever-so-slightly, all with a heavy air of exhausted patience, growing parental displeasure, and grief, a father's grief at the loss of his firstborn son.

"Father, I killed her and I destroyed other lives in the doing. I have to go. There's no place for me here now," Marcus said. He didn't add, "If there ever was." Even though that truth had lived long in his heart.

And in other hearts.

Behind him, Marcus could hear his mother's sobs. Before him, his father asked, his hand leaving his sword to rub at his face, his eyes, "Where will you go?"

Marcus couldn't answer. He just shook his head, turned away from his father to kneel on the rushes at his weeping mother's feet. "Will you give me your blessing, Mother?"

Shadows seemed to close in around them, take what was left of her strength. But whatever else she was, she was her husband's wife, giving him honor in all he did, even if it broke her heart. "I cannot," she whispered.

Getting to his feet, Marcus reached out, brushed his mother's tear-wet face with gentle fingers, and said, trying to smile, to hide the searing grief in the depths of his eyes, "Be well, Mother."

"Don't go."

But she was too late. Marcus, his loneliness and sorrow walled away inside him, was already gone, leaving behind all that remained of his childhood.

Chapter One

GLARING AT THE inoffensive instrument, Tish Warton returned the telephone to its cradle with a deceptive gentleness. She sat it down carefully, even if she was scowling so hard it was making her face hurt. Smiling, nearly angry enough to set off the smoke detector. Muttering dire imprecations, she stood at the desk for a long moment, tapping her fingernails on the battered surface, and twisted her face into a snarl that would, if she had anything to say about it, frighten a witch.

If not Jillian Cobb, her friend since the first grade and current business partner. The whole scene had been played out so many times for Jilly, with so few variations, that it had to be like watching a hundredth rerun of a situation comedy. One which involved some fairly complicated mother-daughter shenanigans revolving around a whole lot of mutual love and respect. Not that Jilly ever complained. Or not usually.

This time Jilly raised an eyebrow when she repeated Tish's display of verbal venom. "Stubborn as a blue-nosed, cross-eyed jackass? Devious as a misbegotten, drunken snake? Really, Tish, is that any way to talk about your mother?"

Her ire smoldering, ready to burst into instant flame, Tish gave Jilly a quick look. It just plain wasn't funny, but she knew how Jilly's mind worked and fully expected her to be unable to contain her wild laughter an instant longer. She had to be about ready to explode, at least, according to Tish's unscientific calculations. But it wasn't happening. Her entire attention, or so she, no doubt, hoped the irate Miss Leticia Warton would think, was focused on the six-foot-tall, frosty-black, grizzly bear she was assembling on the work table.

It was a Bubba Bear, their trademarked creation, the cash mainstay of JAYTEE Enterprises, the custom toy business they had started two years before, with high hopes and a relatively small bankroll. Their hopes were still high, and the bankroll had gained a very respectable amount of weight.

Jilly knew her entire family, mother, stepfather, and two beautiful stepsisters. And for some reason Tish couldn't fathom, the family, as a whole and as individuals, never ceased to amaze, amuse, delight, and bewilder her (and Jilly usually wasn't averse to showing her emotion of the moment).

Muttering maledictions under her breath, most of them still directed at her mother, glaring at Jilly and everything else in the cluttered workroom, Tish could almost read her friend's mind. She ought to be able to. Jilly had said the same thing often enough: Trouble, when it was applied to Tish and the rest of her family, should be outlined in red and carry a subscript that said, "Danger. Innocent bystanders beware."

Her rose-colored work-smock hanging open and billowing out behind her like Superman's cape, Tish left the desk in a rush, stalked over to the table. Hooking her thumbs into the belt loops of her faded, skin-tight Levi's, she stood there, not exactly giving Jillian Tish's patented version of the evil eye, but feeling rather like a militant zealot ready to snatch out her bombs and blow up everything in sight.

Clearly not even slightly intimidated by Tish's stance or glower, Jillian took a deep breath, let it out, and took two more. Then she said, her voice trying to bring in a host of giggles, "I don't know what your mother said to upset you this time, but, Tish, whatever it is, don't you think you might be overreacting? Just a bit?"

"Me? Overreact? Don't be absurd. I know you think I'm silly and she's a sweetheart, Jilly, but my mother is a devious woman. A fiend hiding behind pink lipstick and beige hair. But she's not going to get away with it this time. I'm onto her tricks. We'll just see who can outwit who. Whom? Doesn't matter. When I get through with her, my dear mother is never going to meddle in my affairs again."

She whirled around, setting off a small storm of lint, fuzz, and fake bear-hair, sneezing twice before she looked over her shoulder and said, "Come on. Help me find today's newspaper. We don't have much time."

Jilly clutched the bear, pulling the nearly stuffed body against her chest and hugging it like they were the dearest of friends, but she stayed where she was and demanded, "Time for what?"

Scrabbling through packing boxes, material, and bear clothes, Tish found the newspaper. Spreading it out on the floor, she crouched down over it before she turned her head, gave Jilly a big grin, and said, "To get ready for the ball, of course."

"Ball? Are you nuts?"

"My exact response." Licking her forefinger, flipping through page after page of the paper, Tish found what she was looking for. She gave a little grunt of satisfaction and ran her left index finger down a row of classified ads.

Jilly asked, "What are you talking about?"

"You know what. My mother and that damned charity ball she's helping to sponsor. The Halloween Masque Ball to benefit unemployed Ladies of the Night or something like that. A worthy cause, according to my mother. It's tonight. At the Civic Center."

Jillian rubbed her forehead against the bear's face before she asked, "So, that's what this is all about. You're going? Why didn't you say something?"

"We're going, as in you and me. And I didn't say because I didn't know anything about it until my mother called and informed me that we were expected to be a functional and fully costumed part of family party. Meaning, Mother, the two Steps, you, and me, plus escorts. Sweet, huh?"

Shaking her head in obvious bewilderment, Jilly tried again. "It's rather short notice, but going to a ball with your stepsisters and mother doesn't sound like anything to get upset about. It's..."

"Escorts?" Irritated that Jilly didn't understand, Tish held up her left hand, wiggled her ring finger, calling attention to a small engagement ring. "She wanted me to think it was a family thing, a way to show support for her latest good deed. But, she's not fooling me. It's because of Carl."

Hugging the bear a little tighter, swallowing before she spoke, Jilly said, "That's silly. Your mother knows you and Carl are getting married in less than a month. She..."

"Oh, yes, she knows, but that isn't going to stop her. She believes Carl isn't the right man for me, that he doesn't love me, and she's determined to prove it. So I can go out and look for my very own Prince Charming."

Tish knew from the sour expression on her face that Jilly wanted to say, "Carl Engran is a fortune-hunting, woman-chasing jerk," but she didn't. Maybe she figured she had said it too many times already. Or maybe she knew Tish was every bit as stubborn as her mother, and twice as devious. Arguing with her only increased her determination to do exactly what she wanted; even if the whole world thought she was making the mistake of her life. Which she wasn't.

"Look, I know what you and my mother think, but Carl isn't a tomcat, all hormones and self-interest, putting the moves on every woman he sees. You just don't know him. Jilly, he loves me and... Damn it, I'm twenty-eight-years-old, I should be smart enough to pick out my own husband. Shouldn't I?"

"Well, you should be, but, Tish..." Not really looking at Tish, Jilly sighed heavily and squeezed the bear a little tighter. "Your mother loves you, that's why she..."

"Why she's trying to fix me up with a sexy hunk with more muscles and better buns than Carl?" Tish asked sweetness fairly dripping from her voice.

"She said that?"

"Of course not. My mother said, and I quote, 'Since Carl is out of town on business and unavailable as an escort, I would be happy to provide a suitable young man to do the honors.'" She paused, rubbed at her eyes, and chuckled before adding, "But, knowing my mother, you can never be sure exactly what's in store, so her suitable young man might very well be a super-intelligent nerd, or..."

"It doesn't really matter. I'm going to..." Tish almost wiggled with delight as she planned her next battle in the mother-daughter war.

"Oh, Jilly, she is going to be soooo sorry." Tish felt her own set of giggles bubbling up inside her when she grinned at Jilly and said, "OK, drop the bear. The ball begins in less than five hours and we've got a lot of work to do."

"But... Tish, what about..." She held the unfinished bear out in mute appeal.

"There'll be time for Bubba later. Right now, we have bigger fish to fry. There are two yard sales and a big estate sale on Middlemarch Road." Tearing a section out of the newspaper and stuffing it into her pocket, she jumped up, pulled the bear out of Jilly's arms, tossed him onto the worktable, and grabbed Jilly by the hand. "Come on. It's getting late. We have to get there before they close."

They had told the clerk they were leaving and were out the front door before Jilly asked, "Yard sales? Estate sale? Tish, you're making even less sense than usual. Why are we going to...?"

"It shouldn't be too hard to figure. It's the Halloween Masque Ball."

"Masquerade?"

"Precisely. Now do you see?"

Jilly asked what had to be a purely rhetorical question. "This ball is a big society bash, Tish. You're not going to do something to embarrass your mother, are you?"

WANDERING AIMLESSLY, OR, at the very least, hoping he was giving that impression to anyone or anything that might be watching, Marcus strolled through the plots of intricate plantings making up the knot gardens. Pausing now and then, before he went on into the formal rose gardens beyond the thickly grown ironwood hedge that defined their mutual boundary.

Once there, he stopped for a moment to appreciate the delicate shading of a fluttering cloud of giant pastel butterflies. Trimmed in gold, the mauve, pink, and lavender creatures were larger than dinner plates and more beautiful than the massed profusion of multi-hued roses that perfumed the air as they offered sustenance to the short-lived creatures of air and dreams.

But their fragile, gossamer loveliness couldn't hold his attention long; Stephen's cryptic message had seen to that. Restless and worried, without knowing exactly why, Marcus rubbed his hand across the front of his tunic, touching the unicorn rampant, embroidered in gold on a field of green, crossed by a bar sinister, that named him for whom and what he was, both in Faery and in the Guard. He thought, if only briefly, of his family and of the secrets that lodged in the hidden recesses of his soul and of the vow he had made to avenge a deadly wrong. The vow was still unfulfilled, but snippets and bits of knowledge were adding up, close to making a whole.

The secrets his family didn't know, could never know unless the Curse could be lifted, but even then... Even then the accused witch, the witch he had killed with his own hands deserved all the honor he could give her. All promises had to be kept, even if they destroyed him and all he held in his heart.

If only he could... He had been down that blind alley before. Too many times. Marcus shook his head, tried to think of other things, things far removed from the past that haunted him and the vow that consumed him.

But the worry plagued him, gnawed at him like a beaver with a new tree. And now, if his hunch was correct, Stephen was going to give new secrets into his keeping, and Marcus wasn't sure he wanted that.

Lost in his own thoughts, he started, and it was only partly in sham, when a man walked up behind him and said, "Ah, Marcus, that's the trouble with Faery, isn't it?"

Recognizing the voice of his Guard Commander, and suddenly wary about what was going to pass between them, Marcus answered far more politely than he was feeling, "Which? Never being sure a thing is what it seems, or everything is so incredible that you know none of it can possibly be real?"

"Either or both," Stephen answered, coming up to stand beside Marcus before he added, after a moment of silence, "I've heard it said that you are like that, the first opinion, at least. The surface betraying nothing of what lies within."

It was, at best, an odd conversation, one that seemed to have depths he couldn't plumb. "Oh?"

Stephen was Marcus's oldest friend in Faery, the man who had found a lonely boy and treated him with far more kindness than he deserved, even after he had heard the sordid details of the boy's past. Or at least as much of it as anyone knew. There were only trust and honesty, in the ways that mattered, between them, but still Stephen sounded hesitant, wary almost, when he said, far too indifferently for the event, "I'm retiring from the Guard."

Although he had been hearing rumors to that effect, but had discounted them. Stephen loved the Guard, served it with a love he had never given any woman. So the news, hearing of the retirement from Stephen's own lips was almost like being on the receiving end of a blow to the stomach. Marcus took a deep breath, held it until he had forced some semblance of calmness back into his voice. "Stephen, why? I thought you had all those plans for reorganization and..."

"According to Tregon, the Full Council met and thought my retirement would be in the best interests of the Guard and of Faery." Of late, Stephen's squat body had run slightly to fat, but now his round face looked strained, haggard, and it seemed, to Marcus, as if all joy and laughter were gone from his gray eyes, leaving only emptiness touched by fear. And something else, something unreadable that begged for understanding.

Marcus didn't understand. He was instantly angry, protective, and ready to do battle, with the Full Council if necessary. "What in blazes are they thinking of? Don't they know you..."

"Keep your voice down," Stephen hissed. "There's more to this than..."

For the sake of his friend, Marcus tempered his tone, if not his fury. "You're the best commander the Guard ever had, what do they think they're doing? The Council of Four won't allow this."

"I appreciate your loyalty, Marcus, but put it aside for a minute and listen to me. As far as can be ascertained, the Council of Four are dead and have been for some time. The Full Council seems to be running things now. I've been given a villa on the Coral Cliffs, as a bonus for my long service, and will be expected to begin my retirement there within the day. I would have been gone by now, but I took the time to say farewell to you. I wanted you to know that..."

He fell silent, stared at the butterflies for a moment longer and then, his voice barely more than a whisper, he said, "Just remember,

Marcus, this is Faery. Things are not what they seem. Be careful. The smuggling is only a small part of the troubles. Your vow..."

He stopped and changed directions abruptly, only a slight movement of his hand indicating the greenish glow of the witch light that had drifted in their direction and was hovering, in watchful, listening silence, a scant yard away. "My boy, I know you have to return to the border within the next week or so, but I just wanted to bid you farewell and to let you know that I'm looking forward to the fishing and..."

"I'm sure you are," Marcus said, following his commander's lead. "I hate to see you go, but I know how tired you've been lately. It sounds great."

"There is one other thing, and I think you should hear it from me. I recommended you as my replacement."

"And?" Marcus tried to keep his voice amused, arrogantly disinterested, to hide every emotion from the spy vision of the light. He still didn't know what was going on, but whatever it was, he didn't want to put Stephen in even greater jeopardy.

"The Council is well aware of your qualifications and record."

"And their decision was?"

Not answering immediately, Stephen seemed to watch the swarming butterflies for a long moment before he said, "There were a number of things in your favor, still more against. Some of the negatives can be fixed, some..." He shook his head.

Marcus tried to laugh, but the sound he made did nothing to convey mirth or uncaring.

"It's just that they don't know you, Marcus. No one really does. Not even me. You have..." He licked his lips, swallowed, before adding, in the barest of whispers, "They are afraid of you, you are getting too close to the truth of things. And beyond that, you have too much hidden away, too many secrets."

Then, speaking much louder and sounding nothing more than paternal, Stephen changed the subject completely. "Why haven't you gotten married?"

Marcus didn't say, "Even if I fall hopelessly in love with my one true love, who would marry someone like me?" Instead he carefully avoided looking at his friend and asked, "Is it important? I mean, given the beauties of Faery, it's hard to chose just one and..."

"Don't," Stephen said quietly.

"What else is there to say? If the job isn't mine, I will abide by the Council's decision. I swore to The Oath and I will continue to do as I have sworn."

The glowing ball of green light was very close, listening to their every word and they both knew it.

"Good," Stephen said quietly, clapping Marcus on the shoulder before he said, as he turned away, "I'll miss you, Marcus, but retirement has its blandishments. Keep in touch."

Marcus didn't say him nay. Ignoring the light, he just stood, surrounded by clouds of butterflies and the sweet smell of roses and watched the man as he walked back down the path. And as one more person left his life, Marcus fought down the demons of memory that slipped out of their dark hiding and returned to assault him.

The long years since he had left hearth and home had done much to deaden his pain, ease his loneliness, and had allowed him to build a bright, uncaring facade, one that protected him while it kept him aloof, set apart from those around him. Some secrets had to be guarded forever. That task he had taken as boy, and he kept it still.

And the present worry about Stephen and his retirement was just something more to be dealt with, probably just a minor thing, a power play in the Council that had caught Stephen by accident. It had to be that. Or the fact that he had stepped on a few toes in his time as Guard Commander and now they were stepping back, showing Stephen, and by example the rest of the Guard, just where the power was lodged. Despite Stephen's veiled warning, Marcus was sure he was outside the loop—as those beyond the border so aptly expressed it. As much as he would miss Stephen, Marcus could find no real ground for the man's fears. Stephen's problems didn't touch the secrets or the vow.

Walking from the rose gardens to the water meadow, he put his worries about Stephen aside and tried to shake the sour mood that had gripped him day and night for the past week. The black mood that said something dire was afoot, some life-changing something that Marcus wasn't going to like one little bit. Trying to shrug away the presentment, some might even call it a foreboding, Marcus strode on. Stopping only reluctantly when a woman, dressed in a fairly immodest glittering gown of iridescent red-orange and matching high-heeled slippers, stepped out of thin air directly before him.

"Brooding again, Marcus?" The question was asked lightly. Everyone knew of his long-ago deeds, or thought they did, and dismissed them as unimportant. After all, no matter what had gone before, he had journeyed to the Crystal Court and taken The Oath. That was what afforded him a small amount of standing and a livelihood in a far different world than the one he had left behind, along with all his rightful property and treasures.

Perhaps his past was unimportant; except to him. "Exercising only, Lady," he answered, giving the short reply a bare modicum of courtesy and nothing of his inner thoughts. But he did wonder why Dier, one of the lessor members of the full Council, was doing in the gardens ordinarily reserved for members of the Guard. It wasn't a usual thing. "And you, Lady?"

"I have been searching for you, Border Guard, you are summoned to duty in two hours."

Supposedly he was on leave and would be for the next several days. And the summons came too quickly on the heels of Stephen's words to add anything to Marcus's peace of mind, but whatever else was happening, he was a Border Guard and he went where honor and duty took him. Nonetheless, his smile didn't quite reach his eyes, even if his bow of acknowledgment was impeccable, as he waited for the woman to continue, to give him his new assignment.

Her answering smile hinted at an invitation, one that had very little to do with duty and much to do with satin sheets and perfumed bowers. Her voice was throaty when she said, "You, my dear Marcus, are going to a ball."

He waited without comment and, he hoped, without obvious response to her unspoken words. The Oath guaranteed him respect and privacy, and he wanted no new dalliance, and never with one such as her, to add complications to his life. He had enough of those already. More than enough, and she damned well knew it. They all did, and each one, in her turn tried to swerve him from his path, turn him into something less than the vow had made him.

She floated a little higher above the sparkling crystals of the path, preened, taking a deep breath to enhance her obvious assets, tossed back her waterfall of sun-gold hair, and pretended to pout. "Still playing at being strong, silent, and unavailable?"

It didn't deserve an answer and didn't get one. He knew she was speaking only partially in jest, but he wasn't, not even slightly, tempted. He lifted his chin, looked down at her, and asked, as stiffly and as coldly as possible, "Where is the ball, Lady, and what am I to do there?"

Seductive intent dropped away from her like autumn leaves in a cold wind from the north. She was nothing but business when she said, "You will have to be transported to the middle-border. It is a human ball. Wear your silver dress uniform. It is to be a masque, and that will be disguise enough."

A small tingle of excitement, something that was almost foreign to his being, made him ask, seeing no harm in repeating what was common knowledge in the Guard, "The smugglers? Is that the intersection point where the magic is being..."

She interrupted. "You and the others in your unit will receive the details of the operation when you report to the Charge Commander at the border, but I can tell you this much. Old Britta wanted a simpler life so she retired there, to that particular world, several years gone. Word was received only a short time ago that she has died and..."

"Her belongings? Are we to retrieve..."

She sighed. "I'm sorry to say it's too late for that. One of our people managed to get there in time to break the wand. Most of the rest of the objects are without enough power to do more than make a few small wishes come true."

Shimmering bluish-green around the edges, she started to fade. "Get some rest, Marcus. One of the seers has tranced out about the problem we're facing there. It wasn't a clear seeing, but she saw enough to give us good reason to believe it is going to be a very long night, full of the unexpected."

Speculating on what he had been told, Marcus stood there a moment after she vanished. Magic smuggling was a nasty little business, but as far as he could see, and despite what had happened to Stephen, it carried no real danger for him, nothing that would even come close to upsetting his carefully ordered life. Or as ordered as any life could be at the court where intrigue and power, as well as illusion and glamours, were very much the order of the day.

Keeping up the pretense of being nothing more than an untroubled and obedient Border Guard, he was whistling under his breath as he walked back to the guardroom. A visit to the border might just be the exact cure he needed, the precious moments away from Faery that would allow him to make sense out of a handful of diverse pieces of information.

And maybe then, the knowing would put finish to the odd, inexplicable megrims that plagued him of late. Or make them worse.

Chapter Two

THE WEATHER AND the setting were perfect for a Halloween Ball. Shivery, quivery veils of fog trailed, wispy as starving ghosts, among the birch trees planted in triune clumps on the well-tended grounds. The white-domed, glass-walled Civic Center, pulsing with cerise, lime, and unearthly blue lights, swelled, like some gigantic, diseased toadstool, from its surrounding beds of fading, head-heavy amber, rust, and gold chrysanthemums.

"What do you think? World class ugly, or what?" Tish asked, gesturing toward the building, as a green-faced, Dracula-costumed parking attendant opened the van door and stood back, waiting, with grinning patience for her to exit.

"You should know about ugly," Jilly snapped, opening her own door, jumping out, and hurrying toward the Civic Center. "And if you think I'm going to walk in there in front of all those people with you looking and smelling like that, you've... Tish, your mother is just going to die. It's not really late, why don't we go back to your apartment and find something else for..."

"Not on your life." Her thin frame bulked out with pads, pillows, skirts, ruffles, petticoats, and various inflatable unmentionables. A shimmering magic wand held in her lace-gloved left hand, Tish used her right hand to poke her gray wig into further disorder before she bent over and pulled at her red-and-white striped socks, coaxing them to bag a little more around her artfully thickened ankles.

Waddling up the walk behind Jilly, trying not to laugh at an anticipated magnitude of her mother's chagrin, she peeked over the top of her wire-framed granny glasses and said, or to be more precise, yelled, "Hey, even if you are getting a little long in the tooth, I can grant your secret wish, make the whole thing come true in the shake of a wand. You want a prince? Just say the word, lovey, and I'll fetch one in a jiffy."

The rainbow beads on her Twenties dress jiggling and swaying, Jilly came to a halt, looked back, and hissed, in a tone that spoke more of real anger than her usual amused tolerance of Tish's eternally escalating game of one-upmanship with her mother, "Stop it. You look more like a bag lady than a fairy godmother. And the only wish you can grant me, is to go home and change."

Ashamed to have hurt Jilly, but determined not to show it, Tish tried to tease her back into a good humor. "And, lovey, how would a flapper like you, with your rouged knees and rolled stockings, know what a fairy godmother should look like? I mean, when you were around, Disney hadn't even started to make me into a stereotypical sweet-little-old-lady."

"Tish. Please, it's bad enough that you..."

The wand, looking like a rod of iridescent glass filled with fire flies, was warm in her hand and she could have sworn tingles and spurts of some kind of power were sparking up her arm. Not wanting to grin, and crack the white face she had painted on so lavishly, but a tad derisive of her own imagination, she licked at her oily purple lipstick. Jilly deserved an apology, and would get one, but later. Tish's mother had to be confronted first. The thought made the wand seem to glow a little brighter. The mingled moth ball, cheap perfume, and mildew odor emanating from her outlandish garb grow a little stronger.

"Stop waving that silly wand in my face!"

"It's not silly. It's magic."

"Bull! It's a stupid toy from a yard sale and it's broken at that. Just get it away from me and..." Jilly, fanning herself with her hand, took two steps back, up the steps that led to the wide glass doors, and sneezed explosively.

"It is not broken. I sawed it off and... Super glue is..." Realizing they sounded more like quarreling children than two spinster ladies. Well, maybe not ladies, but grown women. Tish said, managing to sound sheepish and triumphant at the same time, "Just wait and I'll show you what..."

"Tish, if you're going to do this, just come on and quit acting the fool. People are staring at us."

"It's just my costume."

"No, I don't..." Jilly twisted around, peered at the pooled shadows beneath some juniper bushes. "Listen, it... There he is. That man. The sexy, good-looking one in the silver uniform. See him? The tall, dark-haired one, standing by the doors? And there was another one, older but dressed in the same kind of shiny uniform, with him just a few seconds ago and they were both..."

Tish sniffed, and wished she hadn't. "Probably Mother's suitable escorts.

"I don't think so. They looked more like cops or something—your mother probably saw you coming and is going to have us thrown out before you humiliate her."

"Now who is overreacting?" Tish said, trying not to grin as she stepped forward, and Jilly stepped back again. Together they formed some oddly tuneless dance, measured in stumbles and waddles, beads and moth balls. Every jot and tiddle measured and assessed by the long, penetrating scrutiny of the tall, silver-clad stranger.

Other partygoers, after a quick whiff of Tish's melange of odiferous and disgusting aromas, moved rapidly out of range. Letting strains of violin music escape from the Center, they opened the door and joined the masked champagne-sippers in their various and ever-changing groups.

But, regardless of the actions of others, Tish and Jilly included, the man stood his ground, watching them, or perhaps only watching Tish, without moving a muscle. Even when Tish halted directly before him and raised the magic wand until it almost touched his chest.

It wasn't possible, but it seemed as if time shifted, the sounds of night and music stilled, and Tish and the stranger were enclosed in a space uniquely their own.

His eyes, amber and catlike, not domesticated but jungle cat, in his tanned, unmasked face, were inscrutable, expressionless, but not dead—just enigmatic. After a knowing and very superior glance at the wand, his gaze returned to her face, and he said, his voice as void of expression as his eyes, "The Charge Commander has ordered that you be warned only, so that's exactly what I am doing. It isn't legal, you know."

"What?"

Pushing the wand aside, almost contemptuously, and bringing a curious warmth to her wrist where his fingers touched it, he stepped close enough to inundate himself in the rankness of her personal perfumery. His nose wrinkled at the stench, but his voice was even and almost cold when he said, "As I said, this is a warning only. The next time, I will be forced to take action."

He wasn't the sort of generic, well-spoken, mashed-potato-bland men her mother usually picked as safe escorts, but then again her mother was anything but usual—he could be, and probably was her mother's latest move in her plan to break up Tish's engagement to Carl. Well, it wasn't going to happen. Tish was determined to foil her, make her realize Carl wasn't a womanizer, that he was loyal and honest, and, more important, the man Tish was willing to spend her life with.

She lifted her chin, acid sizzled on every word when she said, "If this is meant to be an intriguing line, one that will pique my interest, and make me a happy camper, it isn't working."

"Madam," he said, standing even taller, looking down his thin, high-bridged nose at her, "I do not consort with criminals, especially criminals who look and smell as if they should have stayed in the midden when they were discarded there."

"Midden? Why you...you..." He was, beyond all doubt, the most obnoxious man she had ever met. Obnoxious and arrogant.

"Midden, yes. I do believe you call them garbage dumps." He stared down, fixing her with a glance, acting as if she were some strange bug hardly deserving his attention; except possibly to swat or stomp.

Never one to stand on ceremony, Tish was instantly furious. And she wasn't shy about telling him, and the rest of the listening world, her exact feelings on the matter, none of which were exactly complimentary or even polite. "You puffed-up, pompous, odious, inbred swine." The magic wand quivered in her grasp and the internal sparks, as if responding to her churning anger, swarmed like a hive of furious killer bees. For a wild moment, Tish considered slamming the glass rod across his face, wiping out his smug, supercilious, superior stare, making him look a good deal less like an aristocratic, dark-haired Prince Charles look-alike, without the jug-ears, and more like a street brawler who weaved when he should have ducked.

Her hand moved. So did his. His was faster. His fingers tightened around her wrist and he pulled her close. "You stupid chit, a trick like that is all we need," he said, his voice icy and his face mere inches from hers.

"Inbred bastard!" Tish tried to remain calm, logical, but her anger was hot, burning and her voice was anything but quiet. Fury sputtered like a hot fire in her veins, blinded her to everything but the moment, and she tried once again to use the wand as a weapon, fighting against the strength in his elegant, long-fingered hands.

He laughed. "Overbred is what you mean, isn't it?" he asked, mockery heavy in his voice and in the upward arch of his left brow. "And, as to the bastard part, that much is, of course, a base canard. My parents were legally married at time of my birth, and had been, I believe, for several months."

"Facts can't change the truth," she yelled, snarling each word like a harridan bent on murder. "You are what you are. Now, turn me loose!"

"It would be my pleasure, madam. In point of truth, your rather pungent odor would put a healthy skunk to shame." He released her, but he didn't retreat. She did.

But not silently. "If she thinks you're a suitable escort, my mother must have lost her mind."

"I haven't had the pleasure of meeting your mother, but judging from the evidence at hand, mental illness must run in the family." He made a sketchy bow in her direction and said, "Have a pleasant evening, Miss Warton, but remember what I said. You will not have a second warning and dungeons are far from five-star destination resorts."

Filled too full of fury to have any intelligent retort, or to notice that he knew her name, Tish shouted, "You're the one that's crazy."

"That is not beyond the bounds of possible, but whatever I may or may not be, I am not a childish, disrespectful brat who should have grown up long ago."

"What business is it of..."

"None whatsoever, not as long as you..."

Jilly touched Tish's arm. Light flashed. Once. Twice. Film advanced. A reporter shouted a question.

The world came rushing back, bringing with it violins, waltzes, a dog howling in the distance, and the curious eyes, ill-concealed grins, and mutter and buzz of gossiping humanity. And the word that was repeated most often, after disgusting, was Tish's own name.

"Tish, you'd..." Jilly didn't get a chance to finish whatever she had been going to say.

Pushing through the circle of whispering onlookers, Lil and Sadie, Tish's beautiful stepsisters, one dressed like Queen Elizabeth I, the other as Catherine the Great, bore down on her, satins and taffetas swishing, eyes flashing fire. After telling Jilly to find their mother, they propelled Tish into the Center and down a side hall before she could find enough breath to even protest.

And the two beautiful women wasted no time telling her exactly what they thought of her behavior. "I swear to God, Tish, if you had a single brain, you'd take it out and play with it. What on earth were you thinking of?"

"Screaming and swearing in public. The pictures will be front page news. Mother should have exposed you at birth. Maybe, if we work it just right, it's not too late to wring your neck. Heaven knows we'd be doing the entire world a favor."

"Don't you ever think about something before you do it? This ball is to raise money to build a shelter for homeless women. You must have known that, unless you've been living in a cave. Mother has been working on it for months. The governor is here, two congresswomen, an ambassador, and a senator, and you come in dressed like a... How could you?"

Lil jumped in. "And just exactly who was that man? The one you were screaming at?"

"I..." Tish was almost reeling from their verbal assault. She loved them dearly, but sometimes the Steps were worse than her mother. "He was... I don't know. Ask Mother. She's the one who thought I needed an escort and..."

"Nonsense! Mother would never allow one of her chicks to fall into the clutches of a hawk...no, of an eagle like that. No way. That man is not only sinfully handsome, he's dangerous and you know it."

"He's a supercilious, arrogant..."

Placing a firm hand in the middle of Tish's back, Lil, with little regard for her own cloth-of-gold gown, pushed her down the hall, almost marching her to the ladies' room and its supply of warm water and liquid soap. "Tish, the man is hot. With one flutter of those eyelashes, he could turn on a great-grandmother who had been comatose for..."

"Are you insane?"

Her golden hair piled high, Sadie grinned wickedly as she tugged at her Elizabethan ruff, and gave Tish a sharp look, one that said she wasn't going to allow any nonsense. "Forget about that. We are not going to let you to spoil Mother's evening by coming in here, dressed like a homeless person, mocking and denigrating everything Mother has worked so hard... Tish, honestly, aren't you ashamed?"

"I'm not a homeless person. I'm a fairy godmother and..."

"Tish!"

"Well, I am."

"No, you're selfish brat with no thought for anyone but yourself," Sadie said, not even trying to take the sting out of her words.

"That's not... You know Mother was..."

"Was what? Was hopeful that just this once you'd act as if you were a lady and give her the love and respect that she has coming? Mother isn't that idealistic." Grabbing wads of paper towels, wetting them, the Steps took turns trying to clean Tish's face. They managed to streak and smear her thick, white make-up until she looked, according to Sadie, "Like something the dog threw up."

Lil looked at her critically, pursed her lips, and said, "Maybe, if you wave that silly wand around enough and talk about making all their dreams come true, people will think you're a fairy godmother. One that has some strange disease and is demented."

"I didn't want to hurt Mother," Tish said, knowing, with a sick feeling in her stomach, that wants and realities are not always the same. Still, she tried to explain. "It's just that I want her to... I'm old enough to lead my own life."

"Old enough," Sadie said with a sigh, "but certainly not wise enough. Please, for the sake of us all, just try to get through the evening without creating another scene, and we can all sit down and discuss this tomorrow."

"Okay, but if Mother thinks I'm going to have anything to do with that man, she's got another think coming."

"Hold still and close your eyes."

Obeying, Tish asked, "Why? What are you..." The cloud of room-deodorizing spray almost took her breath. She shut her mouth and stood there while the Steps emptied the can.

"It'll help," Lil said, sniffing tentatively.

"Nothing short of a lye soap and a scrub brush will help much," Sadie answered and then, apropos of nothing, as they herded Tish toward the door, she asked, "Why didn't you come with Carl?"

"He's out of town. A business trip that was planned a month or so ago. That's why I wasn't planning on coming at all. That and I didn't think it was very important. Mother does so many..." Tish stopped, looked down at the floor, and continued, "I told him it wouldn't be any fun without him and that I would stay home alone."

The Steps were noticeably silent, but even their spangled masks couldn't disguise the quick look they gave each other. A look that increased Tish's unease. "What is it? What are you..."

"Did Mother know?"

Sadie's question was too quiet, too filled with unexpressed wariness to make Tish's nerves any easier. "Why? What is going on?"

Fate, in the form of Tish's mother, Leigh Warton-Simms, masquerading as a Roman matron, intervened before any answer was forthcoming. Her smile a bit strained, she was waiting at the end of the hall. She wasn't alone. Jilly was standing at her elbow, and beyond a small masked crowd stood the silver-garbed stranger, his amber eyes narrowed, his gaze fastened on Tish.

Fury, at her mother, at the unknown man, and at the Steps who were aiding and abetting her mother, swelled inside her. It seemed as if the hall kept expanding, lengthening the distance that separated them, that she was going to have to keep on walking until the end of time. And then, too soon, Tish was standing in front of her mother.

Swallowing hard, trying to quell the sickness knotting in her stomach, spreading upward, Tish forced her mouth to form a smile but she couldn't force her eyes, after a single glance, to meet her mother's, couldn't bear to see whatever was hiding in the depths of the clear blue. "Mother, I..."

Sadie interrupted, "Mother, Tish has done it again. Imagine. She came as a metaphor. A fairy godmother for homeless women, but as you can see, " her voice rose a little, insuring that all of Leigh's followers heard every word, "her wand has been broken and glued back together. She is telling us that wishes aren't ever enough, that we all have to work to make sure that no one is homeless or in need. Isn't that wonderful?"

The last was an appeal to the crowd. They responded with a spatter of applause that quickly swelled into mild thunder.

Smiling, a bit grimly, Lil poked Tish in the well-padded ribs. "Take a bow, Tish," she ordered.

Still not daring to look at her mother, Tish obeyed.

Perhaps the others were fooled by Sadie's lie, but Leigh was not deceived. When the good-natured, laughing crowd had heaped her with congratulations and swirled away, Tish was left alone with her mother. It wasn't a wish she would have made for herself.

Licking her suddenly dry lips, she said, "Mother, for this much at least, I...I'm sorry. You're involved in so many causes that I had forgotten that this one was for the homeless. I honestly didn't realize what people would think when they saw me dressed..."

"Leticia, if I could make one wish for you, it would be that you..." Leigh shook her head. "I'm sorry. I love you dearly, but at this moment, I don't really like you very much. There are twenty-seven women, homeless women, depending on me, on the money from this ball, to give them a new start in life. And you come in, looking and smelling as if you just crawled out of a dumpster.

"Does that show respect for the homeless? For the very people we are trying to help? Leticia, you are twenty-eight, isn't it time you started acting..." She couldn't go on.

Tish wasn't yet ready to acknowledge defeat. "It just that. I know you hate Carl and I thought it was a trick to..."

"A trick? Your wedding invitations have been sent. The flowers and cake ordered. Whatever I think of Carl, and I assure you, it isn't very much, doesn't matter at this point. As long as he's your choice, I'm willing to abide by that. I told you that in September, when we were first planning the wedding. Do you hate me so much that you can't even trust my word?"

"Mother, I love you, and you know it. It's just... You... Oh, God, you said Carl was all hormones and muscles, a tomcat who... I thought you, I... Mother, I'm sorry I..."

"Saying you're sorry won't mend what's broken." Leigh bit her lip, blinked back what might, or might not, have been a tear, and then managed to flash a bright smile at an approaching knight in shining armor. "We'll talk later, dear. For now, why don't you go out into the courtyard and air out a little." She turned and walked away.

"Mother, please." It came out in a strangled whisper, and Leigh, if she had heard her daughter's cry, neither paused nor looked back. In another room the violins still invited and beguiled, but Tish was barely aware of them. She had never felt so alone in her life. Even Jilly and the Steps had disappeared. People, elegantly dressed, exotic strangers behind their masks of feathers, jewels, and paint, moved in intricate patterns, but none of them came close.

Swallowing back the lump that threatened to choke her, desperate to escape the lights and the music, Tish was halfway around the room before she knew she'd been had. Her mother wasn't crushed; she was up to something. Tish knew it. Well, it wasn't going to happen. Whirling, she headed toward the nearest exit. And crashed, full bore, into a tall body. A male body dressed in silver. A hard-muscled, sexy body that had been following her all evening.

GINGERLY, MARCUS GRIPPED the woman's shoulders. Despite his fear of some possible contamination, rising gorge, and extreme distaste, he couldn't allow her to fall. He held her by the shoulders, her thick body and foul smell besmirching his silver uniform, as she tried to regain her footing.

"Damn it, Madam," he bit off the rest of his barely audible curse before it turned into an unmanly howl of pain. The magic wand, fairly burning in Leticia Warton's hand, shooting out showers of golden fire, rapped him across the thigh. He hoped it had been an accident, but truly doubted the truth in that.

Ugly, vile in face and smell, the woman was beyond redemption. Fiery pain shooting up his body, his hands tightened on her shoulders and he fairly dragged her to her toward the door. She fought against his grip and growled, "Turn loose of me! What are you, some kind of pervert?"

It was beyond the bounds of courtesy, so far beyond he fell prey to anger, something that was rare in his experience. "Madam, no one is perverse enough to be attracted to you in your present incarnation. To put it mildly, you reek and your appearance is...ah...ah...not enticing. And, I do not fraternize with the locals." He didn't release her. "And, as I have previously told you: that wand is fully loaded and incredibly dangerous. I must ask you to give it into my keeping at once."

"Ask and be damned. Turn me loose before I..." She struggled to free herself, managing to whack him on the forearm with the sputtering wand. Power jolted through it, enough power to make him jerk back, pulling her with him until his grip slackened for an instant.

Tish broke free, backed away from the enraged man, glaring at him with some very real fury of her own. The man was a maniac, he had to be, but she wasn't about to let him get the better of her.

Cradling his arm, rubbing the spot where it he been struck, the man, rage blazing in the amber of his eyes, glared at her. "You're making a big mistake," he said. "One that is going to cause..."

"Road apples," she snapped. "Just stay away from me. Whatever deal you cooked up with my mother is off. We have nothing more to..." Feeling as if she were going to explode with anger, Tish lifted the glowing wand, shook it in his face, and said, "Just stay away. Is that simple enough for you to understand?"

Before he could answer, she turned and waddled away. She could feel his gaze on her back, knew he wasn't going to obey, but she didn't look back as she found the door to the courtyard and stepped out into foggy stillness. She stumbled in the general direction of a blue-lit, splashing fountain, hoping to find a way back to the van and to escape from everything. Especially from the tall silver-clad stranger who lurked in the shadows, watching her every move, stalking her like some sleek, predatory cat, a hungry cat.

*

Chapter Three

WRITHING LIKE A brandy-imbibing viper, reflecting the pulsing ominous-blue of the submerged fountain lights, the fog twisted and curled beneath shrubs and flowers, caught at her ankles, coiled up around her padded thighs. Too intent on escaping from her silver-clad pursuer to be bothered by lesser irritants, Tish ignored it and the splash and bubble of the marble fountain. She jerked off the granny glasses and stuffed them in one of the pockets of her outer skirt, but she didn't slow her waddling exit from the Civic Center; nor could she halt the flailing anger of her thoughts.

For all of her hurt innocence, her protests, her mother was up to something. Tish was certain of that and, no matter what anyone else thought, it hurt, hurt a lot. It was some devious trick the Steps knew about. And maybe disapproved of. Something that boded no good for Tish and her coming marriage to Carl. That much was sure. But what? What was Mother planning this time?

Tish didn't have an answer—at least not one that would send her back to face her mother and demand she cease and desist immediately. Imagining the look of triumph that shone on her mother's face, and hating every nuance of her own overactive imagining, she was within feet of the nearly invisible forms of a man and woman in a fast-breathing, low-moaning, passionate embrace before she was aware of their existence.

It was too late to stop, to go around the other side of the fountain. All she could do was forge ahead and hope they were too involved with their noisy, body-pawing lust to even notice her passage.

Someone else had a different idea of what was proper to the time and place. Tish had a single glimpse of beige hair and pink lipstick on a Roman matron before time flew apart, shattered into a million painful shards, coalesced into a single, ugly, fury-painted moment, leaving Tish's full attention focused on the scene playing out before her. A scene in which she had a major role, one she had never auditioned for: the wronged woman in all the Country Western songs, the trusting woman betrayed by her love.

Hidden lights flashed on, flooding the area around the fountain in too harsh brightness. Across the catch basin, rendered nearly invisible by the shiny mist of falling water, the Roman matron stood, her fingers dropping away from the light switch. Her face wearing anything but a victorious smile, she was motionless, but only for a heartbeat, before she covered her mouth with her hand, stepped back into the shadows, and blurred into the night and fog.

It was her mother. Tish was certain of that. She had won their current duel, but it didn't matter; not anymore.

Scarcely a yard away, the embracing pair was caught, well and truly, in the spotlight. The silicone-enhanced edifice of her exposed white breast made decent only by the deeper tan of his grasping hand, the woman was facing in Tish's direction. Her heavy-lidded eyes, seen through holes in her red-sequined mask, narrowed, she pulled slightly back from her lusting paramour, and gave a little gasp. Probably a combination of dismay and disappointment, without a hint of embarrassment, but holding still a breathy undertone of unfulfilled passion.

He turned his head. His black domino mask was pushed up onto his forehead. Red lipstick smudged his firm lips. But his startled, disbelieving expression was beyond the power of mere words to describe. His mouth working soundlessly. He stared at Tish for what seemed an eternity. But wasn't. The pitiless light burnished his crisp blond hair, touched his cleft chin, ran down the bronze of his muscled shoulders, gleamed and glittered from his golden chains, the chest-baring black leather vest, and identified him as Carl, Carl the tomcat, Carl the betrayer.

Jagged as broken ice, pain coursed through her veins, clawed at her muscles and bones, settled in her chest, beat with her heart. Muted by the agony, Tish stood there, returning his stare, and waited for the agony to subsided, for her right hand to pull the engagement ring from her left finger, fling it at his feet. For her tongue to slash him to ribbons of regret. For her body to turn, stalk away, leave him there whimpering and moaning, begging her to come back, to forgive his momentary lapse, his single venture into insanity. None of it happened.

"Tish," he finally said, releasing his hold on the woman's bosom, turning toward his soon-to-be-bride, smiling an abashed little-boy smile, "darling, I can explain."

"Bull!" she answered, the pain in her body turning to total and absolute fury. It was fueled in part by the stark knowledge that her mother had been right about Carl's prowling lechery, and had been there to prove it to her daughter, to rub Tish's nose in it, as it were. The fury bubbled, bright and hot, in her body, mirroring the pulsing surge of blinding fire that crackled and sparked within the glass confines of the magic wand, gathering in intensity, building higher and higher like some gigantic storm. One that had to break, to explode from its own interior force.

"Sweetheart, it isn't my fault. A man has certain needs that you shouldn't have to..." His smile was easy, caught-in-the-cookie-jar-ish, begging her forgiveness for his tiny misdeed. He reached out, touched her arm with the same hand that had, so recently, fondled and caressed the masked woman's bare breast.

Tish was not deceived, neither was she willing to forgive. Anger, pain, grief, and shame warred within her as she looked at her betrothed, saw something hitherto unknown. Something she didn't want to know. Seemingly moving of its own accord, the wand lifted.

Running feet pounded across the paving stones behind her. The silver-clad stranger's voice shouted, "No!"

Paying him no heed, Tish found her own voice and the invective suitable to the occasion. "You sniveling, slobbering, slab-sided, slimy toad." The wand came down, raked through Carl's thick mat of chest hair. Power flared, sizzled, sparkled red, yellow, and orange, smelled of ozone, netted him like a spent fish, and made her description of him nothing more than the simple truth.

Greenish-gray skin thickening, thick drool oozing from his now wide, lipless mouth, Carl dwindled and changed, crouched at her feet, looked up at her with bulging toad-eyes, croaked, "Reep," before he made an awkward hop toward the fountain. The fog roiled up around him, almost burying him in whiteness after his next leg-flopping, disoriented leap.

Carl's companion in anticipated fornication gawked at the giant toad, the irate Tish, and began backing away, whimpering, trying to pull her scanty slave-girl costume back into place. "No," she moaned. "Oh, God, no. Please, I didn't mean to... We were just..."

She wasn't anyone Tish recognized, but she had all the earmarks and waggle tails of what she was. Driven by anger not reason, Tish raised the wand again and took a single step toward the woman and said, "You cross-eyed get of a misalliance between a howling hyena and a mongrel..."

IT HAD ALL happened too quickly. Marcus was stunned. All outer appearances to the contrary, the fat woman had to be a... He sprinted across the courtyard, shouting at the top of his voice, feeling real fear for the first time in a decade. "Stop! Damn it, you...you idiot! Are you trying to destroy..."

Arms spread, he dove across the space that separated him from the madwoman's back. He caught her around the thick waist as his shoulder struck her derriere with considerable impact. It forced the words she was going to say out of her mouth in an incoherent squawk of protest as his flying tackle bore her to the paving stones. They landed in a tangled, bouncing, thrashing, rolling heap. He swore mightily, in his own tongue, and called for magical aid as he tried to wrestle the wand out of her determined grip.

"Drop it!" he snarled, his fingers tightening around her wrist, but not daring to touch the blazing tube of glass. It carried enough power to burn him, and her, to cinders, and he wasn't ready to go up in a cloud of smoke. He fought harder. "Drop the damned wand or I'll..."

Her snarl was the full equal of his when she advised him to perform a perverted, obscene, and probably impossible, physical act. Her strength was no match for his, but seemingly her madness fought on her side, allowing her to resist his demands.

"Drop it, you idiot!"

"Make me!"

Disregarding her madness, her smell, even the fact that she was a fat and ugly woman, Marcus tried. He was still trying, even as he called for reinforcements in a strangled voice.

GASPING AND PANTING, from exertion, not from lust, they rolled back and forth, bumped against the base of the fountain, swore, demanded, growled, and displaced the thickening ground fog. Solid as cotton, filled with magic fire that ranged through the entire spectrum and beyond, it billowed up, wrapped around their struggling bodies. Tish thought, if her thoughts still had any hold on reality, it lifted them, bound them to each other, imprisoned them.

Panicked, she fought him, the fog, and her own terrible anger. Only the anger was vanquished, and it only in part. Only enough to allow her to hear what was going on beyond the dense layer of swaddling mist. And to almost smother on the vile odor, hers alone, added to, not lessened by the Steps' ministrations, that was trapped inside their vaporous prison and growing steadily stronger.

His long, lean body wrapped too tightly against hers, the stranger was coughing and wheezing. So was Tish. But she was too aware of the stranger hard-muscled length, his arms around her, his hot breath in her ear, and that awareness added to her anger, made her fight her own, purely physical, reaction and for air enough to breathe.

Beyond the encircling fog, a woman, Tish was sure it was her mother, was saying, "I didn't mean to... Tish? Tish? Where is she? Where did she go?"

Another woman, all traces of lust gone from her shaking voice was whispering, over and over, "She didn't do it. I'm dreaming. Too much champagne. She didn't do it."

The bonds of fog tightened, squeezed harder. The air melted into the mist. Flecked with revolving specks of bright gold, darkness crept in, filled her eyes, her nose, seeped, ever so slowly, into her brain.

Just before it usurped her senses, translocated her in time and space, she heard another woman say, her voice icy with command, "Catch that damned frog and get the three of them out of here. Marcus, you and that fool woman are going to pay for this. Pay dearly."

Tish had just enough strength to say, "Toad. He's a toad," before the blackness grabbed her, shook her, and pitched her, head-first and gagging, into a vast cauldron of nothingness. She sank like an Olympic diver and dissolved, was no more.

WAKING FIRST, MARCUS went from sleep-dazed to angry in a single breath. Choking back a burning oath, he looked at the stinking bundle of humanity sprawled beside him and pulled himself back and away. He knew where he was, if not exactly Why. But he suspected it had something to do with Stephen and whatever the other man had tried to warn him about.

He also knew, even if he didn't want to admit it, that their present incarceration was as much, possibly more, his fault than it was that of the sleeping woman.

The wand had been fully charged. He knew that. He should have taken it at the beginning and prevented the whole incredible mess from happening. It could have been a relatively simple deed. Well, he thought with a wry grin and a glance in the woman's direction, maybe not terribly easy, but certainly not impossible. Why, then, had he been ordered to wait, to warn only? That he didn't know. And, if he hadn't taken the Oath, which was supposed to protect him from diverse magicks, he would have sworn he was under some sort of spell. One cast by the disreputable woman.

He looked at her and shook his head. It wasn't possible. She smelled to high heaven, had a tongue that would melt glass, was ugly enough to turn a dragon's stomach, but still there was something, something that tugged at him.

"I must be crazy," he muttered, pulling the prisoning chains to their full length, scooting back against the wall, and gingerly exploring the bruises and cuts their struggle had inflicted on his lean body.

But he didn't feel crazy; he felt alive. His sense of foreboding was gone, leaving behind a breath of excitement, and something more. Something that didn't have a name. And for that small favor, Marcus was truly thankful. He didn't even want to guess what it was.

LIGHT, SPRING-GREEN and insistent, prowled her face, prodded her gummy eyelids, brought her back from nowhere into the here and now. Wherever that was. Her disoriented mind could find no point of reference. Everything was strange enough to be nothing more than a bad dream, one that might, with a little coaxing, develop into a real, heart-pounding, dry-mouthed nightmare.

Stiff, sore, she moaned as she opened her eyes, tried to move her body, to find some spot of comfort on the stone bench that supported her. There wasn't one. Even the scatter of moldy straw that had seemingly served some other wretch as a mattress, was stiff, poking through gaps in her layers of padding and garments to scratch her skin. And the musical clink of the chains that ran from the cuffs on her wrists to some unseen destination was nothing she had heard before.

Stone bench? Moldy straw? Chains? Dear God, what was... Tish took a deep breath of dank, foul-smelling air, coughed, and tried again. The strange miasmic stink, not all of her making, brought her to reasonable awareness. And touched her with enough wit to exercise a little caution.

Moving slowly, she turned her head, stared at the small, stone cell. Its rough, gray walls, oozing with moisture, partially covered with sick-looking moss, looked as if they had been carved from a single gigantic rock. There was a narrow window high up in one wall, iron-barred so closely that a rat would have had trouble crawling through. The only other opening was a small peephole in the door. The cool green light floated a foot or so beneath the ceiling, bobbing and twisting with every change in the air currents. The hair on the back of her neck prickling, Tish licked her dry lips and tried to look away from the ball of luminous green, to examine the rest of her prison. She couldn't; it mesmerized.

"Turn your eyes away first and then your head."

Squeaking with alarm, the light forgotten in her fear, Tish sat up and looked around. He was sitting in the corner at the far end of her bench, leaning against a dry patch of wall, knees up, manacled hands draped across them. His silver garments were filthy and torn. His angular face was the same, with patches of bloody scrapes across his forehead and a purplish-yellow bruise on one high cheekbone, and smudges of dirt everywhere else.

Despite his dishevelment, the man looked and sounded as superior as any royal prince when he said, "It's a witch light. A cross between a spy and a lantern. Just don't look directly at it, and it won't bother you."

"Where are we?" Tish demanded, a spurt of anger overcoming her bout of caution. "Why have you brought me here?"

His left brow arched. His amber eyes glinted. "I," he said, speaking slowly, as if she were incapable of understanding anything else, "have done nothing. If you aren't truly mad, then it is your stupidity that has landed us in the dungeon. I warned you, but..."

"People who say, 'I told you so,' are insufferable prigs," she snapped, glaring at him as her fear ebbed slightly. Memories reared up in her clouded mind, stampeded, trampling each other into mismatched fragments. The fear came back in a rush, and brought a whole family of brothers and sisters, when she looked down, saw the fragile, glass chains and wrist bands that held her more securely than steel. Above all else, they were impossible. The fear quivered in her stomach, fluttered like a trapped bird in her chest. But she didn't surrender, didn't allow the sobs that crowded her throat to be born. Raising her head, fighting to keep a tremor out of her voice, Tish asked, "Where are we?"

"Never having been imprisoned before," he said, "I really can't say for sure. Other than... Well, you used the wand and..." A look of incredible weariness shadowed his face. "I don't know. Probably somewhere in the northern section of Faery."

"Faery?" Disbelief took away some of her fear, polished the single word.

"That'd be my surmise. All hell broke loose after you zapped your intended and he went hopping off to find a bigger pond. One or two of the higher-ups answered my call, chewed me out good for allowing you to keep the wand, gift-wrapped us, and sent us here."

Obviously he was lying. Why she didn't know, but she wasn't about to let him get away with it. Taking what seemed the best option, Tish said, letting a little smug assurance color her voice, "My mother put you up to this, didn't she? This is all some sort of sick joke to..."

A distorted memory eased in, flooded her mind with weirdness, stopped her words, and made her shudder as she asked, "I didn't really turn Carl into a toad, did I?"

His, "Miss Warton, please," was all the answer he gave.

"Why are you lying? It couldn't have happened. The wand was just a toy. It was broken and... No, it couldn't have..."

"Marcus!" The fluting voice came from the tall, silver-haired, green-gowned woman standing, several inches above the mucky floor, in the center of the cell.

Seeming not at all surprised by her sudden appearance, or her apparent indifference to gravity—even if both scared Tish back into silence—the man smiled, albeit coldly, and dipped his head in what looked like some sort of ritual greeting. "Kira."

She returned his smile; only hers seemed even colder. "The Full Council has heard your case and has found you both guilty of all the crimes, except smuggling magic. Which, it has found, on reviewing the evidence, didn't happen; and perhaps never has. You and your creature are to be summoned to the Crystal Court for sentencing."

"Sentencing? Crimes?" The words came out in a barely intelligible mumble. The woman looked at Tish, made a small gesture, and Tish felt her lips clamp together as if they had been glued.

An odd expression flickered in his eyes, but only for a fraction of a second, but he didn't ask for any further explanation. "So shall it be." He stood, extended his hands. Kira looked at them for a moment before she tapped the fragile links with a sparkling silver wand that glowed with an inner-light. The chains poofed and fell away in a cloud of rainbowed dust.

"There is one more thing. Several of the Full Council have delicate sensibilities, as you know. Therefore, you are requested to bathe it and yourself before presenting yourselves at the Court. Garments, soap, and towels, and privacy, await you in the lower grotto."

His sigh was heartfelt, but all he said was, "It shall be as you wish."

"I don't envy you the task, Marcus. It has a rank smell about it." She took a swaying step closer, peered at Tish. "Are you sure it's well. It has a very strange color and..."

"Paint," Marcus said.

"How odd. Is it one of the barbarians then?"

His voice sounded troubled. "Not exactly that, Lady. But you should know and inform the council, whoever or whatever she is, she repaired and powered the wand."

The floating woman pursed her lips, inspected Tish again, and asked, "Not a Wilding?"

"Perhaps, I really don't."

Tish struggled to say something, to demand her rights, an explanation, but the sticky something still stopped her mouth.

"Oh, dear, if that's the truth of the incident, it does present certain complications." The woman stepped back, faded to transparent. "Bathe it, Marcus, and come to Court. Babbet will fetch you when it is time."

She was just a blurred shimmer of pale light when she asked, "What of the wand? Could you touch it without pain?"

Marcus shook his head. Gnawing on her lower lip, she stared at Tish for a moment longer before she disappeared completely, taking Tish's mouth glue with her. But not the questions that crowded her tongue nor the fear that crawled up her spine.

"What's going on? What was she talking about? What crimes? What sentence?"

Marcus sounded distracted but his voice was courteous when he answered her questions. "What the sentence will be, I don't know. But, your crimes are serious. They have offended the Godmothers, and such crimes are never considered misdemeanors. You'll serve time for this. I can almost guarantee it."

It was all she could do to keep from swearing, screaming at him, and demanding her instant release, but she managed to quell the storm of protest and asked, in a tone that fairly dripped irate malice, "What in blazes are you nattering about? What crimes have I committed?"

Enumerating them slowly, he lifted one finger at a time until he was showing a full hand of crimes. "To put it in your own terms? Using a magic wand without a license. Buying an illegal street wand. Sawing it off. Discharging it within human lands. Posing as a Godmother."

It was no joking matter and obviously that's what he was doing. No reasonable person would accept what he was saying as truth. Tish glared at him. "What am I supposed to say, 'I didn't know it was loaded'?"

UGLY AND SMELLY as she was, the other-world woman brought out the worst in him, made him flippant and not a little arrogant, and Marcus didn't know why. "Ignorance of the law is no excuse."

"Damn it, I... Please, just cut the nonsense and tell me where we are and what's really going on."

She was truly frightened. He could see that even through all the paint that streaked and spotted her heart-shaped face. It was a face that didn't match the bulky, misshapen body. He tried to temper his tone, to give her the information she sought. "I've already told you. You are in

Faery and the laws you've broken are..."

He shook his head. "What you've done is serious and I have only named a few of your crimes, a very few. For instance, I'm not sure what they charged you with in the shape-changing of your lover."

"You...you..." She obviously couldn't think of a name that fit her estimate of his character, or lack thereof.

For a fleeting moment, Marcus fought back an impulse to laugh, caught it before it did much more than twitch at the corner of his mouth, and his voice sounded perfectly serious, even to himself, even when he knew he was teasing her. "By the way, Carl wasn't the frog prince, was he? If he was, it'll probably go fairly hard with you. You'll be guilty of witchcraft and someone will have to find a princess dumb enough to let a smooth-talking frog, with superabundance of testosterone, climb into her bed. It won't be an easy task. I've been gone for a while, but according to the last poll I saw, even princesses prefer sexy men over frogs."

"How do I know if he was the frog prince? If it actually happened, I changed the miserable jerk into a toad. And probably insulted the whole kingdom of toads in the bargain."

She had surely cast a spell over him. That had to be the reason he was behaving in such a manner. There was nothing about her to entice a man, but she made him oddly giddy, made him say things that were in nowise true, "I can't say for sure, but you might be guilty of that crime also. I don't know if toads have a representative at court, but if they have, he or she will be demanding punishment for that crime, too." And was only pleased when she fought against her fear, turned it into something else, something that blazed in the blueness of her eyes.

SWALLOWING BACK BITTER anger, she asked, as sweetly as possible, "And what does Faery have to say about Innocent until Proven Guilty. I haven't been charged or tried or anything. You just attacked me and brought me here. That's kidnapping and..."

"Faery is not a Democracy. It is an Absolute Matriarchy, ruled by a Council of Godmothers. They have the magic and the power to do exactly as they please."

"That's the..." Tish's indignation dribbled away, leaving a residue of anger that was almost overshadowed by the growing realization that she was in the clutches of a madman, one who believed part and maybe all of the nonsense he was spouting. A Council of Godmothers indeed. What did he take her for? The thought found its way out of her mouth before she could call it back. "That's nothing but pure garbage.

Godmothers who have magic. What do you think I am, some sort of simpering idiot who'd believe that line of hogwash?"

"That's not for me to say, Miss Warton." Moving stiffly, he reached down beside the stone bench, took up her chains, and said, much as one would say to a well-trained, but somewhat surly dog, "Come along. Things will appear in a better light after you've rid yourself of that..." His amber eyes inspected her from head to toe, his aristocratic nose lifted, wrinkled ever so slightly, and he tugged on the glass chain, forcing her to crawl off the stone bench and stumble along behind him toward the slowly opening cell door and the shadowy corridor that lay beyond.

The pull was light, easy, but she couldn't resist it, couldn't, no matter how much her brain screamed at her, even take a step away from him. Leading her, like a Judas goat leads sheep to slaughter, Marcus said, "The chains are bespelled. It works both ways. I have to take you, and you have no choice but to follow me to the lower grotto. It isn't far."

Some time back, her mind had gone on information overload and blipped out what it considered of lesser importance. That bit of knowledge whipped back onto the screen. Tish's mouth hung open, but only for an instant before she snapped it shut. Marcus, whoever the hell he was, was going to take her somewhere and give her a bath. Like hell he was.

"You damned pervert. I'll not... You'll not..."

Her vehemence did nothing to slow his pace. He looked back over his shoulder, lifted his eyebrow in a marvelous imitation of Mr. Spock, and said, "Indeed." It wasn't a question.

Indignant, sputtering, determined that he would not do what he intended, she waddled along behind him. Tish scarcely noticed the downward drift of the stone passage until they turned a shimmering, slightly translucent corner, walked down three worn steps, and stopped beside a steaming pool of water.

Another of the witch lights floated several feet above the water, revealing a flat-topped rock stacked with towels, clothing, and flagons of something. Tish barely glanced at the bounty, she didn't dare. Marcus was her main concern.

The end of the chain still in his hand, he had turned, taken two steps in her direction. Devils danced in the depths of his amber eyes as he said, very politely, "Miss Warton, it's bath time. Would you kindly disrobe? Or would you prefer I act as a ladies' maid and do it for you?"

Chapter Four

TENDRILS OF STEAM rose, hung in the air. The green-tinted water rippled and surged, lapped, like a lazy cat, at the mica-sparked white sand that surrounded the irregularly shaped pool, nibbling away tiny bites. Gurgling and running somewhere in the shadows, the heated stream, coming from nowhere visible, filled the bathing pool at one end, emptied it from the other.

It was warm in the grotto. Too warm. Sweat popped out on Tish's face, trickled down her back in an itching rivulet. It wasn't just the steamy heat that was making her sweat—and raising her stink quotient to unbearable levels.

Reflecting green sparks from the hovering, pulsing witch light, Marcus's amber eyes mocked her, dared her to defy him, to make him undress her with his own hands. Tish took a deep breath, coughed as the steam filled her dry throat, and edged a single step back away from the man who seemed, at that moment at least, to be her warden. Or, at the very worst, an errant thought, but a real possibility, a madman bent on her destruction, mental and physical.

Or maybe, a small part of her mind told her, you fell and hit your head and all this is a dream, or a reaction to some sort of medication. Whatever it was, or whoever he was, the whole situation had strong overtones of illusion, delusion, one of those things. It was certainly not her idea of a first-order sexual fantasy.

"Strip, Miss Warton," he said, fairly purring the words, "or I will be forced to assist the process. It would be a deed neither of us would particularly enjoy, I'm sure."

With all the grace of a hunting black leopard—movie version, of course—he stalked toward her, his hands drawing in her chains, until less than a yard of steamy space separated their bodies.

Her breath was coming a little too fast. Whether from anger or fear, Tish wasn't entirely sure. But she wasn't about to allow what he demanded. "Touch me and you're..."

"What?" he asked softly, taking another hitch in the spelled chain, holding her in magic bounds that permitted her brain to scream silent denials, her mouth to snarl threats, but absolutely refused to let her trembling body retreat another inch.

"Damn you, Marcus! Turn me loose! You creep! You...you...sadist!" Fear crept into her voice, and, despite her best effort to appear self-possessed and in control, sent her voice up a notch.

THE EMOTION WAS plain in her voice, so plain Marcus heard it and gave her a quick look. "I'm sorry," he said, trying to sound sincere and reassuring, and feeling a very real shame, "I realize this must all be very strange and frightening to you, and I didn't mean to add to your unease. But, I assure you, part of your fears are totally groundless. Whatever prurient tales you may have heard about the inhabitants of Faery, they do not necessarily apply to everyone. I do not lust after, nor do I have any intention of ravishing your...ah...body."

For some reason, his words weren't composed of the entire truth. For some inexplicable reason, one that he didn't want to explore, she was affecting him in ways he had forgotten existed. It wasn't to be allowed; it had to be some of her Wilding magic. Didn't it? It wasn't to be allowed. He fought back, using words, the only tools at his disposal.

"The sight, and I might add, the smell of you, doesn't nothing to arouse my baser instincts. To the contrary, I find you somewhat repulsive and... That is, you are perfectly safe, from me, at least. How you will fare in the hands of the Godmothers is another matter, but even there, you have nothing to fear in the area of virtue lost."

HER FEAR OF the man dissolving in the flare of her own anger, Tish glared at him and muttered something obscene.

His smile was arrogant, superior, and something of his attitude touched his words, "Besides all that, Miss Warton, aren't you a little behind times in playing the coy and modest maiden? Or doesn't consorting with an oversexed toad count in such matters?"

Her second obscenity was louder and stronger.

He made a tching-tching sound and smiled before said, his tone completely businesslike and demanding obedience, "Now that you've had your little fit of pique, we really must get down to business. You will do what we were ordered to do. If not, possibly, the full consequences of your act of defiance isn't clear to you.

"On the other hand, I am well aware of how malcontents are punished and would rather forego that rather nasty bit of Faery justice. So, if you aren't prepared to tend this rather odious chore yourself, I really must help you. If only for your own good."

"Keep away from me!"

Looking pained and sounding testy, Marcus said, "Miss Warton, surely you are smart enough to realize you are already in enough trouble without compounding it on this level of childishness. The Council will be sending for us quite soon, and prior to that time, they have ordered that you be bathed, so that's the end of it."

He reached toward the ripped and soiled, mangy-looking red shawl that was draped around her shoulders, covering layers of clothing and padding. All of which carried their own distinctive smell; something between rotten garbage and essence of polecat.

Before his hand could touch her, Tish closed her eyes for a moment, clenched her jaw, then lifted her chin, and said, because at the moment it seemed the wisest course of action, "Keep your hands to yourself. I'll take your damned bath."

"I will accept your word as truth and laud your rather tardy wisdom. And tell you also that in Faery your word given is, in effect, a spell binding you to that action." He dropped the chain. It sparkled into a shower of glittering motes and fell to the cave floor, freeing her from all visible restraint.

"However that may be, in your particular case, I would fain to take wagers on its binding force." He stepped back again, but he didn't turn away. The light behind his head, he just stood there like a man carved of dark adamant, all shadows and superiority, and waited for her to keep her given word.

He was far enough away that she could have run, but she didn't try to escape; to where she had no idea, and besides, for some odd reason she didn't, at that moment, feel any great need to escape. Fear and excitement tangled in the pit of her stomach, swelled up into her throat, but Tish, her chin high, her stare unflinching, glared at the man and began taking off item after item.

HE WAS USED to magic and glamours, but this was different. He had difficulty believing his eyes, and controlling his breathing, as she changed before his eyes. Starting with the ratty gray wig, she worked her way down, removing layer after layer of garments, pillows, inflatables, and unmentionables until she was standing in the green glow of the witch light wearing only a lacy white bra, matching panties, and filthy red-and-white striped stockings bagging down over large, grimy tennis shoes.

As the strip (he hoped and believed it was without any intention to tease) continued, Marcus felt himself flush. But even that small shame vanished under the hot surge of desire that almost turned him into a caveman, with every rational thought lost to primal heat. Swallowing hard, knowing he couldn't, not now or ever, act on his desire, he fought for control.

He mumbled, his voice hoarse, "I beg your pardon, Miss Warton, I believe I was wrong about the possible ravishment. You and your virtue do indeed present a problem," before he gave her a small salute and turned away, hurrying toward the darkness at the bottom end of the bathing pool and the privacy it afforded him. He didn't know what was happening to him, what was making him act like an adolescent who had his first glimpse of a naked woman, but it had to stop. Right then and right there.

Practically tearing off his own soiled garments, Marcus rushed into the warmth of the water, hoping it would cure him of what had to be a sudden attack of madness. Or just pure lust. But he was afraid it was more than that, and that fear was a prod toward sanity. Of sorts.

TISH MUTTERED ANOTHER obscenity, one of scatological derivation, and ignored his retreat. She pulled off the sneakers, socks, and the padding beneath them, added them to the pile of odorous discards, took up one of the amphora, sniffed the scented soap, and stuck one sweaty foot into the steam-covered water.

The water rose, not in a vast, breaking wave exactly, but in a large amorphous reaching shape. One that resembled, at least superficially, a transparent, sparkle-filled Bubba bear. There was no time to scream. Or to even feel afraid. Tish sucked in a shallow breath just as the water embraced her, pulled her into the glowing, green depths of the pool. She didn't even try to fight the water.

She couldn't have even if she had wanted to. Tish had fallen instantly in love, or was intoxicated, or had suddenly lost what little sense she possessed. It was all one and the same.

Effervescing, bubbles breaking against her skin, laving her in tingling, sweet-smelling water, drove all fear, all doubts, all anger from her mind. She knew nothing but the moment. Giggling, Tish twisted and turned within the water, came up, inhaled the water essence: small, pink violets, summer-ripe apricots, fresh-mown hay, and the crystal hearts of drifting snowflakes.

Dimly she heard Marcus shout, "What in the blazes have you done?" but there was no answer. There was only the water, her laughing playmate, her gentle friend, her...

Hands grabbed her shoulders, not gently, jerked her up and out of the steamy wonderland, and practically threw her onto the top of the rock that held garments and towels. An uninvited guest, reason came back with a whimper, a shiver, and a crawly feeling up her exposed spine.

Marcus said something. Tish knew he did. She saw his mouth move, heard some sort of sound, but his words made no impression on the numbness that held her, the numbness and the growing fear. Fear of her own odd behavior as much, or more, than of the strange water creature that had... Had what?

Confused, disoriented, and haunted by a feeling of loss, for an instant, she wanted to lean against Marcus's bare chest, let him hold her, keep her safe from...from...

"What?" she whispered. "What was it?"

"Damned if I know. This is the prison grotto and warded against man, beast, and..." Marcus shook his head, sending little droplets of water across her nose and cheeks. Tish shivered again.

He peered at her face, touched her lower lip with his forefinger, twisted her head back and forth, examined her neck, and asked, "Did it hurt you?"

Tish stared at him for a moment before she said, "No, what was it?"

Without giving her an answer, Marcus looked at her a moment longer, looked intently, and finally sighed. "Get dressed," he said, turning away from her. But not before she noticed, in a dazed, almost unknowing way, that he had stripped off his own soiled garment and had, given the evidence of his water-beaded, clean, smooth-muscled body, done a little skinny dipping of his own in the pool.

But he couldn't have. There had only been a few seconds between the time the water pulled her in and Marcus had... "How long was I..." The words didn't want to leave her mouth, didn't want to expose themselves to the sodden echoes of the cavern. It was a cavern that was suddenly a very frightening place.

"It was..." Tish stopped to catch a breath, to force the air into her aching chest, "Was it trying to hurt..."

She remembered the boundless joy, the freedom, and the sensation of love, pure, innocent love, that the water had bestowed on her, a gift freely given, and whispered, "No, it wasn't trying to hurt me. It..."

The water hummed, an oddly plaintive sound, endearing and achingly sweet, and its smooth surface trembled a little before the sound dropped away into stillness.

Wanting to comfort the water, Tish tensed, began to move across the top of the rock toward the water.

Marcus stopped her. "Damn it, stay away from it and get dressed." That was all he said, at least to her, but he shouted something, in a melodious, lilting language, in the general direction of the green witch light and began pawing through the piles of shimmering cloth on the top of the rock, tossing several filmy items in her direction and keeping others to cover his own long, lean nakedness.

Dripping down from her hair, water coated her lashes. Tish blinked once. And wanted to rub her eyes, to verify the horde of suddenly appearing women as real. Slim, elegant women, wearing designer gowns and jewels of every shape and size.

Fighting down the growing sickness in her stomach, Tish swallowed twice and blinked again. Nothing changed. The wands were, each and every one, unwavering, bright with danger, pointed in her still-wet, still-unclothed direction.

One of the women stepped forward. Dressed in a very short, watermelon silk frock, liberally decorated with black diamonds and pearls, and four-inch heels and fishnet stockings, she walked, supported on nothing visible, several inches above the sand, to the foot of the rock and looked up at Tish.

MARCUS TENSED, EVERY muscle flexed and ready, eager to jump into the middle of the confrontation, to throw himself in front of the naked woman. Why he didn't know, except the Warton woman, brash and maddening as she was, looked so defenseless, so much like a kitten facing a pack of dogs, that he wanted to protect her from the very ones he served. It was a very strong want, stronger almost than the vows and secrets that held him aloof and alone.

The woman in red silk smiled. It wasn't a pleasant smile, but it matched the ice in her voice when she said, "Marcus, we were dining. I do not know, nor do I care, what has precipitated your rather rude and uncouth summoning. Perhaps it is a direct result of spending so much time in the company of humans. But, at this moment, that is beside the point. Your human creature is plainly lawless and it has caused more than enough upset; thus proving it cannot be trusted among civilized people. Therefore, it is my judgment that it should be euthanized without further delay. Does anyone care to say me nay?"

His protective instinct overrode his common sense, propelled him into the fray. "You can't..."

She silenced him with a surge of power and a wave of her wand, barely glancing toward him as chains wrapped him from shoulder to knee. "You have no stake in this, Boarder Guard. Does anyone one else object?"

The silence was profound, but not with regret, until one of the Godmothers in the back of the group, her tone petulant, said, "Do we have to stand around in the dungeons discussing this? The damp is taking the curl out of my hair. No one cares. Just dispose of it and let's go eat. I'm hungry."

"So let it be." Blazing with power, humming a death chant, the wand was bare inches from Tish's bare skin when a vast roar filled the cavern. Echoing, bouncing off walls and ceiling, it ached in Marcus's ears, shook in the marrow of his bones, and came from the water.

Water that bulged, rose, sparkled with red motes of fury, and drew back from the shore, piled water on water, and became a towering shape. The pool held only dampness, tiny droplets of water, all else was embodied in the huge liquid shape that moved, with deliberate slowness and awful purpose toward the gaggle of disconcerted Godmothers.

And as it walked, its roar became, recognizably, one word. "Noooooooooooo!"

"Marcus!" one of the women shouted. "Tell your creature to..."

"Water sprite," another said, crying the words loud enough to be heard over the terrible head-hurting roar of the angry water. "Drop your wands. It's protecting her."

"Nonsense. Marcus' creature is a human. Only magic-holders can tame a sprite." The red-dressed woman—one of the Counselors and, for the moment, Marcus couldn't call her name to mind—didn't sound icy anymore, she sounded scared and angry, both at once, tangled one inside the other like ivy-twined roses. Regardless of her state of mind, the wand might have paled a trifle, but it never wavered.

Doing the only thing he knew, Marcus drew on a bit of folklore and shouted, knowing he had to save Tish no matter what the consequences, "Name it and tame it."

TISH THOUGHT THE roared command came from Marcus. It seemed the kind of senseless rhetoric he used. But she wasn't feeling too sensible herself. A water sprite? Not possible. Absolutely not possible. It was all a dream, brought on by breathing in too much mothball aroma. It had to be.

And yet, the water, for all its unnatural antics, its threatening aspect, still seemed friendly. At least, it wasn't trying to attack her; quite the contrary, it seemed to be protecting her from the Godmother's unpleasant intent. In fact, she knew the water sprite was harmless. How could it be anything else? It looked remarkably like one of the bears she designed. Bears meant to ride around in the passenger seats of people's cars. Bears made for rich people's MG's and BMW's, great big lovable masses of fake fur and imagination that were, almost, worth their weight in gold.

Without conscious thought, she stood there, teeth chattering, trying to smile in spite of the chill. Which was not from the cold but from pure fear, fear that she wasn't dreaming, that magic, Godmothers, and water sprites were real. But she didn't hesitate. "Bubba."

The roaring stopped, leaving only echoes to wander the length and breadth of the grotto, and was replaced by a guttural purring sound that, without words or gestures, expressed smug satisfaction. The water tower fell, with surprising gentleness and only a few lapping wavelets, but the sprite, if that's what it was, was still there, watching the Godmothers with watery eyes and waiting for their next move. They seemed well aware of the situation. And not at all comfortable with it. If Tish had to guess, she would have said confusion, hotly flavored with bits and dabs of anger, ruled supreme. Whispers and whisperers skittered and slunk across the sands and into the shadows.

Hugging herself, Tish caught bubbles of sound as they sped by and her brain, the fuel needle pressing on empty, barely running on fumes, tried to sort fact from fiction. It was a game try, but every bit of information was bizarre, better fit to be Conan Doyle's pipe dream than the truth. The water sprite had been tamed, that much was certain. Only magic-wielders could accomplish that feat, or so several of the godmothers kept repeating, after sly, speculative glances in Tish's direction.

According to the speakers, who were quite positive about it, it followed, even if it didn't rest easy, that the human, Marcus' creature, had to be a Wilding. The sprite-taming was proof enough of that, only what were they to do with her? She was a savage, untamed, dangerous, and they couldn't just punish her for her crimes against the Matriarchy and turn her loose. That would be unthinkable. But, what could they do that would...

Head shaking, sighing, and brooding seemed to be a majority opinion. That was followed by the same circular argument that said Tish couldn't use magic, but she had, so something, no one knew what, had to be done. Clearly the discussion was getting nowhere, settling nothing.

Her last meal—a hasty dinner of tuna sandwiches and soda as she dressed for the ball—seemingly had been some long forgotten time in the past, a past that hadn't included sprites or nattering, dillydallying

Godmothers. And clearly aware of only its own needs, Tish's upset stomach growled, perhaps not as loud as the sprite's roar but loud enough to silence the Godmothers. And the sound, rather than embarrassing her, prodded Tish into action.

"If this deciding of yours is going to take all night, or whatever time it is, couldn't we, at least, have something to eat? Or is starving me to death the final solution to your problem?" She hugged herself a little tighter, drew her knees up against her arms, and glowered at them through the strands of her drying hair.

Several of them returned her glower and added a dab of glare to give it power, but more simply looked at her as if seeing her for the first time, or maybe as if the stone had suddenly given voice to unseemly, or unrockly, demands.

"Wilding, what we do is..."

Tish's brain stopped working, but it wasn't connected to her mouth. She raised her head, shook back her hair, and said, "My name is Leticia Warton, Tish to my friends, which you aren't, and I am neither a savage nor a creature owned by your lackey, Marcus."

She heard him protest the characterization, but Tish went on. "I'm tired, hungry, and I want to go home. Right now. Failing that, I want to be taken to...to the United States Embassy."

Her outburst provoked a long, strained moment of instant quiet and quick sideways glances. Then the silence gave way to yet another discussion, this one in a close-knit huddle of regal women talking in urgent whispers. It dissolved almost as quickly as it was formed and a blue-gowned Godmother, with silver roses in her upswept raven tresses and a glitter of what might be intellectual interest in her dark eyes, came to Tish's rock.

"You are still a felon, an enemy of the state, and as such will not be allowed to visit the embassy. The proper authorities will be notified and if any one of them wishes to have converse with you, that is another matter. It will change nothing. As to how you found out an embassy exists in Faery, that is a question that involves a very serious breech in security, and it will have to be answered at some later date. First, we must attend to the more pressing of the problems you have, with your willful disregard of the law and the proprieties, given into our keeping."

Tish opened her mouth to protest, but was forestalled by the woman's relentless voicing of what would be. "The water sprite, Bubba, I believe you called it, cannot stay here. You must do something about it. We cannot have our prison system disrupted by a lonely, wailing sprite."

Shaking her head, trying to make sense of nothing even close to being sensible, Tish said, "Well, what exactly do you expect me to do about it? He was here when I came, and I don't see why I should do anything about him leaving."

Perhaps what she said was true, but now that she had named and tamed the sprite, it belonged to Tish. Or so she was informed as the godmothers, acting with haste, not a whole lot of joy, and some very real agitation, zapped some glaring yellow, unfamiliar clothes on her shivering body; evidently Faery's version of a prison jumpsuit. Then they transported her, and the now unchained, but still dazed seeming Marcus, in identical garb, out of the nether regions and into the drier portions of the castle.

They didn't go alone. The water sprite was chuckling happily as the unsettled, wand-tapping godmothers, ordered it to reduce itself and wrapped the smaller version in a pale-blue, handsomely wrought, by magic, out of nowhere, glass jug.

Tish, for one giddy moment, thought it looked remarkably like a gussied-up vinegar jug, of the gallon variety. But that giddiness gave way to a bad case of elevator stomach as they whooshed up, encased in nothing, through ceiling after ceiling. They finally they came to rest on a shimmering glass floor in a vast, echoing chamber that was, somehow, dominated by a row of plain ebony chairs. They were setting, all prim and proper, on a gold-and-crystal dais at the far end of the crystal-domed room. If the word "room" came anyplace close to describing the incredible, insubstantial structure that seemed as if it were made of glass and air and sparkling magic. And beauty. Indescribable, soaring, unearthly beauty that was its own reason for being.

Although she felt like a gawking peasant viewing skyscrapers for the first time, Tish couldn't stop staring. She was just able to force her gaping mouth closed, but she couldn't fight back the vertigo that was trying to bring her to her knees. Nor deny the firm belief that she was standing on nothing and was going to catapult, head-first and screaming like a lost soul, into the greater nothingness that lay below.

Hot and bitter, liquid rose in her throat. She swallowed hard, trying to keep from gagging.

"Miss...ah...Warton, are you unwell?"

It was a male voice. Although it didn't really sound like him, she thought it was Marcus who asked because he was the only male present. Tish didn't dare turn her head to look at him, she had to concentrate on looking straight ahead, seeing nothing, and on what dire consequences might follow her losing her lunch on the invisible floor of what had to be the Crystal Court. The place she was to face her judges and learn the punishment for her so-called crimes against the state, or nation, or whatever Faery was.

"Miss Warton?"

A hand touched her arm. Tish jumped and nearly lost control of her churning stomach. This time she knew it wasn't Marcus who was worried about her health. Breathing with utmost care, she eased her head around and saw a stranger; one that looked vaguely familiar.

Before she could trace the vagueness to its source, something cold and slimy plopped on top of her bare foot. Tish made the ultimate mistake of looking down. She heard one of the Godmothers shout, "Catch that damned frog."

"Toad," Tish managed to say just before she lost it completely, upchucking all over the transparent floor. Neither it nor the stranger's highly polished shoes were pristine when she was caught in a sticky web of magic and sped, dangling like a trapped fly, out of the Crystal Court and into a smaller, darker anteroom and dropped, without warning or ceremony, into a stiff brocade-covered chair.

She hadn't had a case of the violent barfs since she was in the sixth grade and Jimmy Rhones dared her to eat seventeen, family-sized nightcrawlers. Feeling empty and green, she risked one quick glance down and was rewarded with a glimpse of floor, real marble floor. Her eyes were closed, but her stomach was still grumbling and roiling when she heard squishy-sounding footsteps enter the room, heard the stranger's voice say, in what could only be described as a conspiratorial whisper, "Miss Warton, the Godmothers are quite upset. If there's anything to be gained from this unsavory mess, we really must talk."

"Talk?" Tish croaked rather than asked. At that moment, if there was anything she wanted less than to talk, it was what followed, crowding close on the heels of her own question, and adding anger to the turmoil that had already turned her brain to overcooked gelatin and her stomach to something best left unexamined.

All she truly wished for at that moment was to wake up from her nightmare, to look around the hospital room, and know she was home. And just maybe, at that point, she would vow never to sleep again.

Chapter Five

HIS FINGERS GRIPPED her chin, tilted her face up, just as she heard Marcus say, "No talking," obviously not addressing her. As odious as he was, he wasn't stupid. He knew she was barely able to breathe. Talking was out of the question, as was opening her eyes, looking around, trying to see whether he was addressing the stranger with the soggy shoes, or someone else.

Not that any of it mattered to Tish. She was planning on dying as soon as possible, sooner than that even, if she could keep the room from spinning long enough to figure out how to accomplish the deed without moving.

"Sir, I must protest your high-handedness in this matter. I, Artemus King, am a legal representative of the government of the United States of America and she is a citizen thereof. We both have rights which I intend to exercise. Now, step out of the room and allow us a few moments of privacy, so that we will be able discuss her situation and arrive at some possible solutions."

If such a thing were possible, Marcus didn't even try to be polite. "Faery is, in case that minor fact has escaped your notice, a slightly different universe, a totally different nation. Neither of which comes under your jurisdiction. The laws of Faery are not made nor broken lightly. Miss Warton may or may not be a citizen of your nation, but she has managed to run afoul of several laws of Faery and to break a handful more. She has been tried and found guilty of same.

"Talking will change nothing. Miss Warton is in my custody and will remain so until she is sentenced for her crimes. If you feel justice is better served in some other manner, then I suggest you take yourself and your opinions to the Full Council of Godmothers. And do it now."

None of it made any sense to Tish, and it didn't seem important enough to make her open her eyes. All she really wanted to do was groan, but even that would be too much effort. But, somewhere within her, she really hoped the soggy-shoed man was gone, that no one was around to see her total misery.

IN THE SILENCE that followed, Marcus swabbed Tish's face with a wet, pungent smelling cloth that fairly reeked of lemon and some sort of sweet oil, tilting her head back and forth to seek out new areas of soil and disposing of them in an impersonal and efficient manner. And, as a by-product, not intended by the Godmothers but devoutly hoped by him, returning enough of her energy to partly refuel her animosity, to make her keep on fighting. The way things were looking, and he didn't know the why of it, Ms. Warton's defiance might be her only hope of surviving. And, despite what he knew of his own shortcomings, he wanted her to survive. Even if he wasn't ready to admit it, except to himself, why he wanted it so badly. Or that he wanted her just as badly.

Her eyes open a bare slit, Tish glared at him. "Get your hands off me!" It might have lacked force, but it was definitely a snarl. "I'm not an invalid. I can wash my own face if it needs it."

His own chuckle was, or so he intended, malice incarnate, and it hid some of the conflicting thoughts that were adding new disorder to his inner turmoil. Something was going on in Faery, something that had a definite taint of evil. And, whoever this Wilding was, she very obviously didn't have a stake in whatever power struggle was taking place, a struggle that had already sent Stephen away. But it could destroy her, and somehow Marcus knew he was going to do his damnedest to see that it didn't happen.

He hid his worry behind a taunt, one that only erred on the side of absolute truth. "Oh, believe me, Miss Warton, it needed washing. And, if I may say it, with no insult intended of course, so do various and sundry of your other rather spotted and bedecked body parts. And if that was your lunch, it must have been more than a green salad and a cup of herb tea."

She opened her mouth to growl at him, but his chuckle, definitely wicked, stopped her as he went on with his face washing and Tish baiting.

"Tell me, Miss Warton, does it seem to you that washing is something that you seem to need more often than others of your ilk? That's, of course, presuming that such a thing exists. I rather imagine it would be difficult to assemble a group of your peers. I, for one, would hate being in the general vicinity if such an event actually took place. One of you is a disaster, think of what two or more..."

SHE OPENED HER eyes just in time to see him shake his head. Not entirely sure why he was so capable of pushing her buttons, making her furious enough to bite nails, Tish took a quick breath, but she didn't sputter out an obscenity. Mostly because she couldn't think of one awful enough to describe his character and antecedents. Not without insulting a fairly large number of species in the animal kingdom.

Marcus, who seemed to be pondering the mysteries of the universe, went on in a musing tone, "It occurs to me that perhaps that's why your water sprite is so taken with you. According to the best authorities, sprites are rather like puppies in some respects, and, although I've never owned a puppy, it is my understanding that they enjoy chewing on their owner's smelly shoes and socks."

Instant anger pushed words out of her mouth. "I wish I had that damned wand back. I'd turn you into what you really are: an odious, insulting, mud-wallowing pig." Tish tried to jerk loose from his hand, but he laughed again, sounding sardonic and superior and faintly malevolent, and held her with apparent ease while he dropped the cloth and reached off to one side to retrieve something else.

"Here," he said, pressing the rim of a glass against her lower lip. "Drink this. Godmother Morgain says it's good for what ails you."

Furious at his calm assumption that she would obey his every command, and determined to show him that he wasn't her superior in anything, she clamped her lips together. She'd damned sure not drink whatever foul concoction that he was trying to pour down her unwilling throat. She twisted her head back and forth as she slid further down in the chair, trying to escape from his unwelcome attention.

His laugh was definitely evil. "Drink it, Miss Warton, or I shall have to hold your nose and pour it down you. A task that I would no doubt enjoy far more than you would."

Anger red-hot and sizzling, burning her face, churning in her still upset stomach, she put her hands on the arms of the chair and pushed her slumping body up, stiffening her spine until she was sitting erect. She could almost feel the sparks shooting out of her eyes as she stared at him. "You wouldn't dare," her voice was as flat and cold as an ice-glazed pond in winter.

"No?" he asked, his voice deceptively gentle as his fingers clamped on her nose, cutting off her breath, and tipping her face upward. When finally her mouth opened to gasp in a breath, he poured in a few tablespoons of whatever was lurking in the glass. It was a foretaste of hell, bitter as gall, with a decided undertaste of skunk, and it slid down her throat with all the ease of castor oil coated burrs.

"Gaww." She tried to spit it out and got her second dose of pure nasty for her effort. It went down, but, no matter how her stomach expressed its wretchedness, the drink had taken up squatter's rights and was intent on remaining in its new home.

"Marcus," the voice, coming from somewhere beyond Tish's range of vision, sounded amused and imperious at the same time, "do hurry. The young woman is wanted in the Crystal Court, as are you."

Just the thought of returning to the vast, limitless room with its mind-tricking, insubstantial limits, and nebulous underpinning sent Tish into a tizzy, or somewhere into that general area of near hysteria. "No," she said, managing to get out the single word before her tormentor poured another healthy slug of sewer sludge into her open mouth. It oozed down her throat, silencing any further protest.

The Godmother strolled into Tish's view, inspected her with cold eyes, and said, in a rather stilted tone, one that tried to sound both kind and friendly, and came very close to its aim, "It won't make you ill again. Witch's Brew works almost at once. You should have been dosed before your initial appearance in the Crystal Court, but we don't have much congress with Wildings. As a matter of fact, we actually thought they were something of a human tale, the kind Faery children find so fascinating, until you, your frog, and Marcus came to our attention."

The entire speech went into Tish's ears, but all she actually heard, and repeated, was, "Witch's Brew?"

The Godmother was tall, slim, dressed in peach-colored slacks and a cashmere sweater of a slightly darker hue. Tiny pearls decorated her earlobes, and her hair, reddish-brown and shiny, was pulled back into an elegant style that bore some slight kinship to a ponytail. She smiled, and it might well have been genuine, at Tish's question and said, "Yes, it works wonders for those suffering from magical hormone imbalance. It has very few side-effects, unless it's eaten with apples, and then it only causes a deep sleep. The Wicked Queen gives us a yearly supply as a partial payment on the maintenance agreement for her magic mirror."

Her mind fuzzy, skittering away from what she was hearing, Tish licked her lips, shuddered at the lingering taste of the brew, and asked, for no good reason except the Godmother's words, used in the given context, made no sense whatsoever, "Maintenance agreement?"

"Well," the Godmother looked slightly uncomfortable, "ordinarily we don't push that particular product, but she is rather demanding and quite capable of doing some painful things to one's anatomy. The magic mirror needs tuned up, cleaned, demagnetized, re-voiced, and re-spelled every year or so. Otherwise, it might malfunction and start telling lies or something equally absurd. That would not sit well with her majesty. Not at all.

"Our magic mirror shop does good work; they have the latest computerized equipment and are well trained. So I'm sure she considers a couple of kegs of Witch's Brew, and few other minor items, a fair price to pay for the peace of mind, or should that be ego stroking, a fully functional mirror gives her. She does so enjoy being assured she is the fairest in the land and can afford the luxury, so why should we deny her wishes."

"Morgain?" The call came from brightly lit room beyond the open doorway. "Come along. The Council is waiting for the two prisoners."

"Yes, of course. Marcus? Miss Warton? Shall we go?"

Wanting to clamp her hands around the chair arms and hang on for dear life, Tish took a deep breath and got ready to say, "I'm not going back in there," but one look at Marcus's face changed her mind. She'd show him. Damn the man and his superior smirk, one that the bruise on his face only made more arrogant and rakishly handsome.

Maybe this time, if she lucked-out, she could throw up on him. A good drenching in slightly used Witch's Brew would serve him right.

He returned her look, his left eyebrow quirking up, and his amber-eyed gaze seemed as devilishly insolent as his slouching walk when he came to where she sat and held out his hand as if to give assistance to a helpless female.

Surprising even herself, Tish jumped to her feet without a single trace of wooziness. Whatever had afflicted her before was gone, taking with it the last foul taste of Witch's Brew, but leaving her with a mild case of giddy well-being. She felt equal to, as her stepfather was wont to say, licking her weight in wildcats.

"Miss Warton." Marcus bowed and extended his forearm, just as though he expected to escort her, with her hand resting daintily on his arm. It would be a long and stately stroll the length of the anteroom, which could have hosted a basketball game, fans and all, and into the huge courtroom beyond.

"Keep away from me," she hissed. "I'm neither sick nor infirm."

"No, you're a..."

The dash of ire in his lazy-voiced response brought him a gentle reprimand from the Godmother Morgain. "Marcus, do stop. Miss Warton is perfectly capable of walking on her own. Unless of course you are...ah...if you and she have formed a physical attraction and have begun to dally..."

"Impossible," he snapped, rather too quickly.

"No way!" Tish's denial was as swift as his and louder, but not any more vehement.

Morgain looked from one to the other and back again before she said, her voice neutral, her eyes unreadable, "In that case, perhaps Marcus should go first, I next, and Miss Warton last. It has been a long day, and looks to be even longer, I have several clients waiting, with jewels and gold in their sweaty hands, who are clamoring for magic wishes, and I do not intend to listen to the two of you bicker and quarrel like... Well, I just won't have it, that's all."

"Yes, ma'am," Marcus said, standing very tall and proper, rather like a soldier or one of the British Royal Guards.

Tish saw no reason to say anything at all. She followed along behind Morgain, frothing inside, lower lip stuck out, eyes narrow and mean, hardly seeing anything except Morgain's back. She couldn't see Marcus, but he was present in her fiery thoughts. He was a prig, probably a jerk, and she wasn't going to have anything at all to do with him. No, she wasn't. Not even if he did look like Prince Charles, but with a chin, one that she suspected had a cleft, but only a small one, more like a dimple. Just as soon as this silly charade was over, she was going to demand to...

A hand caught her wrist, pulled her into the shadow of a fluted column beside the doorway. Artemus King whispered, "Please, Miss Warton, listen to me. I know you recognized me. I saw it in your eyes. But, please, don't, for the love of God, tell Marcus that you saw me at your mother's ball."

Dimly, Tish heard Marcus say something to Morgain, but her whole attention was on Mr. King. For a fleeting second, she wanted to apologize for ruining his shoes, but couldn't quite find the right words. Instead, she asked, "My mother's ball? Why were you..."

He didn't answer directly. "My life is in you hands. I implore you, don't destroy me."

"But, why..."

Edging back into the deeper shadow, he whispered, "Not now. They're calling for you. Just promise me that you won't betray my secret."

Perhaps she nodded, Tish wasn't too sure, but she certainly agreed with Alice's assessment of Wonderland. Things were, indeed, getting curiouser and curiouser; and there wasn't a white rabbit in sight. And, if Tish were arranging her own dream, she would certainly have added one. Possibly two. And a nonsmoking worm to keep them both company.

No rabbits came leaping out of the light. There was, however, the pure fear of returning to the Crystal Court to send new tremors and nerve quakes zigging and zinging through her body. Not that she intended to let Marcus and/or the pack of Godmothers conquer her with magical displays and stomach swooping nothing. No indeed.

With a final glance toward Mr. King's hiding place, and an evanescent suspicion that her own mother was somehow involved in this whole unbelievable scenario, she lifted her chin, straightened her spine. She started to step through the door, pausing at the last moment to brush resurgent bits and pieces of her last meal off the front of her glaring-yellow prison suit.

And there was a thing she needed to know. She felt an odd sense of something, responsibility tinged with loss, or anger tinged with fear, or all of the above, coupled with the need to know the sprite was safe. "Where's Bubba? I'm not going in there without him."

Morgain stopped, whirled around, and stared at Tish, or maybe it was a glare, filled with suspicion not query. "Who, or what, in Faery is Bubba?"

Tish could feel the blush crawling up her neck to burn on her face, but she made sure she didn't sound like a wimp when she said, "My water sprite. He was in a jug, a blue one, and somebody took him. He's mine, everyone said so, and I want him back. Right now."

Tish wasn't sure if the Godmother was going to slap her or laugh. Morgain did neither, although the corner of her mouth did move ever so slightly, but that could have been the beginnings of a snarl. She signed, heavily, like the mother of three sets of teenage twins at the end of a day long shopping expedition at the mall. It was truly long suffering.

"Your sprite and your frog are evidence of your crimes and/or your Wilding magic. They are with the Council. Your sprite is lonesome and whimpering a little, but your frog is absolutely unruly. You really must do something about him as soon as possible."

The memory of Carl's rutting behavior came back in a rush, complete with mental pictures of his licentious acts, but Tish felt very little pain. Not enough to ache for a lost love, but more than enough to make her say, and mean, "I won't. Carl is a toad now, and as far as I'm concerned, he'll be a toad until he dies."

Giggles, inappropriate but warming to her spirits and her body, floated up from her chest, and she wanted to say, "He'll be a toad until he croaks, and then he'll be a damned dead toad." But she swallowed laughter and words when Marcus said, as if he could read her mind and had found her thought process terribly trivial, "Please, don't say it."

Morgain gave each of them a look compounded of knowing and what might have been secret laughter and said, "Come along. The

Council is waiting and so are several hundred clients. We really must get this matter out of the way so we can get on with the business of Faery."

The juxtaposition of the two words, gave Tish pause. "Business? What kind of business could Godmothers...?"

"Selling magic, of course. Wishes and... There's really no time for this now. Marcus can give you a full explanation later." Making shooing motions, as if she were herding a flock of recalcitrant lambs, or maybe wind-spooked turkeys, Morgain urged Tish and Marcus into the Crystal Court.

Stepping gingerly, almost afraid to keep her eyes open, warily watching for the terrible onslaught of vertigo and stomach-jump, Tish, the Witch's Brew keeping her magic hormones in check, walked into the pulsing heart of a glorification. Scintillating rainbows moved together, blending their violets, indigos, blues, greens, yellows, oranges, and red into ribbons and spangles of newborn unnamed colors.

Eyes wide, Tish wanted to throw open her arms and embrace the skin-tingling, soul-delighting light show. But, remembering where she was, and why, Tish managed to retain a smidgeon of dignity. But only just as she caught her first whiff of rain-drenched summer earth, dew-dropped rose buds, and red, ripe watermelon, rainbow scents.

She scarcely heard a voice, coming from the fully occupied row of ebony chairs at the far end of the court, say, "It's about time, Morgain. Bring the prisoners before the Council." But Tish felt Morgain's hand on her arm, and felt the Godmother pulling her forward.

Beady-eyed fear-mice began gnawing at the outer edges of her euphoria, but their appetites were dulled by the wonders of the Crystal Court. However, their hunger was revved up and rampaging by the time Tish halted in front of the Council of Godmothers. She tried to read her fate in the row of formidable faces and inscrutable eyes gazing down at her. They made her feel as if each one of the Godmothers held a magnifying glass and was subjecting her to a silent, full-spectrum, Sherlock Holmesian examination. One that would certainly get her a marked-down price tag when they sold her on the open market.

The Godmothers' chairs were setting on a raised dais, putting them about three feet higher than where Tish stood on the transparent, light-shot floor. Directly in front of the middle Godmother, sort of bobbing and bouncing in time to his watery cries, was Bubba's gallon jug, with him inside. When the sprite saw Tish, his sobs turned to a fluting sound, one that sent small bubbles up through the opening at the top of the jug. Several drifted across to touch Tish's cheeks, exploding in a series of wet sprite-kisses that were enormously comforting. And, although she would never have admitted it to Marcus, they felt remarkably like a puppy's welcoming licks.

Tish's wand, fairly bursting with coruscating flicks and spurts of multi-hued light, was lying on a square of midnight velvet spread out next to Bubba's jug. Tish felt an instant need to grab the jug and the wand, but not the barred cage of crystal that contained the pop-eyed, raging toad. Slobbering and slimy, it wasn't a pretty sight; neither were its mad bellowing and insane efforts to destroy the bars and attack its former love.

Whatever pity Tish might have felt for it, was buried in a new wave of loathing and disgust. He was exactly what he had shown himself to be, but Tish was fairly certain that if Carl ever managed to escape from toadism, he would murder her with his bare hands.

"Some toads are poison," Marcus whispered out of the corner of his mouth. "I'd stay well away from him if I were you. Unless you're over your bout of jealousy and are planning on turning him back to a man. Although I'm not sure he would still marry you, it might be worth a try."

Startled at his nearness, Tish turned her head, glared at the man who standing very close to her side, and hissed, "Mind your own damned business."

"You are his business, or, at least, very shortly you will be. And, from what I have heard, neither of you will enjoy the experience to the utmost."

The ominous warning came from someone in the row of seated Godmothers. And there was no way to tell who had spoken. They were dressed in identical, billowing, throat-to-floor robes of a sort of opalescent white that color-shifted to iridescent lavender, pale blue, silver, or green at their slightest movement. Their hair, of various shades and hues of silver, copper, and teak, flowed down their shoulders and was confined only at the crown by small tiaras of rubies and gold.

They looked, despite their rich and colorful attire, like a line of Supreme Court Justices. Justices all ready to dispense justice and having the power to see that each malefactor lived up to letter and word of the prescribed punishment.

Rather belatedly, Tish realized that she was, indeed, the prisoner at the bar. And, frankly speaking, it was scaring the vinegar out of her. The quivery trembles were only momentarily eased by another stream of bubbly sprite kisses and Bubba's lilting water-song.

"It's real," she muttered, sounding like a ninny, and feeling like a house just fell on her head. "Faery and... It's all real."

Marcus's scorn would have withered a whole field of drought-resistant nettles. "Of course it's real, Miss Warton. What did you think, that you had hit your head and were dreaming the whole thing?"

That thought had been lurking inside her brain, that's assuming she still had one, and playing a large part in keeping her sane, or reasonably so. After all, what adult in their right mind would have believed anything about Faery and Godmothers and magic wands that worked and water sprites as lovable as puppies and...and...

Tish risked a quick glance at the tall lean man. And Marcus, if all the rest was real, what on earth was he? An elf? No, that was beyond reason. No elf would act like he did. It would take a human to be that arrogant and insolent and totally unbearable.

Well, a small still voice, one that she had always assumed was her conscience, whispered in the depths of her muddled thinking processes, you know one thing for sure: no matter what you thought, this isn't some scheme your mother hatched up behind your back. Not even she could have managed something like this.

Another small voice, possibly the voice of experience, laughed immoderately. Tish ignored them both. If she started thinking about her mother, she would start to bawl like a lost calf. And her tears would just be a new target for Marcus's scorn, and she wouldn't have that. Although there was no reason why she should care what he thought, was there?

She was so involved in her mental gyrations that she didn't hear one of the Council call her name. Morgain gave her a little push and said, "Don't be afraid. Go to the foot of the dais as you were requested, Miss Warton. Regardless of what Marcus may have told you, you have nothing to worry about here. The Council is always fair. And the punishments meted out here always suit the crime."

Perhaps what the Godmother said was nothing more than the truth, but when Tish stepped forward, her mouth was bone dry and her heart was pounding out the beat to a funeral dirge. A rather fast one, or one that had been adopted by a rock-and-roller.

Bubba's water-song became a croon.

Tish's magic wand began to glow with some weird inner light, a light that might have been greenish-gold or maybe magenta. It lifted a foot or so off the dais. Bobbed up and down in time to some inner rhythm.

Marcus cleared his throat as if he intended to speak.

Straightening her back, Tish looked at the row of elegant Godmothers and, fully aware of her own disreputable state, allowed what her mother called her blind bullheadedness to take over. Her mother meant she was blind to reason, bulling her way through a situation without any thought of compromise.

Anger blazed through her, if only for an instant. It was enough to goad her into action. After all, she had some pride, didn't she? She didn't have to stand there like a bug and let them squash her, did she?

Her jaw squared. Determined to see them in hell before she'd let them see the yellow streak that was jelling in her spine and turning her knees to melted butter, Tish lifted her chin. She said, not a little amazed at the words that came out of her mouth, but not about to issue a retraction, "Well, ladies, I'm tired and hungry and you've already decided I'm guilty of heaven alone knows what.

"Let's get this little farce over with, shall we? What's my sentence going to be? Life in the dungeons? Beheading? Sold into slavery? Branded and lamed?"

Behind her, Tish heard Morgain gasp and Marcus chuckle, or perhaps it was the other way around. She didn't look back; the masters, or mistresses, whichever was proper, of her fate lay in a different direction. And Tish wasn't real sure that her Faery Godmothers had any intention of allowing her to live happily ever after. Or to live at all.

Chapter Six

TISH'S OUTBURST cast a pall of dead silence, which wouldn't have been more funereal if it had come with the heavy odor of lilies and a lament played on the bag pipes, into the Crystal Court. The Council of Godmothers stared down at her for what seemed several eternities, plus or minus a decade here and there. It was a far from pleasant situation; Tish was feeling the effects of it, or the Witch's Brew Marcus had poured down her throat, or maybe both.

The huge room, for all of its light show and vast distances, was a bit on the warm side. Sweat ran in an itchy trickle down her back, between her breasts, and Tish wanted to scratch. But not nearly as much as she wanted to scream and run, get away from the land of Faery and go home.

At that moment, even her mother's nefarious deeds of matrimonial shenanigans would have been homemade biscuits and sausage gravy, ordinary things, human things. Tish wouldn't allow her hands to fight the annoying inch, or her legs to run. But she did swallow the lump that filled her throat too full and said, the squeak in her voice making it a question, "Well?"

The fountaining lights shot high, beams and ribbons of color tangled, fell back, like streamers at a wild party. As she watched, or tried to follow the pulsations, the lights faded to a sort of pastel twilight, veils of pearlescent color that trembled and flowed at the command of an unfelt zephyr. One that had to be as warm as a summer breeze. And the wall, if it was one, behind the Godmothers was the night sky, blue-black, replete with twinkling stars thrown by the bucketfuls across the dark expanse. To Tish, it looked no more real than the rest of the Court. If she was doing the guessing, she would have to say the whole thing was a dream, and not an entirely pleasant one at that.

On the off chance it wasn't, Tish took a deep breath, wiped the sweat off her upper lip, and waited. After another endless time, which in all honestly was probably less then thirty seconds, the silence was pushed aside. "We are not barbarians, Miss Warton," the Godmother in the first chair to the left of center said softly, but with shock plain on her exquisitely made-up face.

Tish didn't say, "You could have fooled me," but she wanted to. Instead she glanced at the hyper toad, read his bugeyed glare as fury, and smiled at him. He swelled up until he was nearly ready to pop. It made him slightly larger, but it certainly didn't add to his attractiveness; which was all ready into large negative numbers.

"However, whatever we may or may not be, you are responsible for the frog," the young-looking Godmother seated at the right end of the row said. "I mean, it was your magic that changed him and we can't undo what other magic has..." She put her hand over her mouth, widened her pale blue eyes, and blushed redder than a politician caught telling the truth.

"Wilding," the center Godmother said, her eyes dark and brooding, her flawless golden skin not at all marred by a tiny, lightning-shaped scar on her left cheekbone, "I am Tregon, Chairman of the Council, and it is my duty to deliver sentences in the Crystal Court. In your particular case, we have met and discussed but have reached an impasse of sorts."

She paused, drug her top teeth across her lower lip, making small marks in her coppery lipstick, and seemed to be choosing her words carefully before she went on. Then, what she said wasn't at all what Tish had been braced to hear.

"We have an extensive law library, good law clerks and researchers, but in this instance, we have had to go beyond the known into the unknown and that creates problems. What we do here has future ramifications. Therefore, we must move forward with caution." She stopped, drew her teeth across her lips again, and leaned toward Tish to look at her at closer range.

Tish's chin came up, her eyes narrowed, and she returned a defiant glare for the Godmother's calm, impersonal inspection.

"Wildings have always been a children's tale and, as such, not in our belief system. However, you exist and your talents, while very crude and weak, exist also. But, you have broken laws and have to be punished. But, the punishment for the unmagicked is different, less stringent, than for those with Godmotherly gifts. Thus far, you are unique in our experience and history, so we must delve further into this matter before we can pass sentence."

Not sure whether the news was good or bad, Tish asked, "What does that mean?"

With a billow and flash of changing robe-colors, Tregon shifted in her ebony chair, interlaced her long fingers, and spoke as if she was imposing a sentence on Faery rather than Tish. "You and your cohorts, the frog, the sprite, and the wand, which will be warded and spelled against use by you, will have to remain here until we finish our search through the attics and sub-basements for additional information about your kind. Also, the grimoires in the walnut room haven't been touched; there are histories, diaries, memoirs, and journals in the archives to read. All of which are time consuming and must be done in and around our other tasks. We cannot allow a minor matter, like this, to interrupt the daily workings of a rich and complex kingdom."

Tears, clamoring to be shed, pushed at the backs of Tish's eyes, but she held them back and faked a cool indifference. The tremor in her voice gave lie to her pose. "So, it's back to the dungeons for me, is it?"

"Oh, no, of course not. We... You will be placed in the keeping of..." She stopped to whisper a question into her neighbor's ear, listened to the answer, and went on, but in a new conversational direction, one that held the bark of command in its dulcet tones. "Border Guard Marcus, you have been found guilty of dereliction of duty. Approach the Council and hear your sentence."

MARCUS OBEYED THE command, even though he thought, and feared, he knew what the sentence was going to be. Even as he stepped forward to stand at Tish's side, so close that his sleeve brushed hers, he had that curious sense that something was happening that shouldn't be. That somehow he and Tish were the focus of something that wasn't going to be to their benefit.

He was well aware that he couldn't escape the punishment; indeed, he deserved it. Even if he had been given orders to the contrary, he should have prevented the wand from being used. He had known it was charged, and warning her clearly hadn't been enough. But, beyond that, he was also sure that he would have reached the same state no matter what he had done, that somehow the whole series of events were preordained, planned. Even the thought frightened him, but he was well aware of how much power the Godmothers held. And how dangerous it could be if, and it was far more than a hunch, it was being misused. Not that he could prove it. At least, not yet.

But, his own growing feelings for the Warton woman, Leticia, scared him more than anything else. Such feelings weren't for the likes of him. Not now, not ever.

Still, Tish shouldn't be... He didn't want to pursue that train of thought either. She meant nothing to him, could never mean anything to him, except... Acting on some vague need, he moved a half-step closer to her.

DISCONCERTED AT THE body tingles his nearness was causing, Tish wanted to ease away. Or maybe move closer. She wasn't sure which. And, she did not like, nor could she understand, her almost instant sexual reaction to a man she totally detested. She couldn't, however, deny the fact that she was feeling decidedly warm.

Gritting her teeth, she fought against the desire that was beginning to brush his long, lean body with an alluring glow, making him infinitely more attractive than she remembered him being. Her heart jumped into the act, speeded up, fluttered like a coy bird, and pumped hot blood to her hands that felt a sudden need to caress him, her arms to embrace him, her mouth that wanted to part for his wild, tongue-tangling kisses. What the rest of her body wanted was something that made Tish burn with...well, maybe not shame exactly, but the wanton images of...of...

"Miss Warton, you're dripping with sweat and your face is bright red, are you ill again?" Tregon's cool voice inched through Tish's fevered longings, and held the pulsing need at bay for a moment. Anything to get away from the man she was wanting to ravish, right there on the invisible floor, in front of Godmothers and all, and thinking maybe what Tregon asked was true, Tish panted out, "Yes. Sick. Have to have air."

"One moment," Tregon said, and there seemed to be a good deal of malicious pleasure in the saying. "Marcus, for your crimes and neglect of a previous duty, you are sentenced to guard, teach, and protect Miss Warton, day and night, until she leaves Faery or until we release you from this sentence."

"No, you can't..." Tish's breathless cry was filled with horror. She tried to step back, to remove her lust-crazed body, with its hardened nipples and burning loins from Marcus's immediate presence, and tripped over her own unwilling feet. Marcus caught her as she fell, put one arm around her shoulders, one under her knees, lifted her up against his chest.

"Where do you want her?" he asked the court.

"Morgain is in charge of the pair of you. Take the Wilding to Morgain's personal apartments in the south courtyard. Morgain will see that the sprite, wand, and toad reach the same destination. Hurry along, Marcus, and get the Wilding safely abed. We do not want to be accused, by her embassy, of cursing her or something. An inter-universal incident is not something I care to cope with at the moment."

The Godmother was still talking when the floor dissolved beneath

Marcus's feet and, with Tish's body tight against his own, the magic non-elevator ride plunged them down. This time it didn't make Tish ill, in fact she scarcely felt it. She was too busy running the fingers of her left hand through Marcus's dark hair while her right hand delved inside his virulent yellow prison garb to rub his smooth, bare, hard-muscled flesh.

"Stop that! What the hell are you..."

He held her out and away from him.

Laughing low and sultry, a seductive technique she had learned from a bunch of Saturday nights watching old movies, and some steamy new ones, Tish wiggled and squirmed her way back into close contact with his body. She put both arms around his neck and tried to pull his lips down to meet hers.

The downward drop ceased. Marcus, with Morgain close behind, stepped out a side door of the massive castle and into a chilly, star-bright night, hurrying across a grassy courtyard toward Morgain's suite of rooms.

"Morgain," he said, through clenched teeth, his voice strangled with what might have been the terminal stages of acute embarrassment, "you'd better do something quick."

"Kiss me," Tish murmured, sort of growling out the words as she slithered up to nuzzle his chin and then to nibble at his earlobe.

"Stop that right now!" He fairly roared the words, pulling his head sharply to one side. He strode striding across the court to where a low-walled pool, its water lilies asleep for winter, sludgy ice forming around its edges, stood beneath a winter-silent fountain.

Tish giggled and tried to whisper an invitation. One that erred on the far side of politeness and wouldn't have required an RSVP; more likely an X or two were the only letters it would have gotten in the real world.

"THAT'S IT," MARCUS said, fighting against his own physical response, the need to surrender to her invitation. This had to be some cruel spell set by one of the Godmothers, and he damned sure didn't like it. At least, not under the present circumstances. Raising Tish's too-willing body high, and, without further ceremony or warning, Marcus dumped her into the pool of dark water.

The frigid dunking chilled her ardor. But, it also took most of what was left of her consciousness. When he pulled her out of the water, she was as limp as a worn-out pair of blue jeans, and fairly close to the same color. And, for just an instant, he thought he had killed her.

She moved and, as if from a great crackle-filled distance, Marcus heard Morgain say, "Marcus, why in Faery did you..."

His own rumbling answer was farther away, and too filled with fury to actually belong to him. "What's wrong with her? What in blazes have you done to her?"

TISH HEARD BOTH questions, but Morgain's answer, if she made one, was lost in the shivering, teeth-chattering nothingness that rolled down on Tish and gobbled her up.

And the next thing she heard was, "She won't remember."

The bed was soft and warm, too soft and comfortable to be anything less than a top-of-the-line cloud. The satin sheets were smooth, the coverlet light and cozy and pulled up over her head—her favorite way of sleeping. The words found their way to Tish's ears, wandered through a maze of haze, and found some still functioning receptor in her brain.

She sat up abruptly, realized she was naked beneath the sliding sheet, grabbed it in both hands, and held it up to her chin. "Won't remember what?" she asked, not even trying to take the surly out of her tone as she glared at Marcus who was sitting beside the bed. "Where are my clothes, you inbred pervert? Why am I in bed? What did you do to me?"

As far as Tish could tell, his amber eyes held nothing but icy disdain and his voice was a perfect match when he said, "I did nothing but dowse you in cold water. It was the only thing I could think of that would allow me to keep my virtue."

"Liar! I wouldn't touch you with a..."

"Clichés aren't becoming to a would-be ravisher of men," he said. "Besides that, Miss Warton, you touched me with a good deal more than a pole, no matter what its length."

"I..." Flickers and snaps of memory danced through her head, unpleasant memories of her hands pawing, her lips parting, her loins... Shuddering, she shoved them away, forced them back into some dark place in her mind. "Why?"

"As I understand it, you overdosed on a love potion and were trying your damnedest to seduce me. Not that your damnedest had any class at all. Frankly, I thought the way you were yowling and squirming, you were acting more like a cat in heat than a..."

"I did no such thing!" The sheet slipped a little more, Tish caught it back. "Get the hell out of my bedroom." A worrisome thought struck her. "Or is this your bedroom. Did you slip me a love potion so I..."

Marcus stood up. "In all honesty, you do have a certain sexual appeal, but force you to have your way with me? Certainly not! There are hundreds of beautiful women in the world, many of whom who would swoon if they even thought there was a chance to enjoy my...ah...my manly charms. Just tell me why I would stoop to dose a cross-grained, unpleasant female, with the temper of a warthog and the personal habits of a swine. If I wanted to make love to you, which I don't, I'm sure you could be coaxed into..."

"Marcus!" The single word had the snap of a command. Carrying a heavy book, Morgain came into the room. "According to the latest issue of *The Godmothers' Desk Reference*, it was the Witch's Brew that did it. It is compounded of some of the same ingredients we use in the love potions, but in much higher strengths. We didn't know it would cause...

"In the ordinary course of things, full strength Witch's Brew is given, diluted with water and in small amounts, to young girls, just on the threshold of womanhood. That's when the Godmother gifts usually appear. But, Miss Warton is sexually mature, and you did give her a full glass, so naturally her reaction was... Well, it's always nice to learn something new, isn't it? And no real harm was done, except to Marcus's male pride, when he realized it wasn't his irresistible charms that were..." Morgain winked at Tish and shot a sly glance at Marcus.

He frowned, wincing a little as the expression tugged at the tender skin around his scratches and bruise, neither of which made him look any less aristocratic.

Tish's smile was too sweet to be believed, and her voice fairly oozed sugar when she looked at the man and said, "I knew it was your fault all the time, you poured it down my throat."

He swore, creating some new and interesting variations on themes that Tish had never even imagined.

"That's enough!" Morgain said, giving him a look that would have frozen boiling water and the steam rising above it. "I have clients waiting and... I'm not sure I can trust the pair of you not to kill each other before I..." She sighed and muttered, "Perhaps I can trade assignments with one of the others. Vian has stable duty this month, shoveling out the horse stalls, I believe, perhaps if I..." She shook her head. "No, that wouldn't be a fair trade, I would hate to cheat her."

Marcus said, "Godmother, I am well aware of my duty to this woman. You can rest assured that I will do nothing that brings her to harm of any sort or kind. I will give you my word of honor on that."

Still looking doubtful, Morgain said, "Well, come along then and

I'll give you a list of what must be done. Miss Warton needs to be taught something about Faery, for her own safety if nothing else and..." Her voice faded and was gone as she, with the tall man following behind her, exited the room, leaving Tish alone.

Her aloneness hadn't had time to develop into loneliness before he returned with another of the sickly yellow prison jumpsuits, its folds were topped by a small heap of frilly underwear, also in yucky yellow. Marcus dropped the stack on the bed and said, tossing the words back over his shoulder, "Get dressed and we'll start your lessons after you have something to replenish your supply of stomach fuel. You know, in case you feel a sudden desire to upchuck again."

Tish grinned at his retreating back and said, feeling as spiteful as she sounded, "This is a switch. Ever since we met, all you've been trying to do is get me out of my clothes."

He stiffened, started to turn, took a deep breath, and stalked out, closing the door very gently behind him, but only after he said, sounding every inch the gentleman, "My punishment is to be your jailer, Miss Warton. I can see it is going to be a worse punishment than even the Council had reason to imagine."

"Oh, if I have anything to say about it, it will be," Tish muttered as she scrambled out of bed, grabbed the clothing, and headed toward the bathroom that she could see through a partially open door. It and the bedroom she had just vacated were both ordinary, rich human, fancy magazine ordinary, with polished oak and flowery prints and thick white carpets and crystal accents and decorator frou-frou. Tish had trouble believing that she was actually in Faery until she saw the jumpsuit reflected in the wall of mirrors.

"A felon in Faery," she reminded herself as she made use of what had been placed at her disposal: new toothbrush, creams and lotions, cosmetics, brushes and combs, curling iron, perfume, and girded herself to face the day. But no matter what she did, the same face stared back at her.

Blue eyes with some almost respectable lashes, especially when they were filled out with a dab or two of mascara and some nice smudgy eyeliner. Short black hair that tousled better than it curled. Full lips. Eighteen freckles across the bridge of her nose. An almost dimple in her left cheek. She looked closer, trying to see some change that magic, if she really had some, had made. There wasn't a thing, not one thing; unless you counted the sallow pallor, the prison yellow gave her normally pale skin.

"I hate yellow," she told the face in the mirror as she took a final swipe at her hair. "I hate yellow, toads, supercilious, arrogant bastards who pretend to be men, and..."

A fragment of memory jolted through her brain, memory of the night before, memory of... Red stained her cheeks and she fled from her own reflection in what-might-have-been a magic mirror. If it was, it was certainly out of whack; she was neither the fairest in the land nor the most modest.

Fully intending to apologize to Marcus for her sex-crazed actions, and to assure him that she was not lusting after his body, she walked through the bedroom and into the room beyond. That room, whatever it was supposed to be, didn't even verge on the ordinary, unless ordinary was a thatched-roof cottage. There were shadows lurking everywhere, an odd-looking broom leaning in a corner, a smoky fire smoldering under a caldron in the fireplace, weird bottles and jars of creepy stuff. A huge white owl, stuffed, she hoped, perched on a treeish thing in the corner. It looked at her for a long moment and then, it might have been deliberate, blinked one yellow eye.

Tish yelped and tried to back away, knocking over a container of...of... She didn't know what, but whatever it was smelled bad enough to be rotten dragon dung. Or fermented eye of newt. Or... She yelped again, and a good deal louder, when a live, fuzzy, wiggly something curled past her ankle and took a claws-bared swipe at her bare feet.

It brought blood.

Hopping on one foot, Tish swore, calling the cat a number of very nasty names, ones that a prudent man would hesitate to include in a prime time drama.

"Is that any way to talk to your familiar?" Marcus could hardly conceal his laughter, especially since it tended to break out between words in a snort of ill-concealed glee. He walked in from some concealed door, or secret passage, or...

Tish didn't know from where, and she didn't care. Still hopping, trying to see just how much blood was flowing from the scratch, she had only enough time to spare him a scowl and an indignant, "It was too damned familiar, if you ask me. Look what it did to me."

"I doubt that it's fatal. Besides, Barney is a nice cat. You must have stepped on his tail or something. He isn't a trained guard cat, so he wouldn't attack an intruder or..."

"Guard cat?" Tish stopped hopping to stare at Marcus, trying to read something in the blandness of his expression. Then she asked, not because it seemed remotely possible, but because it seemed the only answer, "You're joking, aren't you?"

Marcus denied the joke, but of course he could have been flat-out lying when he said, "No. Admittedly," he bent over, reached into a patch of dark shadow, and picked up a huge, orange-eyed ginger tom, holding the cat gently, stoking its soft fur with real affection, "guard cats are much bigger than Barney and they are picked for their hostile attitude. Barney likes people." He gave her a sly look and added, "Most people, that is. People who don't go prowling. People who don't step on his tail." Marcus lifted the cat higher, hoisting the large body up until the cat was semi-draped over his shoulder.

Glaring at man and beast, Tish snapped, "That damned cat doesn't even have a tail."

"Oh," Marcus said, perfectly straight-faced and sincere-voiced, "You must have broken it off when you stepped on him. We'd better find it. Morgain will..."

Knowing full well that he was teasing her, but refusing to rise to the bait, Tish folded her arms and gave him her best glare, and did both in silence. It didn't even come close to extinguishing the devils that danced in the depths of his eyes.

After a moment, he still hadn't smiled, and Tish, despite her beliefs to the contrary, was almost to the point of belting him. She took a deep, calming breath, and when that didn't help, she took another. She still sounded shrewish and fishwife-ish, and didn't give a care, when she said, trying to keep her voice even, "I walked out of the bedroom and was here, in this place, whatever it is. You are supposed to be caring for me. I remember that much from last night."

Red flushed her cheeks, only partially fueled by anger, when he said, his voice too low and intimate by half, "I remember a whole lot more than that."

Feeling an odd tingle, one that should not have been there at all, she knew she sounded a little breathless when she said, "You swine."

His laughter was only slightly strained, or perhaps the shadow-filled room was affecting his breathing also. Or perhaps his reaction was just her imagination, which had a definite tendency to shift into overdrive without consulting her reason. And, the man was having far too great an influence on her lust responses. Which, considering what Carl had done to her, should have been dead and buried. But, they definitely weren't.

Marcus took a step toward her.

Chapter Seven

HEART PULSING IN her throat, lips slightly parted, Tish fought down a rising tide of excitement, or fear, or something as yet unknown, as Marcus came to where she stood. She wanted to move away, but she was already scant inches from the door back into the bedroom. And she sure didn't want to be accused of trying to lure him into her bed with sweaty-body ravishment in mind; not with an arrogant cold fish like Marcus. Besides that, even if she had wanted to, her legs had a different agenda: they planned to stand there and turn to overcooked applesauce, all water, no substance.

In all the romances Tish had read, and there had been more than a few, the hero always exuded an enticing aroma of spicy aftershave, or leather and pipe smoke, or the great outdoors. If he was trying out for the part, Marcus failed in that particular hero category. Although the smell he brought with him was enticing enough, if you were as hungry as Tish was. And if crisp bacon, buttered toast, and oranges were three of your all time favorite foods, along with a long list of other favorites, whose position on her list changed by the day and hour. But, delicious as he smelled, the odor turned on her stomach not her loins—mostly.

Stopping directly in front of her, he lifted his arm, reached toward her. Tish stood, albeit on wobbly legs, her ground.

Marcus reached over her shoulder. She turned her head to see what he was doing. She told herself she wasn't disappointed, when he, instead of sweeping her in a wild and passionate embrace, pushed a single button in the cluster mounted on the wall.

When the deed was done, and his arm was back at his side, Marcus said, "You must have hit the glamour switch when you came out of the guest room."

For less than a half an instant, she thought Marcus might actually be complimenting her. It was, and she well knew it, a faintly ridiculous notion, one that vanished like water vapor under the noonday summer sun. And was just as rapidly replaced by the more substantial thought: it's a hangover, that's what's wrong with me. That's why I'm beginning to feel like a simpering idiot, one without enough brains to pour sand out of a boot.

No, that was out—the hangover part, not the simpering idiot

part—she didn't have the symptoms of a hangover. It had to be something else that was twisting his words before they got into her ears, making her hear something that didn't exist.

Tish shook her head, trying to bring her wandering thoughts into sharper focus. She was far from successful. Her new solution to her discombobulation was a couple of inches off center and stuttered even in her thoughts. He...I...it's the Witch's Brew overdose. It has gotten into my brain and poisoned my emotions, made me oversensitive to Marcus, and... That thought brought a handful of lusty memories and a flush to heat her cheeks.

Unable to look directly at him, she glanced over his shoulder. All her thoughts, coherent and otherwise, blanked out, leaving a disbelieving void, a nothingness that resolutely refused to allow the evidence of her staring eyes to enter into any of its data carrying systems.

Arrogant, superior, and condescending, he stepped back, giving her a clear view of what absolutely could not be: the thatched cottage room was gone, vanished in an eye blink. In its place was a partially glass-walled, white-carpeted, black-leather-divaned living room, replete with skylight, crystal vases of dew-touched red American Beauty roses, gleaming ebony tables, and a spread of glossy magazines. And holding neither owl nor cat, at least, as far as she could see.

Feeling definitely sick again, Tish stood there, speechless, and gawked.

Heavy with patience, he almost sighed, as if dreading a very hard task, as he said, again, "It's a glamour switch. You must have pushed it when you came out of the guest room."

His tone jerked her out of her daze and prodded her into her usual distaste. It was a feeling she didn't mind expressing, even if it meant denying something, vehemently and with great fervor, she wasn't sure was deniable. "I didn't either." A grudging sense of fairness made her add, "I don't have the slightest idea what you're talking about."

And then, because fear was beginning to burn in her stomach, "What happened to..." She looked around, gave a quick shudder, and almost shrieked, "to the other room? And the cat? What did you do with the cat?"

"It's all right. A glamour is a spell to make you see something different than it actually is. You know, like in the movie industry's glamour queens," he said, soothing syrup oozing from his voice, his hand reaching out to pat her shoulder. For one incredible moment, Tish thought he was going to draw her close and rub her back until she burped. She stiffened and glared at him as he said, still in his adult-to-child voice, "Barney is still here. He just... Barney! Where are you... Come here, boy."

The cat, or rather, a cat rose up out of the thick shag of the white carpet under one of the ebony tables. It was a white cat. A medium-sized white Persian with a full plume of a tail, carried high. It ambled toward them and it was within sniffing distance before it looked up.

Tish saw the deep orange of its eyes, the same exact color of the ginger tom's eyes, and began to shake. For some reason, one that she had no way of explaining, the changed cat frightened her more than anything that had happened thus far in Faery. Her lungs seemed incapable of sucking in air, and for just a moment, Tish thought she was going to swoon at the villain's feet, do a fair imitation of the fair ladies of yore.

Or was Marcus supposed to be the hero. She couldn't seem to remember. Thoughts skittered and jumped through the foggy, disorienting vistas of her mind, like mice in a hay stack; one that is being torn open and rearranged by an army of rat terriers.

Light-headed, dizzy, she looked from Marcus to the cat and back again. Nothing changed. The modern room was still there. The man and the feline were still there. She closed her eyes, opened them, and then said, her voice so calm and untroubled it scared her even more, "So, it's true. I really am crazy. The Steps and Jilly said I must be, but I thought they were just talking. What will you do with me now?"

MARCUS DIDN'T LAUGH. Seeing her so upset, and knowing he was at cause, made him feel slightly ill, ashamed of what he had done to her. She was a stranger and he... Taking in a deep breath, wanting to apologize, to ask her pardon and forgiveness, but not daring to let her see even that much of himself. He straightened his back, tried not to look either taken aback or guilty, even if he was both, and said, "Feed you first and then start your lessons. Whether you believe it or not, I am sorry this happened. I'm supposed to guard and protect you, not send you into fits."

Marcus was talking, but nothing seemed to be making its way into the chaos inside her head, or if it was, it was only adding to the eggbeater effect. Her thoughts and beliefs were all whipped to an air-filled froth, an ambiguous froth that had no real identity. Her mouth kept wanting to hang open, her tongue to say nonsense syllables, and for some odd reason, Tish wanted to cry, to bawl like a baby, to weep and moan. And maybe when her tears had been spent, just maybe, with no guarantees, she would be able to look at what was happening to her with a dispassionate eye. Not that she was prepared to believe...

"No. No. No." Her whisper was wafted to the far corners of the room on the nose-tickling scent of potpourri, mingled with new, as in new leather, new carpet, new wood. And wax, as in lemon-scented and fresh from the supermarket. And clean, as in no dust what-so-ever.

"Tish," he put his hands on her shoulders and tried to shake her. "It's all right. The glamours are preset in Morgain's computer. When you push the right button, the computer spells the room. There are nine different glamours for this room. The first one you saw was for peasants. The various magic kingdoms have lots of those. This room, the one you were supposed to see, is for humans and, as you can tell, it hasn't had that much use."

Held in thrall by disbelief, Tish was silent. She couldn't ask questions, not when none of it was true. "I'm just seeing things," she muttered. "I'm just..."

"No, Tish, it's true. At least, it's true in Faery. And fairly common. Morgain even has a remote control, so she can ready it for unexpected visitors. She has clients from all over, so it's necessary to spell the waiting room so they will see what they expect to see and not be frightened. Do you understand?"

HIS TOUCH RELEASED her from her blue and green and purple funk and slung her back into instant ire, but it did nothing to make her believe the bull he was spouting. It was all lies, and whatever had happened was his fault, it had to be. He had done something with the other room, or, her churning mind turned crafty, he had hypnotized her and moved her, not the room and the other cat.

"Don't touch me!" It came out too sharp and too shrill, but she had to get away from him. Maybe then she could return to being the normal, rational, human being that she had been before he accosted her at the ball.

He didn't release his hold, but he did sort of half-turn her body and marched it toward a far door. One that opened into a sunny, utilitarian kitchen. It was dominated by the incongruous shape of a large, cheval glass, setting cozily in its gargoyle-carved, black-walnut frame. Large, and obviously new, it took up floor space at the side of the white table and looked totally out of place against the stark white of the ultramodern cabinets and appliances.

The white tiles were cold under her bare feet, but that felt normal. It was too normal, like the pitcher of orange juice on the white table, the orange peels tossed in the sink, toast with butter still melting on its perfectly browned surface, and bacon, crisp and steaming. The homey sight jolted her back to a bit of normal herself, or what passed for normal in Tish's life.

Pulling loose from his guiding hands, she stalked over to the table, looked at the mirror, and said, witheringly, she hoped, "And I suppose this is a magic mirror. What am I supposed to say, 'Mirror, Mirror, on the stand, who's the fairest in the land?'"

"Well, I'm not sure that's the right password. It is voice-activated, but why don't you eat first. The lessons will probably take most of the day. That is if you prove, which I have ample reason to doubt, to be a good student."

"And you, on the other hand, are an outstanding teacher?"

He seemed to take her jibe seriously, or almost so. "I am, as several of my former students will be happy to attest, a very good teacher."

"Of what?" Tish picked up a piece of bacon and took a bite before she added, without knowing exactly why, "And ignorant young girls don't count. Or any of those poor misguided women you were bragging about who are lusting after your...ah...manly frame."

SHE WAS THE most maddening woman he had ever met, and at the same time the most innocent. And, although he certainly didn't intend to tell her so, the most desirable. That fact alone put her beyond his reach. A man like him couldn't live like other men, couldn't fall in love with someone like Tish, someone had surely bespelled him. Perhaps this was the very thing Stephen had been trying to warn him of that day in the garden. But that didn't seem to add up either. By the First Mothers, he didn't know how to deal with her. Tish made him crazy, made him say and do things that...

Marcus shook his head, trying to drive out what should never be there, hiding in his thoughts, whispering beguilements, holding out hope where none existed. He had to stop it immediately. "Tish, I..."

She was anything but agreeable. In fact, she was downright contrary. "I prefer being called Miss Warton by disgraced Border Guards." She sat down at the table and began filling a plate with the tidbits and yummies he had assembled for her repast. "Although I do have to admit that you are a fair cook. Or perhaps it tastes good because you have tried to starve me and to poison me both since you tackled me, wrapped me in a blanket, and kidnapped me."

It was unfair enough to be laughable, if Marcus had been in a laughing mood. Which he wasn't. What he really wanted to do was grab her and shake some truth into her. Or kiss her until she melted against him and... Shaken by the intensity of his thoughts, Marcus snapped, with far more force than was necessary, "I did no such thing."

ENJOYING THE EXCHANGE, especially seeing him squirm, Tish said, "Really, who knocked me down by the fountain?" She speared a bite of melon, popped it in her mouth, and, after the first taste, wanted to moan with delight. It was, beyond all doubt, an experience to savor, one that was sinfully good. Greedily, she took another bite, ignored the bit of juice that trickled down her chin, and closed her eyes, letting the flavor permeate her senses, intoxicate her with a heavenly sweetness that must be named ambrosia. The food of the old gods. Whose gods she couldn't recall, nor did she waste the moment worrying about it.

Too long denied, hunger attacked with a fury, seizing her body, her mind, everything about her, and dedicating them all to one driving need. Marcus left some time during her wild bout of the grab-and-gobbles. Tish didn't even know he was gone until the table was bare, her stomach was tight, and she was sipping a fragrant brew that bore some small relationship to its more mundane cousin, coffee.

The feast had soiled her fingers, dripped from her chin, filled her to bursting, and restored her sense of humor. Even if it did tend toward the absurd, or was off-the-wall wacky. Wiping her chin and hands on a linen napkin, she grinned at her reflection in the looking glass. "Well, Mirror, you're supposed to be a teaching aid. So, teach me."

It lit up with a greenish glow and said, "Welcome. I am the prototype of magic mirror number 603 and still in the testing mode. Your remote is located in the holder at the bottom of my stand."

Making no move to collect the remote, Tish stared at the mirror and shook her head. Not in disbelief, she was long past anything as prosaic as that; she was into big-time don't bother me with facts, I'm already stark, staring nuts.

The mirror, in a well-modulated, but implacable voice, said, "Do you wish to proceed by voice commands only? Signify by saying yes or no."

She wanted to scream a loud "no" and tell it to vanish, but her "yes" came out as a squeak, almost too soft to be heard.

The mirror's hearing was acute. "My functions," it said, "include: visual communications; pictorial histories, with a voice-over; catalog shopping, in full color with models of the buyer's size and shape; and..."

Tish interrupted with, "Visual communications?"

"With whom do you wish to speak?"

There was only one person, or maybe four if you count Jilly and the Steps, in the entire universe that Tish wanted to talk to, to see, to ask for aid. "My mother," she said, gripping her hands together so tightly they hurt, leaning toward the glowing surface, and, not caring in the least that she sounded like a lost child, repeating her request, "My mother. Please, let me talk to my mother."

"One moment please." The mirror didn't ask who Tish's mother was, or where she was located, it just hummed, faintly at first and then a little louder until a picture appeared. It was a talking picture of Tish's mother, Lil and Sadie, and Jilly, all sipping tea and nibbling at watercress sandwiches in her mother's living room. And, they were talking, laughing, not missing Tish at all.

Unshed tears balling up in her throat, Tish watched, but that's all she could do. Letters formed at the bottom of the mirror, made themselves into words, a message trailing across the mirror's face. "We are experiencing communications difficulties and can accept incoming messages only at this time. Please standby."

Tish couldn't have stood if she had wanted. She was mesmerized by the greenish pictures that moved inside the mirror. It wasn't exactly like on television, but the difference was subtle, not lending itself to real explanation. But, Tish knew she was seeing, like looking through a window and seeing, her family, just as they were, at that moment, wherever they were in space.

"Tish," Jilly said, "doesn't know what she's missing. When do you think she'll get tired of..." Jilly's lips still moved, but now the figures were silent.

Another army of letters started a slow march across the mirror, but Tish didn't get a chance to read the new message. The magic mirror went to silvery reflections, of Tish and the glowering Godmother who had appeared at her side.

Tregon, one hand slapping her wand against the palm of her other hand, her foot tapping out an ominous beat, glared at Tish and the mirror alike. "Just what in the Name of the Seven Founding Mothers do you think you're doing? Where's Marcus? Where's Morgain? What idiot turned you loose with a magic mirror?"

Having no ready answer for any of the Godmother's rapid-fire questions and responding to a growing anger inside herself. It was an anger intertwined with loss and longing. Tish looked squarely at the woman and said, "Before I was so rudely interrupted, I was trying to contact my family. I would hate for them to be worried about me. After all, they are totally innocent of my criminal acts and shouldn't have to be punished for them. As to where Marcus is, I neither know nor care. Morgain went to meet with clients.

"And as to the idiot who turned me loose with a live mirror, I would be forced to admit that you are responsible for that. You sent me here, where the mirror was, and you damned sure didn't tell me to leave it alone."

The silence her answer provoked didn't last more than three heartbeats. Then it was smashed by the high-pitched yowl of an angry cat, a dwindling water-scream of fury and despair, and a man swearing on all things born and unborn, visible and invisible, and shouting Tish's name between every other word. Whether he was cursing her or calling for her aid or telling her to run for her life was impossible to tell. But Tish knew the other cry, and it tugged at her, begged her to come before it was too late.

She looked at the Godmother. "It's Bubba. Something has happened to him. I have..." Tish didn't get a chance to find out what had triggered the cry. At least not at that moment.

"I'll go. You have done enough damage for one day." Tregon pointed her finger at Tish and ordered, "Stay right here. Don't move. Don't talk to the mirror. Don't touch anything." She whirled, in a flutter of green chiffon and paler lace, and made an elegant dash for the door and the site of the unearthly commotion.

Tish didn't even mutter, "Go to blazes," she said it out loud and with considerable force before concern for her water sprite superseded any command from the Godmother and she jumped up and followed where the other woman led. It was a very short journey.

And at its end, chaos was not even trying to resolve itself into any form of order. Ripe with the stench of decayed slime and rotting vegetation and other smells less easy to identify, the living room, still wearing its human glamour, was smashed, shattered, shredded, tipped, torn, tossed, and awash with struggling and/or fleeing creatures. Lamps were broken, or else not turned on, but there was enough greenish-gray light coming in through the glass wall to illuminate a scene from a very sick imagination. Or a staged scene from a very violent horror movie.

Tish saw Morgain first. The Godmother, blood spurting from a cut on her shoulder, oozing from a similar cut, but smaller, on her forehead, was crouched against the wall beside the door, clutching a split and blackened wand, and shaking violently. Tregon was kneeling in front of her, demanding to know what was wrong. There was no answer. Morgain just held out one hand, showed her fellow Godmother a livid purple welt, one that was already visibly spreading up her arm.

"Poison," Tregon whispered before she shouted something that sounded urgent, but she spoke in an unknown tongue, so Tish had no idea what was said.

Something terrible had happened. That much would have been apparent to a mole. Morgain was in dire jeopardy, Tish knew that and she wanted to run to the woman's side and render what help she could. But, somewhere within the destruction, Bubba, her Bubba, was still crying piteously. And now, after one sweeping inspection of the room, she knew why. It made her angry and terrified her at the same time, but not all of her fear was for her water sprite.

Time held her in a single moment, like a special effects bit in a bad movie. She saw everything, wondered briefly how the sprite, toad, and wand, which floated waist-high near the center of the room, had been involved in the mess. They certainly hadn't been there before, and she absolutely doubted that even a Godmother's glamour could hide the toad's fury and the sprite's bubbling song. Not that it was singing

With a catch in her breath, she saw Marcus, who was struggling with some stinking, matted-fur beast-thing, and Barney, whose every white hair was standing on end as he spat, hissed, and squalled his fury at the slavering toad, which seemed to be ready to attack the cat. But she couldn't find Bubba, and that started a new ache in her heart.

But there was no time for mourning, if Barney and Marcus weren't to follow Bubba into nonexistence, something had to be done. With Morgain disabled and Tregon ignoring the whole battle, Tish seemed to be the only one left to do it.

She dashed, with no thought of the consequences, across a floor bright with the slivers, shards, and sharp-edged remnants of the glass toad cage and Bubba's broken jug, and caught the floating wand in her left hand. It remained lifeless and inert. No power pulsed through its sawed-off shaft.

"Damn you," Tish snarled, "do something. I don't care if you're warded and spelled. That thing is killing Marcus and the toad is... Do something!" It sputtered, glowed weakly, looking more like a terminally ill firefly than a magic wand. Still, it was, given the destruction of the living room, clearly the only weapon at hand. And Marcus looked like he needed every bit of help she could give.

Advancing on the struggling pair, and trying not to breathe in the mind-chilling odor of the yellowish-gray beast-thing, Tish raised the wand high and slammed it down, hard, on the head of the thing. Sparks flew. Hair sizzled. It lifted its black muzzle and let out a soundless howl, one that vibrated in her bones, left her shaken, but didn't touch her ears.

Tish's wand came up again, clubbed down, creating new fireworks, and inflicting new pain. Releasing its hold on Marcus, rolling off to one side, the beast grabbed its head with both taloned hands. It began a sideways scuttle that seemed designed to take it as far from Tish as possible and out the front door as quickly as possible. Within seconds, both goals were in its grasp.

A short, black sword, made of some material that didn't resemble steel in the least, in his hand, new bruises and bloody claw marks making a mask of his face, amber eyes blazing, Marcus scrambled to his feet and pursued the beast. He took time enough to say, "Thanks," to Tish before he shouted, "Tregon, do something about that damned frog." Sword at ready, Marcus pursued the beast as it made its escape from the trashed living room.

Knowing, somehow, that he was safe for the moment. And that he probably wouldn't relish her running after him, begging him to stop, Tish's next thought was to save the cat from the dastardly toad.

But, although she was still bent over Morgain, murmuring softly, Tregon had already taken care of that matter. The toad, Tish had difficulty thinking of it as Carl, was once again beating at the bars of a glass cage. His hackles still standing, his yowl modified to a grumble of warning, Barney was prowling just beyond the exterior limits of the toad prison and was, to all outward appearances, not playing host to any new battle scars.

Sadness dropping around her, hurting in her throat, Tish surveyed the wreckage, looking for some sign of the sprite in the litter of broken glass and pulverized furniture. She heard a faint bubble of sound and, hope springing full-grown in her heart, hurried toward the shadows that lay beyond the mound of mangled leather and splintered wood that might have been the couch. There, she found what she was seeking.

What was left of the sprite was housed in the three or four tablespoons of water that remained in a cracked and leaking potpourri bowl. She didn't question how he had gotten there, Tish only knew that she had to get him to more water and do it quickly before he died of water deprivation. Dropping the wand, she picked up the bowl and walked, crooning to him every careful step of the way, across the room. Tregon said something as Tish passed her, but Tish had only one mission in mind, one that didn't include Godmothers or border guards. Although she would never have admitted it, concern for Marcus was tangled in with the rest of her welter of conflicting emotions, but it was not foremost at the moment.

Forged in water and in magic, the bond between Tish and the water sprite was already strong, she knew she sincerely cared for him, felt responsible for his well-being. But she didn't realize that tears were streaming down her face, or that blood was dribbling out of the cuts on the bottom of her bare feet, until she was back in the kitchen, running water into a glass pitcher. One that had, until a second or two before, held the remains of her breakfast orange juice.

Murmuring nonsense, trying to make the sprite whole and healthy, she held the pitcher in both hands and almost rocked it as if she were soothing a sick child. A tremulous smile touched her lips when he bubbled, sending a single small sphere to burst, like a baby's kiss, against her cheek, just as a new contingent of Godmothers entered the scene. Their magic would never be wasted on love potions and easy wishes. This was the big gun, and it would destroy just as surely and perhaps more completely as its lessor counterparts, with their firing mechanisms and explosive devices, on Tish's earth.

Chapter Eight

COWLED, HOODED, and cloaked in dull black, the phalanx of deadly Godmothers, their shiny black boots moving in icy precision, wheeled into battle formation. They halted, every black glass faceplate turned in Tish's direction, every smoldering wand held erect in a black gloved hand. They did it all without making a single sound, thereby lodging a nagging suspicion in Tish's mind that the women must be using some sort of spell to hide sound.

Weird as the thought was, she accepted it as almost commonplace, if only for a fraction of an instant. For the next giddy moment, before fear seized her and began wringing her out like hand wash, Tish murmured, "Darth Vadar in drag? I...I... I've got to stop watching old movies." She managed to swallow the wild giggle that came on the heels of her ill-considered words. But at that particular point in time, it was the only way she had of dealing with the unthinkable, the incomprehensible.

"If you joke, it will go away?" she asked, fully cognizant of the fact that somewhere in her mind the dark Godmothers, possibly all of the Godmothers, didn't exist except in children's tales of happy endings. And those tales never included Godmothers the likes of these. Godmothers using deadly force had to be a paradox or something; it just didn't seem right. But then again, what did? Black-cloaked Godmothers on a search-and-destroy sortie?

As if Tish's thoughts had triggered the act, the foremost of the Godmothers lifted her head within the deeply shadowed confines of her hood like a hound tasting the air for lingering traces of its prey. She made a hand gesture, and the squad of magic-wielders divested itself of two of its members. The rest, still in absolute silence, began a march, one that obviously, even to the casual onlooker, boded no good to malefactors, felons, and other lawbreakers.

In a thrice, they were passing through the door, going, Tish supposed, to the living room and the scene of the battle. If, indeed, that's what had occurred. Or maybe they were going to follow Marcus out into... Small memories of an icy fountain rose to the surface of Tish's mind, but other than that rather unpleasant bit of her past, she had no idea of what lay beyond the living room. If anything at all did.

At that point, Tish was taking no bets on anything, not even her own sanity, which, if she actually had any left, was certainly teetering on the brink.

The black-clad women didn't say a single word, but Tish, although she couldn't see their eyes, knew they watched her every breath, her every nerve twitch. She also knew that, if by chance, she made the wrong move, she was going to be on the receiving end of the powerful magic charging every atom in the air around her. It was far from a pleasant thought, but she couldn't quite figure a way to get around it.

The only thing she did know was she had to sit down. If she didn't, she was going to drop Bubba, splash him all over the white kitchen. Well, that just wasn't going to happen; not to her sprite. Gripping the pitcher so tightly it hurt her hands, looking straight into the blank faceplate of the nearest Godmother, Tish licked her dry lips. She said, speaking slowly and carefully to keep her unruly tongue from uttering what might possibly be her own death sentence, "Listen, I don't know what happened in there or who or what that creature thing was, but I'm scared. My knees are shaking and I want to sit down. Is that all right?"

Neither Godmother gave any indication of even hearing her question, let alone bothering to give her permission. Tish waited a moment longer, forcing herself to breathe despite the band of terror tightening around her chest, but she couldn't stop the little shivers that crinkled up her spine or the panic that was getting ready to ambush her mind.

Marcus, with Tregon and Morgain trailing along in his wake, saved her; from her own overactive imagination if from nothing else. And, for once, Tish was overjoyed to see him, even if he did look more like the loser in a knife fight, or maybe even a knife war, than a conquering hero. The yellow of his prisoner suit was streaked and spotted with blood. She hoped not all of it was his own, that the cuts on his face and hands weren't bleeding enough to drain him dry; even the fleeting thought scared her because if looks weren't deceiving, it could very possibly come true.

She felt her mouth shape itself into a round O of dismay as he walked toward the center of the kitchen and felt an odd little flutter in the general region of her heart. It resolved itself into concern for a man whom she loathed, or maybe only mildly disliked, or maybe could have liked if he wasn't so know-it-all arrogant. Her emotions were all too confusing to even attempt to sort out, so Tish put introspection aside and went on to more immediately important affairs.

"What happened," she asked, scarcely aware that her voice was shaking or of the tear tracks that were still damp on her cheeks.

"It got away," Marcus said, weariness slumping his shoulders, making him look, beneath the blood, slightly less aristocratic, more human.

Still holding Bubba's pitcher against her thudding heart, Tish took a small, almost involuntary, step toward the man. "What was it? Why was it here?" And then, softer, lower, she asked, "Are you hurt bad?"

His voice was equally low when he answered, speaking to her alone, "Would it matter?" And, it sounded as if her answer might actually be important to him.

KNOWING FULL WELL that nothing could ever come of it, Marcus wanted his continued health to matter to her. He wanted everything about him to matter, but he knew it would stop mattering the moment he told her the truth. Or as much of the truth as he could, in all honor, tell of his past. It would have to be soon. Even the thought of telling hurt.

Marcus looked down, saw the bloody tracks on the white floor and almost lost it. She was hurt, bleeding. He wanted to rush to her, pick her up, carry her to safety, if such a haven actually existed in Faery. Which he was beginning to doubt. Something was going on, something that, for no reason that he could see, had Tish mired, or maybe tethered was a better choice of words, right square in the middle. And she was going to need rescuing sooner or later. From what he didn't exactly know. But he would, in the fullness of time, he would know all he needed to know.

But it would have to wait. Right now she was bleeding and needed... Marcus took a step toward her. "Tish." It came out softer, more concerned than he wanted, and again he fought his own feelings. Carl had already hurt her enough, she sure didn't need him to add to her pain. But, unable to control his own tongue, he said her name again. It came out as a question, one with no answer. "Tish?"

Unable to meet his amber-eyed gaze, for reasons she couldn't even begin to examine, Tish glanced down, saw he was following bloody footprints, red prints that were stark and frighteningly real against the gleaming whiteness of the rest of the floor. Prints that led directly to where she was standing.

Abruptly, as if a switch had been turned on, Tish was aware of the stinging pain in her glass-lacerated feet. Was aware that Bubba was crooning sweetly. Was aware that Morgain had dropped into one of the chairs at the table. Was aware that sound, in all of its graduated tones, had come back into the room. Was aware Tregon was talking to the two black-garbed Godmothers. Was aware they had pushed up their black face-covering and were listening intently. Was too completely aware of Marcus. His bloody face. His nearness. His eyes that were too full of secrets, and sadness, old, all-consuming sadness.

Tish was aware, too, of her own babbling as she said, "Your wounds look terrible. I don't have a petticoat to tear a strip off of, like they did in the old days, but there must be a cloth in here somewhere. Let me get it and some water...well, I'm not much in the doctoring department, but I could clean you up and we could see what..."

"Not yet. We have to talk first. About what happened in there and..." He took a shallow breath before he went on and his troubled explanation changed her awareness from him as a person to awareness of herself, her own danger, danger from an unknown source.

"It was a hired mercenary. One of the barbarian beast-men. He was using what had to be stolen magic and..." His tongue slid across his lips and he continued, "You were eating and... I thought I heard something and went into the living room. Morgain was there, the broken frog, I mean, toad cage at her feet and..."

Marcus cleared his throat, took a step closer, and said, "Tish, I don't know how to tell you except straight out. Someone in Faery has...that is, in your vernacular, someone has taken out a contract on you. Hired a hitman to waste you."

"How do you know? Who would do such a thing?" she whispered. "One of the Godmothers?"

He answered her questions in reverse order. "No, they wouldn't have to; if a Godmother wanted you out of the picture, she would have the means to see it done with no one being the wiser."

Against her will, she nodded agreement; even if it did raise huge questions, and real doubts, in her mind. Marcus was the only other person she knew in Faery, and he was supposed to guard her, not kill her. Besides, he was fighting with the monster, wasn't he?

Tish looked at him, tried to imagine him as a murderer, found the idea ludicrous. The whole idea, the contract, the hitman, and Marcus as the killer. She asked, "Just who would want to do away with me?"

"I don't know, but I do know the mercenary was following your scent."

Beyond them the Godmothers were talking rapidly, their voices sounding urgent and angry, but that didn't seem to mean anything to

Tish. At the moment, she was sure he was, in his usual superior manner, making derogatory remarks. Instantly provoked, she glared at Marcus. "Is that supposed to be another one of your cheap shots regarding my unclean personal habits?"

He sighed, wincing a little as he shook his head. "He was in your bedroom, sniffing the bed and the floor. I barely had time to snatch a sword before he came out, heading straight for the kitchen, homing in on you. I was just something that got in his way, a gnat to swat. You were the target."

"But..."

Tregon abandoned Morgain and came to where Tish and Marcus were having their discussion, one that was tending toward the loud and angry, and would, very probably, soon disintegrate into name-calling and other unpleasant behavior.

The Godmother said, "He's right, Wilding. The mercenary beasts are hired killers. And, what makes this very disturbing is the fact that he was armed with silence magic and body magic. If you hadn't hit him with your wand, he, if that had been his desire, and it certainly seemed so, would have killed us all. We are in your debt for that, at least. Your act of courage will help mitigate some of your newer offenses."

Ignoring the last part of the statement—and afraid she would learn what it meant too soon anyway—Tish asked, "If it was that easy, why didn't you use your wand then."

"It wouldn't have worked. The stolen magic belonged to a Godmother and..." She shrugged and shook her head. "You'll learn the whys and wherefores of magic later on in your studies, but for now, just accept my word for it. On the other hand, your wand is fueled with magic from another land and the beast's protection was not intended to turn that magic away.

"If you see the spell as being like armor. It will deflect spears and arrows, which is what it is made to do, but if a foreigner comes along with a revolver, the armor is no good at all. Do you understand?"

"Yes, but..."

"We are willing to overlook the fact that you used a wand you should not have been able to even touch. It was spelled and warded against you and it will take some study to determine what went wrong. I have already set up a committee to investigate the failure of both spell and ward. That can wait, of course, but other things can't."

In a totally human gesture, she held up her hand with the index finger raised. "The first being your frog. He has inflicted a very serious injury to Morgain's person. The Full Council has met and has deemed him a clear and present danger to our society and an undesirable alien and is deporting him as soon as possible, either in this form, or his original form. If you want to do the transforming."

Not wanting to admit she didn't know how, and didn't want to face Carl if she did, Tish just shook her head. Then she added, a jot of her old bitterness and hurt creeping back, enough to make her say, "But, if you do that, you should neuter him first, otherwise you'll be doing a good deal of harm to the entire toad family."

Tregon smiled. It lit up her entire face and her laugh was far from wind chimes in a gentle breeze; it was a belly laugh, a lusty burst of muted thunder. "I'm sure we can do just that. Morgain has certain expertise in sexual matters, no doubt she would be more than happy to supervise the procedure. The healers should be here shortly to tend to Morgain and Marcus..." she glanced down at Tish's feet, "and you. They must know the how of it. We'll have it done in no time. No time at all."

Marcus made some slight sound, one that might have been a quick exclamation of denial.

Drawing herself up to her full height, Tregon looked at Marcus and asked, ingrained authority turning her voice to cold steel, "Do you have any objections to that course of action, Border Guard? Or to any course of action the Godmothers choose to take in this affair?"

His, "No, Ma'am," was crisply given, and as impersonal as glass.

But something about it, or his lack of expression, or maybe just the small voice of her conscience made Tish feel a hot flush of shame. Carl was, after all, exactly what he was. Her own blindness in such matters had been the cause of her...her... Tish didn't know exactly what emotion to ascribe to the breakup of their relationship. She did know, even if she hated to admit it, that she probably would never have gotten entangled with him in the first place if she hadn't been so bent on defying her mother. And, considering the amount of trouble she was embroiled in now, neither Carl's oversexed and under-moral behavior nor her mother's sly schemes to prevent the wedding seemed terribly important.

She actually hated to do it, but Tish was prepared to face the consequences of her own acts. "Uh, Tregon," she said, pausing to lick her lips before she finished up what she had to say. "Carl is, or was before I zapped him, a man and regardless of his actions, I don't think we have the right to take his manhood away from him. I think it would destroy him and... Well, turning him into a toad is one thing, but I wouldn't want to be guilty... I would hate to see myself as a real emasculating female."

Marcus smiled at her, a real smile, one that, despite the bloody scratches and bruises and contusions that swelled, leaked, and turned color on his sun-bronzed face, made him look incredibly handsome—well, maybe not handsome exactly, more like charming. Devastatingly charming. There was so much approval in the smile that Tish felt like she was basking in warm sunlight, but she didn't return the smile.

Not with Tregon frowning and saying, "You're a fool, Miss Warton, and, unless you develop a new attitude toward life and learn to see just how unimportant lesser beings are, I doubt that you are worthy of what little magic you possess. The frog means nothing, so why..."

Morgain, cradling her injured arm in her hand, stood up and took a few wavering steps toward them. "He's her frog," she said, speaking quietly. But there was unseeable force behind what she said, waiting like lightning, hidden in the beauty of towering clouds, to strike, to burn whatever stood in its path.

Tregon snorted. "So, Morgain, you think you can dispute my authority in this as you have..."

"It isn't just me, Tregon. We both know the Laws of Magic. Miss Warton made the frog, and only she can unmake him. He belongs to her, if she does not wish to have him mutilated, that is her choice. It is one that I applaud."

"Morgain, I must... The Wilding is almost a barbarian. How can she possibly know..."

"She can't," Morgain said slowly, "but she can learn."

"Well, all I can say is she'd better be damned quick about it. The way things are going around here, if she..." Tregon had to grace to blush, give a small bow in Tish's general direction, and say, "By allowing my emotions and personal prejudices to rule my senses, I have overstepped my authority and for that I apologize."

She sighed and said, speaking to Morgain, "See that she transforms the frog back into a male human before he is exiled. Also, she has spelled the mirror into working order. She was spying on an earth family, her own I imagine, see that it doesn't happen again. She is not yet to be trusted, so teach her as much as possible as quickly as possible."

Tregon said something else just before she did one of the Godmotherly things and faded to gray and disappeared, Tish thought it was, "Before her wild magic kills us all."

Dead certain the Godmother harbored no liking for her, and not nearly as certain the woman hadn't been behind the attack by the mercenary beast-man, Tish opened her mouth to ask what Tregon meant. Her words were lost in the ring of what could only be a doorbell.

And practically stepping on the heels of the peal, two men, wearing multicolored robes and self-important expressions, escorted by one of the black-clad Godmothers, bustled into the kitchen. Each of the newcomers was carrying his own bulging carpet bag: shag carpet in tones of gray, red, lavender, and green and having a just vacuumed look.

The taller, and older of the two, was lean to the point of bean-polism. His white beard, long enough to qualify him for Guinness Book of World Records and then some. He shambled across the room, head up, faded brown eyes flicking back and forth like an adder's tongue, and lips, what could be seen of them, compressed in a firm line. "I am Saneth, Doctor of Dreams."

Waving skeletal fingers in an unreadable gesture, he said, "My colleague, Mansee, Doctor of Night-forms. We were summoned with spells and gold, as was right and fitting. It is our honor to serve and heal."

Rotund, clean-shaven, and gloomy-faced, Mansee said nothing. Neither did he seem aware of his surroundings. But he stopped when Saneth stopped, smoothed down the unruly skirts of his red, green, purple, and yellow robe, and waited, apparently for further instructions. When Saneth said, "I will attend Her Excellency, the Godmother Morgain. You treat the Border Guard," Mansee obeyed without question.

Tish, feeling the full brunt of her own total unimportance, backed away until she was leaning against the counter and watched what had to be the heights of mumbo-jumbo. Or maybe the depths, because the entire process took place within a circle of blue chalk drawn, with aplomb and flourishes, on the white tiles. But only after the Godmother and Marcus, each in some sort of trance, were fixed, after much fussing and calculating, in the proper healing position.

She didn't see it being lit, or placed in a complicated design around the man and Godmother lying, supine or prone, she never could remember which was which, on their backs on the bloodstained tiles of the floor, but, within a very short period of time, the wafting stink of smoky incense filled the room with drifting shadows, making her sneeze, several times. The moaning chants of dreams and night made her itch somewhere she could neither name nor scratch. The hand passes and bell ringing made her dizzy, muddled her brain.

And the whole ritual, even if she could see it fade the burn on Morgain's arm, heal the bloody scratches on Marcus's face, made her homesick for white coats, stethoscopes, and shots of miracle drugs. And she felt weary, so incredibly weary that she was not sure she could stand much longer.

Setting the Bubba pitcher on the counter, pushing it far back under the upper cupboard, Tish gave it a final pat. Then she began edging, in a lame-footed sort of way, around the so-called doctors and their entranced, or comatose, or whatever they were, patients. One of the silent Godmothers, who with her partner seemed to be standing guard over the occupants of the room, raised an eyebrow and pointed toward the living room. Her feet hurt too bad to attempt even that short journey, so Tish shook her head and eased into one of the chairs at the table; the one closest to the magic mirror.

Inert, the silvered glass filled only with her reflection, it didn't even tempt her; well, at least not much. She already had far too much to think about without adding new complications. However, she told herself, with only a quick glance toward the armed Godmothers, and the doctors' blank-eyed patients, it would be a diversion, one that really might provide her with a means of going home. Wearily, and not understanding why she was yawning, why the billow and swirl of smoke had grown thicker, coiling around her like some monster snake, a night snake who dreamed of rest and healing, Tish reached down toward the cheval glass' stand, intending to pick up the remote and, maybe, if she could figure out how, do a little channel surfing, or mirror surfing, and see what was scheduled for the day.

Her watering eyes closed. She tried to open them again, but the weight of her lids was too great. She was asleep before the rod of black glass was in reach of her questing fingertips.

TISH WAS SLUMPED, unmoving, at the table. For one terrible moment, Marcus was sure she was dead, that the killer had returned while he was entranced and... Then he saw her draw a small breath; his own, one of profound relief, was much deeper.

"She's not for you, Marcus," Morgain said, and for some unknown reason, her voice sounded almost regretful, as if she would have like Marcus and Tish to have a future together.

That didn't make any sense either. Marcus barely knew Morgain. She was one of the richest, most powerful Godmothers in Faery, and, if the rumors were anywhere close to being true, one of the most ambitious. Her name was constantly linked with Tregon's and it was said, to be sure never very loudly, that the two of them would be the next Godmothers admitted to the ranks of the Council of Four. If such ranks still existed.

Still whispers didn't make a true villain. Shrugging off his suspicions, Marcus got up from the floor. The doctors were gone. Morgain was already standing, looking down at Tish, but her words were for him alone. "You have been a good Border Guard, just keep it at that. The Wilding is trouble, trouble for us all."

Marcus couldn't argue with the truth of that; Tish was already troubling him in places no other woman had ever come close to touching. And that could never be. Vowing to keep her out of his heart and mind, Marcus broke the vow with his next breath. "Her feet? Are they..."

Morgain's answer, and further orders, did nothing to ease his terrible awareness of Tish, an awareness that had no real place in either of their lives. Marcus sighed, but he followed Morgain's orders; and barely noticed when the Godmother magicked herself into new garments.

SHE CAME FULLY awake between one breath and the next. Taking in a gulp of fresh, clean smelling air, Tish lifted her head from its pillow of forearm and table and looked around. With the exception of the doctors, and even her memory of them was turning to smoke and shadows, everyone else was still there.

The armed Godmothers still guarded.

Wearing a filmy lavender chiffon gown, with a beaded top and full skirt, both rather scantily covered by scrap of a purple apron, Morgain prowled through the supplies in the kitchen cupboards. She pulled out packages of this and glass jars of that and was clearly planning a meal of more than minor proportions.

Marcus, his face healed and unscarred, his amber eyes too knowing by half, was kneeling, one knee on the floor, the other up, in front of Tish, in the classic proposing-swain pose. But, even though the thought tickled Tish's fancy, that wasn't his plan of action. Lifting one of Tish's feet, examining the unmarred sole for any unhealed spots, he slipped it into a slipper; the fur-lined bedroom variety, not the glass of children's tales. Giving it a little wiggle, to make sure the fit was perfect on Tish's narrow, high-arched foot, he sat it down beside its twin, already housed in the other frivolous pink slipper that looked remarkably like a fuzzy rabbit, one with long, satin-lined ears and stiff white whiskers.

"Bunny slippers?" Tish asked, not quite in control of the chuckle that invaded her voice. "Good grief, couldn't you have gotten something else? Alligators maybe? Or wolves?"

He ignored her remarks, saying only, "The healing took your wounds without you being in the protective circle. Because they weren't aware that could happen, the doctors, after a hasty consultation and a disclaimer of any and all responsibility, said you are to stay off your feet as much as possible for the next day or two because they will still be very tender. Think you can manage that?"

Not sure how or when her feet had been healed, but willing to take Marcus's word for it, she nodded. And then, because for some unknown reason her mind felt clear, uncluttered, ready to deal with the unbelievable in a calm and rational manner, Tish said, "Marcus, what's going on around here? What have I done that's bad enough to make someone want to kill me?"

He got to his feet, stood there, tall, lean, and somehow haughty, and looked down at her for a long moment before he asked, straight-faced and apparently serious, "You mean other than being your extraordinarily obnoxious self?"

"Yes."

The one word answer seemed to disconcert him. He moved sideways, pulled a chair away from the table and sat down facing her. "As to what's going on in Faery, that's a very long story."

"So, the way I hear it, I'm not going to be allowed to go anywhere very soon."

"True, but..." he glanced at Morgain before he slid his chair closer and lowered his voice.

Chapter Nine

STARING AT MARCUS, waiting for him to speak, Tish knew the full meaning of the phrase pregnant silence, in fact, she could almost see it: big-bellied, spraddle-legged, quietly waddling toward some, as yet, unseen destination.

But when it gave birth to a low-voiced question, Tish was too befuddled to be a good midwife, to catch the question and breathe life into it. All she could do was lean a little closer to the man and ask, "Huh?"

Marcus glanced at Morgain again before he said, speaking slowly, trying to make sure Tish understood every whispered word, "What did Artemus King say to you?"

Her own answering silence was anything but pregnant. She could only do a good job of staring at him, blank-faced and uncomprehending. The name, Artemus King, stirred a faint wiggle of memory somewhere in the subterranean reaches of her mind, but it was too niggling to be retrieved and held up to the full light of knowing. And beneath the stare there was an ever-present fear, the need to go home, to leave this place of magic and... She didn't want to add danger, but it was there, wild and terrible danger, danger that seemed, if Marcus could be believed, to be threatening her own life.

Her facade of fearlessness was almost perfect, but Marcus could see deeper than he wanted to, could see her helplessness. He knew, with a growing dread, that he was going to help her. Even if it meant losing whatever was left in his life. There was no other option open to him. This path was a dead end, with broken vows and revealed secrets scattered willy-nilly along the wayside. And all for naught.

He tried again. "Back in the anteroom, after you drank the Witch's Brew. King pulled you aside as we were leaving for the Crystal Court. What did he say to you? What did he want?"

Her face was a study in conflicting emotions. She obviously didn't trust him, but seemingly the memory of previous night was eluding her. "The Ambassador? Is that who you're talking about?" she asked finally, wrinkling her brow and frowning at him.

She had an odd effect on him, made him want to do something drastic; while at the same time wanting to hold her in his arms, protect her from everything, her own stubbornness included. "King works at the embassy, but he's not... I think he's just some sort of secretary or something and not truly representing... Tish, please, tell me what he wanted. It's important."

Burrowing her still tender feet into the soft lining of the pink bunny slippers, Tish, the memory of King and his request suddenly full and complete, looked at Marcus's face, trying to find a friend, a trustworthy companion. Maybe even a lover, she didn't know. But all she saw was an impersonal policeman. A diligent policeman intent on his job. Whatever kind of jobs a policeman did in Faery.

Trying to gain time, to sort out the moral obligations of a promise she may or may not have made to Artemus King, a man she had only seen once. But, he still might be an important person in her own government. Tish blurted out the first questions that found their way to her willing tongue. "Why do you want to know? Do you think King hired the hitman?"

He sighed. It was a martyr's sigh if she had ever heard one, figuratively speaking, of course. Then he said, "Even in Faery, we don't go around accusing people of crimes until we have proof they committed them."

"Is that a fact? Well, you could have fooled me."

His explanation was patient, calm, and barely touched by superiority. Although his voice was a little louder, so much so that Morgain and the guard Godmother both looked toward Tish and Marcus. "Your crimes were fully documented. There were eyewitnesses, a toad, and a Godmother disguise. You were carrying a fully charged wand and had been warned that what you were doing was illegal. What more evidence of wrongdoing do you need?"

It was a rhetorical question. She ignored it. "I need to know more than you're telling me. Fair's fair. I'll tell you what Mr. King wanted, if you'll tell me why you want to know."

She was certainly the most irritating woman who ever lived, determined to drive him over the edge if he didn't put a stop to it. How in hell was he supposed to save her if she acted like...like... He had no reasonable comparison, nor an unreasonable one either.

Feeling as if he were strangling, Marcus made a sound that resembled gaaak and swallowed hard. A small muscle in his cheek jumping, he said, "Miss Warton, I do not, in the normal course of events, approve of physically punishing children. But your mother, whatever her other merits, was severely lacking in judgment when she allowed you to reach this stage of your life without giving you at least one good spanking every second hour and twice that amount on Saturdays. Because if I ever saw a person in need of a few swats, quite a few, it is beyond all questions and doubts, you."

Red-faced and seemingly furious, Tish was obviously taking his words as an implied threat. Which, given his state of mind, they might well have been. She jumped up. He didn't smile when she winced at the pain in her feet. Hell, he didn't want her to hurt. He just wanted her to stop being so damned blind-eyed stubborn. The pain and whatever else she was feeling seemed to only increase her animosity toward him.

She leaned forward, looked him square in the face, and fairly snarled, "So, that's what turns you on, is it? Well, no matter how perverted you are, you are not going to try any of your kinky tricks on me!"

She didn't really mean what she was saying, but screaming at him, accusing him of vile things, seemed to be the only thing she could do. And Tish had to do something. If she didn't, she was just going to curl into a fetal position and smother on her own fear. Taunting him kept her from that fate. At least, for the moment.

His face a dull red, his eyes snapping, Marcus put his hands to either side of his head, gripped it, and roared, sounding like a man strangling on his own evaporating patience, "Damn it! I've had enough!" He got to his own feet and, walking at a near run, made for the door.

The guard Godmother stepped in front of him. Morgain said, sounding oddly carefree for someone who was rebuking a felon bent on escape, "You forget yourself, Marcus. You, as well as your companion, are still under arrest. Your sentence, as I recall, was to guide, protect, and teach Miss Warton. I suggest you do so, and do it with less histrionics."

For an instant, Tish was sure he was going to disobey, but she was wrong. He took a quick breath, twitched and pulled his over large, bloodstained prison-wear into some sort of order on his lean frame, or rather exchanged new wrinkles and baggy places for old, and said, in his patented, infuriatingly aristocratic manner, "Yes, ma'am."

He was, to all outward appearances, in full control of himself and of his wayward emotions before he returned to the table where Tish was standing beside her chair, watching the goings-on with a modicum of interest. And a goodly amount of hardly concealed glee. It was a small victory, but no one had ever accused Tish of being a good winner.

Having pushed his buttons once, she wasn't above trying again.

She'd show him who was superior. She said, too low for Morgain to hear, "Are you sure you've had enough? Because I've barely begun. Maybe you should..."

It must have been a battle he had joined before. "Should what, Miss Warton?" He stepped closer, smiled down at her. The smile was diabolical even before he leaned down, his mouth very near her ear. His voice was a lazy purr when he said, his breath a tickling brush across her cheek, "Should teach you, Miss Warton? Teach you all the marvelously exciting things your oversexed toad never took time to learn?"

Warmth, starting in her nether regions, flowed up to burn her face with crimson fire. She took a step back, bumped into the chair, and sat down too abruptly. She would have denied to her last panting breath, but Tish wanted, or at least her body did, to learn whatever it was he wanted to teach.

She caught her maidenly sigh before it could escape and said, sweetly enough to create a sugar rush in a grown man, "I really don't think that was the sort of lessons Morgain was referring to. But, maybe I should ask her before you start your instructions in...what would you call it, Sex 101, or maybe just the remedial class, since I'm so lacking in that particular area?"

He said, "Gaaaak," or its equivalent once again, sat down facing her, and said, "We'll start with geography."

"Would that be geography of the male or female body, sir?" she asked, trying her best to simper and bat her eyelashes like some idiot maid of yore; probably a milk maid or a goose girl.

To her chagrin, Marcus, with one of those infuriating lifts of his eyebrow, gave her body a thorough visual examination—with no clue as to what kind of grade she was getting on the test—before he sort of smiled. "Sorry to disappoint you, Miss Warton, but I believe we must study the geography of Faery first. Perhaps we can explore your...ah...more erotic proposal of subject matter at a later date and in a less public place."

Tish could have sworn his breath had quickened and that he was leering at her, or pretending to. There was enough warmth in pretense to make her wish, if only for the moment, that it was real, that he found her desirable.

But leer or not, Morgain's cold suggestion, or order, demolished warmth, leerish or otherwise, and brought a definite social chill into the proceedings. "Both of you, that's enough verbal foreplay. Stop it at once, turn on mirror, and ask for a map of Faery. Continue your instruction and learning from that point, and only from that point. Do I make myself clear?"

It hadn't been that at all, and Tish had a hot retort almost out of her mouth when Marcus said, his voice even colder than Morgain's, "I find your remarks both distasteful and demeaning, Godmother. As a point of honor, I believe an apology is in order."

Flabbergasted, but somehow gratified, by his icy rebuke, Tish waited with pent breath and thumping heart, hoping Morgain wasn't going to turn him into a toad or something equally repulsive.

"You took an oath to respect and obey," Morgain said, sounding almost sullen, glaring at him, squeezing the piece of melon she was cubing, unmindful of the thick orange juice that oozed from between her finger and dripped down to decorate her purple apron.

"The Oath binds in two directions, or it doesn't bind at all," Marcus answered, his voice devoid of all expression, his eyes unwavering in their regard of her face.

"Your father will..."

Marcus spoke softly, but there was a scorpion sting embedded in his words. "I took the Oath, not my father. I took it against his wishes, and we both know why. Would you change what is? Would you have me go before the Full Council and ask..."

"No!"

It was a sharp retort, but to Tish it seemed like even the air, which had been hard and brittle, relaxed, took on a gentler state of being, one that held the scent of carnations and nutmeg. One small, iridescent bubble floating up from the mouth of Bubba's juice pitcher and touched her cheek.

Putting her sticky palms together, Morgain gave an almost ritualistic bow in Marcus's direction and said, "It shall be as you request. I ask your pardon."

The silent guardian at the door gave a smothered gasp. Perhaps one that only Tish heard because she was the only one who even glanced in that direction.

Marcus returned the bow and said, "Asked and given."

But there was no direct apology to Tish; however, there was something better. Morgain took up her wand, said something, and Bubba was safely housed in a new jug. This one, the palest of greens and etched with graceful swans around its base, sat in the middle of the table, close enough for Tish to reach out and touch. She did, but only after she had smiled at Morgain and said, "Thank you. It's beautiful."

Morgain's only answer was, "The mirror?"

SEVERAL LONG, EYE-straining, head-aching hours later, Tish was ready to heave a brick through the mirror, zap the Godmother with her own wand, and strangle Marcus with her bare hands. She did none of the above; she just sat there, staring at what was supposed to be a map of Faery. She wondered what earthly difference it made if Faery was five times the size of earth, had lakes, rivers, and small seas, and untold numbers of magic kingdoms scattered through its vast distances, like walnuts in chocolate fudge.

Finally, Tish said, "Now, let me see if I have this straight. The extreme north and areas to the far south and bits and pieces in between belong to various groups, gangs, and tribes of barbarians, outlaws, renegade peasants, and hermits. Besides the magic kingdoms that belong to kings, who all have the requisite number of heirs, dukes, etc., there are mountains, inhabited by dragons, unicorns, virgins, and probably no men at all. If there were any men, there probably wouldn't be any virgins to feed to marauding dragons or to use as unicorn bait. Which, if I have my mythology correct, were killed for their horns, so it could be used to restore potency to men who..."

"Very good," Marcus said, interrupting her spate of words, and obviously not meaning the standard approval phrase one single iota; however small amount that was. His amber eyes looked as tired as Tish felt, and his voice was hoarse with too-oft repeated lessons. "And the Godmothers?" It wasn't a gentle prod at her inept recitation. "How do they fit into the overall pattern of Faery?"

Wanting to say, "Anywhere they damned well please," but holding it back, mostly because it hadn't flown that well the last two times she'd said it. Tish sat quietly for a moment, drumming her fingers on the table top, and trying to put the vast chunks of information Marcus, aided and abetted by the damned mirror, which was smugness incarnate, had shoved inside her head.

"Well?"

"Except for a few granny women and witches, wicked and otherwise, and an occasional, and probably unacknowledged, Wilding, the Godmothers own the entire magic supply of Faery. And from the way you tell it, they own Faery itself, only giving away bits of it as a reward for outstanding service, or selling portions of it to deserving and/or rich humans. The Godmothers run the whole magic show; they do not franchise, divest, or sell shares. It is a privately owned monopoly; and probably a bureaucracy of unbelievable complications. There are probably power plays, infighting, and graft up to your..."

"Don't confuse the government of Faery with your own, Miss Warton. It isn't true, and it isn't likely. As I said, Faery is a Matriarchy, ruled by a Council of very powerful women."

Too tired to be angry, but not willing to allow him a single point in their continuing game of one-upmanship, Tish snorted. "Yeah, well, that's what you say, but it'd be my guess that all that power might make them blind to what's happening right under their magic noses."

For some reason her outburst sparked his interest. "What do you mean?"

She hadn't actually meant anything, but she wasn't about to admit it. She countered with a question of her own. "If they are so all powerful and the rest of that junk, why were you guarding the border between my world and yours? Surely it wasn't just so you could tackle me and carry me off to Faery, or was it?" She stood up, twisted and turned to stretch the kinks and knots out her cramped muscles. Then she looked around the shadow-filled kitchen, for the first time in what seemed to be hours, and, judging from the evidence at hand, very probably had been.

Adding to the illumination provided by the magic mirror, a green witch light bobbed above the white table, giving the illusion of mold and decay to the leftover scraps and pieces of a meal. One that Tish remembered ingesting along with a heavy sauce of Faery knowledge.

A bubbling snore wafted up out of the top of Bubba's jug, making Tish smile fondly. The white cupboards were ghosts, pale and green, looming out of the thick shadows.

But, as far as Tish could tell, she was alone in the kitchen with Marcus. She hadn't heard either Morgain or the guard Godmother leave. Or maybe she had been bespelled not to be aware of their departure, or the arrival of her loaded wand, which was lying within touching distance of Bubba's jug and her hand. It looked, for all the world as if someone had placed it there for some, as yet, unknown reason. It was a welcomed sight. Something else wasn't. It was setting behind the jug and almost hidden, and was the beslimed, foul-smelling toad cage; complete with bulging-eyed, slavering toad who was crouched, like the obscene idol of some best forgotten god, at the bottom of its glass prison.

As if he were suddenly coming awake, Marcus shifted in his chair. Stephen's words of carefully veiled warning come rushing back to flutter in his mind, join with his own sense of something being wrong, terrible wrong. He looked at Tish in a bemused fashion, and said, keeping his voice calm and low-pitched, "It's possible that you're entirely correct. Absolute power might make you blind to... Yes, it might explain everything."

"Corruption in high places?"

"Probably in low and foreign."

Umbrage was hers by right and claim, or so it seemed. If it wasn't, she certainly didn't know it. "I'm not corrupt. I don't have anything to do with..."

She was spitting like an angry kitten, and Marcus almost smiled when he said, "I hate to do anything to lower your self-esteem, but I would like to call to your attention to one very small fact."

SOMETHING HAD happened between them. Tish didn't know what it was, but she felt an easing on his part, a bit of a chink in his armor, a hint of approval in his eyes. It pleased her. Thinking she detected a whiff of anticipatory relish in the tone of his remark, Tish decided to play straight woman and allow him a tiny victory. "Oh," she said, trying to act as if she meant it, "what's that?"

"You are not the only foreigner in Faery."

"So, you do think Mr. King is involved in some criminal act, one that involves smuggling magic into human worlds? Is that why you were at Mother's ball? Were you trying to catch Mr. King in act, as it were?" Smugly, sure she had tricked him into admitting more than he wanted to, Tish smiled.

Her smile faded, and she whispered, "Damn," when she discovered who had been tricked into admitting what to whom.

"So, that's what he wanted from you. You saw him there, didn't you? And recognized him here? King asked you not to tell me, didn't he?"

Knowing when to capitulate, Tish nodded, perhaps not too graciously, and said, "Could we continue this tomorrow? I'm really tired and sleepy."

And it wasn't just an excuse; lassitude had fallen on her like a thick, heavy blanket, weighing her down, telling her she needed to rest, whispering, "Sleep," with an implacable force.

The overwhelming sleep-attack wasn't natural. Even Tish, no matter how much she wanted to disbelieve it, knew what it was. "A spell," she muttered, staggering a little as she walked back to the table, caught the back of her chair with her right hand, holding herself up.

"Yes." Marcus, yawning widely, nodded his head, but he didn't sound anywhere near as sleepy as Tish felt, so sleepy her bones were turning to dust, sifting out of her toes, leaving no anchors for her muscles, nothing to keep her on her feet. The floor beneath the soles of her bunny slippers looked as inviting as a heated waterbed.

Marcus reached out, caught Tish by the arm, and tried, with as much success as snake giving hand signals, to seat her in the chair. "It must be clients, important ones, coming here. A love problem. Morgain does most of those. She's..." he tried to stand up but sat down rather quickly, having no more control over his legs than he did his tongue. "Morgain is the sexpert."

Tish wanted to say, "And you're the pervert," but she was using what little strength she had left to reach for her magic wand and to curse the Godmothers, one and all, for daring to send her to an early bed, like a naughty child.

"I won't have it," she said, growling out the words with a tongue that was already too numb to answer her commands.

Her fingers, tingling with sleep, scrabbled across the top of the table, found the barest tip of the sawed-off wand, and she spat out, "No spell. No sleep."

Overriding an indignant squawk of protest, a flare of eye-hurting green, and a fade to black from the magic mirror, Tish's wand, sparking and blazing like wildfire, did the rest. Like a chaff in a dust devil, the terrible, mind numbing sleepiness swirled up and away, and vanished. Not just Tish's spell-induced sleepiness either.

Marcus, looking too frisky, and maybe a bit miffed, leaped out of the chair, took a deep breath, and then another, and just managed not to yell when he said, with greater nastiness than he needed, "What in the Name of the Founding Godmothers have you done now?"

Tish lifted her chin, and said, fairly certain her sweetness would counteract his vitriol, "They can do what they want, but I'm not ready to go to sleep just now."

"You... You..."

Expecting to see steam puffing out his ears, Tish watched him closely. It was the first time she had ever seen a person in the red-faced, gasping, hands-clenching throes of apoplexy. He was livid, speechless, and, quite possibly, ready to do her in, which wasn't the future she had envisioned for herself.

"Stop it," she said, waving the wand in his general direction. "Stop it, or so help me, I'll zap you with the wand and turn you into a toad, a girl toad, and put you in the cage with...with...with Carl."

"You have already done enough! More than enough!" Morgain snapped, charging into the room like a whole band of cavalry, bugler and all. "Put down the wand!"

Tish looked at her, saw a dumpy, apple-cheeked woman in a dress of iridescent gossamer and rosy tulle, complete with pale pink floating panels and what looked like a hoop skirt, ribbon roses, ruffles, furbelows, ringlets and puffs, and a sparkling crown of diamonds and gold.

Her smile was grim, and her jaw ached from being clenched so tightly, but Tish's voice didn't come close to wavering when she said, "I think not. I'm tired of being pushed around, ordered about, and treated like the world's biggest ninny. If you don't want me to go someplace, say so. Just don't try any more sneaky stuff like sending a sleep spell to keep me out of the way while you do whatever."

Suspicion flared and Tish pursued the burning tidbit it dropped at her feet. "It was a set-up, wasn't? A test to find out just what I could do? That's why the wand was left and... The Godmothers have found out something, haven't they? They know what they're going to do with me, don't they?"

Morgain's voice was only faintly troubled when she said, not really answering Tish's questions, but giving some hint that news might be in the offing, "Miss Warton, we will have to discuss this later this evening. I have clients coming at any moment, very rich and important clients who are willing to pay for a very large job. One that involves some very difficult..."

Cocking her head, she listened to some slight sound coming from the room behind her. "Will you be willing to stay in here and wait until..."

Remembering something Marcus had said in the grotto, Tish knew that her given word was a spell that would bind her, so she looked at Morgain and shook her head. "Sorry, but..."

Glaring at Marcus, silently accusing him of Tish's attitude, Morgain said, "Well, be quiet then and..." she licked her lips before she added, "And catch some flies and feed that damned frog."

Bugs, spiders, and mice were really high on Tish's jump-back-and-scream list, and she wasn't about to touch one of the little creatures with her own hands. Trying not to shudder at the mere idea, Tish said, "I can't..."

"You woke him up. He's your frog. Feed him." In a flutter of skirts, petticoats, fripperies, and dangling things, Morgain spun around and, with scant inches of space on either side of her hoops, stalked through the doorway. The room beyond was, probably as a result of the glamour, without form or substance; at least, to Tish's eyes.

On the other hand, the toad had entirely too much substance to please Tish, substance that had to be maintained with creepy, crawly, germ-carrying flies. "I won't do it," she said. "I don't care if he starves to death."

"Have you ever thought about taking a course in interpersonal communications, or courtesy, or..." Marcus asked. "You do realize, don't you, that Morgain is one of the most powerful women in Faery."

"So, what's your point?"

Devils were line-dancing in the amber depths of his eyes and he sounded as if the prospect was eminently pleasing when he said, "She could turn you into a fly and feed you to the...ah...toad."

He looked at her for a moment longer before he shook his head, apparently in regret, and continued, "No, not even old Carl deserves something like that. Besides, it would probably make him sicker than a rat imbibing rat poison."

"Morgain didn't make me go to sleep, did she?" Tish asked, sorely tempted to stick out her tongue and say, "Nah, nah, nah." But, she just grinned at him before she turned away and headed toward the door to the living room.

Horror soaking every word, Marcus, making a dash in her direction, "What in blue blazes are you going to do now?"

"Why, doing what Morgain told me of course. There are no flies in here, so I'll have to go outside to catch..."

He grabbed her shoulders. His mouth was close enough to tickle her ear when he hissed, "You can't just go barreling through there. You heard what Morgain said about a..."

Pulling free, Tish turned to face him, smiled, and said, "Stop worrying so. I won't go in until whoever it is leaves, but I can't know when that is if I don't listen, can I?"

Not letting the fact that his nearness was doing something untoward to her breathing deter her from her plan, Tish said, "If she catches me, I'll just tell her it was a learning experience, a hands-on lab in the workings of Faery."

"One that will, in all probability, get us both strung up by our thumbs," Marcus said, following Tish when she put her finger to her lips and snuggled up to the blank-seeming of the doorway. A blankness that suddenly developed two peepholes when Tish gave it a little tap with her wand.

"Are you sure you want to risk..."

"I want to find a way to go home," Tish said slowly. "Mother must be worried sick by now."

"No," he said, his face too close to hers again, his whisper meant for her ears alone, "she isn't. She thinks you got mad at Carl, broke off the engagement, and took a vacation. At last report, she is taking credit for the whole thing, in a very ladylike way of course."

She had no reason to believe him, but she did; not that it made her feel a whole lot better. In fact, she really didn't know how she felt, except being a little hurt that her own mother would accept her absence so calmly. Trying not to allow the hurt to turn into self-pity, she sat silent for a moment. Marcus, inadvertently, rescued her from a bout of poor-me-ism and maybe a tear or two.

Leaning against her shoulder, he applied his eye to one of the peepholes and made a faint sound, possibly of surprise. "Dear God," he said, speaking more to himself than Tish, "why are they here after all this time. What does this mean?"

"What is it? What's happening?"

Marcus was, seemingly, too engrossed in what he was seeing to answer.

Chapter Ten

THE MURMUR OF soft, well-bred voices, the slight clink of silver against china, polite, tea-party sounds whispered in from the living room, but Tish was having difficulty listening. And breathing. The sound was there but the words weren't. And the kitchen was suddenly far too warm for comfort and, for some unknown reason, the air didn't seem to hold enough oxygen for her needs. She decided it was probably some sort of spell; not that she knew what kind, but it, while not exactly unpleasant, was creating barriers to her eavesdropping.

Besides that, Marcus was standing too close, way too close, leaning against her as he watched, with great attention, what was happening on the other side of the spell curtain. "It is them," he said, his low-voiced comment seeming to hold more sadness than pleasure. "I certainly hope Morgain can deliver what she sells them. Because if she doesn't..." Marcus shook his head and sighed.

"Who are they? What's Morgain selling?"

Making a shushing sound, Marcus pointed to the other peephole, silently telling her that if she wanted to know what was going on, to see for herself. Licking her dry lips, trying, if not very hard, to edge away from his lean body, Tish did her own looking; not that she saw anything terribly alarming. Or interesting.

The living room, wearing its new glamour, was, in essence, an early Nineteenth Century drawing room, with polished floors, silk-brocade on the walls, spindly legged furniture, with several additions: a terminally cute Godmother and two medium-sized women dressed completely in black. They were also wearing heavy black veils. Mourning veils, Tish thought, which hid every glimmer of their features.

Morgain, her ribbons and frills aflutter, simpered and cooed, playing the perfect air-head, as she poured tea from a silver pot and busied herself with lemon, milk, and sugar. Offering a cup to each woman and urging them to take some of the dainty watercress and cucumber sandwiches from the silver tray, she seemed as beglamoured as the room.

And for some reason, probably some of the glamour spell spilling over, Tish didn't find it all that disconcerting, or frightening, or even weird. She was more interested in Marcus's reaction to the veiled women, who had each accepted a cup of tea and were holding them in gloved hands, not even pretending to drink. Possibly, Tish thought, because to do so would mean they would have to lift their thick face coverings; something they seemed to have no intention of doing.

"Who are they?" she whispered.

"The Uglies, I think, or someone dressed like them," he answered, all too obviously not wanting to answer at all.

She did a quick review of her lessons, found no reference to any such people. "Uglies? Who are they? Why are they veiled? Is it a religion? Or did somebody die?"

"Just the witch." His tone was too carefully absent, trying to sound as if his thoughts were a few mega-miles away, but his answer seemed more a non sequitur than anything.

"Huh?" She shook her head, pulled away from the peephole to stare at him. "What are you talking about?"

"I told you. The witch died."

"What witch?"

"Shhh, I want to listen."

"Marcus, what witch?"

"I'll tell you later. This is important. The Uglies have finally decided to act. Morgain is going to be doing some heavy bargaining if she gets out of this deal with any profit. And, this time, no matter what anyone else does, I am completely out of the picture. The outcome of it will rest on someone else's shoulders, and for that I give profound thanks to the Founding Mothers."

He still sounded more sad than thankful, and Tish wanted to know why. "But..."

"You're the student, Tish, so pay attention and see if you can learn something."

Tish didn't take umbrage at his tone, but there wasn't actually anything to pay attention to, except the twitter of Morgain's voice and the soft muffled replies of the two veiled women, none of whom were even close to being intelligible.

Tish strained to hear a moment longer, realized the futility of the task, straightened up, and said, "I can't..."

Never moving from his own peephole, Marcus whispered, "Tish, I really need to hear this, can you turn up the volume or something?"

"How?" Tish asked, fully aware of his body warmth and how it was adding to her own. She didn't really like her own physical response that much; especially to an arrogant, superior devil of a man like

Marcus.

"You have a magic wand. Use it."

Perhaps what he said was true, but that didn't mean much to Tish. Magic wand or no magic wand, she flatly didn't know how to make the conversation between Morgain and the other two women any louder. She even tried, by both pointing and shaking the glass wand, and a combination of both actions, the wand and saying, "Louder."

Exactly what she expected happened: nothing. "Now, what?" she asked Marcus. "Why is it so blasted important?"

Stepping away from his own peep hole, Marcus said, a certain amount of urgency in his voice, "The Uglies are leaving. Hurry back to the table. I don't want Morgain to catch us before I find out just what it is she's planning. There's something going on that doesn't quite..."

Limping along on tender feet, Tish did as he asked; nor did she object when he put his arm around her waist and almost carried her to her chair. She wasn't all that thrilled to be hustled along like a grain sack, but it was a good deal less wear and tear on her feet.

And they were barely seated before Morgain, sans her Faery Godmother frump and flutter, came marching in, resembling a very well-dressed thunder cloud, with a red face and a slinky, go-anywhere, little black dress and the required string of perfectly matched pearls. "You heard, didn't you," she said, stopping in front of Marcus, glaring down at him.

"No."

"Don't you dare lie to me." She raised her wand, threatened him for a second or two before she let her arm drop.

"I saw the Uglies," he said, "but, as I'm sure you made strong spells to insure, I couldn't hear a word that was being said. But, I can guess what they want and..."

She smiled, grim as any reaper, and said, "One way or another, their wishes are going to be granted, either by me or some other Godmother. They have saved, borrowed, and begged enough gold to insure that. Especially since I made them a rather nice deal, one with a fairly substantial discount and a few time payments."

Marcus was on his feet in an instant, glaring at the Godmother, cold fire blazing in his eyes. "I won't be a party to any tricks. Haven't they suffered..."

"You will!" Morgain spoke flatly. "You will do exactly what you are told."

For Tish, it was like watching some game that she had never seen before, didn't know the rules, and wasn't all that fond of either of the players. Although at the moment, she would have preferred that Marcus win and win big. The cold expression on Morgain's face was enough to... She shuddered. The small movement was enough to make Morgain turn her wrath, if that's what it was, in a new direction. And Tish was the sole recipient.

"Against my vote to the contrary, the entire Council has chosen your fate. Tregon is waiting to deliver the verdict. And, my dear, I am happy to say you will hear it alone, without either your paramour or your Embassy representative in audience."

Imagining being flayed, drawn and quartered, or some other horrendous punishment, fear drying her throat, but not willing to give either Morgain or Marcus a glimpse of her terror, Tish stood, lifted her chin, and said, as calmly as if it was an everyday occurrence, "Very well. I'll go, but I do not have a paramour and as far as the Embassy is concerned, except for Mr. King, I doubt they even know I'm here." She tried to smile and managed a small one before she continued with, "So, how do I get there?"

"A guard is in the courtyard." Morgain waited until Tish was almost to the living room door before she said, sounding both snide and smugly malicious, "Take your toad...or should I say, your lover...with you."

The petty act transformed Tish's fear, at least, a portion of it, into anger. Anger gave her the strength to walk back, without limping, smile, stick the wand through one of her empty belt loops, pick up the toad cage in one hand, Bubba's jug in the other. "If I don't get to see you again, Morgain, I would like to thank you for your hospitality and courtesy to an unwilling visitor from another land. I'm sure it will not go unrewarded."

Marcus made an exclamation of some sort, but Tish ignored him and turned and marched back to the door, feeling Morgain's burning gaze on her back the whole way. And wondering, at the same time, what had happened that had turned the Godmother from a reasonable seeming woman into a harridan. Or maybe it was a harpy. One of those unpleasant creatures anyway.

It wasn't a question that was answered very soon. In fact, it was shoved so far back in her mind, to accommodate the happenings of the next few hours, that she forgot it even existed until later. A very long time later.

FEELING AN ODD little pang in the general region of his heart, Marcus watched her go. And wanted to run after her, scoop her up, run as far and as fast as he could, take her someplace where danger didn't exist. It wasn't possible. And even if it were, Tish wouldn't go. Not with him, not after she learned what he had done.

"Fool," Morgain said, her voice almost shrill with real anger, "your pretty little human won't be around long enough to enjoy your manhood. Tregon will see to that."

Fearing the worse, he was instantly alert, waiting for her to drop another hint, to give him some clue as to what was happening in Faery, to tell him what he could do to...to... What? Marcus didn't know.

Morgain turned away.

Marcus wasn't ready to admit defeat. He opened his mouth to demand answers, but Morgain was already shimmering around the edges, getting ready to do her Godmotherly vanishing act. Before he could say a word, she said, leaving the words and a traveling spell behind at her going. "You are called to the old stables. Report immediately."

Having no real choice in the matter, Marcus went.

TISH'S GUIDE, TALL and lean, but having nothing more than a pale imitation of Marcus' aristocratic bearing, was wearing a silvery uniform, differing only slightly, in ornamentation and insignia, from the one Marcus had worn to the ball. She wasn't feeling all that chatty, just nervous and needing to fill the silence with sound, but he resisted all her efforts to get him to say a single word, delivered her, and her wand, toad, and sprite, up for justice in a place, a room, a vast echo-filled edifice, that almost defied description. At least by one of Tish's national persuasion and limited architectural experience.

Eight or nine stories high, hollow in the middle, replete with swooping stairways that led up to nooks, crannies, hideaways, and bowers. Stained glass windows of every size and shape were positioned, tucked, set, and otherwise disposed within the confines of the towering walls that weren't exactly on the up and up. But, then again, neither were they on the straight and narrow. It was probably the most attractive building she had ever seen; although there was no reason why it should have been.

Scarlet-clad Tregon, with four Godmothers, all dressed in pale-blue, floor-length gowns, standing like bridal attendants behind her, was waiting at the head of the first stair on the right. The guard, with a smart salute given to no one in particular, left Tish at the foot of the stair.

Marching in slow time, to the soft strains of some sort of music,

Tregon, and the other Godmothers, descended the red carpeted steps until Tregon's crimson shoes touched the gold-veined marble floor. Then the lessor Godmothers halted, allowing Tregon the honor of crossing the small space that separated her from the felon.

Every step she took increased the pressure on Tish's frayed nerves until she was ready to run and scream. But she didn't, and she wouldn't. She'd see the whole sorry lot of them in hell before she'd admit they were scaring the marrow right out of her bones.

She hardly had enough breath to incline her head and say, "Tregon," when the other woman gave a stiff bow and said, "Miss Warton." But, for a reason she couldn't fathom, it seemed right and proper for what seemed to be a very solemn occasion, one fairly fraught with formality and ritual and importance.

"A verdict has been reached, one that has been deemed fair to all concerned." Tregon paused, looked at the toad with considering eyes, and added, soft-voiced, for Tish's ears alone, "I would have wished for a different fate for him, but..."

Her grin wasn't exactly impish as she pitched her voice so Carl could hear, "He would make such a good eunuch, don't you think?"

He shivered. For the first time since his transformation, Tish thought of him as a real person, realized what she had put him through, knew he still carried his human mind and emotions in his toad incarnation. Pity and genuine regret did a little shaking of their own, and Tish said, "I have to send him back as Carl."

"Well, don't just stand there, do it."

"How?"

"It's your magic, the how of it is entirely up to you, but you'd better warn everyone if you're planning on letting him out of the cage first. His bite is a lot worse than his warts."

She wanted to reassure the shivering toad, but all Tish could think of to do was set down the cage, and Bubba's jug, take out the wand, poke it between the glass bars, touching the toad with the end of it, and say, "Dirty, lying woman-chasing bastard that you are, be Carl."

He was, and he was furious. Splintered and powdered glass on his shoulders, dusting his hair, showering down with his every move, Carl started screaming imprecations, calling Tish names that no one should say aloud; or even think for that matter. And saying, every third phrase, "I'm going to sue you, your whole damned family. When I get through your rich-bitch of a mother won't be so high and mighty."

Pulling the small engagement ring from her finger, Tish tucked it in his vest pocket. And looked at his muscles and mat of chest hair without a moment's regret; except for her own foolishness. "Go home," Tish said, all pity gone, whacking him much harder than was necessary with her magic wand, and breathing a big sigh of relief when he vanished. And only her overactive imagination took a moment to enjoy the mind picture of Carl, his lawyer bending double with laughter, demanding to bring suit against Tish because she had changed him to a toad. Using a magic wand, no less.

Tregon cleared her throat, bringing Tish back to the present reality; if, indeed, that's what it was. "We can cloud his mind if his threats give you worry."

"No," Tish answered. "Who would believe him anyway? And Mother has friends in high places, she can... Mother is in no danger."

"Not from the toad anyway," Tregon answered somberly before she smiled and added, "Good job, by the way. One of your creatures has been dealt with, now, what do you intend to do about your...ah...Bubba?"

Bubba did a little answering on his own and his howl of protest had all the Godmothers within hearing-distance holding their ears and demanding he stop immediately. He did, but only after Tish picked up the jug by the handle, lifted it up against her chest, and said, daring Tregon to contradict her, "He's mine and I'm going to keep him."

"Quite so." There was a moment of silence before Tregon said, "The archives yielded evidence of three cases that fall into the same general category as yours. Two were resolved the same way."

Clutching the wand in one hand, Bubba's jug in the other, Tish tried to look as if she was not nervous, hadn't a dab of fear, at all, but she couldn't stop herself from asking, "Which was what?"

Long blue skirts swaying, the other Godmothers descended the stair and ranged themselves, two to a side, hands crossed at their breasts, wands pointing over their left shoulders, on either side of Tregon. As if it were a Sacred Rite, one formalized by time and use, Tregon assumed the same stance before she said, "Leticia Warton, inasmuch as you have been born to the magic, however limited it may be, and have demonstrated it responds to your will, we have been instructed to inscribe your name in the Hallowed Rolls of Godmotherhood and grant to you all the rights and privileges inherent therein. Do you understand what I have said?"

She wasn't entirely sure she understood anything, but Tish nodded.

"By the Word and the Wand, knowing that you will receive further teaching and instruction into the arts and crafts of our

Sisterhood and must, also, fulfill certain obligations that will mark each step along the way to growth and wisdom, do you have any questions at this time?"

Too full of questions to catch a single one in the dashing, diving swarm, Tish said, rather weakly, "No."

Tregon's voice deepened, grew more resonant, hummed with power. "By the Wand and the Word, knowing undisciplined use of magic can not only destroy you but everyone and everything around you, not just here but in your own world as well, do you agree to Swear the Oath of Office, accept the Godmother Sanction, knowing they will bind you until time ends and Faery is no more?"

It was no small oath. Tish took a deep breath, thought of her mother, the Steps, Jilly, Bubba, and even Marcus, none of whom she actually wanted to hurt. But, still it was a frightening thing, one that raised little goose bumps all over her body, made the hair on the back of her neck stand up. Scared her silly.

"What will happen if I don't?" It came out in a squeak and it echoed up through the empty spaces of the huge building, and came back, time and again, to haunt her with its wimpish sound. But wimp didn't embarrass her at all. Well, not much. One small vain part of her wanted to sound as powerful as Tregon.

"One of the others chose that option," Tregon said, sounding sincerely sad about that long ago event. "Her magic was removed, but..."

"But what? Did she die?"

"No, but everything that made her unique and special did. She lived a very long time, and it was said that she seemed quite happy to be tending the sheep in the meadow. She sang little songs and wove garlands of flowers for the lambs. Is that what you want?"

It wasn't a threat, and Tish was wise enough to know that, and to know, also, that she was a danger to all around her, and that if she chose to go free, they couldn't stop her. Her magic might be small and untutored, wild even, but it was alien magic and theirs couldn't do much of anything to counter it.

Time did one of those odd stretchy things, extending the moment beyond the possible. Hugging Bubba's jug against her chest, Tish bowed her head. She could almost hear her mother saying, as she had said so many times before, "We all have to grow up, Tish. We all have to make hard choices and live with them. We all love you, but we don't always like the way you act. Isn't it time you accepted some responsibility for your acts?"

Sighing, wanting time to stretch farther and farther until it snapped, left her in nowhere, a place she didn't have to... Left her in childhood, eternal childhood. Is that what she wanted? Wasn't that what the woman who tended the sheep got? Singing songs and picking flowers? Forever?

But, was being a Godmother, a Faery Godmother with a magic wand and sprite, any better?

As if to bring their own answers into her interior monologue, the wand grew warm, began to vibrate like a purring cat, and Bubba began to sing, a high sweet song that held not one tad of sadness.

Tish raised her head, rubbed her thumb across Bubba's jug in a sort of caress, did the same to the wand, and said, knowing she was doing the right thing, "Tregon, I will Swear the Oath, accept the Sanction, and do whatever I have to do to tame my magic."

"Vest her for the Ceremony," Tregon said, stepping back as the blue-gowned Godmothers, each smiling a shy little smile, stepped forward and began tapping Tish here and there with some very tickling wands.

Her yellow jumpsuit vanished, was replaced by a silk robe, sort of like a graduation gown, but fuller, and tied at the waist with a golden cord. After a giggling examination of her pink bunny slippers, they left them alone. Tish's hair was wanded into a soft riot of curls and a small crown was set, very firmly, and by hand, on her head.

A looking glass, magic or otherwise, she didn't know, was held in front of her face and one of the attendants wafted make-up into place with a gentle but incredibly expert hand. Except for the barest glimpse of her freckles, and her eye color, Tish had difficulty even recognizing herself in the beauty reflected in the glass.

"It's a glamour," she told herself, trying to catch back the words when she realized she had spoken aloud.

"No," the make-up artist said, "it's you with a little enhancement." Then the hand mirror faded and was gone, allowing the Godmother to retreat and find her place with the rest of the Godmothers after saying, "She is ready, Tregon."

Tregon led the way, with Tish two steps behind, through a doorway of magic and wishes and what happened beyond was secret, terribly secret, bound by oaths and promises. Tish vowed to keep the secrets, accept the Godmother Sanction, until she could use it with honor.

And yet, the whole shebang had a curiously dreamlike quality, one that made Tish feel that she was somehow being conned, that it was a dog-and-pony show enacted just for her; but for a reason she couldn't even guess.

The Ceremony lasted for hours, or so it seemed. She was limp with exhaustion when it was done, but it was not yet time for Tish to go to her rest. There were urgent tasks to be performed, new lessons to be learned.

"There are those who would hold earnest discourse with you, Leticia," a small, wispy, nearly invisible Godmother said, coming close to whisper the message, and to whisk Tish away from a group of well-wishers, or curious questioners.

Whisked was the operative word. Between one breath and the next Tish, with Bubba safe in her arms, was transported—through time and space, she suspected—from the Hall of Oaths to a garden, an old-fashioned garden with pinks and zinnias and sweet peas. Roses, heavy with bloom, crawled up stone walls and sprawled over sundials. Bees, filling the scented air with their droning, wandered from flower to flower in a slow dance.

An old woman, dirt under her fingernails, strands of gray hair escaping from the single braid that hung down her back, almost to her time-thickened waist, was patting the earth around a newly planted something-or-other that Tish couldn't put a name to.

A basket of red, pink, and yellow roses hanging from her left arm, another old woman snipped more blossoms and slipped them into her basket before she looked up and smiled at Tish. Her wrinkled face held nothing but welcome, sparkling eyes, and beauty.

"Come, Leticia," she said, leading the way to an arbor heavy with purple grapes. A table, spread with a white cloth and holding a water-beaded pitcher, five glasses, and a plate of cookies. They had to be still warm chocolate chip from the look and smell of them.

Two women were already seated, both old, neither beautiful, but nothing about them, from the snapping black eyes to the diamond and ruby rings on their fingers, was feeble or weak. Looking enough alike to be twins, their identical nods only added to the sameness, but beyond that brief acknowledgment, neither woman even glanced in Tish's direction. Still she was pretty sure they could tell her how many hairs she had on her head and what she was going to eat for breakfast the next morning. Clutching Bubba's jug a little tighter, she returned the women's nod and waited, her stomach churning just a little, to find out why she had been summoned.

The gardening Godmother, coming up behind Tish and putting her hand on Tish's arm, was the one that spoke first. Her voice cracked by time, but holding power beyond measure, she said, "My dear, among other things, we, the Council of Four, had you brought among us so that we could warn you of your continuing peril."

Not knowing what was expected of her, Tish waited for the Godmother to continue. It wasn't a long wait.

Cocking her head to one side, looking like a bright, inquisitive bird, the old woman said, "Another mercenary beast has made his way into Morgain's quarters. He was destroyed by a squad of the Guardians, but not before he said, "Kill! Kill, Leticia."

Ice formed in her stomach, her chest, her mouth, and Tish could hardly ask the questions that needed answers. "Marcus," she whispered, "was he..."

"No. Neither he nor Morgain was there at the time. He is uninjured."

A bit of the ice melted, giving Tish the strength to ask, "I don't belong in Faery. I have no idea what's going on here. So, who wants me dead? And why?"

Chapter Eleven

"WHO WANTS YOU dead?" one of the hitherto silent Godmothers asked, her voice pure music, high, sweet, and wonderful to the ear. "That, my dear, is not a matter for your concern."

Tish couldn't see the truth of that. It was, after all, her life that was being imperiled and she wanted to know the who and the why of it. She opened her mouth to protest, to demand answers, and was silenced before she could make a sound. And by just a Godmotherly frown and a gentle rebuke.

"Leticia, you have jumped, blind-eyed and incredibly obstinate, into a situation that is none of your doing, and if you are not extremely careful, the situation is going to be the end of you. Without your participation, we will see that it is resolved, with the guilty punished and the innocent rewarded. But in the meantime, we must, given the Oath we have all taken, which, as you will very soon discover, binds both ways, keep you safe."

A bee buzzed around the top of Bubba's jug. Tish brushed it away "But who..."

"Don't interrupt, dear," the gardener said, patting Tish's arm, acting exactly like a slightly doddery grandmother might behave toward a wayward granddaughter whose manners were in the lacking category, possibly because her brain had long since ceased to function. Tish wanted to smile and agree with dear old granny, but she knew an act, especially a good one, when she saw it. And, these ladies, despite their looks, were sharper and shrewder than anyone she had ever met.

"And powerful, too," the other silent Godmother said, smoothing out the turned up corner of her lace collar and rocking ever so slightly in her white wicker chair, her sprigged muslin dress fluttering with the movement. "Don't ever forget that. So many folks do and it does cause problems." It wasn't quite a threat, but it had all the ingredients to make it a very strong warning.

She shook her head, smiled at Tish, and added, "No, I don't read minds. I read faces and yours, Leticia, is of the large-print variety. Now, just be a nice child, have a cookie, and listen to what we have decided is the best course of action in this particular instance."

Setting the basket of cut roses on the gravel floor, just inside the shady arbor, laying her scissors along side, the first Godmother smiled her lovely smile. She said, "But first, I really believe we should do something about your clothes. I know you would prefer blue jeans and a sweatshirt. However, given the situation, and our plans for your future, I believe you would be less noticeable, and that, too, is important to the outcome of our plan, if you are dressed thusly. It is the proper riding costume for that particular kingdom of very clothes-conscious humans."

If she had a wand in her hand, Tish didn't see it, but she certainly felt the ceremonial gown and crown dissolve, only to be replaced by some very heavy, very cumbersome, long full-skirted, tight-bodiced something. Beneath it were several layers of something else, undergarments, Tish thought, of terrible complexity. There was a corset, maybe, and a camisole, several petticoats, long drawers, thick, itchy-wool stockings, and knee-high riding boots.

"Doesn't she just look a picture," the Godmother said. Tish was hard pressed to tell if the woman was cooing or hooting, but suspected the worst.

One of the seated Godmothers opened what had to be a reticule and took out a large square of parchment, a quill pen, ink, and a sand shaker. Every item was far too large to fit into the small confines of the purse. "It's really an eelskin briefcase, but I'm sure you'll forgive my little conceits," she said, smiling at Tish and reading her expression rightly. "The contract is written. An interesting wish was made, a very substantial fee was offered, and it was accepted, on your behalf, by the Council of Four and over the strident objections of some of the other Godmothers. A finger count, no more. We are accepting our usual percentage, thirty-five I believe, for acting as your agents in this matter.

"According to the law, we must also withhold an additional fifteen percent to pay the liability insurance inasmuch as you have no performance record and are not yet bondable. Dear, this is a very important wish. Other than that, it's a standard contract. The wishers want to purchase a Prince Charming as a consort for their sister and we, acting as your agents, have agreed to supply one. In this case, they have requested a legitimate prince, preferably one that is heir to the throne. If that isn't possible, then a second or third son, as long as he is totally legitimate, will do. The matter must, however, be completed with considerable dispatch."

It sounded so boringly businesslike that Tish felt like she was having trouble with her ears. And every fairy tale she'd ever read, and made fun of, came dancing through her mind. "A Prince Charming?

You're selling a prince?"

"Not us, dear, you are selling a prince; well, to be perfectly factual, you are selling a wish, and the wish just happens to be for a prince. It's your first job as a Faery Godmother, which, under the terms of the Sanction, you agreed to take in order to further your knowledge of magic and the land. Now, just come over to the table and sign the contract. We have spent enough time dillydallying; we do have an entire country to govern, you know."

Tish didn't even try to argue. It was too late for that; she had taken the Oath and had bound herself to its rules and regulations. It and the Sanction were making themselves known in several unpleasant ways, not the least of which was an unbearable itch under her shoulder blade, a sharp pain in her big toe, and a chorus of whining gnat voices inside her head.

She walked over to the table, set Bubba down, and picked up the quill pen. After dipping it in the glass ink bottle, she signed the document with a flourish, felt immediate relief from the strictures of the Sanction, stood up, and asked, "Now what? Where's the client? How do I get the prince?"

"I believe the Uglies have returned to their home, but Marcus can, and must, tell you the full story, for both your sakes. And, as far as the prince is concerned, it is up to you how you go about procuring him. Ordinarily, princes, on the open market, aren't terribly expensive, but an heir to an established throne? It might be a bit of a problem, but we have great confidence in you, dear."

It was taking a little time to sink in, but if the Uglies and the availability of princes bypassed her warning systems, the man did not and she wasn't sure whether she was glad or mad. Or maybe a little bit of both. Or maybe neither. Tish didn't know and wasn't real sure she wanted to find out. "Marcus? But what does he..."

"He'll be going with you, dear. We fear his life is in danger also, but don't tell him. He thinks he is going only as a guard to protect a Godmother on a Wish-quest," the gardener said, patting Tish's arm again, and handing her a cookie. "He's waiting just outside the garden gate with the horses."

Tish almost choked on the cookie, spewed out crumbs, coughed, and said, "Horses? Like to ride?"

"Of course. Automobiles and airplanes haven't been invented here; perhaps they never will be. With the exception of gold and silver, we have no metal to speak of. Why, even the horses are shod with enduro-glass. Now, Leticia, we must run, but you are welcome to take the rest of the cookies. And do share some with Marcus.

"Your gold has been credited to your account in the Royal Treasury. But you will be unable to draw on that account until you successfully accomplish your task, make the Uglies wish come true. In the meantime, so you won't be completely without funds, we are giving you a small stipend, in the form of a credit card. It should be enough to pay for any Quest incidentals you need to purchase."

She handed Tish a clear glass card that had her name imprinted in sparkling letters embedded within the glass, and a stack of computer paper, printed with what looked to be price lists. She added, "Magic carries a certain responsibility. Use it wisely, dear, and try not to disappoint the Uglies. What has happened to them is a tragedy. It has taken their girlhood and a good part of their young womanhood. Now, if you'll excuse the rather crude expression from your home world, their biological clocks are running amuck and you are their last hope."

The gardener said, with a sad little sigh, "And, just imagine, it was all because that silly witch died."

It was a rerun, and it made no more sense now than it did the first time she'd heard it. Tish asked, hoping the Council of Four would be more informative than Marcus, "What witch?"

"I believe her name was Roseallen, or was it Alrosen, something like than anyway."

Tish's mouth formed a new question, but it wasn't uttered.

"You have a long trip ahead of you, so you'd better run along now. Marcus can answer all your questions. If he doesn't know, you can always find out more from Cinderella."

It had happened again. Now, Tish knew, beyond any doubt, that she was brain-injured and lying in a hospital, being kept alive by some sort of really strong, really weird, experimental drugs. She was dreaming; she had to be.

"Cinderella?" she asked, not because she wanted the Godmothers to add to the delusion, but because the word was in her mouth and she had to spit it out.

"The Uglies's stepsister. She's the one they're very anxious to marry to a prince. Because of the Curse, you know. The poor Uglies cannot regain their former beauty until Cinderella is married to a proper prince. It's all in the Curse. Marcus will tell you the whole story."

Tish didn't know which Godmother had spoken, and she really didn't care. Trembling slightly, her hand reached out for Bubba's jug just as another of the Council said, "As a parting gift, dear, we will glamorize both your wand and the...ah...Bubba. In their present form, they do not add to your gentlewomanly appearance—and the inhabitants of the Kingdoms must see only what they expect to see. It's written into the original deed and strictly adhered to by all."

Action followed her words. The wand, Tish thought, was some kind of riding whip or crop or something of that general description. Bubba, compressed smaller still, was a medallion or glass doodad on a golden chain—one that floated up and clasped itself around her neck. It wasn't, by far, the most unpleasant thing that had happened to her that day. It was, however, the last contribution, and by far the most welcomed, made by the Council.

"Dear, the water sprite will need to be kept entirely away from water. If not he will... Well, he will swell up and..."

"You dehydrated Bubba? He's instant Bubba now?"

"How quaintly you express your understanding."

Even if she had wanted to, Tish had no time to ask further questions. The four old women had vanished without a trace. And the orderly, well-tended garden was also beginning to fade around the edges, allowing a dry, winter-killed meadow, with a few wooded hills just beyond, and a small stream to show through. It was rather like a double exposure, one that was disconcerting, to say the least.

And, no doubt coming to lead her down the garden path, was Marcus, with two very large black horses in tow. His greeting, after he had eyed her dark-blue riding habit, complete now—although she didn't remember either plopping into place—with a plumed hat and black kidskin gloves, wasn't any glad thing. If she had been forced to describe it, Tish would have had to say it was flat-out surly. And, she thought with a small internal smile, she had in some strange fashion won another point in their continuing battle.

"Just precisely what are you got up for? Why are you here? Where's the Godmother I'm supposed to meet?" And after a deadly pause, Marcus asked, his voice carefully without expression, his amber eyes intent, "You're not going with us, are you?"

Her inspection of him was not as leisurely, but just as thorough. Boots, soft leather, bright with polish, came halfway up his surprisingly shapely legs, in their dark green tights. Those probably had another name, but they certainly looked like tights to Tish; Robin Hood tights at that. The tights disappeared, about mid-thigh, under a tunic, or maybe it was a tabard. Tish's knowledge of swashbuckling garments was severely limited; she had never particularly liked the old movies of a sword-fighting hero who saves a simpering, but pure and innocent, virgin from the clutches of the lecherous villain. Whatever it was, it had some sort of gold crest embroidered on the front: a unicorn standing on its hind legs. It was belted around his slim waist with a fine gold chain. For all its fragile appearance, the chain supported a scabbard, worked in gold and set with jewels, and its black glass sword. A short cape, or cloak, completed his attire.

Not at all willing to admit, to him or anyone else, that he cut a dashing figure in his princely attire, Tish said, "I thought we were supposed to be unobtrusive. Anybody catching a glimpse of that getup you're wearing will run to the nearest phone and call the..."

Brought back to her present world by her own words, Tish said, "No phones, either, I suppose?"

"Just the witch lights and there aren't any of those in the Magic Kingdoms. At least not any that are available for public use," Marcus answered, tying the horses' reins to the lattice of the arbor and walking across the crunchy gravel to where she was standing. "What do you mean we? Just exactly what comprises the we in your query? Not, as in, you and me?"

Tish nodded, handed him several cookies, and said, "Here, the Council of Four said to share these with you."

Seemingly bemused, or maybe only thoroughly confused, he took the cookies, holding them in his gloved hand, staring down at them as if they were artifacts from a strange civilization. "You actually saw the Council?" Awe and disbelief were mingled in his voice, with disbelief the heavy component. Which was probably made him ask, "Are these magic?"

Fighting back the giggle, hysterical, she feared, that jumped and jiggled in her throat, Tish said, "No, they're chocolate chip. Eat one. They're good. See." She suited her action to her words and bit into another of the still-warm cookies.

He was more hesitant. "You actually saw the Council of Four?"

"In person," she said, or rather mumbled, around a second bite of cookie. "Why? Doesn't everybody?"

Marcus, looking like he'd been hit between the eyes with a sledge hammer, sat down in one of the wicker chairs, and fairly gaped at Tish. "No one has seen them in years. There's even a rumor going around that they're dead. Are you sure you saw..."

The memory of the vast power surrounding the women made Tish very sure, but, taking more delight than was kind in his dismay, Tish said, after she had poured herself a glass of ice-cold milk out of the water-beaded pitcher, "Yes, I'm sure. And they are very nice old ladies. Real dears, as a matter of fact."

Amber eyes darkening, a small muscle jumping in his jaw, he said, sounding for all of Faery as if he were strangling, "Dears? Are you crazy? The Council of Four are the most powerful people in the five explored universes and you...you..." He shook his head and clenched his hands, making dust out of cookies, and sort of moaned, or maybe it was growled, deep in his throat.

Tish washed down delicious cookies with equally delicious milk and watched him turn red and redder. Finally, just when it seemed he was ready to start hissing like a boiling pot, Marcus caught his breath and said, "I really don't know what you are talking about, and I doubt that you know either, so perhaps we can solve this particular dilemma if we take it one step at a time."

"It seems perfectly clear to me," Tish said, nibbling at another cookie, "but if you are having trouble understanding, then I see it as my duty to help you."

Ignoring her jibe, Marcus said, "I was ordered to present myself here to accompany a Godmother who was embarking on a Wish-quest. However, nothing was said about you. Why are you here, Tish?"

"Make that Godmother Leticia and it'll help sweep the cobwebs from you mind," she answered, grinning at him as the red receded from his face, leaving him noticeably pale and perhaps, judging from the sweat that sheened his upper lip, a little too warm.

"You?"

"Me."

"Wish-quest?"

Tish didn't say, "Whatever that is," instead, she said, trying to sound as if she knew exactly what she was doing, "You got it."

A breeze, springing out of nowhere, swooped into the arbor, whirlwinded its way around the basket of roses, stripped them of their petals, and bounced and tossed the rose perfumed sweetness in a shower of pinks, whites, reds, and yellows over Tish and Marcus. When that was done, the wind died. Instantly.

Tish was quick to take the hint. Stuffing the credit card and the price list into the pocket of her skirt, she said, "We'd better go, hadn't we. The Council said it was a long journey to where the Uglies live."

"The Uglies? That's the wish you have to make come true?"

"That's what they said. You're supposed to tell me what's going on there. You know, about the dead witch and..."

He made no move to get up from the chair. "This," he said slowly, "is the last straw. They cannot do this to me. I have taken the Oath and... I am not only going to see my attorney, I am going to grieve this through my union."

Glancing at the horses, who had grown increasingly more restless, Tish was almost ready to breathe a sigh of relief when she said, "Good, if you're not going, then I don't have to go either. I mean, the Council certainly can't expect me to go alone. They'll just have to find another place to keep me safe from those beast-things."

"So, that's why you are going, but... You are no longer a prisoner, are you?"

She shook her head; the motion setting the plume in hat to bobbing, and said, "Nope, I am now a Godmother in good standing, with a credit card, a contract, and everything."

It was his turn to shake his head. "But why the Uglies?"

"Why not?"

It wasn't a question he chose to answer. Instead, he dusted the cookie crumbs from his palms, stood up, and said, "Well, let's get going. Where's the toad and Bubba? Are they supposed to go with us also?"

"Bubba is, but not the toad, he's long gone." Tish frowned. "I thought you said you weren't... What made you change your mind?"

He couldn't say, even if it was partly true, "The scared look in your eyes, the way your chin tilts up and you defy the world." Nor could he give even the faintest hint of his other feelings, feelings that had to be repressed. She wasn't for him, and never could be. And even the thought made him vaguely sad, filled with a longing to be like other men, free to follow the path his heart chose.

Stifling what wanted to be a sigh, Marcus took the course of action he felt was safest and less hurtful, for them both, and pulled his facade of uncaring firmly into place.

"Your total, unblemished, shining ignorance." He lifted his eyebrow and smiled down at her, the same arrogant, superior, overbred smile that had, on past encounters, always put her hackles up, presuming she had hackles. "Besides, judging from the looks you've been giving your palfrey, I believe it will be worth it just to see you on horseback."

"Horses make me sneeze and breakout in a rash," Tish said, sounding as if she was trying to make every word sound like the whole truth and nothing but the truth.

"Horse make you scared silly," he countered, not sure of his ground but wanting to push her into even greater disregard for him as a person. And, he assured himself, he was doing it for her.

"Horse pucky," she snapped. "I'm not afraid of..." She turned away from him and practically stalked toward the four-legged beasts, stopping just out of biting and kicking range. "Big, aren't they?"

Her comment sounded almost too innocent, but Marcus's retort was caught in his throat. All his attention was on the pair of pink bunny slippers lying, forgotten, on the ground. For some reason, the sight touched him deeply, made his throat ache. Giving a hasty glance in her direction, wanting to keep his sentimental gesture hidden from her scorn, Marcus bent quickly, picked them up, and stuffed them into his belt pouch.

And then, feeling silly and slightly embarrassed, but determined to show nothing to her, Marcus walked to where Tish stood and said of the horses, "They are the finest steeds from the Godmothers' own stables. And, by my reckoning, the rent for them is setting you back several large chunks of gold."

Her look of total astonishment told him he had turned her thoughts in a new direction, but she was devious and her new directions had a tendency to twist and turn their way back to where she began.

"Rent? They are renting me horses?"

For an instant, she truly thought he was going to pat her on the head and say, "Poor baby," but he didn't. He just smiled and said, "By the week, I imagine, but you'd better spend a little time looking at your price list when we get to the inn. From what I've heard, Godmothering is not for the cheap, or the faint of heart."

"Inn? I suppose I'm going to be paying for that, too?" Tish knew she sounded too indignant for the subject, but she had just realized that what she was seeing atop one of the tall, black horses, a mare and a gelding actually, was a sidesaddle. "I absolutely, positively am not going to risk my life on that stupid contraption. You either get me a real saddle or..."

"Or what? You'll fire me?"

"Does that mean I'm paying for your services also?"

"It depends on what sort of service you have in mind," his tone was definitely suggestive. But before Tish could come up with a smart reply, Marcus's hands were around her waist. Well, not exactly around, even with the corset, she was a trifle larger than a handspan. He boosted her up into or onto the dangerous saddle, surprising her with the effortless strength embodied in his lean frame. And Tish thought probably she surprised him with her balance and her seat on the mare. Even if it did take a little scrambling to get her leg hooked around the horn and her voluminous skirt arranged across the mare's back.

"Oh," he said, sounding ever so slightly crestfallen, "you really aren't afraid. I had forgotten that you are a child of privilege. I should have known that you would have had riding lessons."

"And shots for my allergies?" Tish said, sniffing tentatively, wondering why she wasn't sneezing her head off and weeping like an idiot. But, for whatever reason, it just plain wasn't happening.

But other things were happening. The arbor, with its heavy load of purple grapes, was becoming something else, or nothing else. A pile of dirt, some stones, and bare vines, old gnarled vines that twisted and twined back on themselves, brown brambles with inch-long barbs and the dried husks of some kind of berry. The beautiful garden was gone, leaving a mountain meadow, sere grasses, an ice-rimed stream, and a wind cold enough to cut to the bone.

Tish was glad for the meager warmth provided by the riding costume, and for the greater warmth that radiated up from the mare, but she still needed more protection. She wasn't at all adverse to using the magic wand to get it. "A cape, a cloak, whatever it is, I need it now."

A heavy dark-blue cloak, replete with a fur-lined hood wrapped itself around her. She didn't even wonder what had happened to her plumed hat as heavy metal, probably gold, fasteners, snuggled the cloak close. After she had stuck her gloved hands through the slits in its sides, it closed itself down the front, cutting off the wind and adding immeasurably to her comfort.

That is, until after both beasts were trotting toward the line of foothills that bordered the meadow, and Marcus, riding beside her, said, with a nod toward her gloriously warm garment, "You really are something of a spendthrift, aren't you?"

She didn't even try to defend her actions, after all it was her gold she was spending for the magic garment, wasn't it? Or, at least, it would be as soon as she did whatever it was she had to do on this thing Marcus called a Wish-quest.

And, she remembered that he was supposed to fill her in on all the details and tell her what it was, exactly, that the Uglies were paying her to do, make come true, or whatever it was. After all, if she was going to sell them a top-quality Prince Charming, she certainly needed to know more than she did at the moment. The first question that came to her mind was one she had asked before, "What about the witch?"

It was the question Marcus had been both dreading and fearing—one that he couldn't answer fully and in all truth. He glanced back over his shoulder, loosened the sword in its scabbard, and said, trying to keep disinterest foremost in his voice, "She died."

Tish wasn't deterred. "Why?"

He wanted to lie and say, "I haven't the faintest idea. Old age maybe. Or something else." But he couldn't lie, to her, but he could and did evade the question with another truth. "It doesn't matter. It's the Curse that caused all the problems."

The wind picked up, throwing a scattering of hail in her face. Tish realized the sky that had been clear and incredibly blue only minutes before had darkened, lowered, and looked ready to rain, snow, and sleet on her parade. And do it with a real vengeance.

Wanting to question Marcus further, she shouted, "What Curse? What are you talking about?" The wind howled, grabbed her words and ran with them, taking a good share of Tish's breath along with her words and making her burrow a little deeper into the shelter of her new cloak. Defying all reason, the cloak did not billow and flap in the gusting wind, it just huddled close to her body. She was trying to keep her balance on the mare when Marcus slowed his own horse, leaned close, and shouted, "Hurry. We have to get to the trees before the storm hits."

Suiting action to his words, Marcus whacked Tish's mare on the rump with his gloved hand. She jumped forward. Tish gripped the saddle horn with both hands and hung on as if her life depended on it. It probably did.

Chapter Twelve

THEY RAN BEFORE the storm. Or maybe the storm, lashing them with icy whips, drove them across the wide meadow and into the meager shelter of the leafless trees. Tish would probably have opted for the second description of what was happening. That is, if she'd had time or energy to do anything except flatten herself against the mare's neck, hang on to the saddle with both hands, and swear at the poking, jabbing, suffocating ache the too tightly laced corset was causing in her contorted mid-section.

Tish thought the mare's hooves were pounding, certainly she could feel the jolt of every step, but other than the increasing howl of the storm, she could hear nothing. Her head was down, her face fairly buried in the mare's tossing mane. From what sideways glimpses she could manage, Tish was fairly certain that the mare was running blind, that a white wall of wind-driven, earth-scouring snow was all around them, hiding everything, themselves included. Presuming, and it was a big presume, that Marcus and his gelding were anywhere in the near neighborhood, it was hiding them also.

Tish wasn't about to worry. At least, about mundane things like his safety. If what she was beginning to suspect was true, then neither of them, except in a severe case of damned foolishness, was in any real physical danger from the storm. It had come up too quickly, was too furious, to be anything but Godmother magic. And judging from the strength of it, more than likely the Council of Four had generated the force.

It was probably designed to either harry Tish along the way, or to protect her from whomever or whatever was bent on her destruction. Or maybe it was a little of both. No scent, hers or anyone else's, would remain after the wind and snow had done their thing, and, as a matter of fact, she was wasting no time in dawdling along the way. Still, she muttered, if only in her interior monologue, they didn't have to make it so damned cold and uncomfortable, did they?

And, an eternity or so later, she had another thought, one that she couldn't help saying aloud. "This is costing somebody a pretty penny. I sincerely hope it isn't me." She thought she heard a chuckle in the howling voice of the storm. It added nothing to her comfort.

Although not actually frozen, or even terribly cold, her hands, with the glamoured wand hanging from her left wrist, were cramped and incapable of movement. Her arms were aching, she could barely breathe, and her mind was empty of all thoughts except one: to stay on her precarious perch, to stay atop the galloping mare. The punishing jolt of flying hooves finally slowed to walk and then stopped completely. Totally disoriented, too stiff to move, she stayed where she was, huddled close to the mare's back, and waited mutely for whatever was going to happen next.

"Your ladyship," Marcus said, his weariness and chattering teeth not coming close to hiding the careful respect in his voice, "we are at the Dancing Bear. Will you dismount and join me within where there is warm shelter against the wind?"

Tish tried to straighten, felt a strong jab from whatever kind of hellish bones were in the corset, and swore, only her numb lips making her rather racy use of the language unintelligible to an average listener. Marcus was, in nowise, average. He reached up, loosened her death grip on the saddle horn, and lifted her down from the back of the mare, but not before he whispered, his mouth very close to her ear, "Watch what you say, my lady. The hostler is listening."

Legs trembling and weak, stomach and ribs aching with every breath, every movement, Tish didn't much care who was in audience, but hostler wasn't a word in her common, everyday vocabulary. She looked around the...the...whatever the muddy, smelly plot of walled ground was supposed to be, situated as it was behind a wooden structure with a thatched roof and in front of a long, low building that had the look of a stable.

"We have arrived at the inn, my lady," Marcus said, repeating his earlier announcement. He released his hold on her waist and extended his crooked arm in a courtly manner. "Shall we go in, my lady, and allow the hostler to curry and feed our beasts? And perhaps take a bit of refreshment ourselves?"

Hostler? She saw him then. A stablehand who had, from the looks of his manure-soiled, run-over boots and filthy clothing, spent more time with horses than people. Not sure of the proper etiquette the moment demanded, she gave a small, she hoped haughty, bow in the man's direction.

Grinning mightily, with a show of perfect teeth, he tugged at his forelock and trotted over to take charge of the mare and gelding. Tish fought down a mad impulse to giggle. It wasn't a hard fight when the slightest tremor of her flesh set off new barrages of pain in her ribs and mid-section. She took Marcus's arm and let him lead her into the inn. It certainly wasn't of the four-star variety, more of the deficit-star, hovel-type of gentry accommodations.

If, based on the romantic nature of her past reading, Tish expected a rosy-cheeked, head-bobbing, obsequious innkeeper, her expectations were quickly quashed. The innkeeper, large and female by nature, dour and suspicious by inclination, waited for them to cross the smoky, ale-stenched commonroom, with its odd whiffs of scorching mutton and a surfeit of garlic. Looking Tish up and down, she said, almost visibly sniffing, "We don't got but the one room left, it being the 'best,' and dear by some reckoning. 'Tis at the head of yon stair and sleeps five by most count. Iffen you'll be wanting it by yer lonesomes, and that ain't our way, and I be making no promises that 'tis so, it'll be a silver penny. There be no bathing tub and no emptying the chamber pot out the winder. Will you be for taking it?"

It wasn't a question that needed a real answer, not with the storm that still growled and prowled without, and she knew it. The woman, saying her name was Mistress Near, held out her grimy paw and waited for it to be crossed with silver.

Marcus tossed her a shiny bit of metal. Catching the coin with a grace that belied her bulk, the woman bit it, testing for authenticity, before she said, looking square at Tish and only letting a little scorn color her deep voice, "We don't got a woman to do for you. Yer man'll have to lace you up and tie yer strings iffen you ain't got the know-how for to be doing it yerself."

Forestalling the angry denial that fought to escape from Tish's mouth, Marcus gave the innkeeper a small bow and said, "We thank you for your courtesy, Mistress Near, and your hospitality. If it meets with your pleasure, we have had a very tiring journey and would like to retire to our room for a brief rest before we enjoy our evening repast. Which will be?"

"Mutton stew, yer honor, and ash cake," the woman said, "and you and yer woman'd best not dally none with yer heighing down 'cause folks about here do be liking our custom and what there is won't be long a-going. And there be pipers and a bard coming by this night. The lady mought not find it to her liking, but other folks will and a-plenty. The listening do make thirsty work." Her greedy smile wasn't meant for them, but for the coin that she obviously saw pouring into her coffers that night. Tish, for one, was just as glad, seeing as how the smile made the woman look an awful lot like the shark in *Jaws* just as he was getting ready to take a big chunk out of whatever was closest, and enjoying every bite.

Not wanting to shudder, and arouse new hunger in her own torture device, Tish lifted her chin and commanded Marcus, with a look, to see her up the stair and into whatever privacy the "best" room afforded. When she saw the stuffy little low-ceilinged room, with the thatch of the roof scant inches about Marcus's head, and the one, sheetless, dirty, not over large bed, she almost wished he hadn't.

And, if the corset hadn't been cutting her in twain, she would have demanded they get on their rent-a-steeds and ride out. There had to be a better place to stay than this room, with its strong odor of unwashed bodies and, probably, bedbugs lurking in the dingy mattress and tattered gray coverings.

There was one window, covered by a shutter that allowed streaks of grayish light and fingers of icy wind easy entrance. Other than the bed, the only furniture was a knocked-together table holding a stub of a candle, a pitcher of water, a basin, and underneath a glass something. From her reading, Tish vaguely remembered it was called a slop jar, and not to be confused with the covered chamber pot that was clearly visible, and odorously plain, under the edge of the bed.

It was severely lacking in the nice department, but none of that mattered. Almost before Marcus had closed the flimsy door behind them, Tish had dropped her gloves and the disguised wand onto the bed. She pulled off her heavy cloak and tried, frantically, to reach the row of tiny buttons that marched up the back of her tight bodice. It was an impossible task, and it had to be done, and done quickly, if she was to survive.

Turning her back to Marcus, not caring what he might think or say, she said, "Please, I have to... This infernal corset is killing me."

"Why, I'd be happy to oblige, your ladyship," he drawled, his voice sounded a little too pleased, and too warm, to suit her present mood. But she managed to hold her tongue as his fingers, carrying little tingles with each touch, eased their way up her spine. But it did seem a very long time before her bodice fell free.

Stepping away from his nearness, she pulled off the bodice, learning in the process that it and the skirt were two separate entities, and revealing a lacy, beribboned camisole and the damned corset. It hooked up the front, with glass hooks and eyes, but it was laced up the back, and the laces were wound around her middle twice before they were joined in the back and tied in some sort of knot. And she couldn't remove offending garment without first removing her skirt, three petticoats, and having the corset unlaced. The first two she could do, the third meant she had would have to submit her body to Marcus's long-fingered hands one more time. It wasn't an entirely unpleasant thought, but whatever else it was, it was far better than the alternative. The damned corset had to come off, and it had to come off right then and there.

Taking a shallow, very painful breath, Tish said, loosening the waistband of her skirt and petticoats, trying to sound as arrogant and Godmotherish as possible, "Unlace my corset."

His chuckle was pure evil and so was the purr in his voice when he said, "Am I to assume that this comes under the heading of servicing a Godmother and is above and beyond my usual duties of providing protection and..."

She didn't look in his direction, but Tish did grit her teeth before she snarled, "I'll pay for it. Just do it!"

He let his fingers do the talking, and what they said to Tish as they moved warm, languorous, down her back, pulling, tugging, and loosening, had more to do with desire than comfort. Tish wasn't a whit pleased at her own body's quickening reaction. Heavens above she didn't even like the man. She disliked him intensely, didn't she? Then why wasn't she pulling away, acting like a woman of character instead of a lusting... The shadowy room hid the warmth that rushed up to burn in her face.

Marcus was battling his own feelings.

It was fairly dark in the room, but there was more than enough light for him to see the raw places and red welts the torturing corset had inflicted on her waist and ribcage. And to hear her sharp intake of breath and small cry of pain as she unhooked the corset, letting it, along with her skirts, drop to the floor, as she pulled up the camisole to look at her abused flesh.

"By the First," he said. All laughter and mockery gone from his voice and face, he knelt to look more closely. For one wild, insane moment, he wanted, with every atom of his being, to kiss it and make it well. And beneath the need to take care of her, to ravish her, to cherish her, was the growing realization that he was falling in love with her.

And that small knowledge made him ill, loving had no place in his life. He couldn't inflict his past on her, couldn't take away her joy and laughter, couldn't... Couldn't stop his lips from brushing the tortured skin, if only a feather's touch, a small memory to... He refused to allow his growing need to govern his actions, but he did let his lips have one final taste of paradise.

And she had fallen under the same spell. Tish wanted him to kiss her aching ribs, and she didn't want his lips to stop there, wanted him to go on to other body parts, most of them in sudden need of some kind of attention from his mouth and his hands and...

But she didn't want to respond to the knock that rattled the door an instant later, didn't want to hear Mistress Near say, "The storm be blowing bad. The stable be full of sleepers. The pipers and bard be needing a place for their sleeping. I be giving them a bit of yer floor."

Marcus took a deep breath, swallowed, and said, "My lady requires her privacy. She isn't well."

"They be quiet modest men. They no be a bothering for the lady. They be bringing their traps and such up real soon like, get you decent."

"We paid..." Tish started, but left the rest of the words unsaid. Talking wasn't going to change a blasted thing. She was fuming, ready to... She didn't know what she was ready to do, but whatever it was, Marcus wasn't helping matters one little bit by standing there, staring at her as if bemused, or maybe it was bespelled.

"What is it?" she demanded, standing there in her knee-length, ruffled drawers, her skirts pooled around her booted feet, fanning the throbbing injuries with the tail of her camisole, a dimity camisole and sheer beneath its pink ribbons and handmade lace, and the only covering on her upper body.

Finally, after giving himself a little shake, Marcus said, his breath coming just a little too fast, his voice sounding hoarse and wanting, "Godmother Leticia, the men are on their way up, hadn't you better..."

"Get dressed?" Tish knew she was dithering, but she was feeling a little wanting of her own, or maybe it was only lust she was feeling, and she couldn't seem to pitch the warm fantasy for a dash of reality. But it came on its own when there was another knock, rather a light tapping, on the door and she realized she wasn't dressed for receiving visitors. As a matter of fact, she was barely dressed at all. "You'll have to..."

"No time," Marcus grabbed up the corset, poked it under the grimy covers and whispered, "Your wand. Use it."

Tish was sure she could hear watery chuckles and feel Bubba's pendant moving against her chest when she grabbed up the wand, waved it wildly, and said, "Dress me, and do it quick."

Buzzing like an out-of-tune radio, it did exactly that, and perhaps a bit more by taking the sting, burn, and pain from her corset-wounds and doing a bit of unasked-for-healing. And if it had to add a few inches, here and there, to her riding habit, no one knew or cared. At least she could breathe, and do it with only a memory of pain.

When she was decent—except for some far from fleeting erotic thoughts—Marcus motioned her to seat herself on the bed. She took up the lady-languishing-after-a-hard-day-in-the-teeth-of-the-storm pose all on her own. It was very effective.

The three new tenants were two cold-looking redheads, each carrying a pack and cased musical instruments, and an older man, carrying a heavier-looking pack and what looked to be a small harp. After a quick glance in her direction, tiptoed in, placed their belongings in the corner behind the door, nodded to Marcus, and hurried out, closing the door quietly behind them.

It had taken very little time for them to fulfill their needs, but it was time enough for Tish to get her own needs, or maybe it was only wants, under control. And Marcus seemed to have accomplished the same feat, because when the door was shut and the men's footsteps were vanishing down the stair, he said, rather abruptly and from the far side of the darkening room, "Tish, I..."

She forestalled whatever he was going to say with, "Marcus, we need to talk. The Oath and the Sanction are waiting to tie me in knots if I don't do whatever it is the contract called for, and I don't..."

She sighed and refused to let her weary body stretch out on the bed, get a little of the rest it craved, and deserved, before she said, hoping it sounded like an order and not a plea, "Tell me about the Uglies. Just exactly how am I supposed to catch Prince Charming so I can sell him to them? I guess they must really hate their sister, why else would they want to marry her to a pervert like that one?"

Coming over to the bed, he eased his body down onto the mattress at the far end, toyed with a ragged edge of coverings before he said, "What do you mean by that? Prince Charming being sexually abnormal, I mean. Or is that just another of your slang expressions?"

Drawing on her rather limited memories of the fairy tales her mother had insisted on reading to her, even when Tish insisted that she didn't like them all that much, she said, "No, not slang. But, from the stories I remember, I thought he... Well, in 'Cinderella,' for example, the man had a foot fetish. He didn't marry his bride because he loved her body, or her mind, he just fixated on her feet and that's what turned him..."

"Leticia," he said, "Cinderella hasn't happened yet. It's your Wish-quest, remember?"

"What do you mean? I read the story, saw the movie, and..."

"Those stories are from your land, not mine."

Maybe what he said was true, but not willing to accept defeat, Tish said, "Okay, but what about the other stories about him. In 'Sleeping Beauty,' the man broke into her bedchamber and started taking advantage of a sleeping girl. He only married her because he got caught when the whole damned castle woke up and there he was in the process of ravishing her. If he didn't want to get tarred and feathered, what else could he do?"

The corner of his mouth twitching, Marcus was staring at her, his amber eyes dancing, but he didn't say a word when Tish, fully enmeshed in her own tirade, continued, "And then there's 'Snow White.' Snow might have been a little strange herself, living with all those little men, but Prince Charming got his jollies from kissing a girl he thought was dead. We have a name for that sort of behavior and, if I'm not mistaken, it's consider a criminal act and..."

"They're not all the same prince," Marcus said gravely.

"No? Well, they all have the same name, don't they?"

"That's explainable."

"So, do it."

"The first King Charming was quite prolific and he was very rich. Do you remember the magic kingdoms scattered through Faery? The ones we saw in the magic mirror? Well, he bought the first one from the Godmothers, or charmed them out of it. Anyway, it was his and when his heirs came along, he had enough money to set them up in independent kingdoms. They did the same for some of their offspring, the legitimate male heirs anyway, and pretty soon there was a bunch of Charming princes, all running around trying to find brides."

"Or at least someone to fornicate with, or ravish," Tish said, "not particularly caring whether they were asleep or dead."

"That is base canard."

Smiling, only a little maliciously, Tish said, "Is it? But you just said the first of the Charmings was a randy buck with more riches than morals. He went around siring a bunch of perverts and weirdos, most of whom now have magic kingdoms of their own. The ones that haven't overpopulated their holdings with..."

"I told you no such thing. Where do you come up with..."

"Does it matter? I mean, is this going to help me find a prince for Cin? Or are you just arguing for the fun of it?"

"Fun? Leticia, you have a warped idea of what constitutes fun."

"Yeah, well, maybe warped is going to fit in real well with this caper. Uglies, perverts, and Cin. It sounds like it would make a good prime time soap, doesn't it?"

It had grown steadily darker as they talked, but the wind could no longer be heard howling its way around the building. In a way, Tish was sorry it stopped because now she could hear rustling and squeaks come from the thatch so close overhead.

And she didn't want to turn her imagination loose on that bit of evidence, especially since even the thought of mice, with their sharp little claws and beady little eyes, made her quiver. The real thing brought on a bout of screaming and jumping; not at all becoming to a Godmother, especially one on her first Wish-quest. Surely that demanded a little more courage, if she wasn't to disgrace the office, and she wasn't about to do that. Or so she told herself, knowing, full well, that the only real use for intentions is to make good paving stones.

"Listen," he said, standing up and extending a hand to assist her to her feet, "we'd better go down and eat. We have a fairly long distance to travel tomorrow, and I believe you could do with a little sustenance and a night's rest."

She wasn't about to argue with that.

He had a further word of advice on how to survive the rigors of a Wish-quest in the wilds of Faery. "The fare is rough, not at all what you're used to eating, but..."

Unable to resist temptation, Tish asked sweetly, "Are you afraid I'll do a repeat performance of what happened in the Crystal Court?"

"Well, it doesn't hurt to be prepared."

"I was air sick," Tish said and then added, because confession was supposed to be good for the soul, or something to that effect, "and scared spitless."

Not even smiling at her honesty, Marcus pulled her up and lead her to the door, "Well, I only wanted to warn you about the food and the lack of...ah...hygiene and refrigeration."

"Rank?"

"Totally."

"Eatable?"

"Barely."

"Are you going to..."

"My lady, I certainly don't intend to starve."

"What you can eat, I can eat." That overbold statement proved itself a lie when Tish took her first bite of greasy mutton stew; the only bite she was able to down. At that, mutton grease, heavily flavored with garlic and onions—probably to hide the odor of meat too long dead—congealed on the roof of her mouth, adding nothing good to the taste of the bug-laced ash bread. But she did manage, being careful not to look at the thick chunk of bread, to swallow most of it, if only by washing it down with two and maybe three small tankards of sour, watered wine.

The common room was too full by half. Men were crowded together on the benches around the trestle tables, more standing against the walls, and they were all swilling ale. The heat, from the two fireplaces and the packed bodies, was unbearable, as was the smell. But the noise, barmaids squealing, pipes piping, men shouting, laughing, calling out requests to the bard, was beyond endurance. Despite food and the din, Tish felt her eyelids growing heavy, her mind shutting down, and she managed to hide a huge yawn behind her hand, or almost.

Marcus put his hand under her elbow, leaned close, and said, pitching his voice to be heard below the noise, "Come on, it's beddy-bye time."

It was a wish come true. But the wish changed into something else after they had threaded their way through the throng of men and climbed the narrow stair. Tish was in the room, waiting for him to light the stub of candle, just how he did that, she didn't know, before she remembered there was only one bed.

The two pipers and the bard were going to take up what little floor space there was and that left what? "Where are you going to sleep?" she asked.

"With you, of course."

"But..."

"Tish, in this kingdom, a man and a woman do not travel alone together and rent rooms in inns unless they are legally wed. People who are legally wed sleep together, otherwise people talk. Is that what you want, to call attention to your quest?"

It sounded too damned reasonable to suit her, but she was too tired to dredge up a decent snarl of maidenly indignation. She glared at him and said, "I'm sleeping with my clothes on."

"There will be three other men sleeping in the room, strangers. I certainly expect you to observe the proper wifely decorum. Besides that, just exactly what kind of monster do you think I am?"

"Just remember, I'm sleeping with the wand real handy and Bubba may be freeze dried or whatever, but he's in the medallion, and he doesn't..." The wand was ample protection, Tish knew that. What she didn't know was whether Bubba was alive or dead, or had been changed into some sort of monster. And she absolutely did not want to think about it. Not knowing was better by far than what might be the truth.

Sounding like he was strangling, or maybe would like to strangle her, Marcus said his famous gaaak word.

Later, when she, boots off and clothing loosened, had scooted to the back of the bed and was hovering on the brink of sleep, she asked, because it seemed important at the moment, "The Uglies? Don't they have names?"

"Quincy," he answered, "and Sage."

"Pretty names," she murmured.

"Beautiful," he said, and the sorrow in his voice wrapped itself around Tish's heart and followed her into her dreams.

They were far from pleasant. Unseen things wept and she tried to find what was lost, spiraling down into a darkness fraught with lurking terrors. Things reaching out to snare her feet. Faceless shadows waiting to swallow her up. Icy cold fog that twined around her, pulling her deeper and deeper into nothing. And always the tears, the bitter tears of a woman.

Tish's own soft cry, of fear, of regret, of something unknown to daylight, roused her briefly. If only enough to think she dreamed yet again when a man, a gentle-spoken man, tucked her heavy cloak a little more closely around her chilled body, snuggled her a little closer to his own warmth. He whispered, "Hush, my dearest love. It's only a dream. Nothing will harm you while I'm here."

Warm and comforted, Tish slept again, or still. And neither knew nor cared which.

But Marcus neither slept nor was comforted. Not by choice, he had given his heart into her keeping and at that moment, he liked neither her nor himself. What his father had always called the Family Blessing, love in a lightning flash, eternal love for one woman, seemed more like a curse.

One that would surely be his undoing.

Chapter Thirteen

THE NIGHT, WITH its troubling dreams and odd comfort, and the inn were both far behind her when Tish, her sleep-rumpled habit and finger-combed hair hidden beneath her hooded cloak, urged her rental mare up beside Marcus's gelding and asked, "Just where is it we're going?"

Marcus didn't look like a man who'd spent a restful night, but then again, the pinched look to his face might have been caused by the mush of undercooked grain they'd choked down for breakfast and the icy cold that held the mountainous countryside in an iron grip. His breath coming out in puffs of white, Marcus sounded as grouchy as she felt. "The next kingdom, which I'm happy to say, is blessed, even if it is ruled by one of your infamous Charming perverts, with a more equitable climate."

"That isn't what I meant."

"Oh?"

"No, I meant, when we get there, to where the Uglies live, where are we going to stay? Do the Godmothers stay at the local bed-and-breakfast and zip around doing the wish thing or do they..."

"No," he said, too obviously trying to add some patience to the long-suffering tone of his voice. "There's a safe house, all spelled and warded to keep it reasonably unnoticed. You'll have to wear an invisibility cloak when you go out, although I doubt it'll keep folks from knowing that you are..."

Giving a quick look in her direction, Marcus sighed and shook his head before he continued with, "We'll both stay there, and we'll take the back ways to get there. It's better that no one sees us until you come up with a plan to accomplish the wish."

Skipping over what she considered his odious and insulting implications regarding her ability to be discreet, Tish asked the next question on her "just-curious list." "From the way those people at the inn were talking last night and this morning, it seemed like they didn't actually believe the Godmothers exist. That they, I mean, we are just some sort of a myth. If that's true, then why did the Uglies pool their life-savings and travel to...wherever we were, and buy a wish?"

He guided his horse around a frozen puddle and up a slight grade before he said, "It is an act of faith, or, at least, I believe that's what they call it in your world. You know, like writing letters to Santa Claus and really expecting to get your wishes for Christmas."

Tish wasn't about to accept anything that simple for an answer. "That's not the same and you know it. Only children..."

"Tish, if you have a terminal illness and the only cure is in something most people call a sham, or a myth, or even silliness, but you believe it is true, then you have to take a chance, don't you? Maybe it isn't true, but you actually don't have anything to lose, do you?" It sounded like an argument he had used before.

"But the Uglies don't have a terminal illness, do they? I mean, they're just..." She realized that she didn't have the slightest idea what she was talking about, that she not only didn't know who they were or exactly why they wanted a legitimate prince for Cinderella. She had assumed it was the same as the tale, but was it? "Marcus," Tish said, trying to keep any hint of uncertainty out of her voice, "please. You have to tell me."

What he had avoided for years was staring him in the face. This infuriating woman from another world held his heart, but he couldn't give her the secret, couldn't watch her eyes fill with disgust, hate, couldn't watch her turn away. But, regardless of what foul deeds he had done, he couldn't lie to her either. All that left was to... He didn't know what it left, or even why Tish, with him as guard, had been sent on this particular quest.

He took a deep breath, turned in his high-cantled saddle to face her and there were no devils in his eyes when he said, "Don't they really have what some might call an illness? Isn't anything that prevents you from living an ordinary, happy life a form of sickness. Sage and Quincy were beautiful once, and now... They don't even have names. They have become what they are: the Uglies."

And he knew that once again the sorrow, deep and abiding, was in his voice. But beyond all else, he wanted this woman, the person who had brought laughter, fury, and wanting back into his life, to understand and forgive that which was probably beyond her understanding and unforgivable.

Tish wanted to know what caused his sorrow, what brought the brooding darkness to his eyes, his face, but she was not without a small amount of sensitivity. For this one time, she tried to think before she acted. It was more difficult than she had ever imagined to keep the spate of questions locked behind her teeth. She probably would have given way to their insistence, if the narrow, rutted road hadn't curved sharply to the left, rounded a small stand of leafless trees, and revealed a striped, peaked-roofed guardhouse and two red-uniformed guards watching their approach with narrow-eyed, stiff-backed attention. And glittering, sharp-edged pikes, of lethal-looking glass, at the ready.

Tish's stomach jumped, tightened, and fear began to race, using racing spikes, up her spine. They had the hard-bitten look of soldiers, experienced soldiers, with battle scars and skill at killing. "Marcus, what..." Her whisper broke, was lost in the stillness that surrounded them, a stillness that held nothing more than the muffled sound of Marcus's gelding as he walked it toward the guards.

"Stay here," he ordered, just as if she were actually planning on riding forward.

"But..."

"This is my job, let me do it."

Tish reined in her mare, but she was, nonetheless, close enough to hear the taller of the two guards, the one with an evil grin and pocked skin, say, with welcome in every tone of his hoarse voice, "Marcus? Lad, be it truly you? Ha' you come back to us then?"

Marcus's answer was inaudible, as was whatever else the red-coated men had to say. The exchange lasted less than five minutes, and at its end a troubled-looking Marcus waved Tish forward to where he waited. Then, without another word being spoken, they rode together past the guardhouse. Both guards stood at attention, watching them go, and Tish was fairly sure that the respectful salute they gave was not intended for her.

"What was all that about?"

Marcus gave her his best haughty look, peering down his narrow, aristocratic nose, lifting his eyebrow. "To what, exactly, do you refer?"

She was tired enough and hungry enough and irritated enough to zap him with the wand and send him to...to... Tish couldn't think of a single place far enough away to suit her mood, so she smiled sweetly and said, "Well, those two men treated you as if you were their long-lost prince, or something. Just how, exactly, do you account for that bit of oddness? It would be my surmise that you are not a stranger to this magic kingdom. Is that surmise correct? Or was it your innate charm that captured their goodwill at first glance, making them lifelong friends?"

At the end of her questioning, scorn crept up and devoured the sweetness, making her sound a bit more fishwife-ish than she intended; not that she gave a damn what Marcus thought. He was, without a doubt, the most arrogant, infuriating man on the face of the earth; and on the face of Faery, too.

It didn't add to her good humor when Marcus said, using his most obnoxious teacherly voice, "Those in service to the Godmothers travel to many places, and I have been in their service for some time."

"Oh, sure, evade the question. What are you in training for, Marcus, are you planning on returning to my world and becoming a politician?"

"Godmother," he said, with a token bow that did not detract from his superior tone, "I am abjectly pained to have incurred your displeasure by my attitude and feel that I deserved to by punished by your own hands."

She knew there was a joke or something equally repulsive behind his ridiculous speech, but Tish couldn't resist asking, "Do you want me to turn you into a toad?"

"I was thinking more on the lines of a spanking."

"You really are a pervert, aren't you? The way you act, one would think you were trying to be one of the Charming boys," Tish said, putting a good dash of vinegar in her words. She thought a spanking, with stinging nettles, or even poison oak, might bring him down a peg or two, make him seem a little more human. If that's what he actually was.

Marcus gave her a look, not leering or lecherous, just a considering, slightly abashed look, and changed the subject. "We may have more problems than we bargained for."

Again fear jumped through her, but even fear has a saturation point. She just tightened her grip on the reins and asked, "What now?"

"Do you remember the map of Faery and the kingdoms?"

Geography had never been her best subject and maps had always had the look of impressionistic paintings, paintings done by a Sunday painter at that. Barely able to conjure up some vague memory of a big blotch of green speckled with small blocks of other colors, Tish shook her head.

"Many of the kingdoms are clustered together, with the one we just left being the northernmost of this particular group. This kingdom, Byrum, is one of the largest. It is separated, on the east, from its neighbor by a range of towering mountains, with only the Pass of Kilmont allowing congress between the two kingdoms. At the moment, Lunt, the kingdom to the east, is building an army and preparing to invade."

"There's going to be a war? But why?"

Marcus's answer didn't come close to making her understand, but it did distract her.

"Byrum is a plum. My guess is the King of Lunt has decided it's time to do the picking."

"Marcus, I still don't understand."

"Wars are not always understandable, especially in the kingdoms." He rode in silence for several moments before he said, "Perhaps this will add to your knowledge."

The wind picked up, swirled its icy breath around them. Tish snuggled deeper into the shelter of her cloak, but Marcus didn't even seem to notice. His voice was calm when he went on with his lecture.

"The magic kingdoms, the more expensive ones anyway, come fully equipped with castles, hovels, manor houses, noblemen, knights, soldiers, damsels in distress, fair maids, peasants, roes and hinds, feudal systems, a monarchy in place and waiting for the king, and other things designed to keep life interesting."

He was up to something. Tish knew that, but she didn't know what. It was a game that she was very adept at. She knew the next move was a question, a comment, or something, but she didn't say a word. Burrowing deeper into the warm depths of her cloak, she just bent her head forward and rode on in silence, and frowning when he could no longer see her hood-veiled face.

Evidently he was playing a different game because he went on with, "Some of the designs-to-keep-life-interesting are deadly, some mere annoyances, and some can break limbs as well as hearts."

He paused. It lasted to so long that Tish lifted her head slightly, tipped it to one side, and peeked at him from beneath the dark screen of her lashes. He had the look of a man on a memory trip, one he had taken years before to attend a funeral, if they actually had funerals in Faery. Again he did his eerie, mind-reading trick and said, "The magic kingdoms are not strictly a part of Faery. After the Godmothers grant the final deeds, the kingdoms are nearly autonomous. The king is the absolute ruler and the line of succession is, for the most part, based on primogeniture, but limited to the first born legitimate son. Meaning the father and the mother, the king and the queen, have been married for the requisite nine months and twenty-one days."

Only vaguely aware that primogeniture excluded daughters from the line of inheritance; as well as sons beyond the first born, Tish sniffed audibly and muttered, "What about queendoms, I'll bet the powers that be aren't too keen on anything like that. What about the daughters? Are they supposed to either languish as old maids or marry one of those damned Charmings?"

Ignoring her, Marcus continued, "The dragons are bad enough, but..."

She didn't want to believe him, but she hadn't wanted to believe in Godmothers and beast-things either. If she really was in Faery, or a magic kingdom, than anything, including being snatched up by a hungry dragon and eaten as a midnight snack, was not only possible, it was truly probable.

And now, along with being in the midst of a war, being attacked by dragons seemed to be one of the hazards of her new employment. Which didn't sound all that enjoyable, and, as far as that goes, probably didn't offer hazardous duty pay either. Jerking her head up, scanning the clouded sky with anxious eyes, Tish asked, "Real dragons?"

"Quite."

"Fire-breathing and everything?"

"Fire-breathing, virgin-eating, whatever else your mythic tales relate."

Not sure if he was joking, and unwilling to take a chance that he wasn't, Tish asked, "Wouldn't we be safer under the trees or something?"

"Possibly, but you have the wand, don't you?"

"You don't expect me to... You're supposed to be along on this trip to protect me and you want me to..."

"Godmother, my task is to protect and teach, but the charter does not mention dragons, besides that, what I started to say, before you so rudely interrupted, was: Dangerous as dragons are, they aren't as subtle or deadly as court intrigues."

Convinced he was toying with her, Tish asked, "And just precisely what does all this intriguing information have to do with the Wish-quest I somehow acquired? You know, the one I have to complete or the stupid Sanction will curl my toes and make me wish I was a toad. Are you trying to tell me that it's dangerous just to go zap some stupid whiny girl with the wand and comb her hair and gussie her up, add a little powder and paint, a glass slipper or so, and send her to a ball to fall in love with a prince?"

"Is that what you're planning on doing?"

She wanted to scream at him but, by taking a deep breath, shifting her tired derriere on the unforgiving bit of saddle, she managed to hold her voice down to a mild shout when she said, "It's what's already happened. I told you that."

"And I told you: It didn't happen here. Cinderella is still unmarried, still fat, still reading sexy novels, still grimy with smoke, and still refusing to settle for less than her ideal Prince Charming. Which, as I understand the terms of the contract, means you have to not only furnish the prince, which isn't going to be that easy, but you have to get them together in a proper, and legal, marriage bed, and not forget the happy-ever-after bit either. Otherwise the Uglies will stay just that and you won't get the gold; which, if I'm any judge, you are going to need to pay off your credit card."

She started to say, "What I do with the credit card is none of your business," but she hardly had her mouth open before Marcus reined in his gelding, held up his hand, hissed her into silence, and whispered, "Listen."

As lost and lonely as the howl of a masterless dog, faint and faraway, a horn sounded. If Tish had any guesses to make, she would have called it a hunting horn, a horn that was wound to call in the questing hunt, to tell them the spoor had been found, the quarry ran ahead. She flat-out didn't have a clue as to how she had acquired that particular bit of information and didn't have time to sort through her mental processes to find out.

"Us?" Tish mouthed the word as she strained her ears, listening for the pound of hooves, or, what was worse, the pound of beast feet running across the frozen earth. It had to be something like that, didn't it? Armies used bugles, and dragons didn't hunt with horns blasting, did they?

His lean face turned to granite, his amber eyes dark and grim, Marcus nodded, and pointed to a narrow track that led away from the road. "I don't know for sure, but that would be my guess. Let's not make it easy for them. Go down that way, Tish, and hurry!"

"What about you? What are you going to do?" Tish's hand went up, pressed the Bubba medallion against her chest, felt nothing there, no bubbling kisses, no murmur of comfort. Nothing.

For a brief second loss knotted in her throat, made her want to weep. If not for herself, then for the sprite. Her sprite who was now a close relative to instant potatoes.

"Trying to save our lives."

"No," Tish whispered, listening for Bubba's water voice, and remembering what the Godmothers had said: Keep him away from water. An idea, and a bit of hope, pushed through her fear and loss, diminishing both, if only a jot or so. "Marcus, you have to come with me. We have to find a stream."

"You've seen too many western movies. If what I think is following us, riding in water won't even come close to hiding our scent. Some of the mercenaries can trail a bird through a cloudburst."

"The beast-things? Have they followed..."

Marcus was furious, blazing with anger, and his voice was hot with it when he said, snarling out the words that spoke of betrayal, "Not followed, Tish. Somebody knew exactly where to send them to find you. Somebody wants you dead."

"And you," trembled on her lips, but she held it back. Not even wanting to think what it meant beyond their immediate danger of dismemberment and death, Tish shuddered. The betrayal involved could have only come from a Godmother, one of the Council of Four, or maybe all four. No one else knew where she had been sent, did they?

Tish tried to think it through, to reason it out, but the dryness in her mouth, the pounding of her heart, and the acrid bite of fear got in the way. Dithering, hyperventilating, she didn't know which to fear most, the mercenary assassins or the Godmothers, but the beasts where closer, and, from the yipping sound that came with the faint breeze, it sounded as if the beast-things were hunting in a pack.

Only Marcus's rock-jawed assurance, the black glass sword hanging at his lean waist, and her own Bubba idea kept her from fainting dead away and falling to the earth, waiting like a terrified rabbit for the hunter to come. "Marcus," she said, "shall I cast a glamour over us or use the wand to..."

"This is a magic kingdom, the beasts will be able to smell any magic you... Just go. We can talk later." He raised his hand to swat her mare's rump, but Tish wasn't ready to obey his command to run for her life.

It was a lie, but she didn't mean for either of them to die alone. Besides, given the givens, a simple plan was better than no plan at all. And she had seen what one mercenary could do, so she wasn't real fond of the thought of meeting a full pack. So, going by the maxim, when in doubt lie, she did exactly that. "Bubba says to..."

Hope sparked small fires in the amber of his eyes and Marcus's voice held a touch of awe as he asked, "You can talk to the sprite?"

She wasn't entirely sure what to say, but a lie worth telling was a lie worth embroidering. And, she did, sort of, know that Bubba loved her, after his fashion, would protect her if he could. He had before. "Not exactly, Marcus, but he wants us to..."

Marcus was much more trusting of sprites and magic stuff than she was. He just gave a quick look up the road they had just traveled, shook his head, and said, "The pack is coming fast. We have to get out of here right now. So, lead the way, do whatever it is that Bubba wants."

"I don't know which way to..."

"Bubba does."

Evidently, Bubba did, or else she got there by accident and a good deal of wild riding down a twisting, turning track, that was barely wide enough for the mare to pass between the stands of stiff-branched trees, clinging vines, and spiny brush. Limbs raking her face, threatening to scrape her off the saddle, Tish hung on and muttered something. She probably couldn't have told an onlooker whether she was cursing or praying.

It didn't matter, what did matter was the hunting horn that had grown too loud, too quickly and the pound of running feet and the yelping cries of the hunters. They were so close, Tish didn't dare look back. She had to go on, to find what she had been ordered to avoid.

And when the mare was sweating, rolling her eyes, and stumbling every third step, when Tish had almost given up, she almost raced the weary mare into the loud, cold depths. The mare balked at the edge of the small river, planting her feet, shivering, refusing to take another step down its frozen banks. Frantic, Tish almost fell off the mare's back. She looked back, caught a quick glimpse and a choking whiff of the beast-things. There were, at least, four, and they were not more than fifty feet from where she stood.

Stumbling forward on legs that had lost all will to move, she opened the clasps on her cloak, grabbed the medallion in her left hand, and, doing what she thought was right, waded out into the swift current of the small river. She shivered as the snow-melt climbed up her legs, stumbled on round rocks, went to her knees, and jerked the chain from around her neck, dipped the entire necklace in the milky water.

It exploded, fountaining up, higher and higher, knocking her to her knees, turning the water into something unknown and unknowable.

And she knew the sprite had returned to his natural element, the foaming, growling race of water, and was gathering its strength into his own, transforming it and himself into a huge weapon. And, despite the Godmothers' dire warnings, she knew Bubba, regardless of what it did to him, to his very existence, was a weapon meant only for her defense.

"Bubba," she whispered as the water lifted her up, bore her to the far shore and deposited her, with surprising gentleness, far above the high water mark. Marcus, without aid from the sprite and leading her mare, crossed a shallow portion of the towering stream, soon joined her. And it was the man who tossed her up onto the sidesaddle, urged her on down what had to be a deer trail, a tiny ribbon of a path that led, always and forever, away from the river and the carnage that was about to transpire there.

Away from Bubba, but not away from the tears that were running down her cold face, tears of grief for a water sprite. But not away from her water-soaked garments that were slowly turning to ice in the winter air.

She didn't know how long they trotted, twisting and turning their way down the narrow path that led beyond the bare-branched trees into thick evergreens. Tish only knew that she was freezing, inside and out, that she had gone from teeth-chattering cold to the near edges of hypothermia. And if her confused mind was able to think, she would have known that she had to either get warm or die.

Warm came first, but not by much, and not soon enough to keep Marcus from lifting her down from the mare, cradling her against his chest, and carrying her into a small house. It was one that should have belonged to a wicked witch in a children's scary tale. Or so it looked to her, not that her perceptions were on the up and up.

Whatever it was or wasn't supposed to be, the house was warm and dimly lit and warded and glamoured and hidden from sight by a whole bunch of magic spells, all tangled together like a cat-wrestled ball of yarn. Her eyes closed again when he left her in a chair and they didn't open when he came back. How long later she didn't know. He held a cup of something to her icy lips.

"Witch's Brew?" she asked, when the heated glow inside the cup transferred both heat and spreading glow to the inside of her body.

"Merciful heavens, no!"

His response was so vehement, Tish managed a small giggle before she closed her eyes again, drifting, not asleep, but not awake either, wandering in the grayness between until Marcus tugged at her arm. "Tish, you have to get out of those wet clothes."

Lassitude had captured her muscles and bones turning her into gruel, too weak to stand alone, to lift her arms, to do what he asked. "Can't. Too tired," she murmured.

And she was much too weary to object, if she had wanted to, when Marcus practically ripped off her partially frozen cloak and attacked the sodden skirt and petticoat that were underneath. And she was asleep almost before he had her bundled into a fire-warmed quilt-heavy bed, with cloth-wrapped, heated rocks at her feet, and her magic wand snug in the palm of her clutching hand.

But she fought back the thick, mind-claiming strands of sleep long enough to ask, "What about Bubba? Did they kill him?"

MARCUS TOOK A quick breath before he touched her face with gentle fingers and said, "I don't know, Tish. Sprites aren't..."

It took great effort to shape the question, but she had to know. "Aren't what?"

His answer came slowly. "Aren't considered tamable. No one knows anything about them. Bubba was the first one tamed."

"Was?" It was a sad little question, one that ached in Tish's heart for what seemed forever before it found its way out into the room.

Marcus had no answer to give her.

And he sat long before the fire, remembering things that were a past that couldn't be changed. He would have to tell Tish, he knew that, but how? And when?

The Wish-quest demanded that she know enough to keep her safe and his own honor would see that it happened. But, what of the love that had cast its pall over him? Was it real? Or had the Godmothers somehow conspired to...

Marcus shook his head. The Oath he had taken as a Border Guard was supposed to protect him from magicks and spells, but... And, the Council of Four? Tish had no reason to lie to him about their being behind this quest, but she didn't know the real Council. Maybe someone had...

Again he shook his head. Someone was out to destroy Tish, and him, but who? That was the question, and Marcus didn't like the answers he was getting.

Answers that had to involve Godmothers, deadly Godmothers.

A chill gripped him. Getting up, he walked over to where Tish lay sleeping. He pulled the covers up a little closer to her chin, touched her cheek with a gentle finger, and tried not to sigh. He wanted to rant, to curse the fate that had led him into love, a love that could only bring pain. But another Curse was the root of the whole problem, and it was that Curse Tish was supposed to circumvent. She was a sparrow flying into a hurricane, but hurricanes always won. Didn't they?

At that moment, Marcus would have given his life to save hers, but no takers were at hand. Still, there was one thing he could do, and he vowed he would do it first thing on the morrow.

Chapter Fourteen

"TISH! TISH! WAKE up!" The whisper was urgent. It penetrated the muffling layers of sleep and brought her to instant waking.

"What? The beasts? Have they..." Fear pounded in her chest as she threw back the covers and swung her pajama-clad legs toward the floor almost before her eyes opened. Almost before she saw him leaning over the head of the bed.

"Shhhhh!" Marcus held his fingers over her lips. "It's all right. It's morning. There are no beasts. Bubba must have taken care of that threat. There's no real danger at the moment."

Just the mention of her lost sprite filled Tish with loss, but not to the point that she lost all her senses. Marcus was, by more than a gnat's whisker, too twitchy to be telling the entire truth. Trying to find the reason, by not doing the obvious and asking him, "What the hell is going on?" Tish looked beyond him, examined the small room for some clue to his odd behavior. From what little she could remember of the night before, it looked the same: a rustic rendition of a child's concept of a witch's house.

Shadows, lots of them, several in very unlikely places, such as in front of the window. Dark scary things, like bats and dried toad parts, hanging from smoke-darkened beams. A smoldering, more smoke than flame, fire in the fireplace, over which hung a cauldron of some sort of smelly concoction. A squat-legged table, three or four chairs, some bottles, vials, packets, and other things best left nameless, lurking-in-the-shadow things. It was spooky as a graveyard at midnight, but nothing seemed terribly amiss. Except that Bubba was gone, probably forever, and she was trapped in a universe where magic and witch houses and Godmothers were real.

"Everything seems fine, so, why are you so antsy?" she started to ask before her question was interrupted by a timid knocking at what had to be the front door. It startled her. Tish stared at the door for a moment before she looked back at the man. "You said this was a safe house that was warded and spelled and all the rest of that junk. So, who would come calling at this...this ungodmotherly hour?"

He didn't sound superior, odious, or anything other than perturbed and distant, like maybe he didn't like what he was thinking. "It would have to be someone with a spell to see through the glamour. Someone looking for a Godmother." He barely glanced toward the door, but she knew it had his full attention when he said, "You have to get dressed."

"I am..." Tish stood up, looked down at herself, and was flabbergasted to see her own flannel PJ's, the fuzzy pink ones that Jilly had given her for Christmas. "Where did these come from? How did you..."

"I didn't. I put you to bed in your birthday suit, with hot rocks at your feet and enough covers to warm an ice dragon."

She remembered that much and was too grateful for his doctoring to turn viperish, but she couldn't understand unless she asked, "Then how did I..."

"It's your wand and your credit card. What you do with it is your business—but it's a costly business."

"But I was asleep. They can't make me pay for sleep-charging, can they?"

"If it's an imported item, with all that excise tax and import duties, they can and they will."

"No, they won't," Tish snapped, moving a little away from him and closer to the silently burning fire, absently noting that everything in the room was silent, including the sound her feet should have made on the slick wooden floor. "Now, what am I supposed to..."

The knocking on the door was a little louder, a bit more demanding.

"Whip up a Godmother outfit." Marcus said, edging toward the rear door, the one in the shadows beside the fireplace, with unseemly haste. "Something like the one Morgain was wearing when the Uglies came. That's what all the Godmothers wear when they're dealing with the inhabitants of this kingdom." The door opened at his touch, revealing a dark space with the lingering manure-odor of a stable, and he slipped through with a wink and a wave, closing the door behind him.

The knocking came again, by now it had despairing sound. Or so Tish thought as she was experiencing her own moment of despair. Morgain? What was she wearing? All that came to Tish's mind was some vague picture of hoopskirts, ribbons, and fripperies by the score. She gave a quick glance toward where Marcus had done his disappearing act, scowled, made a silent vow of vengeance, and tapped her pajamas with the wand, saying, "Deck me out, wand."

It did, and Tish was more than a little glad that there weren't any obvious mirrors in the room. It was terrible enough to try to walk in the swaying skirts of lavender tulle, tight bodice of a darker hue, white elbow-length gloves, floating panels of purple, pink, and dusty rose, ribbons, ruffles, lace, white kid slippers, fringed shawl, and the rest of getup. It was a hybrid of Scarlett O'Hara's ball costume and the one worn by good witch in the Wizard of Oz.

Tish suspected it wasn't a viable fashion, but, even if it didn't come close to rivaling Morgain's, it was the best Tish could manage. Or maybe, considering the discomfort of the things, the worst. It did however give her a new respect for the women of the Good-Old-Days.

Gripping the glowing wand, and giving it a good dose of bewitching, glitzy glamour, up to and including a bright star at the end, expecting to feel the pinch of the Sanction at any moment, Tish arranged her face in what she hoped was a Godmotherly expression. She said, "Sound on," and marched toward the door, feeling a good deal like a martyr on her way to the bonfire. And she was only a trifle gratified when the fire began to snap and crackle, the contents of the cauldron to bubble, the wind to moan around the eves, and the knock to grow definitely louder.

Her stomach quivering, Tish opened the door, stared at the two black-veiled visitors, and asked, just as if she was back home and working behind the counter in BearHeaven, "May I help you?" And blushed at little at the stupidity of her welcome. If that's what it was.

The women—Tish guessed they were the Uglies by their top-to-toe black—lifted their bowed heads and one said, "You're not Godmother Morgain. We paid a goodly sum of gold to... Who are you? What have you done with Godmother Morgain?"

They began to back away from the open doorway, and Tish could almost feel their despair and their growing fear. Fear of her. It irritated her already raw nerves. "Stop acting like complete ninnies!" she said, opening the door a little wider. "And come in."

One of the Uglies drew herself up to her full height, about five inches shorter than Tish, and said, sounding every bit as haughty and aristocratic as Marcus, "I beg your pardon."

"So, damn it, stay out and freeze, I don't care," Tish wanted to say, but feeling the Sanction grip her with ice-cold fingers and start to twist various parts of her anatomy kept the words safely inside her mouth. Nonetheless, the Sanction's manners-reminder was painful enough to make her say, if not with a great deal of graciousness, "I am Godmother Leticia. The Council of Four thought I was better suited to help you realize your wish than Morgain. Now, will you come in out of the cold?"

Even with the thick veils firmly in place, Tish could almost see the doubt in their eyes as they came closer, hesitation marking every step, until she stepped back, giving them free access to the door. They stopped just inside. Tish walked over to the table, magicked up a teapot with her wand, and said, "Make tea."

Moving about with a swaying of skirts and a billowing of doodads, she found cups and saucers in the pierced-tin piesafe in the far corner, a bowl of sugar setting on the same shelf, and carried the whole mismatched selection to the table. All the while ignoring the two black cloaked women huddled together by the front door.

Feeling the beginning of a growl in her stomach, Tish zapped up some sugar cookies and some semi-dainty cucumber sandwiches before she said, "Tea's ready. Will you join me while we talk."

"About what?" The question was cautious and seemed to come from either of the two women. It was impossible to tell which one, the thick veils hid all evidence as to facial expressions or lip movement. They both came, if only slightly, a little closer to the laden table.

After a little mental fingernail biting of her own, Tish decided to tell the truth, or more properly a sterilized and sanitized version of the truth, sort of like a TV movie based on actual events. "We need to talk about everything. You see, I am relatively new to this particular kingdom and have not heard all the background material pertinent to your specific wish."

"But, why do..."

"It is my understanding that you wish expedite this matter as speedily as possible. In order to achieve that goal, I need to know what happened prior to..."

"Godmother Leticia, I don't understand what it is you are asking from us. Please, I know you are used to more elegant language, but we are simple countrywomen and..."

Remembering, just in time, that hoopskirts present a problem to the inexperienced, Tish tilted them up in the back before she perched on the front edge of one of the chairs and tried to project a Godmotherly image, hoping her skirts weren't going to pop up and slap her in the face. It seemed to have been the right thing to do, because other than a little twitching and bouncing around her knees, nothing untoward happened.

Taking a deep breath, Tish leaned forward to pour three cups of tea, and magicking hers into coffee as it hit her cup. She left her scattered wits roaming free and asked the first question that leaped out of the shadows of her mind, "What about the Curse? And the witch?"

She almost asked, but only because she was curious, not because she cared anything about him, "And where does Marcus fit into the puzzle. Why is he so sad about it?" but the Uglies, or one of them anyway, started talking before Tish could get the words out.

"We've had a number of years to consider what has happened to us and why. Originally, it was supposed to be a joke, I think, not that it has been," the Ugly said softly, coming to the table and easing into one of the chairs opposite Tish. "I would hate to think anyone hated us enough to do what was done."

She reached a gloved hand for one of the cups of steaming tea, held it in both hands as if she were trying to warm herself.

The other Ugly, and there was really no way to tell which was which because they were dressed in identical rusty black, loose-fitting garments that bore some slight resemblance to dresses, followed her sister to the table, took an uneasy seat on the other chair. Her voice sounded much the same as her sister's when she said, "We were considered the most beautiful young women in the kingdom. There was no Wicked Queen to be jealous of us. Our queen was, and is, happily married to a very faithful king. Our own mother was one of her ladies-in-waiting until she married the baron, Cinderella's father, and moved to his country estate. They weren't terribly in love, or so they told us, but they each had a daughter or daughters and each thought their offspring needed a parent of the other gender."

Tish sipped coffee and munched cookies as she tried to sort through the rather stilted description of the Uglies's mother's marital arrangement and said nothing. She waited, not very patiently, for the two of them to complete the tale of witches and curses and Cin and whatever else was involved.

"We were older than Cinderella, by several years, and of an age to be trothed to the man of our parents' choice. Since our own father was dead, the baron took on the task of finding us husbands. And marriages that would be advantageous to everyone, himself included. To add to our beauty, he contributed much gold and jewels to our dowry."

Tish wasn't sure who was talking, in fact, she thought one talked for a while and then the other took up the tale in mid-sentence. Which made her ask, "Are you twins?"

"Twins? Two born at the same birth?"

"Yes, and looking much alike."

"It is not common; some even say it bodes ill for those of such births. But, as you say we were mirrors one of the other," one said, and then either went on or the other said, "And our images, ugly as they are,

are still the same as the other's."

One of them, the one holding the tea, shivered and said, "I am Sage. My sister is Quincy. And we... Godmother, please, marry our stepsister to a legitimate prince, relieve us of our terrible burden. And do it soon, before this war... Princes are often killed in such... We beg you."

Although she couldn't explain why it was affecting her so much, Tish fought back the urge to cry, kept her voice level, if only by taking several sips of coffee before she said, "That's what you paid for, that's what you'll get." And she didn't say, "At least, I hope you do."

"How soon?" It was a muted chorus, but one that held a seed of hope.

Not knowing she could do anything at all, Tish made herself sound confident and positive when she said, "Well, I can't give you an exact date, but I do know that the sooner I have the facts, the sooner I can do the deed."

Both nodded, one continued, "The marriage between our mother and the baron was of convenience, and neither of them expected to fall in love. They were beyond the years for that. But it happened, and they had eyes only for each other. Sage and I reveled in their joy and, of course, were old enough to take part in all the court festivities, many of which were to display our beauty to prospective suitors. We were very happy and much in demand.

"Cinderella was not. She was still a child, spoiled and jealous perhaps, but a child. Spotty faced, unpleasant, prone to the furious storms of becoming a woman, but she didn't mean what happened. She couldn't have."

Fighting down the impulse to give voice to her own long-suffering sigh, Tish dropped the last cookie back onto the plate, picked up her fire-filled wand, tapped it against her palm, and asked, too sweetly by half, "And, just exactly what did happen? Where does the Curse come in? What happened to the witch?"

"Godmother Leticia, we beg you to please try to understand and not blame..."

Impatience overpowered her pity, and Tish barely kept from snarling as she said, "I just want to know what happened. I can't uncurse the Curse unless I know all the facts. Can you understand that?"

Like chastised children, the Uglies bowed their heads and whispered, in unison, "Yes, Godmother."

And they sat there, mute as statues until Tish was ready to scream or poke them with the wand or something equally drastic. Her, "Well?" was fat with irritation. All her furbelows and ribbons and floating panels, swirling and lifting with the motion, Tish leaped to her feet, paced to the fireplace and back, trying, not too successfully, to get her growing temper under control, and stopped in front of the cowering women.

"Are you trying to tell me that Cinderella had you cursed? Is that how..." she took a deep breath and, damning the consequences, went on, "Is that how you got to be the Uglies?"

This time both women answered at once, each saying something different. One said, "It was her nurse, you see. She was a hill woman and she thought her dearest child was being..."

The other said, "We don't know for sure if Cinny had anything to do with it or not. She says not, but she was rather a spiteful child and not terribly truthful."

"I see," Tish said, although obviously she didn't. "Either Cinderella or her nurse or someone else had a curse put on you. Is that correct?"

"Yes, Godmother."

"How?"

"The veils."

Feeling disoriented, lost in a maze that had no exit, Tish shook her head, hard, then shook it again before she could bring herself to even consider what, of the swarm that buzzed inside her head, questions needed asking first. The Uglies were hurting all right, but that didn't make them any smarter. And if she was ever going to get this wish-thing done, then she absolutely had to know what had happened. And they weren't helping at all.

Tish didn't like feeling out of sync, out of the loop, out of control, whatever it was she was feeling. And she knew that a goodly share of her growing frustration was Marcus's fault. He was supposed to have told her all the background, given her any information she needed to complete the Wish-quest, and he hadn't. No, good old Marcus had taken a vanishing powder the instant he heard the Uglies knocking on the door.

Now, the whole damned mess belonged to her, and if she took a wrong step, the Sanction would leap in and start twisting her nose and pulling her hair and doing other less pleasant things. Inwardly fuming, Tish jumped up, whirled around, marched to the fireplace again, stared down at the dark, smelly mass bubbling in the cauldron, and tried to come up with some sort of sensible plan.

But the question that soared out of her mouth when she swayed back to the table and the seated Uglies was, "What veils?"

Both heads came up, miming shock, disbelief, and maybe a whole lot of distrust of the Godmothers in general, or maybe only of Tish in particular. And in one voice, the Uglies said, "Why the pure white wedding veils, of course. When we wore them to the Unicorn Spring for the Blessing of Virgins, they...they..."

Soft, anguished sobbing shook the two women, stole whatever else they were going to say. In greater ignorance than before, if such a thing was even possible, Tish could feel her jaw beginning ache, from grinding her teeth together. She tried to think of a sensible solution to the whole stupid mess. Not that sense had anything to do with what was happening, or had happened.

So, if sense wasn't involved, then nonsense must be. Tish's overactive imagination leaped into the fray, with a vengeance. "Forgive me for being slow in understanding," she said, gritting her teeth again, "but customs differ in all the kingdoms and I wasn't sure what was right and proper here."

"Oh," one of the Uglies said, or maybe it was only a bat squeaking in the thatch of the roof. That errant thought didn't do much for Tish's state of mind either.

After a quick glance upward, to make sure all the hanging things were still securely attached to the beams, Tish said, "Now, if I have everything correct. Either Cinderella or her nurse went to visit a witch..."

"The Red Witch of Metan Forest," an Ugly contributed. "She was the strongest witch in the kingdom."

"I see. Then, whoever it was that went to the witch's house bought a curse for the two of you and then had it put on your wedding veils."

"Yes!" they chorused. And then, taking turns, they added to their tale, "The baron had plighted our troth to two young noblemen, both elder sons, both very handsome. One had blond curls and a darling beard. The other had dark wavy hair and a little mustache. They danced divinely and were rich and rode to the hounds and..." Sighing, the Uglies fell silent.

By guess and by gosh, Tish tried to take up the threads of the tale, one that no longer struck her as pitiful, but made her want to shake some sense into the vain, silly creatures. "All right, your troth had been plighted and you were ready to wed. Part of the ceremony included putting on your wedding veils, and with the young girls of your wedding party as witnesses, visiting these Unicorn Springs to be blessed, correct?"

They nodded.

Taking a deep breath, and telling herself not to smack them with the wand, Tish made a wild guess. "And when you got there, the unicorn wouldn't touch you."

"It fled and our veils turned black." It was a double wail of shame and sorrow. "And beneath the veils we were..."

"As we are."

The snapping of the magic fire, the huff and yowl of the wind, and even the beating of Tish's heart seemed too loud in the silence that followed. A cold and barren silence that was anything but pregnant.

The tale was fairly awful, especially when Tish's imagination peopled the scenes with bevies of attendants, giggly girls looking like a garden of flowers in their gala attire. And then, horror, hands covering mouths, shrill cries, girls running, screaming. Sage and Quincy looking at their reflections in the spring and seeing nothing but ugly.

It wasn't a pretty picture, even if it existed only in her mind, but it wasn't furthering her Wish-quest either. "Was Cinderella one of your wedding party?"

"No, Mother thought she was too young and..."

The other Ugly said, her voice considering, "But she was there, at the Unicorn Spring. I saw her, in the weeping willows just beyond the reflecting pool. She was..." her voice trembled, "she was laughing. But, when Mother and the baron came, when the strictures of the Curse burned like fire in the air, Cinderella was gone. So was her old nurse. Mother found them later, but neither one of them would admit to doing what was done. But they did! They did!" She threw the cup of tea, smashing it against the stone hearth of the fireplace, and began to sob bitterly.

Her sister made no move to comfort her.

Neither did Tish. She just glared at the mess, banished it, right down to the last splash of cold tea, with her wand, and said, with the expletives deleted, "So, that explains the Curse, but what happened to the witch?"

"The baron, accompanied by our plighted husbands, went to see her, to offer her gold to reverse the Curse, but she was gone. Even her house was gone. It was like she had never even existed, but we... The strictures of the Curse still burned over Unicorn Spring, and we knew we had to find the witch before it was too late, before... According to the Curse, we would remain unwed and ugly until Cinderella married a true prince, the heir to a kingdom; and she was still a child."

She stopped with a small whimper of sound.

Tish slapped the wand against her palm and tried, valiantly to keep from zapping the two Uglies back to their own house and herself back home. Only the Sanction stopped her, and it was up and rearing, gnawing and tearing, ready to rend her flesh from her bones by the feel of it. "Okay! Okay!" she muttered, "I'll do what I promised, but, by damn, I don't have to like it, do I?"

The Sanction gave her a final warning shake—invisible, of course—and released its hold just as one of the Uglies said, "What did you say?"

Thinking fast, or pretending to, Tish said, "I just asked, how did the witch die?"

The answer, coming softly she had to strain to hear it, wasn't something she wanted to know, or believe. "He killed her."

"Who?"

"Marcus. He killed the Red Witch, confessed his terrible crime to the king, and then he ran away. Leaving us to suffer for his crimes. It was a cruel thing. A terrible thing. And all the guilt lies at his door."

Marcus had to be a fairly common name, but, as much as she wanted to hang onto that fact, to make another Marcus responsible for the witchicide, Tish knew, right down to the bottom of her toes, that her Marcus was the villain. Her Marcus had done the terrible deed, had condemned the Uglies to a life of whimpers and whines, and unwedded sorrow. "Are you sure?" she asked, and for some odd, inexplicable reason, Tish felt tears clot in her throat, burn behind her eyes. They were tears for the man, for what he must have suffered.

"Of course! What difference can it make now?"

"None I suppose, but..." Tish sighed, but made no move to stop the Uglies when, after a head-lifted, listening attitude, both women got to their feet and sort of clung together for a moment before one said, "Godmother, we have to go. But, please, we beg you, get a prince for Cinny. If you don't, we'll stay this way forever. It's the only way to break the Curse."

"I'll do my best."

"It better be good enough," one of the Uglies said, and to Tish, watching their almost running exit from the room, it sounded more like a threat than a warning.

Not that any threat coming from a pair of vain, self-pitying jerks came close to striking fear into her heart, or whatever it was the more purple-prosed romances had to say about it. She drank the rest of her coffee, grimacing a little at the bitterness, and magicked up another cup. She needed coffee to aid her thinking, and as far as she could tell, she had a lot of thinking to do.

And most of it was trying to bring tears to her eyes. Sniffing, she grabbed her cup, jumped up from the table, and began to pace, but no matter how she tried to reshape it, it always came out the same.

Marcus had killed the witch.

"Well," Tish told the cottage, "I know full well that there's more to this whole thing than those silly women told me. But, whatever it was that happened back then, Marcus has some explaining to do, and he's going to do it right now."

Setting the coffee cup on the table after she drained it dry, Tish squared her shoulders, wiped away every trace of her tears, and headed for the back door. Marcus had been ordered to protect her and teach her.

Even if he was devious, almost as devious as her own mother, and too smart by half, he wouldn't have gone far. Tish knew that, knew that whatever else he had done, he would protect her with his own life. And she wasn't entirely sure he would do it from duty alone, but what could that matter.

Shaking her head, she reached for the door knob.

Chapter Fifteen

MARCUS WAS GONE. Although the mare was in a stall in the stable abutting the back door, his rent-a-gelding and riding gear were as absent as the man. Shivering a little at the nip of frost in the air, Tish swayed her hoopskirted way over to the mare, scratched the animal's forehead, and then went a little further afield to do her searching.

A thick fringe of evergreens, or maybe, judging from their hue, everblues was a far better descriptive word, anyway a species far removed from anything that grew on Tish's earth, screened the rock-walled, thatch-roofed house from any and all gazes—curious or otherwise. And they were so thickly grown that Tish had to search for the narrow path that slanted through the tall trees. She worked her way to the other side only to discover another grove of tall, dark trees, leafless, brooding trees that exuded a sort of go-away aura. They discouraged even her from doing any more poking and prying; which, given her tenacity, wasn't an easy thing to do.

Shadows crept long and longer, inside and out; or so Tish discovered when she, reluctantly, gave up the Marcus hunt and went back inside. With a wave of the wand, she banished the ones within the cottage, filled it full of warm golden light, but that did very little to reduce her unease. It was the unease, and an unsettled feeling that the beast-things might be lurking about, or so she told herself, that made her jump at the slightest sound. Inch open the door, peek out into the growing twilightish gloom, straining her ears to catch the faintest hint of any untoward noise.

Her imagination played vivid scenes of Marcus in all sorts of dire incidents, most of which were fatal, all of which left her alone in the cottage, at the mercy of her own ignorance. And, although she tried to banish them, Tish couldn't seem to think of happier things. Needless to say, she was worried sick about the man, and she wasn't about to admit it, even to herself. And wrapped tightly around the worry that rampaged, bloodily and gorishly, through her mind was the question of the dead witch. It was a murder she couldn't bring herself to lay at Marcus's door. There had to be an explanation, a real one, and she wanted it.

Needless to say, Tish had worked herself into a state by the time

Marcus finally decided to make an appearance. Stomping back and forth, she consigned her Godmother garb to Hades and magicked up something simple and comfortable in the T-shirt and jeans department. Snarling at the witch-fire, and listening to her stomach growl for real food, like a cheeseburger and fries, or pizza, with Canadian bacon and pineapple, she refused, with loss aching in her throat, to allow herself to even think about Bubba and how much she missed him. Marcus's crime was another matter; no matter how she tried put it out of her mind, it nagged at her. And, regardless of the spin she tried to give it, it just plain, flat-out didn't make any sense. Especially since her informants were vain, silly twits like the Uglies. Tish wanted to cry, to scream, but all she could do was pace, mutter, and plan a few curses of her own.

At long last, carrying a leather sack, chock-full of something lumpy, and a wooden bucket, filled to the brim with water, he slipped in through the back door. Tish, her hands on her hips, her chin high, looked at him squarely and practically shouted, "I've been worried to death. Where in the hell have you been?"

His eyebrow quirked up and he stared at her. And then, before he could even open his mouth to answer, despite every promise she made to herself, Tish said, her voice breaking, just a little, "Oh, Marcus, you didn't kill the witch, did you?

It wasn't a question or an accusation. It was a cry of pain and they both knew it. Even the wind seemed to be holding its breath, listening like the fire, but all Marcus did, his eyes bleak, his lean face harsh with regret, was step around her, take the bag to the table, the water to the washstand. Then he said, "I have confessed, before the king and the entire court, that I killed her, Godmother. And, despite the grief it has caused the Uglies, I would do the very same thing again."

"And run away after the deed was done?" It was only a whisper uttered through a mist of tears. Tish refused to even examine any reasons that might account for her tears.

"Never that."

"But they, the Uglies, said you..."

"So, it was them at the door. I thought it might be, but there was something I had to do and..." Somehow Marcus's hands, too warm and too tingling with energy by far, had gotten cupped around her shoulders, holding her while he looked down at her. It was a very long, very breathless time, before he pulled her closer, held her against his chest, and said, "I'm sorry that you had to face them alone and without knowing more about the story. But, Tish, they don't know what happened there in the wood. No one does, except one other man, and he will never tell."

For just an instant, Tish let her head rest over the general region of his beating heart and then she asked, "Why? Why won't he?"

She felt his chest rise and fall just before he said, "He gave his word. No matter how much I have hurt and disappointed him, he is a man of honor. He would never break his given word."

"Who is he?"

His hands tightened on her shoulders. Without answering her question, Marcus held her away from him, smiled down at her, in what seemed an oddly tender way, and said, "It probably was the wrong thing to do, but I brought you a present."

"A present? But..."

Evidently deciding to make light of the moment, he released her and moved away. "I know full well that I am going to regret this, but it seemed proper at the time. Close your eyes."

She didn't have to obey his request. It was too late for that; she had already seen the bubbles drifting up from the water bucket, heard the wild glad song. "Bubba! You found Bubba!"

After Tish had touched the wooden bucket, listened to Bubba's speechless joy, and crooned her loving welcome, she said, without moving away from her water sprite, "Oh, thank you, Marcus, I was so worried about him. Where did you find him? Was he hurt?" She felt a little silly to be making over a water sprite as if it were her child, but not enough to stop babbling.

Marcus's reaction wasn't exactly what she expected. As a matter of fact, it was more like a warning than the words of a man who had just gifted a woman with great joy. "I know there is some sort of bond between you, Tish, but Bubba is not a stuffed animal. He is..."

Instantly irate, Tish glared at the man. "Bubba is what? He saved our lives and..."

"I know that. That's one reason why I decided to go back to the stream to see if...if he had managed to survive," Marcus said slowly, turning away from her and walking over to the fireplace to rub his hands together as if he were warming them at the witch fire. "But, Tish, I saw what he did and..." He shook his head obviously trying to banish some too graphic memories.

"Which was what?"

Marcus presented his back to the heatless fire, took a deep breath, and said, making no effort to spare her, "There were five of the mercenaries. Bubba killed them, tearing them into several pieces, depositing body parts at least fifteen feet up in trees, and destroying... Tish, the beast-things are thinking creatures, not animals, and Bubba never gave them a chance. He is so powerful that he..."

Tish was furious. "And, just exactly what were they planning on doing to me? Bubba saved my life, and probably yours, and if you don't appreciate that, well, it just shows how ignorant and ungrateful you are."

"Possibly I am, but he's dangerous. He could turn on you just as easily as..."

"Bull!" Tish patted the side of Bubba's bucket. "He would never hurt me, and you know it."

"No," he said, "I don't know it." But, his words were lost in the sudden roar of the fire, howl of the wind, and a high keening cry from the sprite. A warning cry that made Tish's neck hair stand on end, her bones begin to melt, and her breath refuse to leave the shelter of her lungs.

But it wasn't the keening wail of the sprite that jerked Tish into action, it was another cry, one that was almost inaudible, but somehow managed to claw its way into her brain, her muscles, her very soul.

The sawed-off wand spat red fire and was burning hot when Tish, scared down to the dirty soles of her bare feet, grabbed it off the table and held it tightly in her sweaty hand. "What is it?" she asked, forcing the hoarse whisper out of her dry mouth. "What's happening now?"

"Fire drake!" Marcus had his black glass sword in his hand and was standing near the back door, looking up toward the thatch roof. "If it blasts us, the whole house will go in seconds."

The agonizing scream came again. Louder. Gigantic fingers raking down a blackboard. The high-pitch squeal of electronic equipment gone mad. Head hurting. Bone aching. Terror's ultimate voice.

"It's a big one." Marcus swallowed hard before he shouted, "He's going to blast us. Get ready to run."

The explanation made no more sense than the blackness that suddenly gripped the room, thick blackness that had more substance than shadow and smelled, if only faintly, of scorched ozone, sulfur, brimstone, and rotted meat.

The blackness thickened, moved sluggishly. Tish's wand was the only source of light, and it was able to illuminate only a few scant feet beyond its tip. "Marcus, what is it?" Tish's voice traveled no further than her wand's light, but the man had come to where she stood. Sword at ready, he looked at if he intended to protect her with his life.

"What is it? What's a fire drake?"

The life-destroying sound grew to a roar, deafeningly loud. It sizzled, hissed, exploded against the thatch in a firestorm. The roof was an instant inferno, and burning far too quickly for it to be a natural fire. Smoke, thick, choking, filled with chunks and bits of fire, sank into the room. Coughing, eyes streaming, Marcus grabbed Tish by the arm, jerked her toward the back door, toward the stable where the horses were squealing in terror. "Come on! We have to get out of here."

"Get the horses out. I'll get Bubba!" she said, the words coughed out of her aching lungs. Pulling loose from Marcus, she whirled around, grabbed Bubba's bucket, and stumbled toward the door that was completely hidden in the thick dark and the breath-stealing, acrid smoke.

The heat hit her like a blow. It was so hot Tish thought she was going to faint. And, at that moment, she didn't really care if she did. Bubba sent up a bubble. It burst against her face, under her nose, giving her a breath of air, enough to push her through the door and into the chaos beyond.

Another bubble of air, and possibly a mental prod, made her remember the wand that was vibrating in her hand. She pointed at Marcus first and said, "Have air," and was gratified to see a big bubble of clean freshness surround them both.

The horses were next. "Go with Marcus," she commanded after giving each of them an envelope of air, and only one small part of her brain was amazed that fire-spooked creatures obeyed. Safe in her own bubble, Bubba's bucket secure in the crook of her arm, Tish held the wand like a weapon and followed Marcus out into the beginning of evening and through the hedge into the dark and brooding forest beyond.

It was still telling her to get lost and was doing everything it could to warn them away. Tish shivered. The forest, whatever its reasons, was definitely morose, probably in need of a good antidepressant and an even better shrink, but the forest wasn't on fire, wasn't roaring, and probably wasn't one of Marcus's hellish fire drakes. Even at its worst, the forest was a real improvement over their last resting place.

Trying not to notice anything about the forest, Tish banished the cocoons of air that had served them so well before she followed Marcus into a small clearing, stopped when he stopped, and asked, "So, what's a fire drake?"

"A dragon." He looked skyward, pointed toward to distant specks, warring, struggling specks that seemed to be shooting out plumes of fire. "Two dragons in this case."

The pair dropped closer. Tish saw silver scales on one, copper on the other. And blood. And smoke. And she heard fury. They were too big, too fearsome, to be believed. And she didn't believe what she saw, not by one scale, or tail, or grasping claw.

"It's a glamour," she said.

"Do you know that for true?"

Tish didn't want to know it for true. Dragons might be better than what she was beginning to know. But, this time she had no choice but to tell the truth. "The dragons are not real. They're..."

His question came too quickly. "Godmothers?"

Sadness was bitter in her mouth. Tish wiped away some of the sooty smoke that masked her features and said, "One of them is Morgain. The other is Tregon, I think. Why are they fighting?"

"I don't know." Slowly, he brought the sword down until its point rested against the ground. "A dragon-glamour, but that's not... What are they doing here? This is a magic-kingdom, out of the Godmothers' rule by deed and contracts both legal and binding. And if what you say is true, and I'm not doubting your word, it breaks all the covenants between the kingdom and Faery. Somebody is going to pay for this, and pay big."

"Who?"

"I don't... Who hates you?"

It wasn't a question Tish wanted to answer; not that she could. She shrugged her shoulders, sat Bubba's bucket at the base of one of the huge trees, and waited for a long moment before she said, "Maybe it's not just me they hate. Maybe it's us. Both of us."

Swooping, tails lashing, fire spouting, the dragons flew high and gradually, as the evening progressed into twilight, moved to the north, out of sight. Tish thought, not knowing if it was good or bad, that Tregon was winning the battle, that the copper dragon was stronger in magic than the silver.

Shivering, wishing the T-shirt was heavy enough to cut the chill a little better, Tish glanced toward the man who was silent as winter, still, frozen in place, staring toward the darkening sky. The horses had moved away to crop the short yellow grass that grew here and there in the clearing, but Marcus just stood there, leaning on his sword, looking a little less superior than was his wont, and a whole lot dirtier.

Full, total, complete, without a star or dragon to mar the black, night had stolen in and pulled down all the shades. Tish was sitting on the ground beside Bubba, hugging herself for warmth before she finally called Marcus's name.

He didn't answer.

"Marcus," Tish said again, louder. "They're gone. And the safe house is toast. I'm cold, dirty, and hungry. What do we do now?"

"Tish," he said, sounding like he had just woken up from a Rip Van Winkle nap, "we need to talk."

"We need lots of things," Tish snapped, "and talking is way down on the list."

"No, someone is trying to kill us. We need to..."

"Marcus," she said, being only sweet and reasonable, "if you don't put your brain in gear and tell me what we're going to do next, I'm either going to freeze to death or starve. That should take care of all our problems. Is that your plan?" She knew she was being unfair, but damn it, he still had on his cloak and her teeth were turning to ice, right along with the blood in her veins.

"No, of course not, but aren't you engaging in a bit of hyperbole?"

It was actually too dark to see his expression, but Tish imagined he had that nose-in-the-air look, the one that said she was some sort of weird creature that obviously didn't belong in the same universe with intelligent creatures. She shook the wand, demanded a witch light, and then glared at the floating ball of green when it appeared.

He was at her side in an instant, growling out a command as he came, "Get rid of that thing. Do it now!"

"Why?"

It was his turn to be reasonable, but he was far from sweet about it. "I told you before. The witch lights are spy..."

Tish zapped it out of existence before he could finish his sentence. Not that he needed to. She knew what he was going to say, knew that the Godmothers could use the witch lights to spy on them. She knew, also, that she had been incredibly stupid to have given them the opportunity to see that their dragon flyby burning hadn't claimed its intended victims.

She stood up, bumping into Marcus in the process, and said, whispered rather, "We have to leave, don't we?"

"That would no doubt be the best plan, unless, of course, you'd prefer to be warmed by a dragon's breath rather than my own manly form."

He had reverted, become the old, odious Marcus, and for some unknown reason, that pleased Tish no end. He might be a prig, but he was competent. And he had been in this kingdom before, so it was up to him to find them shelter and then get her warm again. Tish didn't quite blush at the direction her thoughts were taking. She didn't allow them to roam further either; she was too cold to venture into erotica, too tired, too dirty, and too...

Running out of toos, Tish asked, "Where? And, is it okay to zap up some warmer clothes. Can the Godmothers trace magic?"

His chuckle was positively infuriating and so was his answer. "That's rather a moot question at this point, isn't it?"

Even if it was true, reasonable, and a proper deduction from the evidence at hand, he was still an overbred, pompous ass. And just as soon as they were somewhere safe, she was going to tell him so—and do it in no uncertain terms, maybe pitch in a few really choice swear words. Words she hadn't learned at her mother's knee.

Even as she fumed, Tish used her magic credit card, probably maxing it out, on a new riding habit, sans corset, drawers, socks, petticoats, boots, a snugly warm, hooded cloak, and a stoppered jug, in a leather carrying case, for Bubba. She glamorized the wand, giving it the form of a lantern, like one of the ones that populated old Dracula movies.

And, as warmth began gnawing away at the shivers and shakes, she said, "Where to now?"

Marcus was a little slow in answering. He waited until she was sitting astride on the mare's bare back before he said, sounding more troubled than was his wont, "There's a hunting lodge less than a league to the west. We can stay there for a day or so, but..."

"But what?"

"If the Godmothers are trying to kill us, I think we should leave the kingdom entirely. And do it immediately"

Tish's thoughts had been veering in that selfsame direction ever since the dragon attack, but before she could give voice to her heartfelt agreement, the Sanction shifted into overdrive, tweaking, pinching, twisting, and hurting her more than was strictly necessary to remind her that she had a Wish-quest to bring to a satisfactory conclusion. One that she had given her word to complete.

"I can't leave," Tish said, knowing full well that the anger in her voice wouldn't change a single thing. She was caught, well and truly, in the Godmothers' net, and she was going to stay caught and until the Uglies weren't and Cin was wedded to a prince.

"The Wish-quest?" Marcus's question, coming out of the darkness behind her, sounded sad.

"Yes." Her snapped answer had no sadness in it, just resignation.

"Let's get to your hunting lodge and..."

"It belongs to the king."

"So, if he finds us there, is he going to chop off our heads?"

Marcus sighed, but said nothing more. He just mounted the gelding and led the way through the dark and brooding forest. The trees fairly dripped pessimism, whispered doom, and did all the other ugly forest things that cursed woods are supposed to do: spooking unwary travelers and giving them a good, or maybe it was bad, case of the despairs.

Tish didn't see any ghostly shapes flitting from tree to tree, nor did she hear any banshee wails, but she was feeling terribly despondent by the time the darkness gave way to a lighter gray and the dense, droopy-limbed woods. They were going to fail. She knew that, knew too that the Godmothers, one or all, were behind what was going on, were trying to kill her and Marcus.

And Tish had no idea why, and twist it and turn it as she might, Tish had no solution to the troubling problem when Marcus pointed out their destination directly ahead.

The hunting lodge didn't live up to its advanced billing. It certainly didn't look as if it should belong to a king; unless, of course, he was bankrupt. Opulent, it wasn't. In fact, it was barely within the category of building. Tumbled-down shack would probably be a better description of the lodge. Barely larger than a tent, built of small logs, it could have come from a period in Tish's world's Old West, at least outwardly.

Already afflicted with a case of melancholy, Tish looked at the small structure, almost invisible in the gloom, with a sinking heart. "Marcus," she asked, "are you sure this is... The chimney is falling down and..."

"I haven't been to this kingdom since... I don't suppose the king comes to these woods anymore, not after what..."

She jumped to a conclusion. "The Red Witch died here?" Tish wanted to look around, see some evidence of what had transpired, but she was just too weary and too depressed to care about a long ago tragedy. Even if Marcus had somehow been one of the principle players.

"Not far."

"Cinderella lives nearby?"

"Very close."

They both sat for a long time without speaking. Rain, cold as sky-tears and sorrowing as the forest, began to ooze out of the dark sky before Marcus dismounted and came to lift her down, saying, "We'll stay for a day or so. We have to. Maybe we can devise a plan that will..."

"Maybe," Tish muttered. She stumbled along behind him as he led the horses around to the back of the lodge and into a cave that was a small, surprisingly clean and well-stocked, stable, as the warm yellow light from her wand-lantern was quick to reveal.

The oat bins were brimming. The stalls freshly cleaned and strewn with loose hay. Water gurgled into the hollow stone troughs. Looking around, holding the lantern high, Tish felt a trickle of fear easing its way up her spine. "Somebody's been here," she whispered. "Are you sure it's safe for..."

Looking weary beyond words, Marcus said, "It's a replenishing spell. It was a gift to the king on the day of his coronation."

The Godmother rent-a-horses rubbed down with handfuls of hay and settled for what remained of the night, Marcus took a deep breath, like a man readying himself for a plunge into deep water. "Tish, I..."

When he didn't go on, Tish, who wasn't noted for her sensitivity, had enough sense to refrain from voicing any of the questions that had laid siege to her mind. Instead, she said, "I don't suppose there's the same kind of spell, only for humans, at work inside the lodge. I mean, one that will spew out some food that's suitable for humans and some blankets and..."

Stopping suddenly, she tipped her head to one side and asked one of the questions that had been clamoring at her. "That's something that's been bothering me for a long time. You are human, aren't you?"

Marcus laughed. It was almost real. And so was the leer in his amber eyes. "Whether or not I was human didn't seem to be a factor the night you were trying to seduce me."

Wrinkling her nose, she grinned at him. "As I have been trying to tell you, I wasn't myself at the time, but seduction isn't exactly what I have in mind at the moment."

"What then? It would at least get us warm."

"So would a big roaring fire. Now, tell me, is there a spell on the lodge?"

"I don't know." A gust of wind-driven rain spattered across the floor, bringing with it a heavier downpour of total despair, a concentrated dose of forest sorrow. He took another deep breath before he said, only a faint tremor in his voice betraying his agitation, "It...it didn't happen here."

Feeling defeated, ready to cut and run, but quickly nipped back into duty's path by the Sanction, Tish swallowed hard and lifted the glowing wand a little higher, trying to banish the awful fingers of...of...whatever it was that was doing its level best to pitch her into a deep blue pool of despondency. "Get," she mumbled, somehow relieved that the wand burned a little brighter, cast a brighter, more comforting light.

"Marcus, are you..."

He didn't answer. He just stood there, staring at nothing, looking like all the paintings of lost souls Tish had ever had occasion to see. That, and whatever was creeping in on the wind, fairly gave her the heebie-jeebies, or one of those odd-sounding, nerve-jumpy things where even the shadows had fangs and evil intent. "Marcus," she said again, "what is it? What's happening to us?"

He sort of moaned, like he was in a world of hurt.

Trying not to stare at him, but feeling oddly compelled to comfort him, to ease whatever it was that was tearing him apart, Tish took a step toward him. "What, Marcus? What didn't happen here?"

Foreboding settled around her, smothered her in its thick, dark folds, and Tish wished, desperately, that the words had never been said, the question never asked. She moved closer. Touched his arm. "It's all right, Marcus. You don't have to tell me."

The bleakness in his eyes was echoed in his voice when he said, "Yes, I do. You have to know it all. It's the only way to keep you safe."

Chapter Sixteen

"MARCUS." IT WASN'T quite a question and more squeak than an actual name.

In the outer darkness, the wind moaned like a demented demon, raising its voice to a howl of anguish, flinging the night sky's icy tears in through the open mouth of the tiny cave. Dust, bits of hay, seeds, and other debris rose, swirled in a mad whirlwind, scoured the stable interior with angry, flaying gusts.

Blinking against the bite and sting, trying to catch her breath and to hold the wand-lantern high, Tish was slammed in the back by a strong blast of wind, shoved across the stony floor until she was halted by Marcus's tall, hard-muscled body. Unable to move away, she huddled against the man.

"Marcus," she said again, screamed rather, in order to be heard over the wind, and accidentally touching his hand with the disguised wand. "What is it?"

Either her words or her body pressed against his galvanized him, tore him out of whatever blackness that was consuming him. He was, instantly, Marcus, the man of duty, the man in charge. "Hurry!" he shouted. "It won't harm the horses, but there's no protection for us in the stable. We have to get out of here, or it will choke us to death on our own tears."

Before she could catch her breath, or say him nay, his arm was warm and strong around her shoulders. Every inch the hero of all her imaginings, protective and strong, Marcus half-carried, half-led her out into the tearing, snapping teeth of the storm. It was a storm that had magic written large and cold on its icy breath. And it was the magic, dirty, stinking magic, evil magic, that made her furious.

"Damn you," she snarled, gripping her wand even tighter, ordering it to protect them in their wild dash toward the ruin of the lodge. It sputtered and shot fire at her command, vibrating in her grasp, sending out a golden cone to spill down on Marcus and Tish. It smelled of summer and heat, and held the storm at bay as they stumbled across a swath of winter-killed grass and into the recessed doorway of the dilapidated lodge.

It held faint lines of magical force in its log walls, but despite that, she doubted that it was strong enough to shield them from the strengthening attacks of the predatory storm. But Marcus seemed to believe that it was the only place near enough to offer them any sort of shelter from whatever it was that was intent on their destruction.

Between one heartbeat and the next, or so it seemed, they were safe behind a thick, cross-barred door of solid oak. Safe in absolute silence and thick musty darkness. A darkness made even darker by the faint light cast by the wand-lantern. Silence and darkness within a space that was, she recognized, without even wondering how she knew, heavily spelled and warded to keep the evil out, to shield those within its walls from the howling, mind-searing magic spell that could have only been cast from the murky depths of a very sick mind.

A counterspell embedded into the very heart of the building could, and would, in time even take away fear and leave nothing behind but a strong sense of well-being. Tish was somehow aware of the truth of that also.

"What was that storm thing? Who would want to do something like that?"

"The Red Witch," Marcus said slowly. "She cursed the forest and set a ravening spell to eat the minds and souls of unwary travelers. She was... Poor, poor woman, she... Don't blame her too much, Tish, she bought some bad magic from a..."

"From a what? I thought you said all the magic in Faery belonged to the Godmothers." There was a long silence and her voice was far too weak, too frightened, to even come close to belonging to her when she asked, all her suspicions, her growing knowledge in the simple question, "You did say that, didn't you? The Godmothers supposedly do all the magic selling?"

Marcus didn't answer.

Tish took a deep breath and forced a modicum of patience into her voice when she asked, "Look, whatever it is, it's your business. If you want to tell me, that's okay. If you don't, that's fine too."

He didn't want to drag the sordid mess out into the open, relive the pain, but, sooner or later, Tish had to know. Still, Marcus tried his best to be reasonable, even though he knew it was more than that. There was no real reason, except his fear of her knowing all about him, and he didn't want to face that. At least, not yet, not until he'd had a few more minutes of...

Giving himself a stern mental shake, Marcus said, and it wasn't nothing more than the truth, "It's a long story and we are both weary and..."

She wasn't one for hiding what she felt. Somehow that cheered him; even if it was as irritating as hell. He smiled a little when he heard her say, "Okay. Now that you've shoved that little bit of information under the rug, what are we going to do to pass the time?"

It wasn't even close to being an invitation, and Marcus knew it. But, a delaying action seemed best under the circumstances and he wasn't averse to using any means at his disposal to ease her fears and keep her safe a little longer.

"Well?" she asked, her voice sounding too loud in the quiet of the place. After a brief second, she was glad it was loud, glad that all sorrow, despair, and mind-harrowing, body-chilling, filthy magic had remained outside the closed doors.

The relief was so great, it made her giddy, flighty even. Grinning just a little, she said, "Okay, Marcus, bring on the food and the fire and I'll light your lights." Suiting her actions to her words, Tish lifted the wand high and said, in her most commanding tones, "Lights! Camera! Action!"

It worked, at least in part. She didn't see any cameras, but the light filled the room, from bottom to top, building deeper and deeper, like water being poured into a bowl, but Tish almost wished it hadn't. The stable might have a replenishing spell, but no such things existed for the lodge. It was a wreck.

It actually looked as if someone, or several someones, completely crazy someones at that, had taken out their swords, since chain saws probably didn't exist in Faery, and slashed and hacked and cut everything within reach. And when ribbons of leather and fabric, mounds of feathers, splinters of wood, and shatters of glass were all that was left of the small room's furnishings, the crazies had tried to pull the stones from the fireplace, the logs from the walls.

They hadn't succeeded, or at least not entirely. The walls were still intact as was what appeared to be a sod roof. The fireplace, however, had suffered far too greatly to even be risked for a tiny fire.

Not even trying to hide behind a facade of Godmotherly gentility, Tish swore, long and loud. And when she ran out of breath, Marcus was looking at her with what appeared to be demon-eyed admiration.

But there was no admiration, no despair, no emotion of any kind in his voice when he asked, "Tish, I have to know. Are you sure the fire drakes were a Godmother glamour? Really sure?"

Poking the toe of her boot into a tangle of unknowable substance, Tish thought for a moment before she said, "Yes, I'm sure. I think...Marcus, the Council of Four were really sweet, do you think they would try to..."

Unwilling to believe the four beautiful old women would have sent dragons to kill them, but unable to see any other alternatives, Tish kicked the pile of junk, kicked it hard, trying to vent her mounting frustration.

Dust motes rose up in a cloud. Tish sneezed loudly and then sneezed again before she took off on a new tangent, drew some conclusions of her own, and asked three more questions before he could answer her first one, "What's really going on around here? Why were you at my mother's ball? Why didn't Artemus King want you to know he was there also?"

His mouth opened, but Tish flung a new question into the breach, one that made him shake his head and walk, picking his way across the trashed room to stand in front of the ruined fireplace, with his hands spread on the mantle, his back to the room. And to Tish.

"Why did the Council of Four give me this Wish-quest when it was supposed to belong to Morgain?"

The silence was unbroken. Marcus stood like a man turned to ice. Tish waited for several minutes before she moved to a corner, scraped away most of the debris from the hacked floor and sat down in the reasonably clean place she had made for herself.

Huddled in the warmth of her cloak, refusing to allow her mind to wander too far from the narrow limits she had given it, Tish tried to reason out the whys and wherefores of their predicament. With no luck. Too many pieces were missing.

And, decidedly against her will and at the most inopportune times, the Sanction leaped into action when she ventured onto forbidden ground, gave even the vaguest thought to waving her wand and getting out of Faery. That wasn't to be allowed. She couldn't come close to even thinking about cutting her losses and running for her life, leaving Marcus, overbred idiot that he was, to stew in his own juice and going home to her mother.

"The whole thing is his fault anyway," she muttered, fully aware that it wasn't. He was just doing his job when he tackled her after she had toaded Carl and had come close to zapping his female companion into a cross-eyed hound of the female persuasion. Still, if Marcus had...

She glanced at his back, scowled, and said, and doubting parts of the truth of her own words even as she said them, "Damn it, Marcus, you'd better be thinking fast. The way I see it, as safe as it feels, we're trapped in here and my magic credit card may not be usable much longer, not if the Council of Four is behind whatever is going on."

"What?" Marcus turned away from the fireplace, looked toward her resting place.

Cold, hungry, frustrated, and wanting to have a rip-snorting fight to clear her head, Tish rubbed her fingers down the leather bag that was Bubba's new home, felt a faint reassuring hum. It soothed her for the moment, made her wise enough to know that it was neither the time nor the place to start in on Marcus. Not when his face was shadowed and drawn, his amber eyes dark with old secrets, painful secrets. Not when she felt a small twinge of pity in her own heart, one that made her want to ease his pain, not add to it. It was a tender feeling, one that she had never, not even once, felt about Carl.

She wanted to examine it, but her mind was filled too full, was too chaotic for her to entertain any degree of coherency. Her thoughts took a jump and she changed direction in midstream as it were, following what had to have been a huge shove from the Sanction. "Okay, fella, if you don't want to talk about witches, let's take up the next item on the agenda. How many princes are there?"

"What?" he asked again, sounding a good deal like a man just waking up from a not too pleasant sleep.

Tish's patience wouldn't have filled a thimble, and what little she did have was worn fairly thin. "Damn it, Marcus. Pay attention. Someone is out to gun us down, or flame us into crispy critters, or suck our brains out through our ears. I can't leave this kingdom until Cin and her prince are in bed together legally. So, all I want to know is: How many Princes Charming are there in this marvelous kingdom?"

"Four."

"All born on the right side of the blanket?" Tish asked, feeling her tension easing just a little. If there are four, surely one of them wouldn't mind tying the knot with Cin.

"Yes."

"Okay, we start with the oldest one and work our way down. Right?"

"No." It was flat and definite.

Tish wasn't willing or able to let it go at that. "Why not? Is he married or something?"

"No."

Anger chased the chill from her bones. The man, if he was a man, was too damned obstinate and obtuse to be believed. "Marcus," she said, pitching her voice low and as emotionless as possible, "you were ordered to accompany me on my Wish-quest. Your duty, or so I was led to believe, is to inform, protect, and teach me. You aren't..."

She stopped, took a quick breath to try to push back the anger that was rising hot and bitter in her throat, and said, actually she snarled, "I demand that you live up to your oath."

"The Council told you about that?"

"The Council told me diddly. You're supposed to be doing the telling, not moping around like whiny old Heathcliff, the man not the cat, and acting like your world has come to a whimpering end. Now, I don't give a...a fig what kind of demons you have in your past, or how many witches you've put an end to, I just want to have a future."

She knew she was screaming at the top of her lungs and just plain didn't give a damn. What she really wanted to do was...was...

Marcus crossed the narrow, littered space that separated them, went down on one knee in the filth, and bent his head, holding one hand, flat and fingers spread, over his heart. It was a scene out of a very poor movie, and at any other time, Tish would have laughed in derision.

But not this time. Not when Marcus said, sounding so sincere she was instantly suspicious, "I ask your pardon, Godmother Leticia. I have been remiss and will do my best to rectify that flaw in my character as soon as..."

Drawing her booted feet up under her cloak, Tish reacted, to her own suspicions, not his seemingly meek apology. She said, with more force than was strictly necessary, "Stop acting like a...a...pompous ass, get up off your knees, and tell me about the damned prince."

"Damned describes him more truly than you can possibly know," Marcus said softly as he, more or less, complied with her order by twisting his lean body around and taking a seat close by her side. Maybe too close for his own peace of mind. He was already more than half in love with her, even though he had fought the feeling every step of the way, and he wasn't the man for her. Even if every muscle and bone in his body ached with wanting, needing, Marcus forced himself to put duty and honor first. And honor's stern voice told him to keep his distance.

"So?" she asked after a moment, disturbed by her own wanting to either move closer or move away from his disturbing presence. She could do neither.

"The eldest prince is not available on the marriage market."

"Why?"

"It's a long story and..."

"Don't give me that guff again. I don't care if it's a ten-part mini-series with a cast of millions, I want to know what's going on. Now, damn it, tell me."

His eyebrow quirked up. "Mini-series?"

"Soap opera?"

He chuckled and his voice sounded almost normal when he made his own suggestion. "Faery tale?"

"Of course. As long as it comes complete with a Prince Charming to give it sex appeal." Relaxing just a little, Tish almost snuggled against him before she stopped herself and zapped them each a big cup of steaming coffee, her standard remedy for moments of crisis. And this certainly fell into that general category.

"Tish," he turned his head and looked at her, "shouldn't you save what credit you have left? The Godmothers are not exactly kind creditors."

Tish had her own idea about the Godmothers, especially the Council of Four, ideas that were based partly on fact, partly on guess, and partly on growing certainty. "Tell me about the prince," she said, "and forget about the Godmothers. I have a feeling they aren't going to be too quick in denying me anything I ask for."

"You think they set you up?" He sounded like she had advocated overthrowing the government by force of arms. It was an idea clearly not to his liking.

"What I think is..." Tish stopped. She needed information, not to air her own suspicions. "Quit trying to change the subject and tell me about the prince, all of the princes, and everything else I need to know to get Cin out of the fireplace and into the royal bed."

"That's a tall order for a weary and hungry man." He took a sip of coffee.

"Do heroes eat fast food?" Tish asked, not at all averse to taking a magical trip to Burger King to grab a couple of Whoppers and a bunch of fries. Which she did.

He was staring down at his hamburger before he had time to say, "Tish, I'm far from being a hero."

"So," she said, mumbled rather, around the bite of juicy goodness that filled her mouth too full, "it's your Faery tale, what are you, the villain?"

"Are those the only choices?"

"Mostly, I guess. In the stories Mother insisted on reading to me, the Prince/Hero always came in to save the poor maiden from the wicked witch, or the evil fairy's spell, or her wicked stepsisters. Is your Faery tale any different?"

"Ours might be."

Her burger and most of her fries were gone and Tish was beginning to feel ready to challenge a wicked witch to a duel, but she just asked, "Ours?"

Wiping his hands together, he said, "When the bards tell of our deeds, I suspect they will tell of a beautiful Godmother who didn't actually need a hero to rescue her from witches or dragons or..."

She knew he was stalling, but nonetheless one word of his nonsense warmed her as it wound through her head to come out of her lips, "Beautiful, huh?"

"All heroines are beautiful, aren't they? At least, the bards always tell it so."

"Verbal cosmetic enhancement?"

"Happens all the time, with no gender bias."

"I'll keep that in mind as you tell me your story, bard."

Wiggling a little to find a softer spot on the scarred floor, Marcus said, "Well, Godmother, if I'm going to be talking away the night, I'd like to be a little warmer and a lot more comfortable."

Her own hamburger gone, along with her share of the fries, Tish wiped her greasy fingers on the skirt of her riding habit. She asked, wishing the words back no sooner than they were out of her mouth, "What did you have in mind, a heated waterbed and a down-filled sleeping bag built for two."

"That would be...ah...very cozy." There was a universe of meaning in the soft purr of his voice.

"No, it wouldn't," Tish said, fully aware that her own red cheeks were probably hot enough to warm the entire room. "Blankets and a few pillows are the size of it. I want the story, not hanky-panky."

"Well, Godmother, in this as in all things, your wish is my command." Marcus made her a slight bow. It seemed to hold more regret than mockery. And thanked her for the warmth and comfort of their shared nest of the thick, fuzzy blankets and big pillows Tish had magicked into being before he started telling what was, indeed, a very long tale.

Sitting on two pillows, one directly under her, the other under her extended legs, leaning back against another, Tish dimmed the lights and closed her eyes. She forced herself to ignore his lean body stretched out beside her own and to listen carefully, to hear what was said and left unsaid.

Marcus hesitated, but only briefly, before he forced some lightness into his tone and began talking. "As all such tales do," he said, "it begins: Once upon a time there was a magic kingdom. The king was old and his only son had looked far and wide to find a princess beautiful enough and gentle enough to be his beloved bride."

"Marcus," Tish said, and warning was heavy in her voice, "don't make it any longer than it needs to be. Just give me the bare facts, if I want to know more I'll ask."

She sounded so irritated, he wanted to smile and smooth down her ruffled feathers, but, of course, he could do neither. She was being Godmotherly, and in that particular mode, she was his boss, one his own Oath to the Guard made him obey. He got on with his tale, omitting only what he considered necessary.

"When he finally found his one true love, he loved her a little too quickly, or so it was bandied about, and their firstborn son came a month or so too soon to be considered the rightful and proper heir to the throne."

"Is that all? Why didn't you just say he wasn't legitimate and thus out of our market?" Tish allowed her disgust to show. "If Cin wants the, what-do-you-call-'em, the Heir-Apparent, we just have to forget the Bastard and go for the second son, right?"

Marcus sighed, heavily, and it was a sound laden with portent, not that Tish put any great value in signs and portents, but she couldn't resist asking, "Now, what's wrong? Is the second son a real pervert, already married, exiled, in love with someone else? What?"

"No, it's just that... Prince Rupert, called Rue by his family, is almost as romantic as Cinderella is reported to be and will only consent to a love match; or so he says. And this is a very rich kingdom, so I really doubt that he's up for sale."

"Pish-tosh," Tish snapped, something she had read in an old novel and liked to throw into conversations at strange moments. "We'll just give him a shot of lust, a lust spell, and let nature do the rest. The king probably won't object too much. According to everything I've ever heard, royal marriages are always arranged to suit the best interests of the kingdom. There has to be some interest of the king's that the marriage of Cin and Rue will further, add to, or otherwise benefit those involved. Right?"

Marcus shook his head slowly. "You are a devious woman, Leticia. It's too bad that you aren't the one looking for a husband, I'm sure that any prince in the One-Hundred Kingdoms would be here to plight you his troth in the twitch of a gnat's whisker."

"And I would be expected to simper prettily and say, 'Charmed, I'm sure?' Damn it, Marcus, stop trying to flatter me and get with the program. That Sanction is starting to tweak parts of me that don't need tweaking. I want to finish this gig and go home."

"Gee, my lady, I thought since I had already compromised your virtue that you were going to stay in Faery and marry me. That's usually the way of it in bard's tales, isn't it."

It was a thought, but not one she wanted to pursue at the moment, especially since Tish knew he was teasing her. "Don't be silly! Godmothers don't get married, do they?"

"Of course they do. Where do you think little Godmothers come from?"

"I don't..."

His interruption was too quick by far. "Would you like me to demonstrate the proper technique for setting about acquiring one of the little magic-wielders?"

A small pulse was throbbing at the base of her throat and for one awful moment Tish was totally tempted to whisper, "Yes," in her sultriest voice and let him have his way with her. With her very active participation, of course. But the moment passed, or rather fell victim to the harsher acts of the Sanction. And it was the Sanction that made her say, "Not on your life."

His chuckle didn't come close to being a caress. "Later perhaps. I don't ordinarily give rain checks, but in your case, I'm sure it can be arranged."

Muttering an obscenity, Tish said, "And, I'm sure if I need such service, you'll be happy to accept my credit card." She squirmed into a more comfortable position in their shared resting place and said, or rather ordered, "Tell me about Cinderella and the Uglies, and don't leave anything out. I really need to know what's going on because..."

Her voice shook, if only for an instant and, to her horror, tears welled up in her eyes. Every fear that she had ever known was battering at her defenses, and Tish wasn't sure that she could keep them at bay.

If he had been the hero in one of her books, he would have been described as sensitive and caring. As it was, he did one of his mind-reading tricks, let his warm hand rest against her cheek. "It's just some of the ravening spell trickling in through the fireplace, but it's not enough to hurt you. It'll be all right, Tish. I give you my word."

And she remembered what he had told her, knew his words were a spell binding him. A few of her fears fluttered away. But only a few, the rest stayed to jeer and jape, telling her she was never going to get home. That she had no Ruby Slippers. That Marcus was...was... She didn't know what he was and didn't dare ask again, didn't want to know if he was an elf. Or something worse.

He slid his arm under her shoulders, gathered her close, rocked her like a child. "Try to get some sleep, my lady Godmother. We can talk in the morning. I'll tell you everything then."

The comfort-and-safety spell on the lodge grew stronger, laved her, but it was Marcus's arms that held her, made her safe. At least for the moment. Tish allowed her eyes to close, her body to relax against him, but her mind was too full to accept sleep.

It was her mind, or maybe only her overactive imagination that was conjuring all sorts of dire happenings, that made her ask, "Why did the Red Witch buy the bad magic in the first place?"

"Shhhh. Rest now."

She tried, for maybe fifteen seconds, before she said, "Tell me. I have to know."

"She was the baron's first wife."

The information penetrated her weary brain with incredible slowness, but when it finally homed in, it hit her like a baseball bat. She jerked free from Marcus's embrace and sat bolt upright. "Am I understanding this right? Are you trying to tell me the Red Witch was Cinderella's mother?"

"Exactly."

Not always dense, Tish saw the implication and asked, "The baron, he divorced her, or put her aside, or whatever men do to get rid of their unwanted wives in magic kingdoms?"

Raising up on one elbow, Marcus said, "Godmother Leticia, what I tell you now must be held in the strictest confidence. Will you so swear on your Godmother's Oath?"

"That bad?"

"Perhaps worse."

Shivering from more than the icy cold, Tish asked, "Is that the only way to get the Wish granted and us out of here with our hides mostly intact?"

"I believe so."

It was only a short time before Tish said, "I do so swear."

She knew it was what she had to do, but when Marcus reached up and pulled her back into their shared blankets, Tish lay stiff and still, waiting for him to tell the rest of his Faery tale. And suddenly it was a tale she didn't want to hear.

Chapter Seventeen

IT WAS SO quiet that Tish could hear the ravening spell sniffling and prowling outside the stout walls of the hunting lodge. Her imagination saw it sending out dark tendrils of desolation to probe for weak spots in the logs, the sod of the roof, to inch down the chimney, crawl through the cracks in the ruined fireplace.

Shivering just a little, knowing, probably from the Sanction, she was going to have to battle the outer spell sooner or later, she gave a silent order to the magic wand. She told it to strengthen the wards, to keep them safe inside the lodge until she had more information. Not that any additional amount of information would add a jot or a tiddle to her shrinking supply of courage. She really didn't have too much to start with, not for magic battles and curses and things that go bump in the night, evil things.

And Tish knew the wand would obey, that there would be no further interruptions or distractions, from the ravening spell anyway, while Marcus told his highly involved Faery tale. That is, if he would just get on with it, would tell the damned thing and be done with it.

But, in all truth, she was feeling more than a little ambivalent about that, too. It was pretty obvious that the telling was going to hurt him, or had already hurt him. For some odd reason, she wanted to protect the man, not add to his hurt. Still, she had to know if she was ever going to do the deed she had been sent to accomplish. And, in the doing, escape from the pinching of the Godmother Sanction.

Tish wiggled around on the pillows. In the process of trying to find warmth and comfort, she somehow managed to move a little closer to the man who was sharing her bed. His body heat and the hard-muscled length of him made her too aware of her other area of ambivalence: her response to him as a man. Her feelings seemed to be veering from the distaste to something far stronger, and more on the intimate side. And, after her so recent experience with Carl, she wasn't ready to be romantically involved with another man. Still, she was having warm thoughts in that direction. It was just plain foolishness on her part. Tish didn't like it, didn't want it, wasn't going to allow it. Not now. Not ever.

"So, tell me," she finally said, pushing all other thoughts back down into a dark recess of her mind and putting a lid on them, "if the baron didn't really divorce the Red Witch, Cin's mother, then what did he do with her, lock her up in a tower in the big middle of Dire Wood and tell the world she died?"

Suspicion and distrust were heavily mingled in his exclamation. "How, in the name of blazes, did you know that? Who told you that? It's not a thing that's been bandied about..."

For just a second, Tish thought he was going to get out of their blankets and go stomping off into the darkness. He certainly rose on one elbow and stared at her like he was seeing her for the first time.

Tish wanted to laugh at his obvious consternation, but she just said, and it was nothing more than the truth, "Look, Marcus, my mother is a fairy tale nut. Out loud and every night, she insisted on reading the Grimms and all the rest. Maybe here Cin hasn't latched on to her prince yet, but lots of the other junk must have happened. Evil barons and pure women locked away in towers are the stuff of which my childhood was made. Jeez, I used to have knightmares; that's terrible dreams about depraved knights, in case you're interested."

He sighed as he lay back down, tucked the covers more securely around them. "Godmother, this truly isn't a laughing matter. Lives were destroyed and..."

"Tell me the whole story then instead of acting like an outraged Victorian prude. I give you my word that I can listen to the tale without giving way to the vapors or any of those other maidenly things, like swooning."

"Ah, yes, the modern, independent woman."

She turned to her side, glared at him, and said, "Stop stalling and get on with it, Marcus. Come morning, I'm going to have to do battle with the ravening spell before I can even start with the Wish-thing for the Uglies. I want this whole damned thing done. I want to go back to civilization where there's soft beds, showers, and..."

His voice was softer and had an odd note, one she couldn't quite recognize, but thought it might be skepticism, "Did the Council of Four tell you could go back to your own world?"

Suddenly everything clicked, formed a picture, one that had no claims on pretty, inside her head. She knew what those wily old women had done to her, if not why. Tightening her grip on the wand, Tish said, chill touching every word with black ice, "No, but they won't stop me. I've finally figured out how things work here, and according to my best drawn conclusions, they will not only let me go, they'll pay me to take the trip."

"Tish, I don't think you..."

"Don't think," she snapped. "Talk."

"Yes, ma'am," he said, sounding suspiciously meek.

Marcus wasn't feeling meek; he was furious at the Council and frightened for Tish, both at the same time. How could they have done such a thing? She was no more suited to fight the spell than a mouse was to make war with a tiger. It was beyond...

He wanted, desperately, to take her in his arms, to protect her from all dangers, but he couldn't. That was beyond his power. All he could do was stand beside her and die with her when the ravening spell attacked in the morning. It wasn't an event he anticipated with any sort of relish.

Tish jabbed him with her elbow. "Stop stalling. You know I have to know about your dark deeds, so get it over with, will you?"

The telling had to be done, Marcus knew that, but he didn't want to see the revulsion in her eyes, feel her draw away from him. He drew in a deep breath, let it out in a silent sigh and began.

"As I said, the baron was married to the Red Witch; of course, when he married her she wasn't a witch. She was the only child of a base born but very rich merchant. She was also legal heir to several thousand hectares of mountainside, low land, and commercial property in the king's city of Matol. It was only after her father died that the baron set her aside, locked her up in the Nightwind Tower, and gave out that she had been killed by a rampaging boar. He brought in bloody bits of her clothing to prove it."

Sounding as if she were trying not to yawn, Tish asked, "Why didn't he just kill her and be done with it?"

"I don't know for sure. Maybe he hated her enough to keep her prisoner for life after he found out the property didn't come to him as a part of her dower. The witch's father, a canny man, had made sure, early-on in the marriage, that it would go to her children. The baron wasn't a wealthy man, but he was over much given to wager and chance. And he needed the income, which, after the supposed death of her mother, belonged to Cinderella. He was her guardian and made use of it as he would.

"Then, dear Godmother, he had the great misfortune to fall in love with a woman at court. And that love was his undoing, as it were."

"The Uglies's mother?"

"Very true. A lovely woman with two incredibly beautiful daughters that were very near handfasting age."

Tish closed her eyes, opened them again, and asked, "Which

means?"

"Fifteen or sixteen. In that general neighborhood."

"So," Tish asked, sounding like a lawyer on one of the TV programs on her world, ticking off points on her fingers, "he married the mother and then set about finding husbands for the kids, but the Red Witch found out and cursed the wedding veils?"

"Well, not exactly. The Red Witch, so-called because her knee-length hair was the color of an autumn sunset, wasn't really a witch. But she did have a string of matched lavender pearls, which are very rare and extremely valuable, and a ruby the size of a pigeon egg."

"And..."

"After Cinderella's old nurse, who brought food to the tower on a weekly basis, told her about the happenings with the baron, she used the jewels to buy some magic."

Tish let the light in the room fade a little more until only a vague twilight filled the room before she asked, "From whom? Which one of the Godmothers sold it to her?"

Marcus didn't try to deny a Godmother was involved, or maybe more than one Godmother. "After it was all over, Tregon conducted a long investigation, but she found nothing to indicate who the Godmother was. All that came to light was: It was a Godmother who did the selling, and what she sold was poison. Spoiled magic that had turned evil. The Red Witch used it to curse Sage and Quincy's wedding veils and to set the ravening spell. But the magic also destroyed others, many others." Marcus managed to keep from saying, "Aided and abetted by me."

With her usual sensitivity, Tish said, without a thought of what he might be feeling, "I thought you killed her." And then she was sorry and shamed enough to reach out, put her hand on his arm, and leave it there without saying anything more.

Even when Marcus was silent for a decade or so before he said, "I did." He took a deep breath. "I had to. May the First forgive me, I had to."

Hurting for him now, Tish whispered, "Marcus, don't..."

If he even heard her, the man ignored her soft protest and continued, his voice strained, raw with old pain. "I was a boy, not near a man-grown, but already a sworn liegeman to my king and to his second-born son, Rue the Heir-Apparent, and as such, it was my duty to join in the search for the Red Witch and to try to reverse the spell afflicting the Uglies. We had searched long and hard, looked for days. Several men had already fallen to the terrible hunger of the ravening spell, which grew stronger with every soul it ate."

As if naming it had called it into new life, the spell attacked the lodge, shook the log walls with the force of its fury, and jarred loose clods of dried mud from the sod roof. Tish tightened her grip on the magic wand, and perhaps on Marcus's arm, and brightened the light a little, but Marcus was too lost in his story to even notice.

And as he talked, Tish's imagination began to supply details. She actually saw the trails of fire and smoke from the wind-whipped torches, smelled the fear and the sweat and torn forest duff, heard the horses neighing, the men shouting and swearing, and the high, thin wails of despair as the soul-eater caught yet another man. She saw, too, the bright velvets, drawn swords, the drab garments of the club-carrying peasants, and the dark head and pointed beard of the baron as he angled his destrier away from the searchers, heading into the heart of the forest where he knew the witch was waiting.

And then, with her heart throbbing in her throat, her hand moving up, clutching Marcus's shoulder, Tish saw Marcus turn his horse, the great blood-red stallion, Sunfire, and follow, heedless of his own safety, where the baron led.

"Why?" she whispered, knowing the baron was the evil villain of the tale. "Why didn't you tell the king or the oldest prince or someone who..."

"There was no time," Marcus said slowly, "and I guess I was more than a bit of a fool. It's difficult to explain, but..."

Feeling an odd pang of bright-green jealousy, Tish said, "You were in love with one of them, weren't you, Marcus? Which one? Sage? Quincy? And you wanted to prove how brave and honorable you were to your lady love, isn't that about the size of it?" And she flat-out hated the pleading note that had crept into her voice, the breathless note that said, "Please, please, tell me I'm wrong, tell me I'm the first woman who ever came close to touching your heart."

Realizing that she was beginning to fall in love with him, and hating the very thought of it, Tish muttered an obscenity and jerked her hand away from his arm. It couldn't be happening. It had to be a rebound, or something equally mundane. It just plain had to be. She absolutely, positively wasn't going to fall in love with a pompous ass like Marcus, even if he did look like a royal prince, one that resembled a young, amber-eyed Gregory Peck more than jug-eared Prince Charles.

But, that didn't matter. She didn't even know if he was human, and here she was snuggled up in bed with him listening to him talk about his lost loves and wishing he would... She edged away from him and forced her skittish thoughts into less erotic channels, made herself listen to what he was saying.

"They were more beautiful than anyone had a right to be, and... But, no, I wasn't in love with either of them."

Tish wanted to heave a very relieved sigh, but she didn't. But she did put her hand back on his arm and she did pay a good deal closer attention to what he was saying.

"My first duty was to my...ah...my king and the cursing incident and the disappearance of the Red Witch was wreaking havoc in the kingdom. It had to be brought to some sort of reasonable conclusion. It was my duty as much as anyone's to do my best to save the kingdom. And, I wasn't averse to playing hero. You're right, I did want to prove myself honorable and brave, but not to the Uglies."

Her heart gave a little swooping dip and she scarcely had enough breath to ask, "Who then?"

"My...ah...my king," he answered after a moment.

"The baron knew the woods better than I. It took me several minutes longer to reach the tower than it did him. Those minutes were all he needed. She was tied to a stake in front of the dark stone of the short, squat tower. A flaming torch was in the baron's hand. He threw it into the pile of tinder-dry wood at the Red Witch's bare feet just as I rode into the clearing."

Marcus took a breath that was nearer being a sob of pure anguish than anything else she'd ever heard, or wanted to hear, and said, very softly, "I'll remember his laugh and her scream for as long as I live."

Aching to wrap her arms around him, hold him until his pain was gone, Tish fought against her own unruly feelings, steeled herself against the primal force that was squeezing the blood out of her heart, and remained where she was. Unmoving, unaware of the tears that were dripping down her face, tears for the man as well as the boy.

"The baron turned his horse, rode off into the darkness, still laughing that horrible laugh. I couldn't follow him, Tish. I couldn't follow him and kill him. I had to stay where I was, had to pull the Red Witch out of the fire. She screamed when I slashed the ropes, screamed again when I lifted her up, and carried her to the catch basin of a spring. The water was icy, but it couldn't come close to easing her pain."

He swallowed hard. "Her feet and legs were burned to the bone, the flesh fell away when I..."

Tish shuddered, dropped the wand, turned toward him, wrapped her arms around his shaking body, and whispered, "Don't. Don't go on."

He had to. The pain had been locked inside him too long. It broke free, poured out with his words, "I sat beside her all through the night, listened to every word she said, listened to her tale of woe and revenge, Tish. And then, when her agony was beyond human endurance, when she asked me for blessed release, I cut her throat with my belt knife. The Red Witch died in my arms, and I swore I would avenge her."

"Godmother Leticia, as horrible as it might seem to you, I hadn't a thought for Sage and Quincy, what their sufferings might be. All my thoughts were centered on the woman betrayed by husband and, Godmother, condemned by her betrayer to die a harsh and agonizing death. I was blinded by my tears and fury filled by heart too full when I gave her my word that the baron would die and the Godmother who betrayed her trust would be brought to justice."

Quite sure her mother would never approve of the man or his deeds, knowing the Steps had spoken truly when they said he was a dangerous man, Tish held him a little tighter. And she did it only because he was another thinking, hurting being, not because of anything her oversexed hormones were trying to tell her about love everlasting and the rest of that junk. "Did you... The baron, did you..."

"No." He took a deep breath and hurried on with the story, wanting to get it out. All of it. To let her see just what kind of a miserable excuse for a man he really was. "I buried the witch in a secret grave. Doing so at her request so that Cinderella would never have to know the full extent of her mother's deeds; the mother she believed was long dead. As I said, when that was done, I went to the king and told him, and only him, the full story. He wanted me to stay at court, but..."

"The oath bound you to another career choice?" Tish asked, loosening her hold on him and wiggling into a more comfortable position in their shared bed.

"My...ah...my king was mightily upset, but, scarce-grown lad that I was, I defied his orders and went to do what..."

"Then, I hope you went into the forest and killed that damned baron?" Tish wondered, if only briefly, why there was no horror in her voice. Why she approved, without a moment's reluctance, of him and his deadly quest, and actually wished she could ride with Marcus to the kill.

"No, I didn't have to kill him. He did that himself. He..." Marcus did a little wiggling of his own, turned so he faced her, and said, actually sounding sad about the whole sorry business, "The ravening spell hunted him down. He ran to a place of spelled safety and was trapped inside."

"Here?" Tish asked with a shudder. "He came here? Is that what happened to..." She wanted to gesture at the ruined interior of the lodge, but it was too cold, too dank, and too close.

"Here," Marcus answered. "No one knows for sure how long he stayed, but when I finally found him, the lodge was as you see it and his sword, notched, gouged, and tip-broken was lying on the hearth of the fireplace. His cape and shield were outside, but of him not even a scream remained. The Red Witch had gotten her own revenge, and, I am ashamed to say, I was glad."

"What's wrong with that? The bastard deserved..."

"Godmother," he said, not actually rebuking her outburst but explaining his own shame, "the spell is evil. It has grown steadily stronger and is threatening the whole kingdom with the icy heart of eternal winter. It should never have been cast, but now that it has, it will freeze the kingdom out of existence just as surely as night becomes day. And by killing the witch, what happens is as much my fault as it is hers."

"So," Tish said, rubbing her finger on the smooth leather housing Bubba and feeling his reassuring hum, "that means the king will be really grateful when I zap it out of existence in the morning. Maybe he'll give me a prince for doing the deed. Then I can..."

His hand was on her shoulder. His voice filled with real concern. "You can't fight the spell. It has already destroyed three Godmothers, each of whom was far stronger in their magic that you. Tish, you can't. I refuse to let you risk yourself..."

It was a gratifying response, but Tish couldn't allow herself to fall into the love-trap her body was trying to set. "It's out there. We're in here. We have to go out. I have to zap it so we can."

"But..."

"No buts." She said, not caring if she sounded surly. He was too damned close and she didn't even like him, did she? But, more than that, she didn't want to explore her feelings, wasn't ready to feel. It was probably just the idea of facing the ravening spell that was turning on her procreative urges. That's what they said, wasn't it? They being the folks who studied such things. That fear and danger heightened all the senses, made people do things in the moment. Well, as far as she could tell, she wasn't a bit afraid.

Bubba and the sawed-off wand were all the weapons she needed, and she could outfox any old spell in Faery; no matter how many other

Godmothers had turned up their heels, turned in their wands, did whatever dead Godmothers did. She knew that. Knew it with a surety that was almost frightening in and of itself.

"Leticia," he said softly, "please..."

"Go to sleep," she said, turning over with what could best be described as a flounce. "This is my Faery tale, my Wish-Quest, even if the bards do tell it later as the highly romantic story of how Cin and Rue got their happy-ever-afters. And I am going to do what I know is right."

"You can't undo another person's magic spell. It's a rule in Faery." His hand was on her waist, his breath warm on the back of her neck.

Heat was building within her, and it made her furious. "I'm not from Faery," she said through gritted teeth, "and the damned Sanction is giving me no choice in this. Now, get your hands off me, turn over, and go to sleep."

"Yes, Godmother," he said, sounding neither disappointed nor glad. And when he did exactly what she had ordered, Tish felt a small cold chill of loss. And a slightly larger one of disappointment.

It was a very long time before she went to sleep, and only an hour or so before she woke to the dawn. It was a waking she would have preferred otherwise, but taking a deep breath, Tish, in the full grip of the Sanction, got up. She noted, without comment, that Marcus, his back ramrod stiff, his narrow nose held high, was standing before the fireplace. Only his disordered hair and shadowed eyes gave any hint of his own inner turmoil.

Having been raised tidy, Tish consigned the magicked blankets and pillows back into the never-never from whence they had come. Then, feeling like she was readying herself for a shootout on Main Street at high noon, she swirled her cloak around her, freeing her wand hand and the snarling spitting wand, touched Bubba's leather bottle for luck, and headed for the door. All without a word to the silently watching man and without a look to see if he was going to be her backup when she braved the day and met the ravening spell face to face.

Throat dry, heart pounding, fear and the Sanction twisting inside her stomach like a convention of mentally disturbed snakes, Tish still had enough sense leftover to know Marcus was directly behind her, sword in hand, and death in his eyes.

What happened next was totally anti-climactic. If she had been watching it in a movie, she would have booed and hissed at the top of her voice. And even if it did mean that she would live to fight another day, Tish couldn't help feeling that it could have been just a little more dramatic.

A short second of ravening spell meets wand fire, spell dies, didn't quite meet the full hero requirements. Especially since the spell just coughed once, a tired, pitiful, little sound, and turned to nothing. Absolute nothing. Leaving her with her wand hanging out and her mouth open. And safe from the soul-eating evil of the spell.

"Now what?" she asked, not entirely sure she had come out the victor. "I mean, Marcus, is that all there is?" She turned to face him.

Dry-mouthed, wanting to jump ahead of her, protect her from the spell at the cost of his own life if needs be, Marcus saw the blackness of the spell and the golden light that was Tish, or maybe her wand, clash, flare high, and then he saw her kill the spell. Her bravery in the face of the unknown and unknowable humbled him. There could never be another woman in Faery like her. Love, with all its many and unfathomable permutations almost overwhelmed him, made him unsteady.

He went down on one knee, bent his head in homage, to the woman, and said, "Godmother, I ask you pardon for my disbelief."

Instantly angry, but unsure why, Tish glared at him, turned on her best fishwifery, and fairly screamed, "Get up, damn it. Don't you ever go down on your knees to me again unless you are proposing marriage." And then, catching the import of her words, Tish blushed hotly. But she didn't stop scowling and she didn't look away, not even when she saw the twitch that tugged at the corner of his firm lips when he said, "I give you my sworn word, Godmother, that I will do exactly as you ask."

"Good," she answered as he got to his feet, with more grace than any one man should possess. "Now, is the spell really gone? Can we go on with the Cinderella story?"

The forest and wind answered before he could. The giant, brooding trees were, right before her eyes, donning a brilliant coat of green, new green. Leaves unfurling like tiny flags were joined, here and there, by blossoms, white, pink, yellow, and any number of changes in between. The breeze, warm with the breath of coming summer, carried the fragrances and the sound of birds and bees and forest animals. Even the squeak of mice—not one of Tish's favorite sounds, but she was too disconcerted at the moment to pay them overmuch heed.

"The king will...you have done this kingdom a great service, Godmother. It will long be in your debt for the return of summer and hope," Marcus said, smiling down at her. Then, he stopped smiling and looked, for all of Faery, like a man who had just be struck by a heavy thought, one that had all the voltage of a lightning bolt.

"What now?"

"The impending war. This will only make it more possible. A kingdom filled with summer is a lot more valuable than one in the grips of a ravening spell. I...Godmother, by your leave, I really must go see the king and inform him of what..."

"Sounds like a winner to me," Tish murmured, "but only if you ask him if I can have a Prince Charming as a reward for my good deed. Oh, and you'd better get me someplace where I can check out Cin and see what needs to be done in that department."

"You could go with me to..."

"No," Tish said, trying to squirm away from the pinch and bite of the Sanction, "I can't do that. I'm sick of being pummeled and twisted by that idiot Sanction. I want to get this show on the road. Snap to, Marcus, we've got a wedding to plan."

She thought she heard him say, "Too bad it isn't our own," but decided the twittering birds, buzzing bees, and fecundity of the forest had infected her with its reproductive drive and was making her indulge in what could only be called, irony of ironies for a Godmother, wishful hearing.

Summer was in full force by the time Marcus, leading both of their Godmother rent-a-horse horses—one he intended to ride, the other to hide—left her on the side of a small, wooded hill. Her present abode, safe house, what-have-you, was a barn. Not a large one, with a lightning rod and weathervane on the roof, but a barn nevertheless, with hay and a small pen for a goat or a sheep or some other small beast, a loft with more hay to serve as a bed, and log walls to keep her movements away from prying eyes. And best of all, it overlooked the manor house belonging to Cinderella and the Uglies and was only a hundred feet or so from a small stream, complete with a bathing pool.

Their plans were all made, hashed and rehashed, and there was nothing left to do but the doing. The plan bore a close resemblance to the Cinderella stories of Tish's youth, with a few minor embellishments to make allowances for lust and war and ugly spells and unforeseen circumstances.

Giving her a small salute, saying, "I'll be back in three days at the most. Take care," Marcus tugged on the reins and started on his journey to see his king. Before he had taken more than a step or two, Tish asked, "What about the Uglies' mother is she still around?"

"Yes. Evidently she loved the baron because she grieved his loss for years and rarely goes to court anymore, but she is still here. And, I should warn you, she firmly believes Cinderella is totally to blame for what happened to Quincy and Sage. And possibly for what happened to the baron also because she doesn't know the true story of his perfidy. If the house and the land weren't Cinderella's sole property, I'm sure the girl would have long since joined the Beggars' Guild."

Tish wanted to question him about that, and several more areas, but the Sanction had more pressing, and tweaking and pinching, ideas, so she stood there, watching him go, and wondering just how she was going to turn a fat, dirty girl into a sex queen, a love-object no hot-blooded, lusting Prince Charming could possibly refuse. And not only do that, but do it before the Sanction decided to bring in the big guns and do her own body parts some very real harm. It wasn't even close to being possible, Tish knew that, but she had to try.

And, if Marcus did his share, it just might, and it was an awfully large might, be possible.

Chapter Eighteen

EVEN IF IT was early morning, and still yawning time for Tish, the sun was hot. Magicking up a glass of orange juice and a couple of pieces of buttered toast to fortify her for the day, she ate and drank without appreciation. Or without missing Marcus too much. Thinking, yearningly, of shorts and halter tops, maybe even a real skimpy bathing suit, Tish did the best she could given the givens and the task at hand.

After changing the material in her riding costume from wool to something that looked the same but was definitely air-conditioned, zapping up clean underwear, and changing her socks from wool to cotton, Tish had set out to inspect the merchandise. And now, as a direct result of her own unspelling, she was trapped, without a cloak of invisibility in sight. And she would have magicked one into instant being if she had any idea of what they looked like. She didn't even smile at that paradox.

The heat wave, or the advent of the long delayed summer, had provoked a house cleaning without peer among the inhabitants of the manor house. Servants, both male and female, were scurrying and running, draping newly washed clothing everywhere until every available shrub, lawn, and tree limb was festooned with drying bed clothes and people garments. Hangings, tapestries, and rugs were receiving vigorous beatings. Other servants were winching water up out of the well, carrying bucket after wooden bucket into the house itself until Tish could envision dirty water cascading from every wall and nook, taking away the soil accumulated during the years of witch-spelled winter.

It made her want to preen a little, to take mental credit for her share in bringing back the sun, but she had no time for such posturing. And besides that, there wasn't a good deal of room in her hiding place on the upper side of the swimming hole in the stream. The only place left for her to hide after several men had invaded her barn, showing the full extent of the wild cleaning spree, and began to tidy it up and dung it out. They even carried in several cart loads of new-mown meadow hay that promised Tish a sweet-smelling bed for her night's rest, providing she got to take one.

But that was beside the point and not actually one of Tish's current worries.

Accompanied by an old woman, a servant by the looks of her, carrying a padded chair, a basket of food, a collection of books, some blankets, and several other items Tish couldn't put a name to, Cinderella had escaped, or been forced to evacuate, the manor house, probably to evade those bug-eyed monsters of the cleaning ilk, and was currently making herself at home on the other side of the gurgling stream.

And, upon her first viewing of the soon-to-be heroine of the genuine Faery tale, Tish had a distinct sinking sensation in the general region of her stomach. It was followed by an attack of pessimism so strong that it might have sent her screaming into the forest, begging the spell to come back and the Sanction to return to its Godmotherly home. It was far from enjoyable, but both of her reactions reinforced her belief that the Council of Four, for some deep, dark, nefarious reasons of their own, had set her up, made her the cheese on their mousetrap, and it wasn't a terribly pleasant thought.

Especially when she remembered the beast-things and the dragons, both of whom seemingly intent on making a wall-hanging from her head and hide, but there was no time to indulge in vengeful ideas. That would come later, when this was over. That was presuming it would be. Which, as far as Tish could see, which was just to the other side of the water, made her far more presumptuous than present truths gave her the right to be.

Cin was miles from being a vision of delight and last in the running for Ms. Summer Centerfold of Faery. Even air brushing and a staple in her belly button wouldn't be enough to make her on the plus-side of presentable.

"Ravening spells are duck soup compared to this," Tish muttered. She crouched behind the screen of thorny, red-blossomed, sweet-smelling bushes, watching a fat Cinderella turn the page in what had to be, judging from its lurid cover, a really sexy novel, stuff another chocolate-covered something-or-other in her mouth, and sigh heavily. But only after she, in a coy, arch gesture, had tossed back her long, greasy, matted strands of smoke-colored hair. It came very near to matching the color of her face and ragged, old-fashioned garments.

Her legs cramping from crouching, her eyes beginning to water from the bright reflections of the afternoon sun on the bathing pool, Tish searched her mind, looking for some solution to the problem of Cin. Cin was truly a problem of some magnitude, or amplitude, or plenitude. Whatever the word, Cin was, judging by the standards of

Tish's world, over-endowed in the fat department and under-endowed in the clean, as a matter of fact, she was as grimy as a chimney-sweep or a coal miner.

Sweat, trickling down between her breast, set up a new itch, which Tish scratched absently as she alternately swore at the duplicity of the Godmothers, and vowed she would get even with them for setting her up as bait in a game she wasn't even playing. But most of all, she worried the problem of Cin. It was, beyond all doubt, a problem that was going to have to be cleaned up and muscled down if Tish was going to be able to go back and face the Godmothers. And it had to be well on its way toward done in two or three days; by the time Marcus came ambling back with the second prince in tow.

The whisper of wind died, leaving behind a cloud of hungry midges whose one mission in life was to feed on Tish's sweaty face and drive her to distraction. She looked, with great longing, at the pool of water, willing Cinderella, and the silent old woman, to make tracks back to the manor house and leave the bathing facilities to someone who might not need them as much but would appreciate them a good deal more.

But Cin, hunched forward now and turning pages a little faster, wasn't about to leave her hiding place, not while there was still candy in the large basket of goodies and loins-throbbing pages to be read in the book. That fact didn't improve Tish's disposition one iota.

Neither did it give her any new ideas, except one: aversion therapy, or at least, her own version of it. And she started first by zapping the chocolate, turning them into bitterness beyond endurance. Then she blanked all the rest of the pages in the novel. One that looked suspicious like it could have come from any book rack in any supermarket in the U.S.A.

And then she waited, and scratched, and sweated some more. She needed to get Cin alone and the only way that seemed possible was to zap her into doing a little sleep walking. And talking. Never having learned the fine art of considering things from all angles, Tish waved her sawed-off wand and muttered, "See you later, Cin baby, when the good folk, like your nurse or maid or whatever she is, are sound asleep and the night invites you out and about. Come and see me, we need to talk."

The wand sputtered slightly and was still, giving Tish the distinct impression that small magic was rapidly becoming beneath its dignity; it had, after all, vanquished a very evil spell.

"Don't believe all your publicity," Tish said, unsure whether she talking to herself or the wand, and louder than she intended, loud enough that the nurse raised her head and peered hard, and nearsightedly, in Tish's direction before she offered Cin another fat candy from the basket.

Cinderella's gobbling turned, rapidly enough to give Tish a tad of sweet satisfaction, into a scramble to rid herself of the bitterness that filled her mouth. She spat, gagged, and bestirred herself enough to crawl to the edge of the water and repeatedly rinse the taste from her teeth and tongue. And her distress was even greater when she discovered her trashy novel had turned snow white, or, more accurately, paper white, right in the middle of a lusty scene of hot hands and searching lips and secret places.

Rubbing away the cramp that was trying to knot up her left calf, Tish grinned at Cinderella's yelp of outrage. "Serves you right," she said, making sure she wasn't overheard this time. "If you want a prince, Cinny, you'd better get up and get to doing—because, dear lady, we have a lot of work to do."

"Ellllllleeeee! Ellllllleeeeeee!"

"Up here. In the bower," Cinderella called, and her voice held more vigor and beauty than Tish had expected. And those two things gave her reason to hope that maybe, just barely maybe, she could pull this wish off, get Cin married to Rue, and give the Uglies a fighting chance to snatch their own happiness.

Sounding breathless, and looking hotter than a desert sun, one of the Uglies, still dressed from head to toe in black, came to where Cin and her companion were sitting in the shade. "Mother is looking for you," the Ugly said, "an invitation just came from the king. Young Prince Rupert is looking for a bride to wed and bed before the border war erupts and the king has commanded all the young ladies in the kingdom to present themselves at a ball to be held in three days."

Her ears straining to hear every word, Tish listened intently, but her interior monologue was blistering enumeration of Marcus's idiocy. How could he have allowed the king to set the ball in three days. Three days! That wasn't even enough time to... Tish sighed heavily, promised herself she was going to scalp him at the first opportunity, and listened harder. There had to be a plan in there somewhere, if she didn't panic. It was an enormous if.

"They can do that without us, can't they?" Cin asked, her lovely voice holding a wistful, yearning undertone.

"It's a royal command, Elly. We have to go. Mother would never disobey. The queen is one of her dearest friends."

"And you and Sage, are you going?" Again the note of yearning.

"Of course, and so are you."

"Me? Look at me? I can't... I can't... Your mother will be more than happy for me to stay home. All I do is embarrass her anyway."

"She actually has no reason to be proud of you; not after what you've done to the family. But if you honestly don't want to go, I'm sure Mother can think of a suitable excuse for your absence. Everyone knows you wouldn't, by any stretch of the imagination, make a suitable bride for Prince Rupert, so there's really no need for you to present yourself to court. Is there, Cinderella?" There was a wealth of scorn in the woman's overdone sweetness, and it was built on a firm foundation of pure hate. That much was obvious to even a casual observer; and Tish was far from that.

Cin jumped to her feet and ran for the manor house, moving faster than anyone could have even guessed. Thus making Tish sure that the girl wasn't quite in the sorry shape she seemed, that maybe with some judicious magic liposuction and a heavy dermabrasion and a complete hair make-over that she would fit into the acceptable category; after a scrubbing with lye soap and a wire brush.

"Ya should no be hurting the lass. 'Twern't her doing that made ya mirror-breaking. 'Twas the master himself that did the deed, putting herself aside like that. But, ya'll no be seeing the baron for his lying and hurting innocent folk. 'Tis always the lass that carries the burden, and she be without the doing at her door. Can ya be blaming her for the eating and the hiding and the dreaming? What else do her be having? There be no ball gown in her closet."

"Mother has warned you, old woman. If you don't stop this lying, then you will have to be sent back to your home village. She will not allow you to cast slurs and aspersions..."

"Slurs and aspersions, be it? Then, why be my innocent lamb wearing rags while ya, yer sister, and yer fine lady mother do be dressed in silk?"

"Good question," Tish murmured, "let's hear the answer."

Quincy, not moving too fast in her black silk, but fast enough to make sure her audience was fully aware that she was leaving in a huff, drew herself up to her full height, lifted her veiled head high, and turned gracefully and marched back down the hill. All in icy, unrelieved silence.

It was an impressive expression of ire, but the old woman wasn't even slightly intimidated. "Phhht," she said, making some sort of gesture toward the vanishing back; Tish guessed she didn't want to know what the gesture meant. "Yer lady mother do be knowing the way of it. Cinderella do be wearing them castoffs from the attics causing she do be too big for aught else, And that be the truth of it, betimes like, she ain't being no bigger than them fine ladies from the court. Why the queen herself, bless her, be a fine size for a woman growed." The old woman talked as she picked up Cinderella's scattered leavings and headed back toward the manor house and her nursling.

Mulling over what she had learned, and swearing at every twinge and ache in her cramped body, Tish straightened up and, moving with great caution, made her way to the barn. She watched from a fringe of trees as the peasants, or serfs, or whatever they were, finished the cleaning, shouldered their rakes, and departed for their own dinners. At least, if her own growling stomach was a proper judge, that seemed to be the logical place for them to be going. It was where she was going, and after that, after the folks in the house were snug abed, she was going to strip off to the buff, zap up some yummy-smelling soap and a fluffy towel, and take a bath while Bubba enjoyed a nice long swim.

She was exhausted, wrinkled as a prune, but clean, when she told the cavorting sprite, "No more for now, Bubba," and crawled out of the water for her date with Cin. Remembering, just in time, to dress Godmotherish, in hoops, panels, ribbons, and lace, she gave the wand some special effects, made sparks fountain up and out, like a sparkler on the Fourth of July. And, not wanting to detract from the illusion of magical power, she gave herself a faint golden glow, a splash of rose-scented perfume, and stood in the bright starlight, watching Cin, her full nightgown billowing out around her, make her slow way up the path.

The girl, no cleaner now than she had been during the day, looked at Tish, opened her eyes wide, fell down on both knees, clasped her hands at her breast, bowed her head, and sort of whispered, "A Godmother? Oh, no. I...I...don't know what to say. I thought you weren't... Oh, Godmother, have you come here to make my dream come true?" She lifted her head, tried to look behind Tish and asked, shyly, "You didn't bring him with you, did you? I mean you wouldn't let him see me like..." Her questions were lost in a wail of despair.

It was so loud that Tish tapped her with the sparking wand a little harder than was strictly necessary. But all they time, she was wondering how she was going to take away some of Cinderella's hurt and make her into a suitable bride for a future king.

With a wry grin, safely hidden by the starlight, she could almost hear her mother say, "Leticia, you have gotten yourself into this mess, now use your head to get yourself out. And, remember, always start at the beginning."

It didn't make any more sense now that it did the hundred or so times her mother had said it in the past, but just thinking of the nonsense advice made her feel a little more confident.

But, the first words she said, pitching her voice low, trying to sound Godmotherly, "So, my dear child, where exactly do you think we should begin?"

"I don't know!" The self-pitying wail was creeping back into the girl's voice. It irritated Tish no end. She took a step forward. Cin scuttled back on her hands and knees, tried to get to her feet, caught her toe in the hem of her nightgown, and screamed as the earth gave way beneath her and she rolled down the bank, catching at nonexistent branches to break her fall. None of it helped, not even getting to her feet, stumbling sideways, and flailing her arms like a dysfunctional windmill. She still fell, head first, into the star-glittered water, breaking the images of light into fragments as she went completely under.

And came up sputtering and trying to scream again as Bubba, seemingly eager for a new playmate, or acting on some agenda of his own, caught her in his watery arms and dunked her under again. And again. And again. Each spriteful dunk rinsing off a layer of soot and grime, but not enough to make any real difference in Cin's unwholesome appearance. But every little bit helped, and Cin was in no danger of drowning; even her whimpering cries had given away to an occasional giggle at Bubba's water antics.

But the bathing and the giggles were enough to give Tish the beginning of an idea. It involved Bubba and a whole bunch of imported shampoo, soap, conditioner, a scrub brush, scissors, deodorant, perfume, a bit of blush, and a full length mirror. But those only came into play after the girl had sweated a couple of hours on a treadmill. Magic might be doing the real weight-loss trick, but Tish wanted the girl to earn a little of what she was getting; or more likely what she was getting rid of. If it worked. If Bubba would do his part. If...

And three short days didn't given her time for very many ifs, especially if Marcus hadn't goofed up the rest of their plan and was bringing Prince Rue by for a tantalizing, lust-arousing glimpse of his virgin bride before the ball.

"Do you be real?" The harsh whisper came out of the shadows, and Tish almost jumped out of her hoops before she recognized the old woman huddled in close to a tree trunk, staring at her with wonder-filled eyes, the need to believe written on every wrinkle of her face.

"Have ya come to... Will the lass be getting her wish, Godmother?"

"Yes," Tish answered, not sure it was the truth, but not wanting to take away any of the old woman's obvious faith. Still she was totally disconcerted when the nurse fell to her knees and tried to kiss Tish's hand. She stepped back, said, "There's no time for that. I have work to do, and you need your sleep. Go back to your bed."

"I be willing to help, iffen it be yer grace's want," the woman said, getting to her feet with agonizing slowness and breathing hard from the effort.

Biting back a whined, self-pitying, "Nobody can help me," Tish tapped the wand against her hand and considered. Maybe the old woman could. She had to know more about the mores, customs, and dress of the kingdom than Tish did. Based only on the anxious looks she kept sneaking of Cin's ablutions, she did seem to love the girl.

"Ball gowns?" Tish finally said, speaking her thought aloud.

"I be no sempstress, yer grace, but I be knowing the style of such fripperies. The mistress be having one made right now. For the king's ball." She stopped, shuffled her feet, glanced at Cin again, and asked, her voice careful, her eyes looking only at the ground, "Ya'll no be sending the girl, be ya?"

"Yes!" Tish wanted to snap out the word, hustle the old woman, with her sad, judging eyes and fierce protectiveness, off to bed, after giving her a good shot of forget-you-saw-me, but she had a growing suspicion that the woman was going to be the only ally she had in this mess. And, after what Marcus had done to their carefully thought-out timetable, Tish was more than a little sure that she was going to need all the help she could get to fulfill the terms of the damned Wish-Quest.

"'Twill kill the poor lass."

"What?"

"All them fancy folk'll be laughing at her. She can no stand that and the whispering and pointy fingers. She dinna go to the Red Witch, but..."

"I know."

"Yer be knowing it all?" It was a whisper laden with despair.

"Yes, all of it. The truth about..."

Her hand trembling, the old woman caught at Tish's arm, and her rheumy eyes were wide with fear when she said, the words a bare tread of sound, "Godmother, ya'll know be telling the right of it to the girl?"

"No. There's no reason why she should know. But, I do need your help. I have to get her ready for the ball, and it's going to take some real doing. Cinderella is... She's going to require a lot of work, and I don't want the..." Tish licked her lips. "I don't want anyone to see what I've done to her until the ball. I want her to be the beautiful lady of mystery."

The old woman's cackle was full of glee. She released Tish's arm, clapped her hands together, and sort of crow hopped around on the grass. "Twill show'em rightly," she chortled. "The bitch and her whelps'll..."

"Nurse, is that..." Cinderella's call came from the pool, and she sounded as if she wasn't quite sure whether she still dreamed or had wakened to a slightly different reality. Tish didn't want her awake, what needed to be done had to seem like a dream until...

"Don't answer her," Tish said softly. "Go back to the house and go to bed. I'll make sure she returns safely. Just don't mention our meeting to her or anyone else."

The nurse dropped a stiff courtesy and said, "My word be yers, my lady Godmother." But she hesitated, started to say something else, before Tish took her by the elbow and led her, with gritted teeth and real gentleness back down the path that led to the silent manor house.

Tish's voice was very soft when she said, "I give you my word that Cinderella will not be shamed by her wishing. She might not get her prince, but she sure is going to get a remake, on a grand scale. Now, go to bed. You need your rest because I need you to bring me a ball gown tomorrow night. I need to see..."

"But you..."

"Nurse," Tish said sternly, if not entirely honestly, "I know my business and I must insist that you do as I ask."

"Yes, ma'am."

Tish waited, hidden in the shadows, until the old woman had entered the manor house and closed the door behind her. Then, sighing heavily, thinking furiously, and not paying too much attention to the night world around her, Tish walked back toward the swimming pool and its dirty girl and light-hearted sprite. She didn't have a clue as to the time, but it had to be late, really late, from the way she was feeling.

She was nearly there, just stepping out of the shelter of a small grove of aspen, when the long-fingered hand covered her mouth, a hard-muscled arm encircled her waist, and she was jerked backwards against a lean body. The quick motion made her huge hooped skirt bounce high in front, exposing her knee-length drawers to the warm summer night.

"Not a sound," a voice hissed in her ear.

There was no mistaking her captor. And Tish felt a rush of instant anger. How dare he treat her like...like a babe in some cheap made-for-TV thriller. She fought with him, tried to bite the hand that sealed her mouth, to bring up her wand and zap him into some sort of odious beast, or, at the very least, a pompous ass.

"Tish, please," he whispered. "Don't make any noise. We've got trouble, real trouble." He loosened his hold on her mouth, if only a fraction, and then, evidently thinking better of it, said, "Will you swear not to scream and..."

Grudgingly, she nodded and when his hand was a scant inch from her mouth, Tish said, keeping her voice low, "Damn you, Marcus, what in the name of Faery are you trying to pull? Just look at that girl. How in blazes do you expect me to make her presentable, let alone marriageable, in three days?"

"You'll have to do it a lot sooner than that," he said, not releasing his hold on her waist, still keeping her stiff body close to his. "We've got a real problem and it'll be here sooner than you expect."

Not averse to being in his arms, but wanting to see him face to face when she killed him for whatever new trouble he had brought crashing down on them, Tish pulled loose and turned to face him. "What is it? What have you done now?"

"I didn't. My...ah...my king acted all on his own on this one and you'd better be ready to do some fancy zapping if we're going to give this tale a happy ending."

He sounded as if he really meant it, but Tish was still suspicious. "Just what are you trying to tell me?"

"Although he doesn't know that's his destination, Rue is on his way to inspect his future bride, so Godmother you'd better come up with a plan and do it quick, like in the next couple of hours or so. Otherwise, the king might be exceedingly wroth."

"Why?"

"I told him you could work magic and that we could make this marriage a done deal."

"Done deal?" Tish sighed and shook her head. "Look at her, Marcus. You're going to owe me, and owe me big. This is going to take more than magic, it's going to take a top-of-the-line, first-class miracle."

He looked at Cinderella, gave a small whistle of agreement, and muttered something that sounded like, "I'm sorry, love," but probably wasn't.

Chapter Nineteen

"HOW LONG?" TISH asked, knowing full well that whatever Marcus's answer was, it wasn't going to be long enough, that the Heir-Apparent was going to get the shock of his life when he saw his fat, dirty Cinderella. And that the Sanction was going to have a wall-eyed, screaming, clawing fit.

"Dawn."

"I don't have a watch. And if I did, I still wouldn't know how time runs here. Marcus, just exactly how long have I got to..."

He put his hands on her shoulders. For one breathless moment, before sense triumphed over hormones, Tish thought he was going to draw her into a tender embrace. He didn't. Marcus just looked down at her and said, "You can do it."

"Easy for you to say. I don't know the first thing about changing people..."

"Of course you do. There's Carl. You certainly didn't have much trouble with..."

Tish was affronted. He was teasing her and, as far as she was concerned, this was neither the time nor the place for joking. "That was different, and you know it. Now, tell me honestly, how long before Rue shows his face?"

"Two hours at the most. I have to go meet him and..." His voice took on a seriousness that she had never heard before. "This accidental meeting between Cin and Rue is just incidental to our main goal, Tish. I'll try to detain him as long as possible, but our mission is very important. The enemy troops are said to be massing, in even greater numbers, at the border and we need to look them over. The king has mounted his own assault force, but..." His hands tightened on her shoulders, but only for an instant.

"Negotiations between the two kingdoms are at a very delicate point, and to be perfectly honest with you, the land that Cinderella inherited from her mother is a critical piece in the game. It commands the pass, and if it belongs to the king, or to his son through dower rights, then he can build hill forts on either side and hold his position until the end of time. There will be no war, but..."

"Why didn't he buy the land or something and build his forts there before? Besides, he's the king, isn't he, so why doesn't he just take the land. I thought that's what kings did when they want..."

Marcus sighed. "First of all, he is honest, a good king. He wouldn't do anything like that if there were other avenue available. And, as you may remember, until a very short time ago, the ravening spell held that part of the kingdom in an iron grip, leaving only the road through the pass free and indefensible. Now, that has all changed, so new plans must be made."

Tish understood, even if she didn't like the extra burden it placed on her shoulders. "So, what you're telling me is that a lot of people will die if we don't get Cin and Rue in bed and actively engaged in the consummation of the marriage, thus giving the defensible land into the keeping of the king? And do it quick?"

"Crudely put, but yes. And, to add a complication to our problem, Rupert has made a vow not to marry for any reason except true and lasting love. In Faery, it is a binding vow."

Muttering her finest scatological expletive, Tish took a deep breath and started questioning him about the standards of beauty in the kingdom. "What am I dealing with? Do I need to turn her into Barbie with working parts? Or is Rubens more the rage? Or is somewhere in between more appealing to male libido?"

After a quick, but fairly thorough visual examination of her own slender charms, he stood there without speaking.

"Damn it, Marcus, if I'm going to make this thing work, I have to know. What turns men on here?" He looked at her body again, blushed, and mumbled something almost unintelligible.

But Tish understood, blushed in turn, and said, "Forget it. We don't have time for a roll in the hay. Besides, you've been around me too much. It's propinquity that's turning you on."

And she hoped she was telling the truth, about him as well as herself. Because her on button had definitely been turned to hot and panting. Unfortunately, so had her Sanction button, and it was far more powerful, and painful, than loins-warming lust. "What's the verdict? Does Cin look busty and boyish or..."

Taking his hands from her shoulders, he made some fairly graphic gestures that encompassed a female form that looked vaguely familiar to Tish, like maybe one she had seen in pictures or paintings of another time. "You mean they look sort of like the Gibson Girls of my world's late 1800's?"

"I'm not sure, but..."

"Close enough," Tish said, deciding to just shut her eyes and jump in. After all, if she married Rue, then Cin would set the style, not be a slavish follower. "Go find the prince," she said. "I don't want you hanging around here, making obscene suggestions."

Even in the starlight she could see his eyebrow arching up, hear the familiar superiority in his deep voice when he asked, speeding up her pulse a little with the question, "And, just presuming I made a suggestion or two, perhaps verging on the exciting and erotic, would you be at all tempted?"

She knew she owed him an honest answer, but all she said was, "I expect, with all I've got to do, that I'd have to take a rain check on that, too. The only lust, and slacking of same, that I have time to worry about concerns Cin and Rue. And you'd better hie yourself hither, whatever that means, and let me get on with my Godmothering."

Taking her hand in his, Marcus bowed slightly and touched the back of her fingers with his warm lips. The tingles lasted for a very long time, echoing and re-echoing through her too willing body. They were terribly distracting, turning her thoughts to areas she would prefer to avoid.

He hadn't gone more than a step or two into the darker dark in the heart of the grove before he turned and said, sounding terribly sheepish, "Maybe, just to be on the safe side, you'd better conjure a mild love potion for Rue. I can add it to the waterskin he carries on his saddle and..."

Silently, but a little disappointed that he didn't trust her to pull off the lust part, she did as he asked, producing a tiny glass vial sealed with wax and dropping it into his outstretched palm.

"Godmother," he said, "be careful. If..." pausing he looked at her for a long moment before he said, "Whatever else happens, you should know: I did exactly as you asked. The king has granted you a boon of great magnitude and promised to give you his son for destroying the ravening spell."

His leap in subject was close to being a non sequiter, so much so that Tish shook her head, trying to reorder her wandering thoughts, before she said, "I don't understand what you mean. You already said Prince Rupert was on his way here."

His face was shadowed, but his voice was uninflected, as enigmatic as his words when he said, just before turning and striding away, "My...ah...my king does have other unwedded sons, Godmother."

Suspicion, raw and angry, made her say, "Damn it, Marcus, you haven't set me up with the oldest one, have you? The prince you said was damned?"

A musical chuckle, as maddening as the man, was Tish's only answer. "You're going to pay for this, too," she muttered, but there was no time to plan revenge, or to even wonder what he meant. It was Cinderella time, and poor Cin was blessed with a Godmother who was scared spitless. So scared that not even Bubba's watery song could reassure her that she was equal to the task at hand.

As far as the task itself went, it was definitely labor intensive.

Tish was disheveled, sweating like a hippo, and frazzled; as well as possessing an impressive mound of empty shampoo, conditioner, lotion, soap, moisturizer, and skin-cleanser containers. And dawn was fast approaching before she was willing to concede that she had, with Bubba's help, done all she could for one night.

Forty pounds lighter—a loss Cinderella dreamed of walking away pound by pound—and reasonably clean, the girl displayed an astonishing wealth of red-gold hair. It was silky-fine and had a tendency to curl. With the aid of some magicked rubber bands, Tish had managed to gather Cin's crowning glory into an untidy mass and fix it into a sort of trailing upsweep, with tendrils and tresses hanging down here and there in spiraling curls.

The sun was rosy in the east, at least, Tish thought it was the east, when Cinderella, attired in a delicate white lawn camisole, rich with tatting and ribbons, and knee-length drawers, returned to the warm water for a final dip. The girl, still a trifle grimy but looking more centerfoldish by the minute, was still sleepwalking, still dreaming an incredible dream, and smiling sweetly, when Tish heard a sound, a series of sounds. Stealthy sounds. Cautious footsteps. A branch snapping under an unwary foot.

"Not yet," Tish said, or maybe whimpered, as she dropped down, with her hoops popping behind her, until she wanded them into limpness. Hiding behind some bushes, she looked toward the pond and the very wet girl standing waist deep in water. It was a picture to please any romantic's heart, but Tish, egged on by the Sanction, added a few touches of her own.

To the water, already tinted pink by the rising sun, she magicked on some trails and billows of mist, also pink and looking, just a bit, like whipped cream and almost as luscious as the girl poised, like a shy, timid fawn, in their midst. Her undergarment was water-transparent and plastered against her beguiling curves, showing rather more than it should, but guaranteed to make even an oath-bound prince indulge in a few lusting fantasies and some heavy breathing. Or so Tish hoped.

She wasn't sure if what she hoped had transpired even after the deed was done, even after the prince, his dark hair in disarray, his thin face sweaty with his efforts, looked through an open spot in the screen of trees, flowering bushes, and tall grasses that protected the pond. Day was approaching rapidly, but he was still in the shadow, and what Tish thought she saw, the look of mingled wonder and shame, could have been a trick of the light.

He stepped back, turned abruptly, and was gone after that single look at the girl who might be his bride. A girl who still needed a good deal of scrubbing and conditioning before she would be ready to attend a ball, but who, flattered by the pinkish half-light, certainly wasn't ready for fright night.

Absolutely sure, from her brief glimpse of the man, that Prince Rupert had his inspection, Tish was more than ready to call it a night, or a day. She magicked a glamour around Cin, making her appear to still be her old fat and dirty self, and sent the girl back to the manor house. Leaving Bubba in the stream, to sleep the sleep of the just and to get some well-deserved rest from his arduous labor of cleaning and re-cleaning Cinderella, Tish got rid of the empty bottles and jars. She zapped away her own wet and bedraggled Godmother garb, and welcomed her riding habit onto her weary body before she made her slow way to the barn and climbed the ladder to the loft.

Luxuriating in the odor of new-mown hay, the softness of the thick mat of grass beneath her magicked quilt, Tish closed her eyes. She was hovering on the outer limits of sleep, or possibly had drifted into that marvelous state, when a hand fastened on her arm, shook her, and an urgent voice whispered, "Tish! Tish! Wake up! Where's Prince Rupert? What have you done with him?"

"Huh?" Bleary-eyes, heavy-headed, Tish peered up at him, saw only a fuzzy outline, a silhouette of a man surrounded by mote-filled light. "Marcus?" she asked, trying to fight her way out of the all-enveloping arms of sleep. "What are you doing here? Where's the prince?"

"I asked you first," Marcus said. "I haven't seen him, have you?"

She sat up, rubbed the heels of her hands into her heavy-lidded eyes, yawned widely, muttered, "Sorry," before she answered his question. "I saw him. He was across the pond and... He acted like he was really embarrassed after he saw Cin in the water."

"By the First," Marcus swore, adding a few choice words from Tish's world to give his language some spice, "I have to find him." He started toward the ladder before he paused long enough to ask, "Was she still fat and... Had you had time to work some magic before he..."

Marcus sounded so horrified that Tish was sorely tempted to tell him Cin was still in her natural state when Rue did his peeping-tom act, but instead, telling herself she was just too tired to do otherwise, she said, "It'll take all the time we have before the ball to get her into fighting shape, but he saw her just at dawn. Her clothes were wet and sticking to her bod. I did have enough time to reshape her shape. Even if she is a tad on the voluptuous side, she's still fine."

"Thank you, Godmother," Marcus said, making it sound more like rote manners than any sort of gratitude. "I will see you the evening of the ball."

"You'd better bring a carriage and some horses, and whatever else she needs to make a grand entrance, with you."

"Why?"

"Cin is going to need a ride. I'm not going to let her go with the Uglies, and I'm damned sure not going to turn any mice into coachmen and rats into horses, or whatever it's supposed to be. I hate 'em."

"I don't know what you're talking about, Leticia, but if you want a carriage for Cin, I'll be happy to fulfill your need even if I have to steal one." With that he was down the ladder and gone.

Tish didn't have any time to waste being lonely, she went to sleep almost before her head was back on the bed. It was a sleep plagued by nightmares. She slept, tossing and turning, fighting dragons and running from beasts, through the summer day. She woke up soaked with sweat, a vile taste in her mouth, and in even a viler mood. It had been a hellish night and an enervating day, and the coming night wasn't coming with a host of shining recommendations either.

Every muscle in her body was sore, her head ached, and she was hungry more for the sounds and smells of home than for any more magical food. Beyond that she was sick and tired of the eternal demands of the Sanction. And, although she hated like the very devil to admit it, even to herself, she missed Marcus, was more than a little in love with him. Or maybe she just wanted to somebody to fight with, somebody who knew who and what she was, and still felt free to make, or he meant them or not, suggestive overtures. Or maybe that was seductive suggestions.

Not that it mattered. As soon as Cin and Rue had said their vows, Tish was going to be in the Godmothers' faces, telling them just exactly what she thought of them, and making a few demands of her own. And, if what she had reasoned out was true, every single one of her demands was going to be met with more than smiling faces and alacrity. She was going home, ruby slippers or no.

The very thought of going home, seeing her mother, the Steps, and Jilly made Tish's throat ache, but when she thought of leaving Bubba, and Marcus, behind, it hurt more. So she refused to think about it, pulling what she ruefully called her Scarlett O'Hara act, and knowing that refusing to face facts wasn't going to get her anywhere. The facts would stay there whether she faced them or not.

Not that staying in bed was a better solution either. Sooner or later, she had to get up, zap something to eat, and put on her detested Godmother garb; but only after it had been cleaned and re-frilled. Even if it seemed like only a dream, Cin, with her still grubby complexion and unstyled hair, was waiting for another adventure-filled night of scrubbing and exercise. The nurse was going to produce the ball gown for Tish's inspection. Tish, in her spare moments, was going to have to come up with full ball regalia, with the necessary underwear, jewels, ribbons, and, as far as Tish knew, fans, slippers, and reticules. Then, too, the Uglies, who had bought and paid for this silly quest, were probably lurking around, expecting her to show up with a computer printout detailing her progress in the Cin-wish department.

Catching hold of the errant thought and following it in a new direct, Tish crawled out of her bed, shook wrinkles out of her riding habit, and wondered, briefly and with no real interest, what had happened to the price list the Council of Four had given her along with the credit card. And remembered that it had long since vanished, but she couldn't remember which one of her water encounters had done the list in.

It was just a mental distraction, one that kept her mind, if only briefly, off her newest worry. One that had to do with Marcus, Prince Rupert, and the impending war. If they were lanced, or arrowed, or maced before the ball, what would she do then? Or rather what would the damned Sanction do? Probably a lot more than pinching her arms and legs black and blue and twisting her innards into painful knots. Just like it was doing at the moment, and would continue to do until she had done what had to be done.

Her hair was frowsy, matted with hay and sweat, her body smelled only slightly worse than an old gym sock, and it wasn't yet dark enough for her to venture outside the barn and grab a quick swim. Tish climbed down the ladder, zapped up a big cup of strong coffee, and was considering taking the risk when she heard voices outside the barn. Women's voices. Familiar, petulant, whining voices.

Tish took a quick sip of coffee, swore softly when it burned her mouth, and crept to the wall of the barn, trying to hear what Quincy and Sage, her employers, were talking about now. "Me, probably," she murmured into the coffee cup as she took another, smaller sip.

And she wasn't wrong.

"Oh, Quincy, where can she be?" Sage asked. "We've looked everywhere. The cottage burned and...and all those peasants talking about dragons fighting in the night sky."

Quincy sounded a little less hysterical. "The peasants? Sage, how can you possibly listen to talk like that. They're all credulous fools. The stupid Godmother is around somewhere, and we both know it. The page that brought the message to mother from the queen told me the ravening spell had been destroyed by a young woman, a foreigner of some kind, and the king had given her the bastard prince for a husband, at her request. Of course, that's all nonsense, it has to be nothing more than the court gossip of a pack of idiots. But, then again, I don't know what to think. It is summer again and... And, Sage, the Red Witch's evil spell is completely gone, and everyone knows that for a fact."

There was a long pause before Sage asked, her voice dropping down to a hard-to-hear whisper, "You think that woman was the Godmother? You don't think she's dead? That she burned up in the cottage?"

"I don't know what to think. It's common knowledge that Godmothers don't get married, so why would she ask for the prince as a boon? Every one of the tales about them say Godmothers don't die either, so I guess she's alive somewhere. And it's said that they always grant the wishes they've been paid for, so I guess we just have to wait and see."

Two black shadows, they paced across the open doorway, pausing momentarily at the other side before they turned and made their way back, still talking, still wanting their long ordeal to be over.

Not dressed for receiving visitors, and not in the mood for it either, Tish took another drink of the cooling coffee, and listened, hoping she thought, with a wry grimace, that she would hear some more about this so-called husband the king had promised her. And vowing, internally, to make Marcus pay for whatever it was he had done. Because, as far as she could tell, if it was meant as a joke, it was a pretty weak effort. And, besides that, it wasn't particularly amusing.

"We'll see what's funny when I get my wand on him!" she muttered before she drained the cup and zapped a refill. The way things were shaping up, it was going to take more than a single cup of coffee to see her through the night.

"The ball is tomorrow night, Quince, and after that, I don't see how even a Godmother can help us. Prince Rupert will be going off to war. And, if the king has his way, will probably married to some simpering little chit before he goes. Elly will still be fat and dirty."

"And what about us?" It was a hopeless cry.

"We'll still be ugly," Quincy said flatly, "a lot poorer, and probably not much wiser. Oh, Sage, how could we have been so stupid as to actually believe that Faery Godmothers..."

"Don't cry, sister. Oh, please don't cry. We still have a little time. Maybe it's not too late."

"Maybe." The sorrowing sound seemed to hang in the evening air as the two black-veiled women, shoulders drooping, heads bowed, made their slow way back to the manor house where their mother and dirty stepsister waited.

Tish didn't have time to watch them go; or perhaps she had the time, but certainly not the inclination. One fact, gleaned from the sisters' conversation, as filled with Godmother misinformation as it was, buzzed around inside her head, dive bombed every other thought, and added to Tish's agitation. "Tomorrow," she said, not even knowing she was speaking aloud. "The ball is tomorrow. But, they said... Three days until... Tomorrow? It can't be. Yesterday was one. Today is two. Tomorrow is... Oh, god, it can't be."

She drained the coffee cup, pitched it into the magic world of never-was, and tried to prioritize her chores, while she castigated herself for being seven kinds of idiot and feckless to boot.

"Cin first," she muttered, stalking the length of the barn and back, trying to wish the growing twilight into full black night, needing to be able to get out and about without being seen. "And then the dress. Or, dress first and... Bubba will help. He loves bubbles. I'll just import a ton and... I can make it work. I'll have to."

Ten hours later, hours that were backbreaking, shoulder-hurting, and longer than they had any right to be, Tish was a whole lot tireder and miles less confident. She had done everything humanly, and Godmotherly, possible, but she had a very strong feeling it wasn't going to come anyplace close enough to being enough.

Under her dirty, fat glamour, Cin was a smooth, peaches-and-cream, comparatively slender, if still on the tiny-waisted, busty-hippy side. She was a young woman with shining, red-gold hair that most women would have given their Gold Visa cards to have as their own, but the dress was only partially complete.

Tish hadn't spent several years designing and making Bubba Bear clothes for nothing, so Tish was fairly sure she could make the gown the standout of the evening. Be that as it may, Tish had no idea in the world, or in Faery for that matter, about how to go about conjuring up glass slippers that wouldn't cut Cin's feet to ribbons or shatter when they hit an obstacle.

And she knew there was a way, if she wasn't so tired that her brain was sand in an hourglass, spilling endlessly, then she knew she could remember something about glass. Something the Council of Four had said, something less than important to them, but really important to Tish at the moment.

And it wasn't until the beautiful gown was complete, right down to the last seed pearl and gossamer ruffle dusted with diamond dust, until Tish took a long afternoon nap, until she heard the clop of horses' hooves as the carriage was brought around to take the baroness and her twin-crow daughters that Tish remembered.

"Enduro-glass," she said, giving the wand a shake, "but make it softer, like that clear plastic they make shoes out of at home. And put some sparkles on them, lots of sparkles."

Pleased beyond the scope of the deed, Tish was holding the incredibly beautiful, totally unique slippers in her hands, smiling, tilting them this way and that, admiring them from every angle, when the nurse came into the barn.

"Milady," she called softly, "be ya here. The rest of them be gone and my poor lamb be sitting by the fireplace, poking at the ashes, and crying like one of the lost. Will ya be coming now?"

"You got that right," Tish answered. "Now, catch this stuff as I throw it down." She pitched down an abundance of lace-bedecked petticoats, drawers, fine white stockings, a camisole of great beauty, a corset, a corset cover, and a cloth bag containing combs and hair ornaments. But, trusting no one with the spelled shoes and the left one's need to drop free of Cin's foot at the stroke of midnight and the gown, she ferried them down the ladder herself.

And the only question she asked when she got to the bottom was, "Has Cinderella's coach arrived yet?"

The old nurse's, "No, milady," sent new worry to coil, like cold, overcooked spaghetti, in Tish's empty stomach. Marcus was supposed to be here. Where, in the name of Faery, was he? Had something terrible happened? Was the war...

Squashing her frightened thoughts with a firm hand, Tish, in full Godmother dress, walked to the manor house. Cinderella was going to be at that damned ball if Tish had to carry her there on her own back.

Or, horror of horrors, turn some furry little mice into horses to pull a pumpkin. Even the thought made her shudder with distaste.

Chapter Twenty

CINDERELLA'S COACH, A fantasy in glass, gilt, and pink satin, traveling behind six, prancing, white horses, who were chiming musically, from the hundreds of tiny glass bells sewn to their gilded harness, at every toss of their plumed heads, rolled into the courtyard just before Tish and the old nurse reached the front steps of the manor. It was driven by a handsome, white-liveried coachman, with two tall footmen up behind, and would have been at home in any royal parade in England. Indeed, it was a coach fit for a queen. But it arrived sans Marcus.

There were no servants in sight, which was as it was supposed to be, or was it? Tish frowned as she tried to remember what the nurse had told her sometime in the big middle of the busy night before. She thought it was something about clearing the way, sending all the servants off to a ball of their own so that the Godmother could work her magic uninterrupted. It was a gesture of trust that she really appreciated, but she didn't have the time, then or now, to express her gratitude.

For some reason, perhaps because she heard the sound of horses, Cinderella opened the front door and stood there, mouth open. She stared first at the empty coach, then at her old nurse and Tish, who was resplendent in lavender and green, diamonds and emeralds, and assorted laces, dangles, ribbons, and other frou-frou, and looking like the penultimate Godmother.

The girl's mouth worked. A tiny squeak of sound finally made its way out as she made a deep curtsy and asked, "Is it really you, Godmother?"

Determined to keep up her facade, if only for the sake of the girl, Tish, encumbered by the dress and slippers, bowed her head, but only slightly. She said, "My dear child, I have come to grant your wish. You are going to the ball to meet Prince Rupert. However, I must warn you, as with all things magical, there are certain conditions you must meet."

"Oh, Godmother, I have dreamed of... Anything. I'll do anything you ask. I swear it." The girl clasped her hands together at her breast and her brown eyes were bright enough to light a night sky's prodigal sweep of stars.

"So be it," Tish said, with a gentle smile. "Now, time runs rather quickly. So, it's into the house with you. Your good nurse and I will act as your tiring women, and when we are done your beauty will outshine that of all the other women at the ball."

"Oh." It was a sigh of pure delight. Cinderella dropped another graceful curtsy before she turned, still caught in a dream-come-true daze of happiness, and went, cloaked in her fat and dirty glamour, back into dark interior of the manor house. The nurse followed, but Tish was halted by a soft-voiced calling of her name which seemed to come from the far side of the house. It was Marcus, she knew that but she couldn't see him until he stepped around an incredible topiary hedge and waited there, still partially screened from other eyes, for her to come to him.

"Well?"

"As you requested, my lady Godmother," he said, with a wave toward the magnificent equipage. "I'm sorry if I caused you any undo concern, but I didn't come with the coach because I don't want Cinderella to see me. She might recognize me and...well, it's better if she does not, but, perhaps you should...ah...hurry the girl along. The rightful owner of the coach-and-six might be a bit testy when he finds them gone. That particular moment is one I would prefer not to face."

The idea of Marcus, the sophisticated epitome of aristocracy, being a horse thief was ludicrous, but Tish didn't even smile. Her mind was occupied with, if not more serious, than more important things—even if they were only important to one romantic girl.

"I know you turned horse thief for me, Marcus, but this once, I'm afraid you'll have to take care of your own elegant hide. I won't hurry Cin through either the robing or the anticipation."

"Why? You have the wand, all you have to do is wave it and Cin will be gowned and tressed and on her way."

Tish could exactly explain her feelings, but she tried. "That's the way it's done in my fairy tale, but it was obviously written by a man, because it certainly isn't right or proper. It's more like being sold at a meat market than having all your wishes come true."

"Godmother, once again you have managed to confound me. I haven't a clue as to your meaning."

She thought he was peering down his aristocratic nose again, but he wasn't. He was looking truly puzzled, and Tish wasn't at all sure he could ever understand, but she tried again. "For whatever reasons, Cin has been fat and dirty for a long time, Marcus, and the only thing that kept her going was a dream; and a not very realistic one at that. It's pretty obvious that her stepmother isn't at all fond of Cin. The Uglies blame her for what has happened to them. She hasn't had the happiest life and..."

His next comment surprised her. "And you want to give Cinderella a night to remember?"

Thankful that he understood, Tish went on, "Something like that, but... Well, I remember watching my beautiful stepsisters getting ready for proms and things and... We laughed and talked and admired them and..."

Caught up in her own memories, Tish tried to smile at him, but her voice had a faint tremor when she said, without feeling the slightest bit silly, "Marcus, it's important that Cinderella have the whole thing, from dressing to dropping her slipper. I don't want her to miss a moment of tonight, because after a day or so, she'll be a married princess and then whatever she does won't be for her alone. It will be for the kingdom. And, from where I stand, up until now, Cin hasn't had much of anything to call her own, has she?"

"No, I imagine that is very true. Take your time; I'll face the posse on my own." Marcus leaned forward, brushed Tish's forehead with his lips, and said, very softly, "Godmother Leticia, your beauty is beyond the scope of my experience. And now, I must salute your wisdom and your compassion."

It was an opportune moment to throw in a smart remark, but Tish could only find a hot blush and a stammered, "Thank you," before she whirled, and hoopskirts swaying, practically ran up the front steps of the house and into the drawing room. Nurse had evidently decided to turn it into a dressing room for the night.

The room, looking very much like a Seventeenth Century English drawing room, or so Tish guessed. It had an abundance of settees, wing chairs, tiny tables, and assorted ornaments. But, there was no time to give it more than a cursory inspection, especially since it was just there, and sort of too-clean and blah, and not an actual part of the Cinderella's story, or Tish's Wish-Quest.

Carefully placing the incredible gown and the slippers on a red plush settee, Tish waved her wand, removed Cin's glamour, and got right to work because Marcus was right, there wasn't much time to prepare Cin for her grand entrance into the palace ballroom.

It was, possibly, her last coherent thought. From that point on, Tish's impressions ran together, shifted, kaleidoscoped, and were reduced to bits and pieces, segments of the whole. Watching the nurse help Cin into her pure white undergarments and sheer white stockings. Cinching the girl's waist tinier and tinier with that instrument of female torture, the corset. Adjusting layer upon layer of full-gathered petticoats, finishing with the lace bedecked silk one. Curling the girl's red-gold hair, using a little magic to make the artful ringlets and long, dangling curls perfect and lasting. Adding nothing to the relatively simple coiffure except some sparkling combs, to hold it in place, and the small tiara that the nurse assured Tish was an absolute necessity for a lady of quality.

Close your eyes," Tish said, spraying Cin with flowery perfume before dropping the white dress, with its pearls, lace, and diamond dust, over the girl's head and fastening the tiny buttons that marched up the back, pulling the top down to expose Cin's creamy shoulders and the upper swells of her breasts.

"I want to see," Cin said.

"The shoes first," Tish decreed. And as the nurse knelt to slip them on Cinderella's high-arched feet, Tish zapped a full-length mirror into being, handed the girl a pair of elbow-length gloves, and commanded, with only a tad of pride in her voice as she viewed her creation. "Look."

They all looked, all beheld a vision of loveliness. The grubby, greasy, fat girl was gone, and in her place was a creature straight out of a fairy tale; one from Tish's world anyway.

Tish sighed, and then berated herself for being a sentimental ninny.

"Ohhhhhh," the old woman said, and it was nothing more than a cry from her heart. Her lamb was, at long last, receiving what the nurse knew she deserved. And she wasn't ashamed of the tears she dried on her white apron.

Speechless, Cinderella lifted the skirts, peered down at the gorgeous shoes, turned slowly, tried to see the back of her gown, touched her hair, and finally said, "It's beautiful."

"You're beautiful, Ella, but you'd better get your gloves on and get in the carriage if you want to meet your Prince Charming."

"Oh, yes." Breathless with excitement, and probably the tight corset, Cinderella somehow managed to draw on the gloves and walk to the front door, before she said, "Thank you, Godmother. I will remember this until the day I die."

Tish patted her cheek and tried to sound completely businesslike as she gave her final instructions. "Remember me if you will, but there are other things you must remember first. You must leave the ball before the stroke of midnight, otherwise your fine garments will turn to rags, your skin will regain its grime, and your hair will..."

They were at the coach. The footman had jumped down from his perch and was waiting to assist Cinderella into the pink satin interior. With her dress carefully arranged to keep it from wrinkling, Cin was seated in the coach before she said, with every appearance of sincerity, "Godmother, I will remember to leave and...and everything. Oh, I will. I promise."

Tish leaned in, gave one final order, "And, my dear, if you really want to marry this prince of yours, tell no one, absolutely no one, your name."

"But how will he come courting if..."

"Cinderella, I must insist that you obey me. It is part of the magic spell. Now, what are you going to do?"

"Leave before the stroke of midnight. Tell no one my name."

Stepping back, allowing the footman to close the door, Tish relented enough to say, "Have a grand time, my dear. I'll be waiting, in the old barn, to hear all about your first ball and your handsome prince."

Watching the coach roll away from the manor house, Tish muttered, "I hope I got that damned spell right on the shoes. I hope the left one remembers to drop off her foot at the stroke of midnight."

"Be ya going back to the barn now, milady?"

The old woman's question brought Tish back with a start. "No," Tish answered, "I think, after I run in, disappear the mirror, and clean up any mess we may have left, I'll go for a swim."

"That be a goodly idea," the nurse said, rubbing her back with both hand, "but I be for my bed. 'Tis time and past that I be getting some rest. Old bones..." She shook her head, bent her knees in a quick bob of a curtsy, and said, "If ya no be needing me, milady, I be sleeping the sleep of the just this night."

"Go," Tish said with a smile, feeling as if she should maybe bless the old woman or something, but absolutely wasn't sure how, or what. Instead, struck by a sudden thought, she asked, "How did you know I was in the barn? Before? When you came to get me?"

"I be a peasant, milady. We be believers in such as ya. Ya was seen out and about, but we no be telling the gentry."

"Thank you," Tish said. Extending her wand, she touched the old woman's shoulder and said, "May all your wishes come true."

There were tears running down the nurse's wrinkled face, but there was nothing but pure joy in her quavery voice when she said, "They have, milady. This very day."

"I have always hated this damned story," Tish muttered as she, still in glorious Godmother lavender, trudged up the hill to the pool in what was almost full darkness. She was tired, hungry, and, if the truth were known, lonely as the north wind in winter. The deed was done, or at least set in motion, but Tish felt no sense of completion. She just felt sort of empty and at loose ends and weary of the whole blasted mess.

She tried to drum up a little righteous indignation at Marcus and his sly hints about getting her matched up with the king's oldest son, the Royal Bastard, but she knew he was joking. And if he wasn't, it couldn't possibly matter. As soon as Cin and Rue had joined hands and bodies, Tish was going to be long gone from this magic kingdom. Very shortly after that she was going to be shaking the dust of Faery off her feet for good and always. The prince, if he even existed, was just out of luck.

The only thing she was going to miss was Bubba, and she knew she couldn't take him home with her. What would a magical creature like a water sprite do in the United States of America? He would be as lonesome as she was, and Tish wasn't about to inflict that on man nor beast. As for Marcus, he wouldn't even want to go home with her. She wasn't sure why she was even thinking about him, after all, he had his own life and... And she wasn't sure why even the thought of leaving Marcus made her throat ache with unshed tears, tears for a love that could never be.

HIS LIFE WAS in turmoil. Whether or not it was the doing of the Family blessing, Marcus was in love, totally and completely, and that fact had brought him very near the edge of despair. All he wanted was Tish, Tish as his wife, Tish by his side until the far end of never. But it couldn't be. She lived in another world, and soon, very soon, the Godmothers, if Tish had her facts in the proper order, would be sending her home. There was no future for the pair of them, no...

Saddened by his own dark thoughts, Marcus sighed, leaned a little harder against the sheltering tree, and watched the path for her coming. No matter what else happened, no matter how soon they were torn apart, he intended to have this one night to remember. But when he saw her, his heart didn't do a flip-flop, his chest wasn't constricted, and he felt no up surge of aching desire.

She was so terribly weary, so lost looking, that all he felt was concern. Wanting only to take some of her burden from her, to ease this time for her, Marcus stepped out of the shadows, and said, "Godmother?"

A hand touched her forearm. Tish squealed, whirled to run, caught her skirts on a low-growing, prickly, tree limb, and, with a ripping of material and catch in her breath, went down, hard, on her hands and knees on the stony path.

He was lifting her up, almost before a fiery spurt of expletives and earthy oaths got to her lips, and his apology was lost in her language. Cradling her against his velvet tunic, Marcus walked up the path with her in his arms, his lips against her hair, murmuring something she couldn't come close to understanding.

Her hoopskirt bounced high, exposing more of her drawers than was seemly, Tish didn't even notice. She was too aware of his arms, his chest, the odor of...of Witch's Brew. It was, it had to be. Nothing else could have that particular... Instead of snuggling close against him, Tish stiffened.

It was too familiar, too bitter, not to trigger her memories of another night and her suspicions of the man and his motives on this night. Struggling to free herself from his embrace, she fairly yelled, "What do I smell? What are you trying to pull? Damn it, Marcus, you'd better answer me, or so help me, I'll change you into a...a..." Unable to come up with a proper threat, Tish waved the wand a little wildly.

But for a magic wand capable of menace and mayhem, it was curiously lifeless, seemed to be inert, unable to respond to whatever she wanted it to do, not that she was exactly sure what that was either. Her body, perhaps just responding to odor, was far too hot and too eager to meet with Tish's liking; especially if the man who was causing the heat was going to resort to dosing her with Witch's Brew again.

"Put me down." It was an order. One that she intended to see obeyed; no matter how much her body whimpered and whined in objection.

"As you wish, Godmother." He sat her on the grassy bank and stepped back.

Tish couldn't see his expression—his face was hidden in the night shadows—but his sudden, faintly seen, movement and the total dismay in his voice came close to convincing her she had, perhaps, misjudged him. Perhaps.

"Tish, I didn't... It must have broken when I picked you up. By the First, you can't actually think I would..."

His innocence was so obvious, and he was so patently embarrassed by what he had done, that giggles staged a tap dance on her tongue. She fought to squash them, tried to sound cold, unbelieving when she asked, "Broke what?"

"The love potion you gave me for Rue. I had it in my pouch and...

The glass broke and..." He held the strong smelling leather bag out as evidence for the defense.

The bitter odor burned her nostrils, made her light-headed, a little giddy, but not enough to keep her from saying, despite the laughter that was trying, wildly, to escape, "Get that damned thing away from me."

And then, as a thought stilled her mirth, she asked, "Why didn't you give it to the prince? What if he doesn't even like... Marcus, now what are we..."

"I am sorry that I have offended you. I assure you it wasn't intentional. My motives were both pure and honorable."

"Stop that," she snapped, rubbing at her aching head, pulling off the small crown she had added to the Godmother uniform, and tossing it aside, to settle into the thick grass and reflect a pale imitation of the brilliant star shine.

"Just answer my questions and stop...stop whatever pompous thing you're doing now. I'm too tired to... Just tell me, in plain words, what's going on, so I can figure out what else I need to do to fix it."

Sleepy nightbirds cheeped and twittered. Somewhere, far away, a dog, or its Faery counterpart, barked. A hot wind rustled through the trees, making them whisper at its passing. But Marcus was silent for a moment before he said, "Attacking your questions in the order I believe they were given, I can only say, I didn't give Rue the love potion because he had already seen Cin before I found him that morning. I didn't want the potion to cause him to lust after someone else."

It was a slender straw, but Tish was quick to grasp it. "Maybe seeing her was enough. Did he say anything about her? When the pair of you was going on to check out the enemy?"

"Godmother," he said gently, "whatever false conceptions you have regarding the Charming men, let me hastening to assure you that Rupert is both a gentleman and a prince, he would never peek and tell. He said absolutely nothing. But, I have to admit, he did seem a trifle abstracted as we pursued our mission."

The assurance as to Rue's sterling character did nothing to relieve Tish's worries. It just brought a flock of new questions flying into her already overcrowded mind. But she didn't get a chance to ask even one.

"As to the love potion, I had actually forgotten it was in the pouch until I heard it break when I picked you up. I am really sorry for that. Truly I am." He didn't exactly kneel beside her, but Tish had the feeling that's what he was planning. And the fumes of the potion, or something equally potent, were still wandering in several of her body parts, warning her of the panting consequences if he got too close.

And no matter what her body wanted, Tish was certain that she couldn't allow herself to get any more involved with the man than she was because... She didn't want to think about that because, or about the love that was already putting down roots in her heart. She couldn't afford to fall in love with him. She had to leave Faery, go home, and leaving him behind was going to be hard enough without...

"Godmother?" he asked softly, "what is it? What's the matter?"

She wasn't about to answer that question, so she countered with one of her own. "Why aren't you at the ball?"

"The king thought it would better if no one knew I was... Quincy and Sage were going to be there and, as you know, they have very little reason to like and admire me. There are many others who feel the same way."

"But not the king?"

"No, not the king."

In the silence that followed, the bubble and glug of the stream was far too loud, too intrusive. Tish had to fill the moment with, "That still doesn't explain why you were lurking, does it?"

Again he sounded faintly embarrassed. "I was waiting for you because... Tish, you have been working very hard and... It is my job to take care of you and..."

Pulling up her skirts, rubbing at her smarting knees, Tish asked, "And?"

"My...ah...my king sent you a bottle of sparkling nectar. It bears a small kinship to your land's finest champagne. I purchased bread, cheese, and grapes in Matol so that you..."

At the mention of food, her stomach growled hungrily, but Tish's suspicious mind was growling a different tune. "Why did this king of yours send me anything? Marcus, you haven't..."

"It is a gift of gratitude, nothing more."

"Then what did you mean when you said the king had been more than willing to give me a prince?"

His answer wasn't terribly informative, or satisfying. "Godmother, I was only doing as you asked. You specifically told me to ask the king to give you a prince. I did that."

"I meant Rupert."

"The king didn't?"

"I don't know," she snapped. "I don't know anything about kings..." She whacked, rather savagely, at her recalcitrant skirts with the wand and wasn't displeased when they vanished, leaving her attired in camisole, drawers, and a pair of unGodmotherly fancy, high-heeled slippers.

She kicked them off, stood up, and said, "Marcus, I'm sorry for acting like a...a harpy. But, right now, I smell like a goat, and I'm going swimming with a bar of soap. Get rid of that pouch and that nasty love potion, maybe then I'll feel more like drinking the king's booze and eating your bread and cheese."

It wasn't particularly gracious, but it was the nearest thing to an apology he was going to get; especially since she still had doubts about what he had done. Not that it mattered, she wasn't responsible for any king's son, damned or not. But she tried to soften it with an almost invitation. "Are you going for a swim also?"

"No, Godmother," he answered, "I have already bathed. I will await your coming in the barn. It is there our repast is spread."

He sounded too formal to be believed, and Tish hoped she hadn't hurt his feelings. She didn't want to do that either, but she couldn't keep herself from asking, "On a linen cloth? In crystal goblets and silver plates?"

His chuckle was as warm as the night air that brought it back to her as he strode toward the barn and its piles of new-mown hay. Not wanting to join Marcus and hay in the same titillating thought, Tish jumped to her feet and ran into the water, hoping it would cool her body and drive the erotic fantasies out of her mind.

It was a vain hope, one that a romp with Bubba, complete with watery kisses and bubbling water songs, only postponed, pushed back into the corners of her mind. That allowed her to pretend she was only dressing for the walk back to the barn, and the food, when she zapped up matching lacy briefs and bra and covered them with a thin, silky knit dress that ended just above her knees. And the fragile sandals she magicked onto her feet were just to protect them from stones in the path. The perfume spray on her skin was for her pleasure alone. And so was the transformation of the wand into a bracelet of some magnificence.

The breathlessness as she walked into the barn, saw flickering candles, the spread linen cloth, the crystal flagons, the silver plates, and the grapes, cheese, and bread, and the man, resplendent in green velvet and leather, more handsome than any prince, was only the direct result of hurrying. Nothing more. She wasn't about to...to get involved with...

She didn't even know if he was a man or not. And, to her horror, those were the first words to leave her tongue when he came toward her, offered his arm, and escorted her to a soft mound of hay beside their waiting meal.

"Are you a man?"

"Godmother?"

She didn't know whether his shock was pretense or real, but Tish knew she had to ask her question again, had to have an answer. "Please, Marcus, I have to know. Are you a man, or are you something else?"

His eyebrow was quirked high, but he was all grace and lean-muscled strength as he settled himself beside her, reached for the dark green bottle of nectar, and pulled the cork before he asked, "As opposed to what? An elf? A prince? An ogre? A barbarian?"

Tish looked at the sparkling blue liquid he had poured into her flagon, took a sip of pure heaven, and said, "Are you?"

Smiling lazily, he plucked a frosted grape from the bunch and popped it into her mouth. "Eat," he said softly, "and then, perhaps, I'll give you an opportunity to find out for yourself."

Taking another sip of the marvelous drink, Tish felt its warmth spread through her, join the heat that was already building in her nether regions. She looked at him over the rim of her glass and wasn't at all surprised to hear herself say, her voice only slightly breathy with invitation, "Promises, promises."

And she took another quick gulp of nectar as Marcus rearranged himself, took up a new position on the hay, one that put him in close proximity, close enough to reach out, pull her into a heated, and heat-making, embrace.

And to knock over one of the flaming candles instead. Scarcely believing what she was seeing, Tish watched with growing horror as it, with a fiery insolence, rolled over the edge of the linen cloth, ignited the hay, and flared into an instant conflagration.

Marcus swore. Tish screamed. The fire leaped higher.

Chapter Twenty-one

CRACKLING AND ROARING the fire doubled in size. Hungry, gorging itself on hay, angry red, laced with smoke, it reached out for Tish. Marcus grabbed her, jerked her away from the flames. Tish, when her mind finally kicked in and began to function, pulled partially free from his rescuing embrace, shook her disguised wand-bracelet at the fire, and was weeping, from the smoke, not from fear, when a rain of water, rather over much water, turned the fire into black mush. It also rained on their dinner, on the remaining candles, on the dirt floor of the barn, and on Tish and Marcus.

The fire, the smoke, and the furious downpour were history in less than a second, but the aftereffects of the rain lasted a good deal longer. The barn floor was ankle deep in mud. Tish, still in Marcus's dripping arms, was soaked to the skin, with water dribbling down from her hair, cleaning trails in the haze of smoke on her face.

The seduction scene, if that's what he intended, was shambles, soaking-wet shambles, and for some reason, possibly her weariness, that tickled Tish's funny bone. Leaning against Marcus's chest, she began to laugh. But not before she managed to gasp out, "I'll say one thing for you, Marcus, you certainly know how to get a girl hot and bothered."

His arms tightened, held her even closer, but there was no laughter in his voice when he said, "It's you."

Still shaking with laughter, Tish lifted her head and asked, "What's me?"

"You make me do crazy things. Only an idiot would put lighted candles in a pile of hay, but I never even thought... Tish, I..." His hand left her back, came up, pushed the wet hair off her face. It was a gesture of pure tenderness, caring.

"You make me a lad again, awkward, sweating, fumble-fingered, and I... Tish, if I were in your world, I would want to walk on picket fences, stand on my hands, do anything to impress you, but I..."

Love, wanting, need, desire, wonder, and joy, all tangled in an untidy ball of emotion, lodged in her chest, her throat, her head. No longer caring who or what he was, but knowing he was Marcus, the person she was falling in love with, Tish said, "I believe the loft is still dry, and we really need to get out of these wet clothes. Don't we?"

His lips were against her hair. He chuckled. "Make a light, lady of my heart."

"Why?"

"We need what's left of the food and the nectar."

That wasn't what Tish's body had in mind. "Why," she asked again, wanting him to pick her up, race up the ladder, and...

His chuckle sent new heat racing through her. "My first duty, before any joy, even a roll in the hay, is to protect your well-being. I haven't been doing a very good job there either. You are tired and hungry, and I just tried to incinerate you. Besides, we both need to eat, sooner or later, to build up our strength. We have the night ahead of us and..." he paused before he added softly, "activities involving breathtaking delights."

Tish wanted to melt against his lean body, but she found enough energy to produce a light, even if it, too, tended toward the warm side of the spectrum and sort of pulsed in time to her heartbeats.

The bread was glue. The grapes were fine, and so was the cheese, except for being a wet and sticky on the outside. Marcus had re-corked the nectar bottle; it was in wonderful shape. The linen cloth was toast, one of the wine flagons had disappeared, the other was partially full of mud.

Telling the floating light to go along before them, Tish carried the bottle up the ladder to the loft, leaving Marcus to manage the grapes and cheese. At the top, even before she zapped a thick, soft comforter, to guard their bodies from the stickery, itchy hay, Tish pulled the cork and took a swig of bubbly blue liquid.

"Better eat something first, "Marcus said. "I don't want you drinking the king's nectar on an empty stomach and later accusing me of plying you with booze to have my way with you."

"Isn't that what you had in mind?" With a wave of her bracelet, Tish provided a pallet, complete with down pillows, on a thick bed of hay.

"From our first bath together," Marcus answered.

"We didn't take..."

He stopped her words with a small bite of cheese, but somewhere between that bite and the next, they each drank deep from the bottle and somehow parlayed that into an embrace and a deep, lingering kiss.

Then there was the need to divest their bodies of wet clothing and kisses bestowed on naked skin, one wildly incredible sensation leading to another. And through it all were laughter, tenderness, and gasps of pure pleasure that drove them up a climbing spiral of desire, one that seemingly had no top but just kept swooping higher and higher.

Almost lost in the magical wonder of their lovemaking, Tish finally had enough sense to say, "Wait, Marcus. I have to...safe sex... I'll conjure a condom."

Floating on unseen currents of air, the light bobbed and danced just under the thatch of the roof and cast an intimate light on Tish's magic making. Chuckling, Marcus looked down at the strip of foil packets he now held in his hand and asked, "Six condoms, Godmother?"

"High expectations," she murmured.

"And purple?"

"My favorite color," she said, trying not to giggle, "it goes well with passion."

And that was more than true. But true or otherwise, there was no time for afterplay, new adventures, or basking in afterglow.

Minus a glass slipper, glamoured in grime, Cinderella was home from the ball. Not only was she home from the ball, she was in the barn, climbing the ladder to the loft where Tish and Marcus were just barely anticlimactic.

"Oh, Godmother, I'm sorry to interrupt. I know you're up there, I heard you. Godmother, Godmother, please, I need to talk to you." The ladder made creaking sounds as Cin began her climb.

"Do something," Marcus whispered in Tish's ear.

"I...you..." Tish caught her breath, somehow managed to call, "I'll be right down. Wait for me outside." She tried to inject command into her voice, but, to her ears, it was the breathless squeak of a woman who was, as it where, caught in the act. Or immediately thereafter. And for some, as yet unfathomed, reason, she felt an urge to giggle.

Evidently Marcus was struck by the same urge. She could feel his body shaking, hear small explosions of air as he tried to laugh without making a sound.

"Stop it," Tish said, poking him, biting her lower lip. "She'll hear you and climb on up the ladder and..."

"Godmother, please." Cin hadn't followed Tish's order, she was still in the barn.

"Wait outside. I'll be right down. I was resting, and I need a moment to..."

"Yes, Godmother," Cin said, sounding meek and obedient, but also sounding too close.

"Resting?" Marcus asked, or rather whispered in her ear, just before he nuzzled her neck, provoking other urges in Tish—said urges immediately triggering the Sanction.

"Tell her you'll talk in the morning."

The Sanction objected, painfully, to that suggestion. Tish said, not without regret, "I can't."

"The Sanction?"

She nodded and then shivered a little as his body left hers and she became, almost before she had gotten to her feet, the Godmother, complete with full skirts, crown, and wand.

Not lingering in their shared bed, stooping a little to keep from bumping against the roof, Marcus kissed her before she moved to the ladder and said, very softly, "I'll get dressed and go to the palace. Rue will probably need some nudging to begin his grand search for the mystery woman. But, my love, I want you to try to get some rest and..."

"Who is doing the talking, Marcus the guard or..."

"The lover," he said promptly.

Tish was smiling as she made her awkward way down the steep ladder, fighting her bulky skirts every step of the way—and, if the truth be told, muttering some fairly uncomplimentary remarks concerning Cin, her timing, and possibly her ancestry. But, outwardly at least, she was all Godmotherly concern when she walked with Cin to the pool and sat beside it to rehash the wonders, and terrors, of the night.

The girl, alternating between singing the praises of Prince Rupert, whining about her own ineptness, lamenting the fact that she would never see the prince again, and apologizing for disobeying Tish, took a long time to tell her tale of girl meets prince, they dance, fall in love, clock announces midnight, and girl runs away—losing glass slipper in process. Basically, it was the same tale that had uglied up Tish's childhood, but with a few variations. The coach-and-six, liberated by Marcus, hadn't turned to a pumpkin and mice; the coachman had just turned the rig around and took it back to its owner's carriage house.

The sky was silver-and-rose with fast approaching dawn when Tish finally persuaded Cin that everything was going to work out wonderfully, that the girl should go into the house and catch a few hours of sleep, that the prince would find her, and happy-endings would be the order of the day. Sighing heavily when at last Cin had departed, Tish leaned back against a convenient tree and closed her own eyes. For only a minute, to rest them.

THE SUN WAS standing high in the sky when the Uglies found her and shook her into dry-mouthed, slightly dazed, waking. It was far from a pleasant experience.

"How dare you?" one cried. Tish was too fuddled to even try to sort out their identities and too slow to fit her answer in between the twin tirades.

"Everything is ruined, and it's all your fault," the other Ugly wailed. "Prince Rupert has found another love and..."

"Where were you? Why didn't you do something?"

"Now, what are we going to do? You have taken our treasure and done nothing."

Tish sat up straighter, rubbed her eyes, tried not to yawn, and didn't even try to defend herself. The Uglies, bad-tempered as they were, were going to get the surprise of their lives very shortly. Long about evening if Marcus followed directions and lived up to his part of the plan.

"A herald just came from the palace. The prince is personally looking for the beautiful woman who came late to the ball. He danced every dance with her, and when she ran out, he followed, and he never did come back. Now, he's ready to make her his bride and nobody knows her name, or where she is from, or anything."

"Except that she lost her slipper when she ran out. Prince Rupert has announced he will try the slipper on every woman in the kingdom and marry the woman it fits the very moment he finds her. He is determined that she will never escape from him again."

A sun-heated breeze swirled their dark veils, lifted the edges as if it intended to show their ugliness to the world. Both women grabbed the coverings, held them down, and, after saying, "You are going to be very sorry for this, Godmother," turned as one and marched, in high dudgeon down the hill to the manor house.

Her long nap had done very little to decrease Tish's weariness, as a matter of fact, it seemed to have added to it. But, it seemed nectar didn't provoke hangovers. She smiled, a tad wryly, at the thought and its accompanying memory. She should have been berating herself for making love with Marcus, but she couldn't. It had been an incredible experience that she didn't dare allow it to happen again, didn't dare allow herself to fall totally and completely in love with him. There was no future there. He was a man Faery, and she belonged to earth.

As far as he was concerned, she was probably just a doxy, a one-night stand, and an easy conquest. Trying to push the demeaning thought away, Tish leaned back against the tree trunk and closed her eyes. And resolutely refused to allow the hot tears that were burning in her eyes, clotting in her throat, to be shed.

"No," she muttered, "I'll not sit around like a simpering ninny crying for a man who... I won't, that's all." Suiting action to her words, she got to her feet, zapped the Godmother high-heels into Nikes and shortly thereafter the full-skirted gown into a BearHeaven T-shirt and her best pair of faded jeans. Carrying the sawed-off wand in her left hand, she took off down a path, or a game trail, or whatever the narrow, faintly defined track was that led from the pond into the dark, heavily shadowed depths of the forest. It didn't matter where it led, she was determined to get away from the manor house and walk some of the kinks out of her emotions.

Without the ravening spell to depress it, the wood had lost its morose air and was only a wood, neither threatening nor oppressive. Nor was it unpeopled.

Walking fast, but silently, Tish rounded a corner, looked across a mossy, fallen log into a sunny clearing, and saw Marcus. Wearing burgundy and gold, tights and tunic, a sword, and boots, he was standing with his back toward her, holding the reins of the black rent-a-horse. She started to call out to him, but closed her mouth without speaking when she realized he wasn't alone. There was a Godmother with him.

One Tish recognized, even through the last time she had seen her, Tregon was disporting herself in the night sky, wearing all the scales and wings of a rather fierce dragon, breathing fire, and attacking Morgain in what seemed a life or death encounter. What was she doing here? Talking to Marcus as if he were some sort of dog? Wearing a green silk dress that belonged, more properly, in a fashion designer's Paris showroom instead of the proper Godmother dress for the magic kingdoms.

Whatever was going on, it wasn't right. Discounting any animus brought on by jealousy, Tish knew something was going on, something concerning Marcus.

Feeling a small trickle of fear sneak up to add goosebumps to her skin, unsure whether to retreat or shout a greeting, Tish did neither. She just stood there, screened by a clump of brush, and listened, shamelessly and with growing bewilderment.

"You don't have a choice in the matter," Tregon said, not even trying to soften the command in her voice. "You have been summoned to appear before the Council in the Crystal Court and you will go. Willingly or under constraints, it makes no difference to me."

"I can't," Marcus said, sounding as adamant as stone. "I have an obligation to Godmother Leticia and to..."

"You swore an oath of loyalty and service in return for help in getting what you desired. It is done." Her wand, a rod of ebony glass, took on a sullen glow. "Now stop being an idiot and take my hand. We depart at once."

"What of Godmother Leticia? She needs..."

"The Wilding needs nothing, nor do we have any further need of her. She underwent a sham ceremony, was made to believe she was a Godmother for reasons that do not concern you. She has served her purpose. We will dispose of her in our own way."

"If you believe that, you're in for a real surprise," Marcus said, sounding coldly angry and hotly furious, both at the same time. "Leticia has magic, Tregon. Real magic."

"What would a mere human know of magic? Come along. The Council is waiting to hear your testimony and then, if it needs doing, the Council will send someone here to clean up whatever mess the Wilding has made of this affair. Why has she come here anyway?"

"The Council of Four sent her."

"Don't talk like a fool. The Council of Four couldn't have sent anyone anywhere, they don't even exist. They have been dead for centuries."

Flatly unable to believe what she was hearing, Tish took a step forward, and lifted the wand. "That's a lie," she shouted. "Why are you..." The rest of her denial dried to dust in her open mouth. She had no further need of them anyway. There was no one to hear them; except for green grass, a few flowering bushes, and a chattering squirrel, the clearing was empty. Tregon and Marcus had vanished.

Scrambling across the fallen log, Tish tiptoed, scarcely daring to breathe, to where they had been standing. She saw the crushed grass, a burgundy thread snagged on a briar, some horse tracks, but nothing more.

"Even the horse," she said. "It's gone too. But why? What are they going to do to Marcus? What did Tregon mean? I saw the Council of Four, talked to them. I did. I know I..." Her voice was shaking, so were her hands, her knees, but the Sanction heard the sound of a horn, a herald's horn, and it went into a pain inflicting frenzy.

Sham ceremony or not, the Sanction believed Tish was a Godmother with a Wish-quest to finish and it intended to see that she did just that. But, she told the worry, for Marcus and for herself, that was raging, like an angry bull, through the corridors of her mind, "As soon as this is finished, then it's the Crystal Court for me. I'll find out what's going on, and, if the Godmothers think they are just going to get me to do their dirty work and then dispose of me, they've got another thing coming." Perhaps it was an empty promise, or perhaps it wasn't. Tish would decide that after Cin and Rue had tied the knot and the Uglies took off their veils.

First things first, not that the Sanction gave her any real choice in the matter.

Fuming and grumbling, Tish trotted back down the narrow path, pausing just within the edge of the trees to re-gown her Godmotherly image. She caught enough breath to stop at the stream and call, hoping the sprite was nearby, "Bubba. Bubba, are you there? There were no watery kisses, no bubble of greeting. Bubba was not there. She felt only an emptiness where he should have been.

New fear coiling around her worry, twisting it into ever larger, more frightening dimensions, Tish called again, "Please answer me, Bubba. The Godmothers have taken Marcus and... I need you. Please, Bubba. Please."

The running water gurgled and splashed. A grayish-blue, long-legged bird waded in the shallows. A breeze, hot with summer and not timid, shook tree leaves and rumpled the smooth surface of water. A horn blew in the distance. Faint voices called, a plenitude of voices, male and female, excited sounding. But no Bubba. No cavorting, joy-filled water sprite. He was gone as surely and completely as Marcus. And, except for the wand and the gadfly Sanction, Tish was alone. All alone in a land of strangers.

And, despite her fears, some imp of the perverse, probably her patron imp, made her murmur, "And some of the folk in Faery are a lot stranger than others."

"Indeed."

The agreeing voice was deep, pleasant-sounding, and it came from behind her. Wand up, Tish whirled, ready to defend herself if necessary.

The man had, in the tilt of his head, the aristocratic stance, something of look of Marcus, but didn't actually have any of the missing man's physical characteristics. This man was broad shouldered and heavy, not tall, not lean, not amber-eyed. But, even knowing what the circlet of gold crowning his grizzled, graying hair meant, Tish still felt that she knew him. He, even if he was the king, didn't really seem like a stranger.

Never having learned how to curtsy, Tish inclined her head and said, "Your majesty."

His bow was a little deeper, but holding only respectful greeting, not servility. "Godmother Leticia." And then, before she could say anything more, Marcus's king said, "We, my kingdom and I, are greatly in your debt. The ravening spell was growing stronger every day, very soon it would have devoured the entire kingdom. You have prevented that. I wish I could give you half my kingdom, but..."

She hadn't actually done much of anything, and Tish knew it, but she didn't know how to tell him so with making it seem as if the spell was of no import. And, to this man at least, it was terribly important. "Your gratitude is more than enough, your majesty. And, besides that," she tried to smile, "your son, Prince Rupert, needs to be heir to a complete kingdom if I'm going to be able to lift the Curse off Sage and Quincy."

"You are as kind and generous as you are beautiful."

She blushed.

The king, she didn't even know his name, extended his forearm and asked, "Godmother, will you do me the honor of joining me in my spying expedition?"

Accepting the royal invitation, Tish, feeling stately, paced along at the king's side as she asked, "Spying?"

"Of course. I'm the king. I need to see what's going on in my kingdom, but I don't always want others to know that I'm watching. Marcus told me what you have done, but Marcus has a rather odd sense of humor and...well, Rupert is my son. This girl, Cinderella, has been the talk of the kingdom for any number of years."

Tish started to say something but wasn't quick enough.

"I know she is blameless in cursing her stepsisters. But the rest of the kingdom does not; Marcus made me promise not to tell and I haven't. He bore the brunt of the blame and the shame for killing the Red Witch and leaving the sisters mired in ugliness.

"But, alas, the poor woman could not have lifted the Curse; only a Godmother could do that." He sighed. "It has been hard without Marcus by my side. Very hard. But, Leticia, I am proud of his courage and his honor. He is a good man."

"Yes," Tish agreed, and she wanted to pour out her worries, tell the king that Marcus was in the clutches of the Godmothers, that Bubba was gone, and... But she couldn't burden him with her own troubles. The king could do nothing to help, but she could. And she would. Just as soon as this Wish-quest was gift-wrapped in wedding paper and tied with a wedding knot.

"I would prefer not being seen," the king said as they neared the manor house. "Could you..."

A crowd of peasants, servants, minor nobility, and various hangers-on were milling around in the courtyard, the women and girls giggling, the men trying to catch glimpses of the prince, or pushing their daughters into the long line that was forming. A line of young women, each one eager to try on the glass slipper, to marry the handsome prince, and live happily ever after.

"Want to be one of the group?" she asked, pointing.

"Wonderful idea. Will you do me the honor of being my daughter?"

She didn't quite understand. He chuckled. "I will push you into the line and walk along with you. That way, we can see everything." He waited for a second before he added, "And you will have a chance to try on the magic slipper."

A memory, achingly sweet, of Marcus pulling other slippers, bunny slippers, not glass dancing slippers, onto her sore feet scrunched itself into a ball in Tish's throat. She swallowed hard, fought back the worried tears that hovered behind her eyes, and said, her voice only slightly hoarse, "Your wish is my command, your majesty." The wand supplied the dusty garments and the glamour that turned the handsome king into an ignorant, bossy old man who wanted nothing more than getting his rather stupid daughter, Tish, wed to the prince.

"Get ya in the line," he said, pushing at her. "I be wanting ya to fit yer foot in that slipper. And..." He muttered, "Sorry," as he practically sent her sprawling in his hurry to get his "daughter" to the kneeling prince and the sparkling slipper he held in his hand.

Tish thought the king was enjoying himself far too much to be sorry, but she didn't say a word. Keeping her head down, shuffling along on bare, dusty feet, she cast furtive glances at the five women standing on the steps of the manor house. Two were gowned and veiled in black. One was the old nurse, and she was fairly bursting with ill-concealed excitement, anticipation, and just general joy. The other older woman, probably Cin's stepmother, seemed less in tune with the proceedings. In fact, her mouth would have put a prune to shame and her eyes betrayed her fury. The object of her anger, a dirty, fat girl, was trying to hide her rags, and herself, behind the old nurse. The stepmother's venomous look might make the girl cower, but it couldn't keep Cin's hand from stealing into her pocket to finger what was hidden there.

The Sanction was fairly purring, but Tish was too jumpy to enjoy the moment; not that she would have anyway, not with Marcus gone. When it was her turn to try on the slipper, she made a motion with the wand, lying in concealment up her sleeve. Cinderella's stepmother yielded to the magic urge and pushed her daughters forward. "Let's get this silliness over with," she said. "I am extremely weary and wish to retire to my chamber."

After a quick apologetic look in Tish's direction, Prince Rupert knelt in front of Sage and Quincy in turn. Neither fit the slipper. The stepmother said, "That takes care of the household, Prince Rupert. The sun is quite warm and terribly fatiguing, may we have your permission to retire?"

Before he could give answer, the king gave a cackle of laughter and pointed to the girl on the steps. "What about that 'un, yer honor? She no be trying it yet." He cackled again, acting as if it were the joke of the century.

Sounding kind and gentle, the prince held out his hand to Cinderella and said, "Miss, will you try?"

It was no contest. Her foot slid into the slipper. She pulled the mate out of her pocket. Tish zapped her with the wand, destroying the glamour, allowing her natural, and clean, beauty to be seen by the prince. And everyone else there.

He went down on one knee, proposed on the spot. Cinderella accepted. A brief wedding ceremony, one that involved sharing a bottle of nectar, a vow or two, and not much else, took place. Crying tears of pure happiness, Sage and Quincy pulled off their veils, reveling in their returned beauty.

Tish heaved a profound sigh and started to whisper a quick goodbye to the king. 'Not yet," he said. "You have to get me out of here first."

When they were back to the pool and he had been returned to his kingly self, he said, "Thank you. Once again you have saved my kingdom. Ministers adept at treaties are already explaining the situation to my neighbor. While they talk, hill forts are being built. My neighbor is a wise man. There will be no war now."

Worry tugged at her. "Sir, I have to..."

"My lady queen is preparing a wedding feast and a reception for our son and his bride. You would be an honored guest."

"I can't."

"I believe it is proper to give a gift to..." He pulled a small ring from his little finger, handed it to her, and said the words usual to tales of magic kingdom and quests fulfilled. "It bears my royal seal, if you should ever..."

Tish held it in her palm, closed her fingers around it. "Thank you,

King...King..." Some of her dismay must have shown on her face because he said, "Mark. King Mark."

She wanted to ask him more, but unseen forces grabbed her, whisked her away from forest, pond, and king, and dropped her in a small empty room.

Chapter Twenty-two

TOSSED LIKE A piece of garbage into a can, Tish fell, heavily, with her dust, coarse-woven peasant skirts over her head, muffling her curses. To overuse a cliché, it was the last straw. Since being dragged into Faery, she had been dungeoned, dragoned, threatened, cut, bruised, and just generally misused. But this, Tish vowed, clutching the king's ring in one hand and the wand in the other, was the final insult.

The thought made her smile thinly as she took a slow turn, surveyed the room, or more probably the cell, that prisoned her. She noted each meager detail. No chairs or windows. Walls, seemingly of wood, painted flat white. A thin rug underfoot. A single visible door.

Tish lifted her wand.

"I'm sorry, child," a voice said from somewhere behind her, "your wand will not activate here. You need only ask, and we will be happy to provide your needs."

"Bull!" Tish snapped before she walked to the nearest wall, stood with her back against it, and viewed the still empty cell. Power was fairly surging in the wand, so she knew the speaker was wrong, or lying. Or, just maybe, she was being subjected to either another form of subtle torture or another test of some sort.

Whatever it was, Tish didn't know whether to reveal her advantage or not. And hoped she was taking the path to wisdom and freedom.

Since she was fairly sure the speaker was one of the Council of Four and since she was sick and tired of the whole stupid outfit, Tish zapped her peasant garments into the never-was. She exchanged them for sneakers, jeans, and a T-shirt, before she asked, not caring if it was polite, "Why did you set me up?"

Whispers, hissing like falling sleet, filled the room too full for understanding. Tish waited without further comment. She did magic-up a glass of water and take a drink, to get the magic kingdom dust out of her throat, vanished the glass when she was done, and slid King Mark's gift-ring onto her forefinger.

And any ladylike manners she might have had under ordinary circumstances were lost to her anger, her blazing fury at the old women who had almost gotten her killed. "It better be good," she said, "or I might decide to zap everything in sight. I don't like being used. I did what you commanded, rid the Uglies of their spell, saved the kingdom a time or two, but did that get me any thanks, or even a friendly wave?

"Hell, no, it didn't. It got me zilch, and on top of that, you sent Tregon to snatch Marcus and my sprite. And you made sure she let me know the whole thing was a sham, that I was a pawn in some sort of a Godmother game, and not a real Godmother at all. That's over. I'm telling you right here and right now, that I won't have it."

"We didn't send Tregon," a weary old voice said. "And we know nothing of your sprite. Marcus is safe, for the moment, and you..."

"I was bait. You threaded that damned Sanction through me like a hook. I couldn't have gotten away if I... Why?"

The wall dissolved into haze, motes of light that shattered and were gone. Tish was in a room so like her mother's green-and-gold family room, with its comfortable furniture and smell of roses, that it made her ache with homesickness. She knew that was deliberate, too. Knew the old women were trying to manipulate her again. She wasn't going to have it.

"Stop it!" Tish said. "I am not a child, and I will not be treated like one. Show yourselves and stop playing games."

"As you wish."

The familiar room, with its growing plants, entertainment center, and wall of family pictures was history. Tish was standing in a richly paneled boardroom. It was as brightly lit, freshly flowered, and as windowless as the two previous rooms had been. Carafes of something, from the smell, probably coffee, were on a tray, alongside five dainty china cups, a sugar bowl, and a cream pitcher. The tray was on a huge, ornately carved, oak-looking credenza. The forest green carpet was foot-sinking thick. The Council of Four was sitting, two to a side, near the head of a long, gleaming table.

Tish walked over and took the padded, black-leather chair at the head of the table. "I'm neither happy nor patient, so you'd better make this quick. Start with Marcus. Where is he? What have you done to him?"

Since she had seen them last, the women seemed to have shriveled, grown immeasurably older and tireder and shabbier. Tish didn't believe that either, but she made no mention of their seemingly pitiful state. She just sat there, toying with her wand and staring straight ahead.

"You have shamed us," the Godmother at Tish's left hand said softly.

"No," Tish answered, not sure what the woman meant, but entirely sure of her own place in the matter, "I have shamed no one. Whatever shame you have is of your own doing."

"True," the woman said, her fingers pleating and unpleating the lavender shawl that covered her bent shoulders. "Power tends to corrupt, and we have been powerful for a very long time. Too long perhaps, but that isn't your concern, is it?"

Shifting in the chair, Tish looked at the woman, looked squarely into her eyes, eyes that were clear and focused with not a hint of age or shame to dull their brightness. She asked, "Where is Marcus?"

"Leticia, we had nothing to do with his taking, but I give you my word he is safe."

Tish smiled, but it felt more like she was baring her teeth in a snarl of rage. "As you should know, your word doesn't count diddly with me. I want Marcus and my sprite, and I want to know what the hell is going on around here. If you can't, or won't, tell me, then I'll just have to find someone who can." She stood up. "Tregon, maybe? Or Morgain?"

"No!" It was a barked command, but it held an undernote of pleading. "Sit down please. We'll tell you all you need to know."

"You'll tell me all I want to know," Tish answered, hoping she wasn't bluffing, hoping they would believe her threats, because if they didn't, she was going to have to find out how much magic her wand could undo. Even if she had to prop up Faery and put a brick under it. "You'll tell me and you'll do it now. Those are all the options you have, I believe, because you owe me, owe me big, and it's pay back time."

And she absolutely refused to listen to the small voice inside her head that said, "You have been watching too many old movies, bad movies. They have given you an almost terminal case of melodrama."

"Marcus told you he killed the Red Witch?" another of the Council asked, the one who was busily knitting something white and fuzzy.

"This is getting us nowhere. I..."

"Leticia, please, we are old, allow us to tell this story in our own way. It is complicated and... Dear child, I assure you that in the end you will understand and will, perhaps, be able to forgive us for what we have had to..." She got to her feet and went to the credenza. "Perhaps a cup of that delightful beverage that your world calls coffee and..."

"Cookies," another of the women said brightly. "Leticia likes our cookies. Chocolate chip, I believe, is her favorite."

"Just tell me," Tish said, weariness scraping away at her anger, dulling its cutting edge. She ignored the cup of steaming liquid the old woman had sat in front of her, but the sweetness wafting up from the plate of warm cookies was harder to will away. But Tish, with fear for Marcus's safety a worm wiggling through her anger, wasn't about to be bribed with food.

One of the Godmothers, the one with bluish hair and glasses hanging from a silver chain around her neck, tipped her head to one side, looked as if she were listening intently to some communication only she could hear. After a second or two, she nodded and said, "Perhaps we had better just stick to the essentials. The trial is moving rather rapidly and we certainly want to be there at the end, don't we?"

All four women laughed. It was a musical interweaving of sound and triumph, and it sent cold chills to race down Tish's back, warning her that she was walking on perilous ground. Not that she cared. She still had enough anger in her blood and bones to steal her common sense, her prudence—not that she'd ever had very much of either.

Speaking together, or rather one after the other, sometimes in mid-sentence, sometimes at the ends of paragraphs, the women began their tale. "You know it was a Godmother, or more than one Godmother, who sold the spoiled magic to the Red Witch. A Godmother who accepted a priceless string of matched lavender pearls and a ruby as large as a pigeon's egg in payment for her evil deed. The pearls, the only ones of their kind in the known worlds, were never seen again. They didn't make their way into the royal treasury, which they would have in the normal course of events, nor were they exported to one of the other worlds in which we do a limited amount of trading."

"So," Tish said, taking a leap of logic, "you think they were hid in the safe house in King Mark's kingdom." Remembering the battling dragons, she added, "And you sent me there hoping your traitor would do something drastic. Which one was it? Tregon or Morgain." She took another jump. "Both of them? They were fighting each other because of..."

The old women had stopped doing any of their minor activities and were watching her attentively, making her feel like a child who had learned a poem and was reciting it before a group, a group who wanted her to succeed.

"Very true," the woman on Tish's immediate right said. "There is a little more than that, of course. That particular magic kingdom came with a guarantee, and we, as sellers, were responsible for the ravening spell's damages. Ah, but you don't care about that, you are more interested in what's happening to your young man. He is currently standing trial as an oath-breaker, but we will take care of that very shortly. Long before they can invoke the death penalty."

Fear, sudden and icy, gave new strength to her anger, but it left her shaking, if only inside, in the general region of her thudding heart. "Oath-breaker? Death penalty? What..."

"After he killed the Red Witch, he came to the Crystal Court and swore an oath of service and obedience to the Godmothers, swearing he would do exactly as he was told until the evildoers, the spell sellers, were found and brought to justice. When we sent him off with you, without notifying the full Council, and with a little agitation from Morgain and Tregon, it was decided he had broken his oath and taken off with his light of love. He is standing trial for that.

"However, we are still in full control of Faery, even if we do not always make ourselves known to the masses. Our orders supersede all others. And we do have enough evidence to convict the traitors. Or at least one of them. Morgain, after the dragon firefight, came to us, threw herself on our mercy, and turned state's evidence, as it were, in order to cop a plea."

"Cop a plea?" Tish fought back a wild impulse to throw herself down on the floor, pound it with both hands, and begin screaming at the top of her voice.

"It is a parlance I thought you would understand; straight from your American TV cop shows. Morgain, who is being kept in seclusion, has had her wand taken away and is bespelled. She will never be able to use magic again."

"It is, I believe, a fate far worse than you can imagine. Rather like becoming blind, deaf, and lame all at the same time."

Tish bowed her head for a moment, tried to be patient, to trust old women, four very powerful old women, to do what was right. She just couldn't do it. It was her life they were messing with, hers and Marcus's, and her mother's, and...

"Damn you! Damn all of you to perdition! What right have you got to do this? First you jerk me away from my own world, probably worrying my mother to death, and then you try to feed me to beast-things, dragons, and who knows what else. That is truly despicable. Almost as bad as selling spoiled magic to weeping wives."

"Your mother isn't worried, we made sure..." one said.

Another broke in with, "There are Godmothers living in your world and..."

Tish was outraged, only barely believing what she thought they were saying. "Are you trying to tell me my mother is a God..."

Still another of the Council broke in. "No, but she..."

Suspicious still, fairly sure there was something she was missing, something important, probably something to do with her mother, Tish looked at them, each in turn, before she asked, "Why was Marcus at the my mother's masked ball? And what does Artemus King have to do with this?"

One of the Council got up and started pacing. Tish thought it was the one who had magicked the cookies. The knitting one began to unravel her knitted piece, muttering something about dropped stitches. A third took one of the cookies from the plate and nibbled away at its outer edges, turning it after each bite, looking only at it.

The fourth Godmother sat a little straighter in her chair, folded her hands before her on the table and said, "My dear, your Mr. King is something of a problem. He is involved, as the saying goes, up to his armpits, but his cries of diplomatic immunity have been heard in some very high places. We are sure that it was he who smuggled your wand, various other magical objects, and the ruby out of Faery and into your world, taking them to the home of one of the old Godmothers who had retired to your particular world. Probably without her active knowledge.

"The ruby was being passed that night, at the ball, to persons who had best remain unknown for the present. Just rest assured that he or she will not go unpunished."

"And Marcus was there to try and catch him?"

"Yes, our world and yours touch in several places. A fact not unknown to your government. We trade certain things, including magic wishes and other less costly items. Lately some rather exotic and unlawful magic artifacts have found their way into your land and have caused some..."

Shaking her head, she waited a second before she continued with, "Working at our command, although he didn't know it, and without a full set of facts at his fingertips, Marcus went to the ball to catch the smugglers in the act and stop this lawlessness and greed for all time. Your untimely entrance with the outlawed wand and the magic you did was not only unlawful, it was down right dangerous. Against the direct order of his Charge Commander, who was certainly involved in the smuggling, Marcus had to make himself known to protect your land and..."

Tish shivered. "Now, he's the target?"

"Our problem with Mr. King, while not solved has changed

direction and will no doubt be easier to deal with now. It seems he was found dead in his room at the embassy late this morning. He had fallen victim to a hired assassin."

Tish was beginning to get a glimmer of the truth and she wasn't liking what she was allowing herself to imagine. "One of the beast-things?" She licked her lips. "But why?"

"We're not sure. Murder mysteries are not an ordinary part of Faery. We have reason to suspect that it was because he hired an assassin to, what's the phrase, to waste you because you could place him at the scene of the smuggling crime, as it were. It seems that his partners in crime knew and approved, but decided that Mr. King would best be trusted if he were dead."

The love she hadn't wanted to admit even existed, rose up, tried to strangle her. Tish knew her voice was shaking, but she didn't care. "Now, they, Tregon anyway, is going to kill...kill Marcus?"

The pacing Godmother stopped, turned, and, unexpectedly, smiled. "You love him?" she asked, and there was a pleased note in her voice.

"Yes, but..."

"Good, that will help solve another of our problems."

"Look, it has been pleasant, but I want..."

The Godmother smiled again. "It's time to go, but... Drama is everything in these last-minute reprieves from death—the Perry Mason ending, I believe it's called. You will need the proper garments and, of course, the proper jewels for your day in court. Stand up, please."

Unwillingly, Tish obeyed.

The Godmother, fairly beaming now, waved her hand.

Tish was wearing a white linen skirt, a silky shell, also in white, a long, linen jacket that matched the skirt, white stockings, white shoes, and, around her neck, an opera-length string of perfectly matched lavender pearls.

Looking at herself in the mirror that had made an appearance on the otherwise unadorned wall, Tish fingered the pearls and asked, "Are these the... They didn't burn up in the fire?""

"They weren't there. We recovered them a long time ago, shortly after the Red Witch died and the ravening spell began to devour the kingdom. Several Godmothers had been in that vicinity when the evil deed was done, so we waited. We waited for one of them to go to the house and try to recover the loot."

"So, why did they wait until now?" Peering at the beautiful pearls, but absently noting the change that the Council was undergoing. Gone was old, dithering, pitiful, back was power and authority and beauty real beauty, the kind that goes with age and wisdom.

"Their motives escape us, except where there is treasure, there is power, magic to be bought. Ambition and greed are the driving force usually, but it is possible that they were born bad. It happens. Some children are beaten, here as in your land, and some are loved far too much."

It sounded like one of her mother's axioms, enough so that another suspicion struck Tish, one that had been hovering in the back of her mind. "Did my mother have anything to do with me being here? Did she buy a wish for me to..."

It wasn't a question she got answered.

"Hurry," one of the transformed Godmothers said, and before the word had leaped completely off her tongue, Tish and the Council of Four were in the Crystal Court, standing before the full Council, and watching as pandemonium broke out. Exploded is probably better describes what happened. It was rather like the results of emptying a box of lively mice at a tea party: there was a lot of screaming and scurrying.

Most of the Godmothers were staring at the Council of Four, but one had eyes only for Tish, or more properly for the lavender pearls hanging around Tish's neck. She knew what they meant, and her smile was a death's head when she shifted her gaze to Tish's face and said, "It's too late, Wilding, and you can do nothing to stop me."

They had materialized beside Marcus. He was wearing the disgusting-yellow prison suit, a plethora of glass chains, a smudge of dirt on one cheek, hard dark circles under his amber eyes, smelled of dungeon gunk, and was the most handsome man Tish had ever seen in her life.

But Tregon's wand was loaded, ready to spew death and destruction, and pointed at Marcus. "You have been found guilty," the Godmother said, ignoring all the commotion around her, "and I am prepared to carry out the sentence." The tip of her ebony wand grew red with power, hot, killing power.

"No!" It was the high-pitched scream of an angry mountain lion, and it held in its fury all of Tish's love and impending loss. Almost with conscious thought, Tish stepped forward, placing herself between the chained man and his self-appointed executioner, and raised her wand to defend the man she loved.

"How romantic," Tregon sneered. "A stupid Wilding trying to defend her traitorous lover." Her smile was cold and cruel, but her hand was rock-steady when she said, "Die with him then." Death left the end of the wand, red death that shot sparks and flame and arched toward Tish and the man behind her.

Tish's sawed-off wand accepted the challenge. Blue fire, as bright and sparkling as nectar, fountained up in an almost gentle curve, met the red fire, and quenched it in a single instant. The second gout of blue touched Tregon's face, held her in icy thrall, prisoned her for all to see.

But Tregon was strong enough to break partially free, to send a single whip of magic energy in Tish's direction. It didn't do the damage she intended, Tish managed to duck away in time to keep from getting fried like an onion ring. It struck her hard enough to make her weak in the knees. She retaliated with another blast of blue. It cuffed and hogtied Tregon past all hope of escaping.

Some time during the deadly duel, one of Council of Four made a small gesture in Marcus's direction. It made dust of chains and exchanged the yellow suit for a burgundy and silver tights and tunic, his formal dress in King Mark's kingdom.

Seeming to have no thought for anyone else, he was standing at Tish's side when the magic stoke almost felled her. When he was free, he caught her in his arms, held her close, but when he spoke his fierce words were for someone else. Someone who cowered in her ebony chair and knew, judging from the expression on her face, that she was well and truly caught, that the jig was up.

"Ah, Tregon," he said, smiling his marvelous aristocratic smile, "I believe someone should read you your rights. And, to add to your knowledge, you really should be aware that what I told you was true. Leticia's magic is real. She took the Godmother Oath in good faith and she..." That was all he had time to say.

Everyone occupying the ebony seats, with the exception of Tregon, leaped up and hurriedly departed the dais, leaving the judgment seats for the Council of Four. And bowing and smiling and welcoming and insisting, forming a guard of honor, escorting the Four to their proper places.

Forgotten in the hubbub, Tish found herself in Marcus's tight embrace. He was holding her as if he never intended to let her go, and she was clinging to him in much the same manner.

"I love you," he said softly, "and I would plight my troth on this day, at this hour, and tell you my heart is held as pledge."

It sounded like the words from a formal ceremony, but Tish couldn't repeat them, forge bonds that couldn't be broken. "Marcus, I can't. I have to go home. I don't belong here. I don't..."

"Do you love me, Godmother Leticia?"

Tears of loss, sorrow, tears for all the empty tomorrows, hot bitter tears slid down her face, but, try as she might, she couldn't lie to him, couldn't tell him that she didn't love him. So, she sagged against his lean chest and wept, just like all the sappy heroines in all the romantic novels she had ever read. She wanted to tell all those paper women that she was sorry, that she honestly hadn't known that love could hurt so much.

She heard someone say, "It's the magic. She was hit and she needs to eat. We have some chores here that had best be done in private, Marcus. It would be better for all concerned if you would take Leticia into the anteroom and feed her. Very shortly, we will come and make arrangements for whatever is to be."

The food, fat sandwiches of ham and cheese on thick, crusty hunks of bread, did help, not by lessening her sorrow, but by returning some of her strength. So did the tall glass of icy orange juice and the slice of heavenly melon. But she was far from ready to bid Marcus goodbye and journey back to her own world when the Council of Four, not trying to hide their we're-so-pleased-with-ourselves smiles, came to find Tish and Marcus.

Looking, for all of Faery, like four doting grandmothers, all intent on showering largess on their single grandchild, the Godmothers had evidently elected a spokesperson. The one in the blue chiffon and diamonds stepped a scant foot ahead of the others, cleared her throat and said, "Leticia, you have admirably performed the task set before you. Mark's kingdom is saved, both from the impending war and the ravening spell. Cinderella and Rupert are properly wed, and at the last news from that kingdom, both Sage and Quincy are being courted by nobles of good repute. You have given them all happy endings, and now we would like to do the same for you."

"All I want is to..."

The Godmother's gesture for silence was imperious and not to be disobeyed. Tish subsided into silence and waited, knowing full-well that there would be no happy ending for her, not with Marcus anyway.

"Marcus, it is our understanding that you regard this Godmother with love, honor, and respect. Before I ask the final question, you must be fully informed of the facts. She is very wealthy. Her credit card is now unlimited platinum or will be as soon as we deposit the pearls in her account. She is more powerful than we even know. Knowing all that, is it still your wish to ask for her hand and to live with her in..." she paused, dimpled, and added, "wedded bliss might not be the proper description to use in conjunction with Leticia, but I'm sure you understand what I am asking?"

"Yes," Marcus answered, there might have been a trace of laughter in his voice but there was certainly no hesitation.

"Leticia, what is your feeling in this matter?"

Trying not to sigh, Tish said, "I have to go home."

"Yes, of course. Or, perhaps I should say, for now at least. But, even if Commander Stephen is returned to his rightful place in the guard, which he left at our request, we still have a problem on the border, and we still need someone trustworthy there to protect our interests. Marcus, I know that you have lived up to the terms of your vow, but would you be willing to serve us, for an unlimited period of time, in Tish's land?"

"Certainly."

Joy, unbelievably warm, flooded into Tish, like sunshine pouring through a window. "Marcus can... You're sending him home with..."

"Not without vows, both legal and binding. We cannot send you back unless those are given."

"Vows?" Tish asked, trying to understand what was required, but hanging on to Marcus's hand with fingers that never wanted to let go. "What kind of Vows?"

"Betrothal. Wedding. Troth-plighting. Whatever you want to call them as long as they make you husband and wife."

It was happening too fast. Tish was dizzy with more than magic backlash, but she knew that this was what she wanted, what she had always wanted. She looked at Marcus and nodded.

He went down on one knee, took something from his pocket, something that looked remarkably like one of her bunny slippers, unfolded the scrap of pink, and took out a beautiful ring. "Lady of my heart," he said, his deep voice rich with emotion, "will you marry me?"

"Yes." It was a whisper, and at that, it almost caught in Tish's throat when he slipped the ring on her finger, turned her hand over, and gently kissed her palm.

It was the last thing Tish clearly remembered. The ceremony was a blur of magic and vows, a shared flagon of nectar, a kiss, and a flurry of congratulations and a shower of happy-ever-afters from a bevy of Godmothers who knew how to make such wishes come true.

Time sort of twisted around on itself, and Tish wasn't sure how much of it had passed when the Four came to them, carrying a large basket, smiling a little sadly, and allowing their spokesperson to say, "Leticia, it is time for you and your husband to return to your world.

Your mother has received word of your coming; from the many postcards you have sent detailing your vacation in California and your whirlwind, love-at-first-sight romance with Marcus.

"She is expecting both you and your husband, but it is very hard for us to let you go. What you have done for us will not be forgotten. My dear, you are always welcome in Faery and we will expect you to visit as often as possible. You have endeared yourself to..." Unexpectedly, she stepped forward, put her arms around Tish, and hugged her hard.

So did the other three. And when they were done, they handed Tish the heavy basket and waited expectantly. Something inside the basket whimpered. Tish opened it, looked inside, saw the puppy, an Irish Setter puppy, saw beyond the outward seeming, and whispered, "Bubba? You found Bubba?"

The excited puppy-sprite wiggled through the opening to lick her face with wet enthusiasm. Holding the puppy in her arms, Tish turned to Marcus, and blinked as all of Faery, except the three of them and a battered magic wand, disappeared.

Epilogue

SNOWFLAKES CAUGHT IN dark hair, tangled in her eyelashes, but Tish was snug and warm in a down jacket, jeans, and boots that had joined her somewhere in their instant trip from Faery to her mother's front door. She was too happy to give more than a passing thought to the inexplicable fact that a Christmas tree, bright with twinkling lights and cherished ornaments, was standing in the bay window of her mother's house.

She had been kidnapped on Halloween, and now it was...

"Marcus?" she asked, pointing toward the tree. Bubba wiggled in her arms, trying to divest himself of the red bow around his neck.

His courtly attire reduced to sweater, jeans, and jacket, his arm securely around her, Tish's husband—just the thought sent tingles to chase each other through her entire body—leaned down and kissed the tip of her nose. "Time runs different in Faery," he said, just before he asked a question of his own, "Will your mother be hurt that we wed without..."

Chuckling, aware the wand was now a bracelet encircling her left wrist, Tish reached out a gloved finger, pushed the doorbell, and took a deep breath. "I don't know," she said honestly, "but I honestly doubt that she will be anything but happy for us. Mother does... Her big problem is that she loves me and..."

The time for questioning was past. The door sprang open, Tish's mother, her stepsisters, and Jilly were all waiting on the other side. All talking at once, all trying to hug Tish, Marcus, and even Bubba, and all terribly happy.

"We canceled your other wedding the day after the ball, and possibly you should know, Carl is taking a long rest in a funny farm," Sadie said after the newlyweds had been suitably welcomed, told of plans for a wedding reception, thanked for all the postcards, and hugged again. "After you ran off, Carl evidently tried to follow you. When he came back, he was a wild man. I do believe he went to every lawyer in town, trying to bring suit against you for turning him into a toad. Finally someone took pity on him and had him committed."

Before Tish had time to feel even a dash of guilt, her mother smiled at them both and said, "What possible difference does it make about Carl? As long as Leticia has married her Prince Charming, I am completely happy."

The seemingly innocent remark caught Tish completely off-guard. Wondering just how much her mother knew about wishes and Faery, she didn't know whether to laugh or cry. She looked down at the ring, with a pink diamond large enough to choke a goose, Marcus had given her, the other ring that King Mark had given her, and drew wild, and very probable, conclusions regarding her husband and his relationship with King Mark's oldest son, the Royal Bastard, the damned prince.

"Marcus?" she asked, and there was a world, possibly two worlds, of suspicion in the sharp look she gave him.

Red stained his lean cheeks, and in a very sheepish voice Marcus said, "My lady wife, we have been quite busy. In all the excitement and everything, I believe there are things about myself that I've neglected to tell you."

Finis

Patricia White

A best selling author, Patricia White, lives in the Cascade Mountains, very near an extinct (she hopes) volcano. Keeping her company is a long-suffering husband, a darling daughter, and three really different cats (who may or may not have been the inspiration for White's previous Hard Shell release, A WIZARD SCORNED).

Formerly a teacher (high school English), she has been published in many mediums and in many genres. She is currently working as an editor and trying to write (among other things) another Faery tale romance.

Visit Patricia at: http:// www.patriciawhite.net

Printed in the United States
16115LVS00001B/78